THE LOVER'S VOW
An Oracles Novel

Virginia Addison

Just Add Gin Publishing – Arvada, CO
ISBN: 978-0-692-05616-5
Library of Congress Control Number: 2018931951
The Lover's Vow | Virginia Addison
Digital distribution | Paperback
Just Add Gin Publishing | Paperback edition

DEDICATION

To my sister T.P., the first one I ever told about this book; and to A.K. and L.L., two of my best friends and my proof-readers. I love you, and thank you for your support!

CHAPTER ONE
CALLIE

"Fuck me." The muttered words and a big sigh escaped me as I sank back into my office chair, leaning my head back and staring at the ceiling. Despite loving my job, I'd been feeling restless lately and today that feeling was in full force. I was having the hardest time concentrating on my work and that was a recipe for disaster with my job.

See, when you're paid to help people find "The One", there's no room for error. My dating and matchmaking company had taken off even better than I thought it would, and the applications were coming in fast. I was working on finding another couple of employees to help out in the office, but it was slow going. I had high standards, and was picky about who I let in to my personal life and my business.

Rubbing my temples, I decided to open one last profile application before heading out for the day. I'd almost called it in early multiple times already, but I'd made a goal to get through thirty-five applications before leaving. I'd worked hard in school and the last couple of years to get where I was, and slacking wasn't an option. Plus, working kept my mind off other, less important things. I took a deep breath and let it out slowly, popping my gum a few times before finally clicking on the request from a Joseph Minkly. A gym selfie focusing on flexed arms filled the screen and I rolled my eyes before scrolling down to his bio.

"I go to the gym every night to keep my guns loaded and the hunnies lookin' back." I started laughing so hard I almost swallowed my gum. Was this dude serious? As an opening line to a comedy show it wouldn't be half bad but as an introduction on a dating website, it just sucked. His terrible spelling didn't help either. Did he really expect that to attract girls? I figured he was one of those 'bros' who owned a lifted truck and had to constantly pump iron to make up for their small dicks. I scanned over the rest of his profile, rolling my eyes at his obvious innuendos and eggplant emojis. His pictures were all of him shirtless, only one that actually showed his face, annnnd yep- the requisite jacked up Ford.

I shook my head and emailed my best friend and business partner Char to check out our new profile approval request. I attached the gif of that lady saying "Ain't nobody got time fo dat"- what we usually send to each other when we think someone isn't taking our business seriously. I chuckled imagining his reaction would be similar to mine. I wasn't wrong; a few short minutes later I heard a loud "Oh my GOD" come from his office across the hall from mine.

I grinned widely as a reply popped up in my inbox from him. *"Body is delicious, but maybe he should workout the muscles in his brains once in a while too!"* I laughed loudly, shaking my head. He was the stereotypical gay best friend- he said he'd tried to tone down his "epic gayness" as he called it, but just couldn't help himself. He was sassy, hilarious, and had a razor-sharp wit. He'd come from a "proper family" in England, but since he was out and proud his family had forcefully *suggested* he move somewhere that would accept his

6

"heathen lifestyle". So Charles Sharpe had come to America for college and that's how we met and bonded instantly. I knew we were meant to be when I heard his muttered insults aimed at the idiots in our classes, which sometimes included the teacher.

"Hella! I almost feel bad for men, born with two heads and only half a brain. You excluded, of course." I added a smiley face before sending my response.

"Bloody right!" Char yelled from his office and then I saw him coming across the hall towards mine. I leaned back in my buttery-soft, black leather chair, folding my hands across my stomach. He sat on the couch in my office back against the arm and faced me before continuing. "So do you think this guy is salvageable?" I gave him a dirty look when he started to put his feet on the small coffee table. He paused, toed off his shoes, and then resumed using the table as a footrest. I rolled my eyes but let it go. "Or do we tell him to shove off?"

"Well, we can do our usual 'we're a serious business, not hookup central' and see what his response is. It'd be interesting at the very least to see if this one calls me a bitch too."

"I do love it when they do that. Gives me hope for all of mankind." Sarcasm dripped from every word as he tried to keep a straight face. He only held it for a few seconds before we both cracked up. "Maybe you should meet this one in person, see if there's anything you like."

I raised an eyebrow. "Seriously Char? You too now?"

"I'm sure I have no idea what you mean."

"You know exactly what I mean! You're trying to convince me to go on a date with this dude. He's not even my type! Just for that, you get to be the one that calls him for the initial interview."

He rolled his eyes then narrowed them at me. "You need to get out more. You need to go on a date. Snog someone! It doesn't need to be a lifetime commitment. You haven't dated anyone since that bloody git Carl. Your lady bits are going to dry up before you get a chance to even use them."

"Oh my GOD you did not just say that!" I was trying not to encourage him, but I couldn't help laughing. "You know my parents have been bugging me to find someone for like, the last year. Then they somehow roped in my siblings. I can't have you starting in on me too."

"You know we all just love you and want you to-"

"To be happy, yeah, I get it. But I'm not *un*happy. And besides, if I can't be happy by myself, how is a man supposed to change that for me?"

Char nodded, looking at me thoughtfully. I didn't really want to know what he was thinking. I was tired, and my parents were visiting in the morning and I knew I would hear the same things from them. I shut down my computer and started to grab all my stuff.

"I'm… I'm gonna head home Char. We'll figure out what to do with Broseph another day."

"Ha ha ha, very funny. Broseph." He stood up and pulled me into a hug before I could escape. He didn't say anything, but my body relaxed with the small reassurance that he was still on my side. "I'll see you later, cupcake. And good luck with your parents tomorrow."

I snorted and muttered, "Yeah, because I'm definitely gonna need it."

CHAPTER TWO
CALLIE

My parents spent three hours at my place the next morning before I started to really lose it. They had been hinting about me finding someone the whole time they'd been there, and my mom had now officially stopped being subtle. I just needed them to leave before I jumped off the cliff they were driving me towards.

My mom and dad were very loving, very affectionate, amazing parents. I'd thankfully grown up in a pretty good environment; we'd had our share of issues, but we stuck together as a family and everything had turned out for the better. Unfortunately, that also meant that sometimes my parents cared *too* much. Like I'd mentioned to Char, in the last year they'd started to prod me into the whole find-love-get-married-have-kids lifestyle, and now that I'd recently turned twenty-nine they'd really doubled down. I knew they were doing it because they cared for me and wanted me to be happy like them, but it was driving me crazy that they didn't think I'd a) really been trying, b) wasn't really happy without "love", and c) thought I'd been posting about cats a little too much on Facebook.

In fact, my mom was going on about the whole cat thing at that very moment. I rinsed out the cup I'd been using and started actively maneuvering them towards my front door, all while trying to tune out my mother's words. My dad broke away to use the bathroom and I inwardly groaned since that only gave my mother more time to pester me.

"…And then ten minutes after that, you posted about how cats were better companions than any man because they can't talk back!" My mother huffed as she picked up her purse from the side table by the door. She turned back around to me, a twinkle in her eye as she leaned in and stage-whispered, "You're a Drakos- men don't talk back to us anyway."

"I heard that," my dad yelled from the bathroom he'd been using. He sounded stern, but I could tell he was fighting a grin. "And your mother is right, Calliope. We don't take shit from anyone."

My mom nodded forcefully once, like that was the final word as my dad came out of the bathroom to stand by her and looped an arm around her shoulders. And then, of course, she kept talking. "Callie, we just want you to be happy-"

"Mom, Dad," I interrupted. "I am aware that you want me to be happy. I get it, but I *am* happy! I have a great job with a great partner, I love my family even when they drive me crazy, I'm healthy, I'm independent- I even know how to change my own tire! I'm getting along perfectly fine without a man in my life! Just because I like cats and I live alone, it doesn't mean I'm a miserable old woman. I'm only just barely twenty-nine, and I have plenty of time to fall in love. If I'm even capable of that!"

After several beats of silence, my dad was the first one to speak. "What do you mean 'if you're capable of it'? Why wouldn't you be?"

"Because I've tried, and it never works out! All I ever feel is friendship or whatever with these guys, but it never develops into anything else."

My mother snorted. "Now you're just being self-pitying. There's no need to be dramatic about it. Plus, I know some boys that..."

I couldn't believe it. MY mother, calling ME dramatic! And then trying to set me up in the next breath! I interrupted her again before she could really get herself going. "I don't want your pity dates! And at this point I feel like it's not even worth it. In fact, how about this," my temper finally getting ahold of me I continued, "since you won't listen to me, I vow to the heavens and whatever gods or goddesses are up there, that I'll never fall in love!"

My mom tried to stop me from finishing my declaration as soon as I said the word 'vow' like she knew what I was about to say, but she'd frozen as the last words left my mouth. She looked at me with a strange expression in her eyes, almost a mixture of pity and reluctant humor. I glanced over at my dad who had the same look in his own eyes. They glanced at each other, then back to me and said at the exact same time, "You asked for it." That was nowhere near the response I'd been expecting, and I was about to ask what they meant by that when a sudden, blistering pain exploded in my chest like a hot brand was pressed against my sternum. I fell to my knees, gasping for air.

"Wha... What's happening?" I managed to get out as I stared up at my parents. They were looking down at me, that same look from before on their faces.

It finally started to fade out, only a dull throbbing by the time I managed to stand up. My legs wobbled when I tried to put my weight on them, and my parents rushed to help me stand. I reluctantly leaned on them as they guided me to the nearest couch. I plopped down on the plush cushions, absently rubbing my chest.

"We told you Callie. We told you never to promise anything to the heavens you weren't sure about. You knew why. And you still did it." My father shook his head as he pulled my mother in closer to his side, watching me try to breathe through the last of the pain.

Taking a deep breath, I responded to my dad. "I didn't realize you were serious about it… I thought it was only a family fairy tale." Even as I said this, I could feel in my heart that it wasn't the whole truth. My parents had taught my siblings and I growing up that we had an interesting genealogy- we came from a line of Greek oracles. Both our parents were descendants of these oracles and that somehow made their children doubly sensitive to "oaths accepted by the gods" or something. I'd always thought it was cool, but not necessarily true. Even with that skepticism, I still hesitated to make any sort of promise that my parents had warned, as my dad recently pointed out, I wasn't sure about. Just in case. And I had just ignored my twenty-nine years of caution all because my parents had insinuated I should probably start dating if I didn't want to become a crazy cat lady like our old next-door neighbor.

"Obviously," my mom said, "it's not a fairy tale. Do we seem like the kind of people to raise you based on fairy tales?"

"I… Well… No." It was at that moment that I realized I had officially jumped off the cliff, and I had no idea just how hard my landing was going to be.

CHAPTER THREE

APHRODITE

"Silly human." I chuckled excitedly, not having had a project like this in several millennia. I'd lost count of just how many, to be perfectly honest. Everything got so boring with the same thing century after century, so I tried not to pay too much attention to the ever-passing time. But now- this Callie girl had given me something to do for once and I found I was rubbing my hands together like I was coming up with an evil plot of some sort.

All of us up here in Olympus kept an eye and ear out on the humans who descended from any of our lines. It was entertaining to see what kind of troubles they got themselves into (with or without our help). Finally, it was MY turn to intervene. And what a time to be alive! The twenty-first century really gave me so many ways to prove this human wrong. Never fall in love? I snorted with derision at the audacity.

I sipped on ambrosia and plotted as I watched Callie interact with her parents for a few minutes more. After her parents left, she went directly to bed and continued to rub the spot on her chest where my personal brand marked her as mine until she fell asleep.

CHAPTER FOUR
CALLIE

"I'm telling you Ell, it was so weird." I'd filled my sister in with what happened to me two days ago. She was only a year and a half younger than me, and we'd grown up close. With three brothers all younger than us, we constantly said how glad we were to only have one sister to steal our stuff and argue with. "It felt like a hot poker was being pressed against my ribcage. I don't know what it means... but I know I don't like it!" I vigorously punched the crosswalk button with my elbow, juggling my smoothie, my cellphone at my ear, and heavy bag at the same time. *I knew I should've taken my backpack. At least I would've had a hand free instead of trying to carry a purse full of books I shouldn't have bought in the first place.*

"God Callie, are you even listening to me?" Ellinor protested loudly into my ear, jerking me back to our phone call. The walk signal came on, and I started to cross the street. Thankfully it was almost dark, so there weren't many people to maneuver around.

"Yeah, sorry sis. I was.... Never mind. What were you saying?"

"I was saying that you probably don't even need to worry about it. It's probably just a fluke or something."

"I don't think so. It felt too real to be rand-" My last word ended on a yelp as I stepped onto the opposite curb weirdly, twisting my ankle and completely losing my balance. Suddenly everything went into slow-motion as I fell. My smoothie arced in the air and I watched it come back down, right into the face of an oncoming skateboarder, all while I fell straight into a parking meter. I watched, horrified, as the skateboarder swerved and lost his balance when the shock of the ice-cold drink hit him and then my forehead smashed into the meter.

"Fuck!"

"Shit!" We exclaimed profanities at the same time on impact, and I lost sight of him as my vision went black for a few moments. I came back to consciousness for a second, only to find him lightly shaking my arm to get my attention. As I made eye contact with him, the hot pain from the other day spread in my chest again. *Oh hell no,* I thought to myself right before I completely passed out at the combination of the head impact and the pain in my chest.

CHAPTER FIVE

AIDAN

"Fuck. Fuck fuck fuck," I said again, quieter this time than when that smoothie or whatever the hell it was had hit me in the face, making me fall off my skateboard and onto my hands and knees to the pavement. This chick had taken an even harder fall than me after face planting into the parking meter. It was almost funny, but the brain freeze and road rash kept me from appreciating the humor. Still, this chick had passed out and I had no idea what to do now. I was starting to really freak out when I heard a tinny voice squawking somewhere nearby. I looked around and saw what had to be the girl's phone, screen cracked but glowing. I realized she must have been on the phone when she fell, and I was thankful someone was apparently still on the line. I tried to wipe the lady's drink off me as much as possible and grabbed the phone.

"Hello?" I could hear the tinge of panic in my voice as I answered. "Who is this?"

"WHO is THIS?!" I held the phone away from my ear, cringing as the high-pitched screech came through my end.

"Uh... I'm Aidan?"

"Okay AIDAN, why do you have my sister's phone? What the hell just happened? Where is she?" She sounded really worried and peppered me with questions, not giving me enough time or breath to answer any of them.

"Woman!" I interrupted loudly. "If you'd give me a sec I could tell you what happened!" There was only a grumpy

16

harrumph from the other end, so I continued. "Long story short, she twisted her ankle or whatever, hit her head on a meter, and is fucking passed out."

"WHAAA?!" I jerked the phone away from my ear at her scream. I swear this lady was going to blow my eardrums out! "Call an ambulance! Take her to St. Mark's hospital, I'll be there in twenty!" The line went dead before I could say anything else. I sighed, but did what she asked. Thankfully the hospital she had named was close by, so we got there a mere thirty minutes after I'd called them. I somehow ended up in the back of the ambulance with the mystery girl, my sticky shirt starting to dry, and I looked her over as the medics checked her out and asked me questions about what happened and cleaned the scrapes on my hands.

Even though I couldn't tell much with everything happening around her, I could see that she was pretty. She had dark chestnut hair that I was guessing fell to her shoulders at least. With her dark hair, olive skin-tone, and a slightly larger but perfectly straight nose, I guessed she was Greek. I'd always been fascinated with mythology, and Grecian folklore was my favorite. Because of my fascination with their culture I'd traveled there a few times, so I recognized the features.

We arrived at the hospital and pulled around to the ER, and I pulled my gaze off her face to see a young girl, probably around twenty-three or so, wringing her hands fitfully near the doors. I assumed it was her sister- they had the same shade of hair and skin tone. That and I could hear her yelling at the paramedics about her sister. Damn, that girl had a serious set of lungs on her.

Fifteen minutes later, they'd hooked the girl up to some monitors and were doing more evaluations. In the ambulance they'd determined she had a concussion and they wanted to monitor her, at the very least until she woke up again. One of the ambulance drivers turned and walked towards me where I was standing by the curtain when the nurses had everything under control. I felt awkward being there. I didn't actually know this girl, and her sister was here to watch over her so they didn't need me. But I felt an odd pull towards the woman so I didn't want to leave quite yet, either.

"Sir, I'm going to need to ask you to leave the room. If you could stay for a little bit longer in case we have any other questions about your girlfriend that would be great."

"Oh, I'm not... Well, alright." I started to correct him, but he was already heading back down the hallway and I didn't want to distract him from whatever he needed to do to help my 'girlfriend'. I turned to look at the loud sister who was giving me a narrow-eyed glare, and I assumed she'd heard the girlfriend comment. I shrugged at her and left the room, thinking I would explain to her later what happened and that no, she wasn't actually my girlfriend.

I paced in the waiting room for a few minutes, and then went to find a bottle of water to calm my nerves down. I didn't know why I was so anxious about this girl. I didn't know anything about her except that she was beautiful and she had a sister with a propensity to yell. I collapsed into an uncomfortable chair, rubbing my face roughly in frustration. Leaning back, I imagined her face in my mind again. I wished I knew the color of her eyes and what she looked like when she smiled so I could complete the picture. I started to doze off while imagining taking out her bun and running my hands through it, leaning down to kiss her...

"You're already thinking of kissing her and you don't even know her name?" A feminine chuckle filled my ears as my eyes jerked open. I had thought for sure I'd fallen asleep, but here I was, wide awake in the hospital waiting room with a voluptuous, unnaturally beautiful woman sitting across from me. "Thank you," she said smirking at me. She had a heart-shaped face, large blue eyes that would've looked innocent on anyone else, and wavy blonde hair that fell past her hips. Something about her looks was mesmerizing, to the point where I couldn't help but stare.

"You're welcome," I mindlessly mumbled back. Then I paused, finally getting my senses together. "Wait, I didn't say anything."

She chuckled again. "Not out loud. But you were thinking I was beautiful."

"How the hell do you know what I was thinking?" My heart started to beat faster. *There's absolutely no way this lady can hear my thoughts. It's not fucking possible!*

"Well of course it's not possible for a mortal, but since I'm a goddess there's not much that I can't do."

After a moment's pause, I burst into laughter. "What mental hospital have you escaped from? You might be beautiful, but you're fucking certifiable." My laughter died down as I stared at her serious face. She really believed she was a goddess- and that could spell trouble for me. I didn't want to encourage her crazy, but I knew that if I pissed her off enough she could very well attack me, and I just didn't want to have to deal with that. I slowly stood up, getting ready to find security or a nurse or even a receptionist or something to help me out. Not that I couldn't have handled her by myself, but I'd rather avoid physical confrontation given the chance.

"I wouldn't bother trying to find anyone, you're only dreaming. And I'm controlling it so you might as well be in an abandoned building." She was studying her nails as she said this, and I smothered a disbelieving snort. She glanced up at me sharply and motioned with her hand to me to sit back down. "Listen Aidan, do you hear anything? Peoples' voices? Machines beeping? Phones ringing?"

I paused to listen, and realized it was deadly silent. My jaw dropped slightly when I realized she somehow knew my name and I stared at her in disbelief. I had no choice but to sit down when my legs started wobbling. My mind was racing at the possibility that she was telling the truth, but it was hard to come to terms with it.

"So you're a goddess. What's your name then?"

She rolled her eyes. "C'mon Aidan. You've studied all kinds of Greek mythology and you can't figure out who I am?" She stood and spun around slowly. When she stopped, her arms were wrapped loosely around herself and her long blonde hair settled with the motion. It suddenly clicked- she looked almost exactly like the *Birth of Venus* painting.

"Aphrodite. I should've known." I scrubbed my face with my hands again, finally believing her.

"Yes, you should've. But I understand that it's difficult to accept real gods and goddesses in these modern times." She sat next to me and grabbed my chin in her hand, turning me towards her. "I have something I need you to do."

She let go of my face and leaned back in her chair, eyes focused on mine.

"I don't like the sound of this."

"You don't have to like it; you just have to do it."

I folded my arms across my chest, raising an eyebrow at her. "If you're a goddess then you should know I don't really care to be told what to do."

"And you've studied mythology- you should know I don't particularly care what you like or don't like. You will do what

20

I tell you or there will be consequences." We stared each other down, but I eventually looked away.

"What do you want?"

"That girl that you brought into the hospital, her name is Calliope Drakos. Her family calls her Callie. To make a long story short because I don't have time for all the details, her family comes from a line of oracles tied to the Fates, blah blah blah. What really matters is that she made a vow, and you're going to help me break it for her."

She continued as if everything were normal, ignoring me when I got up to pace again. "I'll give you some vital information, and I'll make sure she wakes up without memory of 'your time together' that way you can manipulate the details as you see fit. The doctors will think its amnesia, and you need to take advantage of it."

"What do you expect me to do?" I scoffed. "Make her fall in love with me?"

"Exactly."

I jerked my head over to her, narrowing my eyes. "No. Not just no, but *hell* no. What gives you the right, goddess or not, to do that? And what makes you think that I can even make her love me?" I was almost shouting at this point, the panic really setting in. "I have my own life, and there's no room for this kind of shit in it. What was her vow, exactly?" I stood in front of Aphrodite, hands on my hips and breathing hard. At the moment I didn't care about the consequences of my anger.

She slowly stood up, fire in her eyes. "I am the goddess Aphrodite, and I do not need a *mortal's* permission to do *anything*. Whether you like it or not, you're in this now. I don't care what happens after you succeed, but succeed you will. Or I'll make sure you never find what you've been searching for."

The air left my lungs and the blood drained from my face. I sat back down once again, defeated. That was the only thing she could've said to make me do what she wanted, and she obviously knew it by the triumphant smile on her face. After several beats of me trying to decide if I could get out of this- and concluding that no, I definitely could not- I nodded in assent, semi-willing to do as she said and she gleefully clapped her hands.

"Alright! So what's going to happen is this: I'll snap my fingers, literally, and you'll wake up. Just so you know, the flood of information coming your way is going to hurt a bit, but you can handle it. It'll include some details about Callie and her family, as well as some suggestions of what to say to all of them. Oh, and it'll also include a playback of when she made her vow, to answer your earlier question. Don't fail me Aidan."

Before I could say anything else, she snapped her fingers and I jerked awake- for real this time. I sat up in my seat, breathing like I had just run a marathon. There were three people standing in front of me, staring at me. One was Callie's sister; the name Ellinor trickled into my mind. The other two were older, but definitely related. Another trickle in my mind told me these were her parents- and that's when the floodgate opened and made my head feel like an axe had lodged directly into my brain.

What felt like hours later but in reality was probably only a few minutes, the barrage of information slowly stopped and I breathed deeply through the last of the pain. I lifted my head from my hands, and looked back up at Callie's family who were still watching me. I could feel sweat running down my face and the rest of my body, but looking sweaty was honestly the least of my problems at the moment.

I opened my mouth to say something to them, but nothing actually came out. My mouth opened and closed a few times, and for some reason Callie's parents gave me understanding smiles and turned to Ellinor.

"Sweetie, go sit with your sister for a bit. I don't want her to come back around and not see someone she knows." Her mom patted her on the shoulder, lightly pushing her towards the doorway.

Ellinor didn't say anything, but she continued to glare at me suspiciously until she turned the corner. I glanced back at her parents whose names, thanks to Aphrodite, I now knew were Alethea and Hektor. It was kind of cool to be able to just know some of these things, and I mentally whispered a quick thank you to Aphrodite for saving my ass in that sense at least. I just wondered how I was going to explain to her parents that Callie and I had been dating and they didn't know it. From the information I had received, I could tell they were a close family. If her sister suspected me, there was no way her parents weren't going to as well. Before I could say anything however, Hektor beat me to the punch.

"Welcome to the family." He and Alethea sat down across from me, throwing considering gazes my way. "First of all, we already know that you aren't actually dating Calliope, and that you kind of fell into this situation."

I snorted, wondering if he also knew how literal that phrase was, and replied. "How do you know that?"

"Because we went through the same thing you're going through now. You just woke up from a dream with a god or goddess talking about a vow, did you not?" I nodded, confused and miserable. "Trust us when we say, this is going to be hard. It's going to suck. But they chose you for a reason, and it'll be for the best in the end."

Alethea nodded and added, "We'll go along with whatever you say. We're here to help as needed, but please," she leaned towards me and grabbed my hands in hers, "please try not to hurt Callie. At least not any more than you have to. We know that sometimes the gods don't give us a choice. What's your name, by the way?"

I breathed out, slightly relieved that I didn't have to try and carry this lie all by myself. I squeezed Alethea's hands and nodded gratefully. "I'm Aidan. I... this whole thing is fucked up. Sorry about the language. But I'll do my best to make things right, no matter what happens at the end." They looked at me for several moments, and then nodded once in sync.

Getting up, they headed back towards Callie's room. "Feel free to take a few moments Aidan, but please come up when you can. Calliope is out of danger and only has a mild concussion. She should wake up soon, and the sooner we get this initial meeting over with, the sooner this debacle can end," Hektor said and followed his wife out to the hall, and then turned back to say one last thing. "And remember, you can't say anything to Calliope or Ellinor or their brothers, when you meet them, about what's really happening. They'll all go through the process and learn in their own times. And you'll know when it's the right moment to tell Calliope."

With that, I was alone once again in the waiting room. I sat for a few minutes, contemplating what was about to happen. I took a deep breath and let it out slowly, trying to calm my pounding heart. I stopped in the bathroom to splash some water on my face on the way to Callie's room, and stared at myself in the mirror. *I hope to god this works.* I paused, and a maniacal laugh surged out of my throat. *Or should I say I hope to goddess this works?* I shook my head at myself, dried my hands, and slowly walked to the hospital room where everything was about to change.

Chapter Six
Callie

"What do you mean you're my *boyfriend*?!" I stared up at the man from my bed in the hospital I'd woken up in not too long ago. My parents and sister had just left to give us a few minutes alone and I was not only confused but a little scared. I stared at the stranger- albeit a very gorgeous stranger- and waited for him to explain.

He shifted his feet, almost looking nervous, and if I wasn't mistaken, slightly pissed. What he had to be angry about though I couldn't begin to imagine. After all, I was the one in the hospital bed, not him! "I'm your boyfriend," he repeated. He muttered something under his breath that sounded almost like *I guess* but I let it go because my head was throbbing and figured I hadn't heard him right. I just couldn't believe him- I had never been seriously interested in anyone, and the one relationship I'd had previously was boring enough to the point where I felt content being alone for the rest of my life with only cats as my company.

I tried to concentrate on remembering anything about him but all I got out of it was more throbbing in my head. I groaned and reached up to rub my forehead with a hand I belatedly noticed was bandaged. I hissed in pain when I touched a huge lump on my head, not completely sure where it had come from.

"Callie? You alright?" He sounded concerned, moving a step closer to me and reaching out a hand but dropped it before actually touching me.

"Yeah, I think. My head is just killing me. What happened? And seriously, who the hell are you?" I sunk deeper into my pillows and met his dark blue eyes. I raised an eyebrow at him, waiting for answers even as I sighed on the inside at the intensity in his gaze.

"Well, you took a hard fall yesterday. You... I mean *we* were walking across the street and you stepped up onto the curb wrong or something. You fell face-first into a parking meter, knocking yourself out. Since you were on the phone with your sister at the time, I picked it up and talked to her. I called an ambulance and, well, here we are." He sat down in the chair next to my bed, running his hands through his thick, just long enough black hair. My mouth dried slightly at the move and I swallowed hard, watching his arm muscles flex. I had always had a weakness for great arms and the slightly careless look. Was it weird that I'd never dated anyone who looked like that? I closed my eyes tightly, trying to get my train of thought back on track.

"Okay, that explains why I'm here. And the headache from hell. But *not* why you think we're dating. Also, what's all over your shirt?" I crossed my arms over my chest. It hurt my bandaged hand a little, but I readjusted their position and that helped. The man's eyes moved over my chest and I saw him swallow hard before quickly moving his eyes back to mine. He ran a hand through his hair again and breathed out slowly.

"When you fell, your drink flew up in the air and landed on me. And I don't *think* we're dating Calliope Drakos, I *know* we are." He kept eye contact with me, expression hard. "The doctors said you hit your head pretty hard. I didn't realize it was going to make you forget our last three months together."

My mouth had fallen open when he used my full name, but then he said we'd been dating for three months and I started sputtering. "There's no way! I couldn't possibly hit my head hard enough to forget months, and especially not with someone who looks like you! I mean... I... I don't even know your name! And you sure as hell don't know me!"

He was grinning now, and I almost fainted at the dimples that appeared. Fuck me, dimples were another of my weaknesses. "Well Callie, my name is Aidan. We've been dating for three months. Your favorite colors are teal and lavender. You hate mornings and love sunsets. You have an obsession with books bordering on unhealthy and you're especially interested in poetry. I know that your purple eyes go almost black when you're pissed. Kind of like right now." He leaned closer to whisper, "And I know that you have a birthmark on the inside of your right thigh that you like me to bite right before I eat your pussy out."

I drew in a sharp breath, shocked and turned on. This guy... Aidan... he knew about the birthmark that only my family was privy to. The mark was simple, just three triangles with one on top of the other two, symbolizing the three fates that all oracles were supposedly blood-tied to. My siblings, my parents and I all had them in various places. While dating, only one guy had actually been in the position to see the birthmark and he'd never asked about it. Then again, I was pretty sure he'd never actually looked at it since he wasn't too adventurous in the bedroom.

The fact that Aidan not only knew about the birthmark but also the fantasy I'd never said aloud blew me away. I was a very private person, and that right there almost convinced me he was telling the truth. *Was it possible?? And if it is, how the hell could I forget something like that happening?*

I was saved from responding to him when my parents and Ellinor came back into the room, checking *again* on how I was doing and all that other caring stuff that family is supposed to do. I answered their repetitive questions half-heartedly, still mostly focused on the source of warmth radiating from the man next to me.

What the hell is happening in here? I glanced back and forth between Aidan and my family, but gave up trying to figure it out for the moment. I was still trying to come to terms with the fact that apparently I had a boyfriend. And that we'd been dating for three months! And that he had met my family for the first time on this hospital trip. None of this was helping the pounding in my head and I closed my eyes, wincing. I felt the air move next to me and assumed Aidan had stood up, confirmed when I heard his tense voice come from above me.

"Callie's had enough for today. We should let her rest and we can all work everything out later." There was silence, and I peeked out from between my eyelids. My parents were nodding, and I saw that my sister was glaring at Aidan. I sighed and decided to talk to her later about Aidan, when I got a moment alone with her. My parents and Ellinor came over to say goodbye, and everything hit me at once. I almost started to cry when my mom softly kissed the top of my head.

"We love you Callie. Let us know if you need anything." My dad and sister repeated my mom's sentiment, and then they left. Now it was just Aidan and me again. I could feel him looking at me, but I didn't want to meet his gaze. I was overwhelmed and I didn't want to start crying in front of him. I was confused and in pain, and I hated people seeing it. I was picking at a loose thread on the ugly hospital gown when he softly grabbed my hand and lifted it to his lips.

My watery eyes shot up to his, and I glanced down to watch his lips graze the bandage. I could've sworn I felt the heat even through the gauze, and my heart started beating hard. The move distracted me from my tears. I slowly pulled my hand out of his grasp and after a light squeeze from him he let me go.

"I know this isn't easy for you Callie. I do want to talk more, but I meant what I told your family about you needing rest. I'm going to find your doctor and talk to him about when you can be released, and I'll be here when you wake up." I started to protest and he cut me off. "Don't argue with me right now Calliope. I already turned your morphine drip back up so just stop fighting me and go to sleep."

Usually I'd keep protesting anyway, but I could feel the pain reliever working through my system and my lids got heavier. I nodded reluctantly, and before I closed my eyes I saw a small smile from him. "Th-thanks," I managed to whisper, and I was pretty sure he responded but I was already too far gone to hear what it was.

CHAPTER SEVEN

AIDAN

I watched her sleep for a few moments before going to find a nurse. I quietly closed the door to her room, and leaned back against it. When she'd first opened her eyes and looked at me, I'd been shocked by the vibrant purple of her eyes. If I didn't already know they were real based on the information Aphrodite had given me, I would've thought they were contacts.

But then the vision of biting the birthmark on her thigh and going down on her had blown through my mind. I'd instantly gotten rock hard right there in front of her family and the doctor. I'd quickly sat down and crossed an ankle over to the other knee to hide the physical reaction. It definitely wasn't an appropriate time, but I'd tuned out the doctor anyway and stared at Callie, watching her eyes flick nervously between everyone in the room while imagining that scene repeatedly. I was willing my body not to react to it all over again when I heard Hektor's voice by me.

"She should be free to go tomorrow. We just talked to the doctor and they said everything looks fine, as long as she doesn't get any worse after they let her go. They also said it'd be wise to have someone with her fairly constantly for the next week or so, just to be sure." His face was thoughtful, staring off down the empty hall for a moment before he continued. "I think you should take advantage of this situation to get to know her, and vice versa."

We were both quiet for a moment while I thought about it. Hektor seemed like the kind of guy that was easy to be around- said what needed to be said and nothing more, and comfortable in silence. I appreciated that about him, especially with everything that had happened in the last twenty-four hours.

"I have a business trip that I was going to take next week, but I suppose I could move it up."

"Your boss wouldn't have a problem with that?"

"I am the boss, so I would hope not," I chuckled in response.

He looked at me appraisingly, nodding sharply. "Well then I think that would work. Calliope has her own business which can be mobile if she needs it to be. I'll talk to Charles and make sure it'll be okay for her to take an impromptu vacation."

I raised an eyebrow at Hektor, silently questioning who the hell Charles was. I hadn't gotten any information from Aphrodite on a Charles, and I was suddenly annoyed at the idea of Callie having another man in her life. *Not that you've got any room to talk, Aidan,* my inner voice scolded. I brushed the voice off and ignored the twinge of guilt as I focused on the conversation again.

Hektor noticed my look and smiled. "Charles is her business partner. He's not... interested in Callie."

"He must be blind then," I muttered to myself. There's no way any man could look at her and *not* be interested. But now that he'd mentioned that he was her business partner, I put two and two together- I had no information about a Charles, but the name Char was ringing a bell. Must be a nickname- Aphrodite was probably somewhere watching this and laughing at her bright idea to try and trick me. Hektor laughed and shook his head, obviously hearing what I'd said.

"Trust me, you don't have to worry about him. At least not where Callie's involved." He held his hand out to shake mine, grasping it firmly in his. "Take care Aidan. Nothing is going to be the same after this, I can assure you. Watch out for Calliope. Her heart is guarded but she's willing to let the right one in." He walked briskly down the hall after those parting words. I watched him go, contemplating how I was going to get out of this mess with as little collateral damage as possible.

I sighed for what seemed like the millionth time, and grabbed my phone out of my pocket to call my business partner to let her know about the trip being moved up. Lucy was my best friend Nick's little sister and we had somehow managed to run a business together for the last five years. Over time she'd become a good friend, a great confidant… and the woman I was already in love with.

You're in some seriously deep shit, Aidan McRae.

CHAPTER EIGHT
CALLIE

I woke up feeling much better than the last few times I'd managed to open my eyes. I'd been in and out for several hours, and this was the first time waking up that I didn't feel completely groggy. That, and now I only had a slight headache and a dull pain in my hand. I was sure the morphine had something to do with that, but I'd take what I could get. I stretched carefully, not wanting to dislodge the needle in my arm or any of the other wires attached to me. Glancing around I noticed Aidan dozing in a chair next to my bed.

I was grateful for the chance to study him without him staring back. He reminded me of Robb Stark from Game of Thrones with slightly longer hair. And taller. And bigger muscles. I sighed inwardly as he shifted and the muscles in his legs bunched, the definition noticeable in his fitted jeans. I realized he must've gone home and showered at some point, since he was wearing different clothes than before. When he let out a small snore I couldn't stop the giggle that escaped. The noise brought him back to the land of the living, and I couldn't help but grin as he jerked awake and looked around wildly before meeting my eyes and settling down.

"Hey there Sleeping Beauty," I joked. He responded with a sarcastic "ha-ha" face, but still smiled. "Did you know you snore?"

He looked at me haughtily. "No, I do not."

"Oh yes you do. You woke me up it was so loud! You could probably wake the dead with your snoring, Princess."

"Impossible," he sniffed, "Princesses do not snore."

I burst out laughing, but winced as the laughter aggravated the pain in my head from too much pressure. He quickly got out of his chair and hovered over me, obviously looking for a way to help. Eventually he settled on brushing some stray hair out of my face. My breath caught at his soft touch, and my heart beat hard when he stopped his fingers on my cheek, seemingly mesmerized. I shook my head to get out of whatever trance I was in and he stepped back suddenly as well.

"Are you okay?" His voice was gruff and he cleared his throat before continuing. "I didn't mean to make your pain worse."

"No, it's alright. I actually don't feel too bad, just a small headache. The laughing didn't help, but it was worth it."

He smiled softly. "Laughter is the best medicine, eh?"

"Whoever said that can jump in a pit and die."

This time he was the one laughing loudly. I watched in fascination as his throat moved when he threw his head back. I was grinning at him when he met my eyes again, laughter still swirling in his blue eyes.

He sat back down in his chair, now visibly relaxed. I suddenly got nervous being alone with him and my eyes flitted around to different things in the room, not really taking anything in. I finally settled my eyes on the stupid loose thread on my hospital gown, fidgeting with it again.

"What happens now? Am I free to go?"

"Almost. They wanted to check you over one last time when you woke up before releasing you. They said it wouldn't be unusual to have some lingering pain but that it should go away over the next few days."

"That's it?" I met his eyes and saw a look in them that made me wary. "There's something you're not telling me."

He ran his hands through his already messy hair, and it annoyed me when it fell back into place perfectly. Then I realized that he looked nervous. "Ah, well... They're not sure how long your amnesia will continue. And they want you to be monitored pretty constantly for the next couple weeks in case any of the effects of your concussion worsen for some reason."

"Okay... so I just have to stay with someone for the next two weeks? That's inconvenient, but doable. I don't see what the problem is."

"I was... Well, I'm hoping you'll come with me on a business trip I've got. I was going to ask you anyway, but I know that you don't remember a whole lot of our relationship right now."

"A whole lot? I don't remember anything. Nothing. I don't know how we met, or what made me think dating you was a good idea." I folded my arms and looked at him stubbornly.

He gave me a half smile, a dimple popping out and softening my annoyance. "You don't think my good looks are enough?"

I sputtered, racking my brain for a response. "I... you... Look, your looks are fine, but dating is more to me than beautiful eyes and bulging muscles."

"Bulging muscles huh?" He flexed his arms and pecs, and my mouth watered, eyes taking in the display. *What I wouldn't give to get my hands on those...* I jerked my gaze back to his, and frowned at the satisfied gleam in his eyes. He scooted his chair closer to my bed so he could talk in a low voice. "Maybe you shouldn't come away with me. I saw that look in your eyes. You'll probably take advantage of me at the earliest opportunity. I just don't know if my delicate sensibilities can handle it."

I laughed nervously while his face moved closer to mine, and I could hear my heart rate monitor speed up slightly. My breath was coming out faster, and tingles ran through my whole body as he leaned down to my ear.

"You wouldn't take advantage of me, would you? You're a good girl." His whispered words made my nipples hard, and wetness flooded my panties as he quickly nipped my earlobe. I gasped softly, trying to hold back a moan as my eyes closed.

His chuckle in my ear a second later made my eyes fly open and I weakly pushed him back. I knew I couldn't actually move him if he didn't want move, but he let me put him at a safer distance anyway.

His eyes glanced quickly to the heart monitor, still beeping faster than normal. I took a few deep, calming breaths and waited for my heart rate to get back to normal before I responded. What he didn't know about me- or maybe he did, I honestly had no idea right now- was that I had a stubborn, competitive streak in me. His teasing had felt like a gauntlet being thrown at my feet. It sounded like a challenge- no, a dare. And I never backed down from those.

"Yes," I said simply.

He looked taken aback. "What do you mean, 'yes'?"

"I mean yes, I'll go with you on this business trip of yours. I could use a break from normality, and I suppose that spending some time with you could help jog my memory about... us." I could see that I'd surprised him and I gave myself a victory point.

"Okay then. Let me grab a doctor and see if we can get you checked out of here. By the way, your sister brought you a new phone since yours was all smashed up." He pointed to my side table and then walked away before I could say anything else and I shook my head. He acted like he was afraid to be around me but I felt like I was the one who should be careful. My body's responses to him were nothing I'd ever experienced, and although I was usually able to keep a cool head on my shoulders, I had the feeling that this guy could turn me upside down.

Aidan came back in with my doctor who I only half-listened to tell me about after care and what prescriptions for pain he was going to give me. An hour and a half later we were leaving the hospital and Aidan was helping me get into his car to take me back to my place. Staring out at the fading sunset, I realized I had just dumped into a whole vat of trouble agreeing to go away with someone who was a virtual stranger to me. Especially with one who obviously had a strong effect on me.

You're in some seriously deep shit, Calliope Drakos.

CHAPTER NINE
CALLIE

The drive to my apartment was quiet except for the directions I gave Aidan. When I asked him why he didn't know where I lived after dating for three months he just shrugged and said, "You always wanted to go over to my place or we went out".

He acted like it wasn't a big deal so I let it go. He parked, and I debated for a few seconds about whether I should invite him in or not before he made the decision for me. He got out of the car and came around to my side, opening my door before I finished gathering the bag the hospital had given me for my things. I looked up at him, his hand out and waiting to help me out of the car. I ignored it and heat creeped up my neck when he moved back and chuckled at my stubbornness.

Although I felt relief at his willingness to give me that space, I was also filled with inexplicable disappointment. If he hadn't moved I would've ended up rubbing my body along his all the way up. I shook my head at myself for being disappointed that I didn't get the chance to rub against him like a cat in heat. I trudged down the sidewalk to my door, very aware of his presence close behind me. I became flustered when he stopped right against my back as I was trying to unlock the door.

I didn't realize my hands were shaking until I dropped my keys before getting them into the deadbolt once. Twice. On my third try, Aidan reached around me and grabbed the keys out of my hand. I held on to them tighter, not quite willing to admit defeat. He tugged harder, trying not to hurt my hand but also letting me know he wasn't going to let go. I rolled my eyes but let him take them, stepping aside so he could get to the lock

"Why are you so fucking stubborn?" I heard him mutter under his breath as he smoothly slid the key into the two locks. I held back a small smile, my lips twitching in amusement at how annoyed he sounded. He'd seemed willing to let me try and do everything myself but now I was seeing some of the frustration leak out. I couldn't deny it gave me just the tiniest bit of satisfaction to be affecting him in any way.

He let me go in first, following close behind. I watched him as he looked around my place, face expressionless. Suddenly I was dying to know what he was thinking, what my apartment told him about me that he didn't already know. I also glanced around, imagining I was seeing it through his eyes.

I lived simply, but comfortably. I didn't have much in the way of things, but everything I did have was centered on comfort. The plushiest couch I'd ever sat on was against the wall facing the door. I'd painted the walls a barely-there blue, and had a large painting of an ocean and sky that blended almost seamlessly with the wall color. A medium-sized TV sat on a simple entertainment center with only a handful of DVDs. I had a Wii so that I could watch Hulu and Netflix, but I'd always been more of a book person. You only had to look at the bookcases against the wall in my dining room, filled to the brim.

Along with the bookcases was a small dining table and four chairs around it, with a seating bar connecting it to the open kitchen. I kept everything clean most of the time, but there were some pillows haphazardly thrown around in the front room, and my laptop sat open with papers scattered everywhere on the dining table.

My home was my sanctuary. It was where I could escape from people, a safe place for my mind so I tended not to invite people over. My family and Char were the only people I'd ever had over- and now it made complete sense that Aidan had never been here before. Knowing myself, I probably hadn't been sure enough about him to invite him in.

Satisfaction filled me when the first thing Aidan reacted to were my bookshelves. His face lit up with a small smile and he went to investigate them. I left him to it, walking down the hallway to my bedroom. I passed the second room which I'd turned into a sort of library-office combo where I had three more full bookcases lined against the wall, and in my room, I had another one about halfway filled.

"When you're done looking at those books, there's more in the room back this way," I called out. I didn't get a response, but I really hadn't expected one. I dropped my stuff on my relaxing chair near the bay window and laid down on my king-sized bed. I sank an inch or two into the blankets and pillow-top mattress and a grin spread across my face at the feeling. This was my favorite place in my apartment, followed closely by the bay window. I absolutely adored my huge, ridiculously soft bed and I didn't think I'd ever get used to the sensation of sinking into it. I hummed quietly in happiness and closed my eyes.

I laid there for a few minutes and I'd almost started to doze off when Aidan's voice startled me. My eyes popped open and I realized that he was quoting something to me.

"'The thing about chaos, is that while it disturbs us, it too, forces our hearts to roar in a way we find secretly magnificent.'" His voice trailed off and he looked up from a book; I'd put together

some of my favorite poems and bound them together and that's the book he'd apparently picked up. His eyes met mine and my breath stopped at the burning intensity I saw there. "This is an interesting poem to leave a bookmark at." His eyes roamed down my body quickly, then around my room. I sat up as gracefully as possible (which wasn't easy, seeing as how I'd all but been swallowed by my bed) while he was looking away.

His eyes met mine again as I nervously ran my hands through my hair, hoping it hadn't turned into a bigger mess than it already was. "I uh… It's one of my favorite poems." I cleared my throat when he just stared at me, seeming to wait for more. "I read it a lot, especially when my life seems to be getting out of hand. It helps me to remember that I'm doing what I love and that chaos can be good for me."

He nodded. Before I could move or say anything else, he was sitting next to me on my bed. He jerked a bit as he sank down more than he had expected to and it made me grin even though his nearness made my heart feel like it was trying to escape my chest. He scowled at me playfully and bumped my knee with his own.

Handing me the book, he said, "Show me another of your favorites."

I swallowed hard, my throat suddenly dry. I could feel the energy between us buzz up my arm when our hands touched while he passed me the book. I rifled through absentmindedly, thinking about the tingle in my arm when I realized I'd stopped at a page. I glanced at it and my cheeks heated with embarrassment. I tried to flip to another one but Aidan stopped me.

"Stop. Read it to me." His voice was deeper than before and I couldn't meet his eyes as I hesitated. When I realized I was being ridiculous, I straightened my spine and met his gaze with determination. I wasn't going to let my physical reactions keep me from being brave. This was just another kind of chaos, one I didn't know how to handle yet. I had this particular poem by an unknown author memorized, and I wasn't going to hide behind my book to recite it. I licked my lips before starting, and his eyes tracked the movement.

"'I wanted him in the bluntest way. I wanted his lips, his hands, his arms. I wanted him in the way the ocean wants the shore, constantly reaching and running back. I wanted him the way rain wants to fall, the way the sun wants to shine, the way the words want to be read. I wanted him to infinity, to the millionth degree, no amount of rain could douse the fire I had in me for him.'" I'd planned on finishing the poem strongly, but as my voice trailed off I could hear the want, the plain desire in its breathiness. I had never experienced something as sensual as this moment, right here. I could feel that I was practically begging him with my eyes to kiss me, touch me, anything.

I glanced down and saw his hands squeezed tightly into fists beside him. My eyes couldn't stop but rake over him and my breath caught in my throat audibly as I saw that he was unmistakably hard. My nipples peaked in response, and I could see the bulge swell even more as I stared. I quickly glanced back up to his face in shock. He met mine on the way up from staring at my breasts and the hard tips poking through my thin bra and shirt.

I felt the bed shift, but I wasn't sure if it was him leaning towards me or the other way around. Or maybe it was both of us. My breathing picked up and I was on the verge of lunging at him when three loud knocks on my door rang through my apartment.

We both jerked back, and I stood up quickly. I practically ran out of my room to the front door. I expected to hear him laughing behind me, mocking me for escaping so quickly but I heard nothing. I tried to catch my breath, checking through my peephole to see who it was.

KNOCK KNOCK KNOCK. "Calliope Drakos, I swear if you don't let me in I'm going to-" I ripped the door open before Char could continue shouting and knocking out in the hallway. I glared at him, partly because he was being obnoxious and partly because he had interrupted my almost-kiss with Aidan. No, wait, I was grateful for that part. Right?

"Charles, what are you doing here?" I had to move out of his way quickly because he had already started to shove his way into the apartment. He looked around like he was searching for something. Or some*one*. My heart squeezed.

"Don't 'Charles' me little miss sneaky pants, where is he?" He folded his arms as I shut my door and tried to put on a blank face.

"Who?" I asked as innocently as possible but Char always could see right through me. He studied me for a beat, then two, then three and four. I started to flush at his scrutiny. His eyes widened and he came closer.

"Were you making out with him just now?"

"NO," I protested too loudly. "Well, not yet."

Char crowed quietly in triumph. "You bitch! I can't believe you've been hiding this from me!"

"Well join the club Char. I can barely believe it either. How did you know about him anyway?"

"Your dad called me while you were still knackered out in the hospital. Said you might be going away for a couple weeks and wanted to give me a heads up."

"Great. Well, to make a long story short, I've apparently been dating this guy for the last few months and now I'm going away with him on some business trip so he can make sure I don't worsen and so we can 'reacquaint' ourselves with each other."

"Ah, I see your dad wasn't exaggerating about the amnesia thing."

"Unfortunately not." We both paused for a moment. It was only when the water from my bathroom shut off that I noticed it'd been running. Char whipped around and I stared over his shoulder as we watched Aidan emerge from the bathroom with the edges of his hair damp. I grinned but quickly wiped it off my face before he could see it. I was betting he splashed cold water on his face to try and cool down. I glanced at his crotch for a second and noticed that the freaking monster in his pants had gone into hibernation for this awkward meeting.

"Holy shit," Char said quietly to no one in particular. I started grinning again. Holy shit was right. Even though whatever was happening annoyed and confused me, it was impossible to deny that Aidan was quite the specimen. It almost made me sick but I was too busy drooling on the inside.

Aidan looked back and forth between the two of us with a raised eyebrow. I shook myself out of my stupor to introduce them.

"Char, this is Aidan, and Aidan this is Char, my best friend and business partner."

Char strutted to meet Aidan halfway. "Well no wonder you hid this guy from everyone Callie, he's a damn god! If I looked like him I'd have my pick of guys any minute of every day."

A laugh burst out of Aidan as they shook hands. "It's good to meet you too Charles. I knew about you, but no one mentioned how handsome you are. If I weren't straighter than a ruler..." Aidan shrugged casually and I swear Char swooned.

Char glanced back at me as I rolled my eyes at them. "That's it babe, he's mine. Claimed. Dibs."

Aidan was grinning so big I could've stuck a quarter in his damn dimples. I glared at Char's hand still grasping Aidan's. A tinge of jealousy went through me even though I knew they were both just joking. However, it didn't stop me from wanting to claw my best friend's eyes out for a split second. He read the near murderous look in my eyes and reluctantly dropped Aidan's hand.

"By the way Aidan, you can call me Char. All my friends do."

"Char it is. So, what brings you here, other than trying to steal her man?" He gestured toward me and Char cut me off before I could retort that he wasn't *my man*.

"Wanted to check up on my girl." I noticed Aidan's hands tense slightly at that phrasing, and I watched as he tried to make himself relax. I could almost hear him chanting *he's gay* in his head over and over. "And, as I was telling Callie when she let me in, her dad called me to check if it was alright that she went on a vacation for a couple weeks. So I came to talk some business with her before she took off. When are you guys leaving?"

"Tomorrow," Aidan answered. He looked at me and I could see the question in his glance to see if I had any more arguments. I probably did, but I couldn't think of any at the moment. "We're flying out tomorrow," he repeated. "Which reminds me, I've got to go talk to my boss about the specifics and getting that extra ticket secured."

Aidan walked towards me and pulled me into a tight hug. I was stiff at first, unsure what to do. After a few seconds I leaned into it and hugged him back. I drew in a deep breath, his masculine scent filling my nose. He pulled back and rested his hands on my hips. Squeezing them briefly, he searched my eyes.

"So, I'll see you…" I trailed off, unsure.

"I'll pick you up tomorrow night; we'll be taking a bit of a later flight. Can you be ready by 6:30?"

I nodded and he smiled. He leaned forward and kissed my cheek, lingering for a few seconds before facing Char again.

"It really was good to meet you Char. I hope to see you again soon."

"Likewise," Char replied cheerily.

Aidan shut the door after himself. I didn't realize I was staring at the closed door, fingers grazing where his lips had rested on my cheek until Char let out a low whistle.

"You've got it bad, girl. I'm still pissed you didn't tell me about him."

"I guess I didn't tell anyone about him," I sighed and turned back to him. I fell down on my couch, head back and hands covering my face. Everything was moving so fast and this was my first real chance to breathe since Aidan wasn't around. I felt the seat next to me dip as Char joined me.

"Callie, love," Char pulled a hand away from my face to get me to look at him, "I'm not judging you for anything… But it just seems a little weird that you didn't tell anyone about this guy before all of this." He motioned towards the lump on my head. "You're a private person, but you usually tell me things. And you're close with your family so it's not like they would disown you for dating someone a little rough at the edges like him."

My brain throbbed hard at his words. I could feel myself on the verge of tears, and I just didn't want to deal with all of this right now. There was no way to prove anything since I just couldn't *remember*. My voice cracked as I replied to Char.

"Can we just leave it alone for now? We really need to figure out a plan for the next two weeks that I'm gone." Char searched my eyes and finally nodded. We made our way to my home office and Char started to tell me about the last candidate he'd talked to and how he might have a couple potential matches for her.

I pushed everything but business out of my mind and it only took us a couple hours to get everything solidified. Char left after a tight hug of support and I went straight to bed telling myself that I could worry about my problems in the morning.

Chapter Ten
Aidan

I sat in the parking lot of my office building around 9 pm, well after closing hours, trying to get my shit together. Lucy was upstairs waiting for me to talk to her about the details of this little extravaganza I was going on, and I was dreading it. I'd been working up to asking Lucy out, and now I had to tell her that I was taking a different woman with me on a two-week business trip.

I was hoping that it didn't ruin my chances with her, but I was also conflicted because I'd almost kissed Callie in her room. I'd wanted it more than I'd wanted anything in a long time. Which confused me because I loved Lucy, and had for years. I'm sure it'd just been the intensity of the moment with Callie that made me feel like hauling her over onto my lap and seeing if the taste of her mouth was as addictive as her voice. I swear Callie's voice was even more alluring than her normal voice when she recited that poem to me. And I already thought her normal voice was hot as hell. It was like she'd put a spell on me with her words, drowning me in the cadence.

I could feel my body responding to the memory again and glared at my crotch. *Calm down buddy, you're not getting near her any time soon.* I shook my head at myself and jumped out of the car to head to my office to deal with this shit.

I walked into the lobby and took a moment to stare at the quote I'd had etched into the wall behind the reception desk. It was something my adoptive parents had always said to me,

49

and seeing as they'd inspired my business, I'd only felt it was right to include it. I read the words and could hear my mom's voice in my head.

"In order to love who you are, you cannot hate the experiences that shaped you." It'd been coined by Andrea Dykstra, and I had heard it said so many times I didn't need to read the words but I liked to anyway. I felt a buzzing in my pocket and pulled out my phone to see a text from Lucy.

Are you going to stare at the wall all night or are you going to come up and talk to me? A smiley face followed in another text a second later and I looked up to the second level with a grin. I saw Lucy waving to me from the glass window of the conference room that she liked to use when her desk space wasn't enough. I jogged up the stairs and opened the door to find architectural plans splayed all across the table.

"I figured since you were moving the trip up by a couple days that I would just double check and make sure I didn't miss anything before you took my babies away." Lucy grinned at me before leaning down to adjust a line or two on the plans. Lucy was the designer of the two of us, which meant she would plan the buildings, what went inside, and how everything was organized.

My part of the job was more hands on. I found the land, made sure everything went smoothly when building, and decided which of our employees would be handling the day-to-day operations for each venue.

Lucy liked to tease that I was the heart of the operation, but she was the brains. Since I had no mind for planning architecture on paper, I was grateful that she did and that I could trust her. I would tell Lucy what I was imagining for a space and she would draw it up almost perfectly. I could read her plans well enough to know if something wasn't quite right and she helped me with making sure we had the right people on our teams.

"This looks great, Lucy. Thanks again."

She waved my gratitude away without looking up at me. "This is the fifth building we've put up Aidan. You don't have to thank me every time. It's my job."

"Yeah, but it's more than just a job to me."

She finally looked up with sympathy in her warm brown eyes. "I know that Aidan. That's one thing I love about you."

My heart beat harder and I could feel my forehead start to sweat a little with what I had to say next. "So... Do you think there's any chance you could book an extra ticket for my flight tomorrow?"

"I can try. What's up?"

"I uh… I'm taking someone with me." She stared at me. I sweat a little more. "I can get you whatever information of hers you need to book the ticket."

Her eyes bugged a little. "Her??"

"Yeah. Her name is Callie. We've been dating for a few months and she just had an accident and needs someone with her for a bit so I decided that she could just come with me plus then I can show her what I do and-"

"Okay Aidan," Lucy held out a hand to stop me from continuing to blab. "I don't need every single detail or reason." She smiled warmly at me. "I'm happy you're dating someone, although just a tad offended I haven't heard about her before now. Seriously though, congratulations! I want to meet her soon." She hugged me quickly and then went back to her plans. I just stood there, completely shocked.

"Um yeah, okay." The words strangled out of my throat. I felt like I'd been sucker punched in the stomach and I couldn't breathe. She was genuinely happy for me to be dating

51

someone else, and all this time I thought that my efforts to make something happen between us was heading in the right direction.

"If you come back in the morning I'll have your tickets and the plans ready to go in plenty of time for your flight. Now go home and get some sleep, I'm sure you've got a long day ahead of you tomorrow." She physically shooed me out of the room, and I was still too dumbstruck to argue or fight.

I'd been best friends with her brother Nick since middle school so I'd known and loved her for well over ten years. And now it felt like it was all for nothing. I stared at Lucy for a minute before heading back out to my car. I somehow made it home safely and into bed without paying any attention to my surroundings. I shot off a quick email to Lucy with Callie's information that I knew (thanks to Aphrodite) to get her a ticket. I stared up at my ceiling and tried to understand how lost I suddenly felt until I fell into a restless sleep.

CHAPTER ELEVEN
AIDAN

I woke up at 4 am feeling worse than when I'd gone to sleep. Every time I blinked it felt like sand was under my eyelids. I trudged my way downstairs to my home gym, knowing I wasn't going to be getting any more sleep anyway. I didn't like people trying to talk to me while I was working out, and I hated wearing headphones even more so I'd invested in a mini gym in my house. I had a weights corner, a stationary bike, and a TRX band. I'd also had a full wall turned into a mirror so I could watch my form. The last thing I'd had put in was a sound system that I could activate by saying its name and a command.

"Dwayne, play workout mix." Yes, I named my sound system Dwayne, after Dwayne "The Rock" Johnson. I had to pick something that I wouldn't accidentally say if I started to sing along, and the guy was cool as shit.

It took me an hour and a half to sweat out my misery. By the time I got into the shower any feelings I had were just a dull ache that I could easily ignore until they decided to surface again. My thoughts wandered to Callie as I got ready for the day and packed for the trip.

I'm sure she was feeling just as conflicted as I was, except she definitely had more of a reason. I almost felt bad for tricking her into all this, but I remembered Aphrodite's threat. Ever since my adoptive parents had passed away within three months of each other when I was twenty-one, I'd begun a search for my biological parents. I met Serena and Caleb when I was 9, and I loved the people that raised me after a string of bad foster homes. No matter how much I acted out with Serena and Caleb, they never hit me or punished me unfairly, teaching me that I could get farther in life by not fighting those who were just trying to help. It was only supposed to be temporary with them, but when the end of my time there came up I couldn't imagine going back into a home where abuse and starvation were the norm. Thankfully, they felt the same way I did and asked if I would be okay with them adopting me.

I never would have thought to look for the people who had abandoned me, but I found a letter after Serena and Caleb's deaths. It was in their bedside table, my name written across it in Caleb's strong handwriting. One of the things they said in the letter was to find my biological parents because I would regret it if I didn't. It had taken me a year to start the search since I'd been grieving Serena and Caleb's deaths too much to care about anything other than work. I'd forgotten about the letter until I found it going through some papers.

The trail had gone cold for a while, but in thee last seven months one of the investigators I'd hired had caught a hint. I felt like I was closing in, and then this mess happened.

I bet Callie had grown up in the perfect home, with the perfect family. Everyone from her life that I'd met so far seemed like they were super close, and it frustrated me for a moment to think that I'd had such a hard time keeping family around.

I grabbed my phone to text Lucy. Ignoring the sinking feeling in my stomach about having to face her again with a broken heart while she was perfectly fine, I typed out my message.

Hey Luce, I'm heading over to the office. Want to grab some lunch before I head out?

Her response came within a minute. *Of course I do! You're paying yeah? My job doesn't pay much. ;)*

Yeah right it doesn't. I'll see you in 30 minutes, mooch.

Sounds good! I'm picking the place, btw. I'm sick of eating Chinese food all the damn time.

You got it, you big baby.

I chuckled as I rolled my carry on and suitcase out to my car. I was planning on heading over to Callie's after leaving work since it was between my office and the airport. Maybe I would surprise her and show up a bit early. I grinned mischievously at the idea, excited to see how she'd react to the surprise. *Here's hoping she yells at me. She's even prettier when she's pissed,* I thought to myself. I sang along to some oldies on the way to work, feeling a bit better about the situation.

"I'll take the guacamole bacon burger, medium with provolone cheese instead of swiss please, fries and a side of mayo." Lucy handed the menu back with a smile to the waitress at Red Robin without even looking at it. She was the kind of person that knew what she liked and rarely drifted from it. She got the same burger every time, but she tended to switch her drinks. This time she'd decided to get the mint brownie shake. She proceeded to eat a brownie piece while I asked for the same of what she had except with onion rings and ranch.

After the waitress left I expected Lucy to launch into a barrage of questions about Callie and our relationship. She surprised me by staying quiet, slowly sipping her shake. I sighed overdramatically and stretched my long legs out under the table, invading her space like I knew she hated. She glared at me but I saw the mirth twitching at her lips.

"Alright, what do you want to know?"

She grinned so big, I was afraid that she was about to pull out a list of questions she'd prepared before the lunch. She'd done that before, so I wouldn't have put it past her.

"Her name is Callie right?" I nodded. "A nickname?"

"Yeah, her full name is Calliope."

"OOH, like the Greek muse of poetry?! Awesome!"

I sat up straight, staring at Lucy. How the fuck did that not sink in before now?!

Lucy looked at the expression on my face and laughed. "What, you didn't think of that Mr. I'm-Obsessed-With-Everything-Greek? You've been dating for three months, I was sure you'd caught on to that by now if not at first."

"God, I feel stupid." I laughed out loud. "She's even obsessed with poetry, you should see her bookcases."

"That better not be a euphemism."

"No, I'm serious. That girl has five or six bookcases in her apartment, all of them over flowing but the one in her room."

Lucy wiggled her eyebrows at me. "Her room, eh?"

"Oh shut up," I growled and looked away, feeling like an idiot for the blush I could feel rising on my cheeks. I was thirty-one, too old to be blushing at the mention of being in a girl's room.

Lucy chuckled but let it go. "How'd you guys meet?"

Slight panic rose in my chest. I hadn't thought about that part, not realizing that people would be asking. I sorted through what I knew of Callie to come up with something believable. Then I struck gold with an idea, assisted by the information filtering into my brain about Callie.

"You remember that event I went to about three months back?"

"You mean the 'charity gala'?" She smirked at me.

"Yeah, the event you told me was for charity but was actually some kind of speed-dating meet-up thing." I glared at her once again for the trick she'd played on me three months earlier. She'd been teasing me about being alone forever shortly before the event. The morning the event was taking place, she told me that she had signed up to go to a charity event but couldn't make it and would I please oh please go in her stead? I agreed without doing any kind of research. I'd put on formal wear because she'd called it a charity gala, so I assumed I'd need to go in something nice.

To my surprise when I'd walked in to the rented-out hotel event space, I'd been the best dressed person there. Everyone looked nice, but no one was dressed to the nines like me. I'd panicked and looked around, my eyes catching on a huge banner over the doors I'd walked in. EROS MEET AND GREET it read, with a shadowed cameo of two people kissing, arrows shooting into their hearts. There were some stations around the room with heart balloons floating above each area, a label attached saying things like "For The Adventurous" and "Walk The Dogs" and I quickly caught on that I'd walked into a trap. Before I could make my escape I'd been greeted by a distracted host, telling me to write my username and age on a tag. She'd turned away, speaking into a headset before I could tell her that I was in the wrong place.

I'd whipped my phone out to discourage a couple females giving me the eye from coming over and called Lucy to yell at her. She hadn't answered of course. I'd ended up staying for a good twenty minutes before I could make my escape from the meet and greet of an apparently popular dating service.

I focused again on Lucy who was trying not to laugh from remembering how angry I'd been at her when I found her later that night. It'd only taken me telling her a few stories of the ridiculousness to see the humor in it.

"I stand by my threat, by the way. Trick me into one of those ever again and you'll regret my payback."

"Ooh, soooo scary," she sarcastically returned.

We fell quiet as our food arrived. Lucy opened her burger and wrinkled her nose at the onions, picking them off with her fork.

"How is it that you always order the same thing but forget to ask for no onions every single time?"

"I have no idea. I just get too excited about the fries I think." Lucy had already stuffed a few said fries in her mouth so she'd answered me while chewing. "Anyway, so did you meet her there?"

"Sort of. When I went home later that night I found a note in my pocket from a 'PoetryInMotion100'. All it said was 'give me a call, I promise you won't be disappointed' and then a phone number. It intrigued me so I called, and her voice was beautiful. Turned out to be Callie, so we chatted for a week or two and met up for a few dates. I found out later that she actually owns the company that put the meet-and-greet together. As they say, the rest is history."

"So you're saying that I'm the reason you have a girlfriend?"

"I *suppose* if you'd like to take credit for that then there's nothing I can do to stop you. However, I'd like to think that my good looks and boy-ish charm won her over."

"Honey," she paused for effect, "There is nothing boy-ish about you. You're 100% man and nothing you can do will change that. It's not your fault, it's just good genes my friend."

I expected to feel warmth spread through me at her compliment like it usually would, but I only felt mild chagrin. *Interesting*, I thought and brushed it off.

"Anywho, I think I like this Callie girl. She's bold enough to go for what she wants and still lets you do the work. Smart girl."

I snorted. "Yeah, and stubborn as all get-out."

"Beautiful too, I bet."

I nodded silently, not trusting my words. She was one of the most gorgeous women I'd ever laid eyes on. Lucy was beautiful, but there was something about Callie that pulled me in. I found my mind wandering back to those moments when she recited the poem to me. Her purple eyes had been fierce and passionate, voice caressing my soul. I was sure that memory I would never forget.

"Earth to Aidan." I jerked my gaze back to Lucy who was waving a fry in my face. "Are you going to daydream all day or eat?"

I dug into my food at her prodding and she thankfully turned our conversation to something I didn't have to really think about. We chatted casually through the rest of lunch and I waved her money away from the bill when it came. We drove back to the office where she gave me the blueprints in a travel-safe tube, and the flight information.

"Hey Aidan?" Lucy casually intoned as I turned to leave. I looked back at her over my shoulder, an eyebrow raised. "Fly safe. Let me know if you have any issues with anything over there. And I don't just mean the business crap."

I was confused as to why she'd be willing to help me with my romance, but then I also supposed that she wasn't interested in me the way I'd wanted her to be. Want her to be. Present tense. I still loved her, no matter how attracted I was to Callie. I nodded my thanks and made my way out to my car. I put the tube in the trunk with my luggage and looked at my watch. It was only 4 pm, and I could be over to Callie's in an hour. I got behind the wheel and started driving, ready to surprise poor Callie an hour and a half early. *I'm sure we'll find something to do.* I smiled as heat traveled through my body at the thought.

CHAPTER TWELVE
CALLIE

I was out of the shower and walking around my apartment in just my towel, munching on a handful of grapes while I air-dried when someone knocked on my door. I'd been thinking about what this business trip would entail, half hoping for some steamy make-out sessions at the very least. Aidan and I had probably kissed before but since I couldn't remember any of it, I felt like this would be the first time. I laughed quietly to myself on my way to the door, feeling like Drew Barrymore in *50 First Dates*. I didn't even think to check the peephole before I opened the door and almost dropped the rest of my grapes in surprise when I saw the objects of my thoughts standing there with a huge grin on his face.

The grin dropped along with his eyes when he realized I was only wearing wet hair and a towel. *OH MY GOD I WAS ONLY IN A TOWEL.* I slammed the door shut with that bolt of realization. Then I just stood there realizing that I hadn't even said anything to him before slamming the door in his face.

Little giggles started escaping from my throat, escalating until full-blown, nearly hysterical laughter had me bent in half. It took me a few seconds to realize that Aidan was calling my name through my door. I looked through the peephole and I saw Aidan run his hands through his hair, then fold his arms impatiently.

"Callie?" He called my name again, not as loudly since he could hear I wasn't laughing anymore.

"Yes Aidan? Aren't you a bit early?" I asked through the door.

"I got here faster than I thought I would."

I checked the clock in my dining room. "You're almost two hours early."

Silence from the other side. I started to turn the handle again and heard a harsh "NO" from Aidan. I paused, surprised at the vehemence in his voice. I checked through the peephole again and saw him staring at the handle of my door, fists tensed at his sides.

"Go get dressed before you let me inside, Callie." His voice was dangerously low, and it reverberated through my body even from the other side of my door. The tingles that I got every time I was around him started when I realized what he wasn't saying out loud. The devious side of me wanted to fling the door open and see his reaction to me in my towel again, but the cautious side of me warned me not to try his patience.

"Okay, give me a minute." I stuffed the rest of the grapes in my mouth and rushed back into my room, quickly putting on the clothes I'd set out to wear for the flight. My shirt was a light green, plain V-neck t-shirt and my black leggings were thick enough that you wouldn't be able to see through them even if I bent over. I ran back to the front door and opened it quickly to find Aidan leaning against the wall opposite my door, playing with his phone.

He looked up and studied me all the way from my toes to my still-wet hair. His slow perusal made me flush but I ignored it and motioned for him to come on in. He walked by me and since his 6'5" frame took up so much space his arm brushed my boob, lighting up my nerves. I was a taller-than-average woman at 5'8" in bare feet, so I loved that he was so tall.

"I'm going to finish getting ready, so feel free to wander I guess."

He looked back at me now. "What if I get bored?"

I crossed my arms and tapped a foot. "Well that's your own damn fault for being so early, isn't it?" My voice was sickeningly sweet, totally overdoing it. Aidan only grinned back at me and shrugged.

"Like I said, I got here faster than I planned."

Rolling my eyes, I walked to the bathroom attached to my room. I had a pretty sweet deal with this apartment. Two baths, two beds, a washer and dryer in the unit, and that bay window. That's really what hooked me on this place. Sure, it was bit more expensive that way, but I liked space.

I quickly dried my hair, styling my bangs and a few face framing strays but braiding the rest. I figured that two simple French braids were the best option for traveling. I couldn't do just one because if I leaned my head back it got in the way with the headrest in the car, so I figured it'd be the same while flying. The only makeup I bothered to put on was a couple layers of mascara and some Burts Bee's Chapstick.

I walked back into my room, contemplating whether I should wear my black sparkle Converse like I had been planning to, or the black wedges with the ankle strap that I could wear for hours on end.

I ended up falling back on my original plan with the Cons. Didn't want to look like I was trying too hard. I shoved the wedges in my suitcase, along with a pair of wicked tall heels in a shade of purple that matched my eyes exactly. I had no idea if I'd get the chance to wear them, but I wanted them just in case.

I was just slipping on the second shoe, using my bed for support when I heard Aidan's voice behind me.

"Are these the only suitcases you're taking?" He pointed toward my luggage lined up by my door.

"Well, technically only one of them is a suitcase. The other is my carry on."

"Semantics. Do you want to take them out to my car?"

"I guess. What are we going to do with the last," I checked the time on my new phone, "forty-five minutes until we have to leave?"

"We could head to the airport now, just get check in and security over with. Then I guess we could find a cafe at the airport and people watch with the rest of our spare time."

I smiled, actually excited by this. I enjoyed people-watching, it was hilarious to see the things people did when they had no idea someone was watching. I agreed and we headed out.

After double checking I wasn't forgetting anything I might need and getting loaded into his car, we started towards the airport.

"What do you want to listen to?"

I shrugged. "Well I'm sure you know I like a little of everything. Surprise me." He tapped his fingers on the steering wheel while thinking.

After seeming to decide he pressed a couple buttons on the touch screen of his dashboard and to my great surprise, Adele's smoky voice filled the car. It was a bit of an older one, but "Chasing Pavements" was a favorite of mine. I started to sing along because I never could help myself from singing along to songs I knew. During the first chorus I looked over to Aidan to see him glancing at me over and over. I decided to make it worth his while and started to get really dramatic, making faces and using my hands for emphasis. He laughed quietly at my antics and I thought that maybe he actually liked hearing me sing.

The song finished just as we stopped at a light and he watched me as I finished the last line. I grinned back at him, admiring his dimples, feeling completely relaxed. I didn't think I had a half-bad voice, and was glad to see he wasn't crying from having to listen to me warble along with Adele.

The light turned green and Aidan focused back on the road. I playfully leaned over to his side of the car and began to poke his ear, inspecting it.

"What the- what're you doing?" Aidan moved his ear away from me as much as he could while still driving, obviously very confused.

"I just wanted to make sure your ears weren't bleeding from having to listen to me sing," I teased.

He snorted. "If you're checking for an effect of your singing, you're looking at the wrong body part."

I tilted my head, confused. He looked at me and then glanced down at his lap. My eyes followed the hint, and I saw the obvious bulge.

"Heavens," I squeaked out.

"More like hell," he grumbled back. I giggled in response and settled back into my seat. Some John Mayer was playing through the car now, but I was only humming along out of reflex. I was still distracted by what was happening in Aidan's pants, to be completely honest. Aidan adjusted in his seat, trying to get comfortable. I laughed quietly under my breath while watching him out of the corner of my eye. *Good luck with that dude,* I thought to myself.

Aidan turned the music down a bit and then looked at me. I could feel a question coming and waited patiently for him to voice it.

"You're okay with all of this? How's your head feeling?" I wasn't sure what I was expecting him to say, but that definitely wasn't it.

"You know what? I'm doing alright. It's still confusing and I'm not sure what this little 'vacation' is going to be like, but I figure it can't hurt. And my head isn't throbbing nearly as bad. I have a feeling it'll start to bother me a bit when we're on the plane, with all the air pressure, but I've brought my pain killers to fix that."

"Okay good. I just wanted to be sure that you didn't feel I forced you into this whole thing. I don't you to accuse me of kidnapping you later." He half grinned, the dimple on his left side staying hidden.

"Well, I might feel like everything was a bit rushed but that's probably only because of the stupid amnesia." I looked him over. "I wish I could remember everything."

His face fell for a split second, then shifted to something more neutral. "I'm sure it'll come back eventually." I nodded hopefully. "So, Char was quite…" He trailed off, trying to find a descriptor appropriate for my best friend.

I chuckled. "Yeah. He's a character. Gayer than a rainbow and sweeter than Skittles."

Aidan laughed at my description. "I can believe the gay part, but I think the sweetness is a front. He seems like the kind of person that could burn you alive with his words alone."

Now I was the one laughing. "You've got that right. That's one of the reasons I call him Char actually."

"I like him," Aidan thoughtfully said after our laughter died down. I smiled happily, glad that he approved. Not that I needed it, I just liked that he got along with someone close to me.

We'd reached the airport by this point, and it didn't take us long at all to find somewhere to park. We did the usual routine of getting our checked bags taken care of and getting through the security check. Surprisingly it all went very smoothly, and I hadn't even had to take my laptop out of the backpack that I was using as my carry on. By the time we'd finished all of that, we still had about thirty minutes to spare.

"Where do you want to go?" He motioned to the many choices the airport laid out for us. I glanced around, and found someplace.

"I've never been to Blue Sky Bar. I definitely think I'm going to need something stronger."

"I know what you mean." I followed him to the hostess standing at a little podium. "Do you have a couple seats at the bar?"

She was staring at him without answering and I could feel my eye start to twitch. I cleared my throat to get her attention and she jerked like she was coming out of a stupor. She glanced quickly at me and back at Aidan. Her face heated but she nodded stiffly and motioned for us to follow her, mumbling something incoherent. Aidan looked at me and grinned satisfyingly. I refused to respond to that look and shoved him to follow her. I heard him laugh quietly and I knew my reaction only encouraged him. She sat us down at the bar, handed us some drink menus and scurried away.

"Could she have been any more obvious," I grumbled to Aidan. I refused to look at him and instead burned a hole in the middle of the menu.

"What drink do you want," he asked. I could hear the laughter in his voice so I ignored him. "Callie."

I looked up. His eyes were intense, holding my stare for a few seconds before I tore my eyes away and looked back at the menu. "Breckenridge Burro," I blurted out before he could say anything else. I didn't want to talk about the apparent jealously I was showing. I could tell he was going to tease me about it and I was trying to avoid that, if at all possible.

"What?"

"My drink. That's what I want." A dimple began to form on his right cheek and I glared playfully at him. "Leave it alone. Now order me my damn drink." I slapped the drink menu on the bar in front of me and stared at one of the TV's across from me.

The bartender picked that moment to check on us. Aidan ordered the Breckenridge Burro for me, and a Highland Mist whiskey. His choice didn't surprise me, he seemed like a whiskey kind of guy.

"You don't have to worry about other girls, baby." I shivered at his voice in my ear. He'd leaned close, casually throwing an arm around my waist and pulling me into him. "I've got you, I don't need them."

I quickly turned my head towards him. "I couldn't care less who you look at, or vice versa, I-" My words were cut off when my lips touched his. I hadn't realized he was still so close, and apparently he hadn't anticipated the movement either because we both sat there frozen, lips touching. Neither of us could pull away, and my wide eyes met his. I exhaled through my slightly open lips and his hand around my waist tightened.

Before I could pull back he nipped my bottom lip with his teeth. I drew my breath in sharply and my eyelids fell to half-mast. He pulled back, staring at me hotly. He ran his tongue over his bottom lip and I trailed the movement, wishing we weren't in public surrounded by people so I could replace his tongue with mine.

"This isn't over Callie. We'll be finishing that conversation soon." His eyes were full of wicked promises.

I was the first to break eye contact, distracted by the bartender bringing our drinks over. I downed half of mine in a few seconds, suddenly parched.

When I looked back at Aidan he was still looking at me heatedly and I said the first thing that came to my mind to break the tension.

"So Scottish whiskey? How is it?"

"It's good. This particular brand is one of my favorites. It's a bit stronger than most, but us Scottish people can handle it with no problem." He said this last part with a flawless Scottish accent.

"Oh, you're from Scotland?"

"Well I'm fairly sure my last name gives that away." When my face fell slightly he realized his error. "Oh shit Callie, I'm sorry. I didn't realize you wouldn't remember. My last name is McRae." He spelled it out for me and I indicated that I agreed, his last name was absolutely a giveaway.

Aidan started to look around the restaurant. He took another swallow of whiskey and then pointed behind me subtly enough that I only noticed because I was watching him. I turned and saw a couple sitting at a table. The woman was picking at a few fries left on her empty plate and glancing around absently while the guy droned on and on about something.

"Wow, she looks totally into this guy." I felt bad for her, stuck on what was obviously a terrible date.

"I bet it's a first date."

I looked back at him. "Why would they be having a first date at an airport?"

"Obviously so she has multiple routes of escape."

I snorted into my glass, half choking on the swallow I'd taken. "That seems pretty dramatic. All she'd have to do is call an Uber, no need to fly to another state."

"I guess that depends on how bad the date is."

I tossed my head back and laughed loudly enough to draw attention to myself. This tended to happen to me, so I paid them no mind. They quickly went back to their own conversations as I turned all the way back around to face Aidan.

"I'll give you points for that one. I wish I'd thought of that before I went on some of my own less-than-pleasant dates."

"Well I'm good for something at least."

"I was starting to wonder why I kept you around, but now I see I had good reason." We teased each other back and forth for another ten minutes before paying our bill and heading towards our gate. We were standing in line waiting to board when a sudden thought popped into my head. I looked up to the message board that displayed where we were flying to and from.

I breathed a sigh of relief- Denver to California. That means I'd packed the right clothes. I hadn't thought to ask before now, and I'd just packed some of my favorite things. It was early fall here in Colorado which meant it was still warm most of the time. Thoughts of Aidan had occupied my mind while packing so I hadn't put thought into whether I was packing the right stuff or not.

"What was that sigh for?"

"Oh, I'm just relieved we're going somewhere where it'll be warm. I didn't pack for cold weather and I'd be screwed if we were going somewhere like Michigan."

"Right, I didn't think to tell you where we were actually heading."

"That's alright; I hadn't thought to ask either. It's been a crazy last couple of days."

"You've got that damn right."

An announcement came on for our flight to let us know boarding was about to begin, and Aidan handed me my ticket. I looked at it out of curiosity, and when I noticed we were riding first class I let out a sound of excitement.

"Is something wrong Callie?"

"Not at all! We're in first class! I've never been on an airplane, and now I'm going first class! I feel guilty having you pay for it though."

"Don't even think about offering to pay me back. Especially since it's your first flight! It's a company trip, so it's the company's expense."

"Well… Are you sure your boss is okay with that?"

He laughed. "Yeah, the boss is perfectly fine with it. In fact, he insisted."

That surprised me. Not many bosses would insist that an employee bring their concussed girlfriend on a business trip. "Sounds like a good company. What do you do anyway?"

Before he could answer, one of the airport workers motioned for us to come forward to start boarding. We showed our tickets and I followed Aidan to our seats. I figured I'd wait for the answer until after we settled. Aidan motioned for me to slip into our row. There were only two seats so it's not like it mattered which of us sat where. I happened to glance over to Aidan while he stowed his carry on in the compartment above. I noticed that his shirt had ridden up just enough to catch a sliver of abs between his shirt and low-riding jeans.

"Do you want me to put yours up here too?"

I nodded and handed it over. I'd planned on keeping it with me but I wanted an excuse to take another look. I had my eyes fixed on where his shirt rode up last, and I caught a glorious eyeful of those lines that all girls drool over- the ones on a man's hips that basically make an arrow straight to their dicks. I was fairly sure Aidan knew I was staring because it seemed to take him longer than necessary to fit my backpack in the storage compartment.

Someone grumbled behind Aidan, waiting for him to finish so they could pass. Aidan grinned at me and I smiled right back even though I was fairly sure my thoughts were obvious with my cheeks flushing.

"Thanks," I said to Aidan when he got into his seat next to me.

"For what, exactly?" He knew I meant the view he'd given me, but I played it cool.

"For putting my backpack up there for me." I winked and Aidan shook his head.

"Oh, anytime Callie. Really," he leaned closer, "*Any*time. Just let me know."

I blushed even more furiously at the meaning in his words. I couldn't respond so I just nodded and avoided his gaze. I pretended not to notice when Aidan grabbed my hand and held it, intertwining our fingers. He gave my hand a small squeeze and I smiled to myself still looking out the window. I gave a tiny squeeze back though, just to let him know I was okay with all this.

The more I stared out the window, the more it hit me that I was on a plane, in first class, with a virtual stranger to me. I surprised myself- I'd never taken a risk like this before. I was the staid one in the family. We were all stubborn but I knew I took it almost to the point to where it drove people away. I could become snarky and a bit of a bitch. That's one reason I didn't really date, and why I didn't have an excessive amount of close friends.

I got along with people fairly well, but not a lot of them got close. I glanced over to Aidan again. He was still holding my hand, and doing something on his phone with the other. I'd somehow managed to find someone who put up with my bull-headedness. He liked me enough to watch over me when I couldn't remember who he was or anything about our relationship. Even though trusting him terrified me, a warm feeling in my chest told me that this was right. It didn't hurt that he was ridiculously good looking.

Soon, everyone was boarded and we started our take off. They gave us the safety and exit demonstration, and then left us to our own devices. I'd meant to ask Aidan again about what he did, but I was dozing off before I even knew I was tired. I promised myself to ask again when I woke up and let sleep take me, the comforting feeling of Aidan's hand wrapped in mine.

Chapter Thirteen
Aidan

I thought about letting go of Callie's hand when she fell asleep, but I decided it wasn't a big deal. She hadn't pulled away and I liked the feeling of her hand in mine. I watched her for a bit, noticing a small piece of hair blow across her cheek with every breath in and out. I reached over and pushed it to the side so that it wouldn't eventually wake her up. My hand moving across her skin was slower than necessary, but I told myself it was only because I didn't want to startle her. Not because she was even softer than she looked, or because she unconsciously tilted her face into my touch.

I looked back at my phone, checking a few other emails. I was about to mark one as spam when the weird username the sender had used, LoveMeLoveMe, caught my eye. Hoping it was just spam, and not who I was afraid it was, I clicked on the email with the subject line 'Congratulations On Your Progress'. I read the short but to the point email in disbelief, checking to make sure Callie was still asleep.

"Aidan- I'll know whether you just delete this email or actually read it. I've been keeping an eye on you and you've done well so far. This is will be easier than I thought! Remember, if you want to know who your parents are, don't mess this up. Love, Aphrodite P.S. Did I mention you've got two weeks to make her say she loves you? XOXO"

I carefully slipped my hand out of Callie's then, shock reverberating through me. Only two weeks to make someone fall in love with me? A someone who vowed to never fall in love? I growled under my breath and muttered, "This is going to be fucking impossible."

A notification popped up on my phone. I found another email from LoveMeLoveMe, no subject line this time. I reluctantly opened it to read *"Nothing is impossible idiot. And I can hear you."*

I scoffed, but didn't say anything this time. I was restless suddenly, frustrated all over again with the situation. I glared over at Callie. If she hadn't made the stupid promise then I wouldn't be in this predicament. I would've never had to lie to and trick her, and I could've worked on getting with Lucy who I loved. I hated lying, and I didn't like that I was being forced into all of this.

I couldn't sit in my seat any longer. I got up and went into the bathroom. I stared at myself in the mirror, then washed my hands and ran them over my face and through my hair. I took some calming breaths, and focused on the reason I agreed to this. I needed to find my biological parents- not just for me, but because Serena and Caleb had wanted me to. I'd do almost anything for those two. Feeling a little calmer, I made my way back to Callie.

She was still sleeping and I deleted the emails Aphrodite sent, just in case. I looked around the rest of the cabin, noticing that everyone else was sleeping as well. I never could fall asleep on a plane and I envied all these people for getting that respite. I looked over at Callie again and jumped a bit when I noticed her eyes were open. She smiled softly.

"Sorry, you seemed deep in thought so I didn't want to disturb you." She'd talked in a low voice, so as not to disturb anyone around us. Her voice had that just-waking-up quality, and it affected my instantly. I adjusted slightly to relieve some pressure and hide my reaction as much as possible. Callie's voice was a lethal weapon and she had no idea. I suddenly remembered something I'd read about the muse Calliope. Not only was she known for poetry, but her name literally meant "beautiful-voiced". Her name fit her more than her parents probably thought it might when they picked it out.

Callie was looking at me with a question in her eyes, and I realized I hadn't responded to her. "No worries, I didn't expect you to be awake when I checked on you so it just surprised me."

We were quiet for a time after that, just looking at each other. I was comfortable in silence, and was grateful that it seemed like she was as well. Then I remembered she'd asked me what I did for work and I hadn't gotten a chance to tell her yet.

"Have you heard of the Rikers Foundation?" I watched Callie think about it, sorting through her mind to see if she recognized the name.

"I'd heard something about them a couple years ago. They're based in Colorado right?"

"They are."

"Well, if I'm remembering correctly, they're an organization that focuses on helping orphaned children and homeless families. That's all I can recall though." She tilted her head. "Why do you ask?"

"Before we got on the plane you asked what I did. So I was just seeing how much you already knew about my job that way I would know where to start."

"You work there?" We'd leaned in closer to each other so we could continue to talk quietly without waking anyone.

"I do. It's a great business, and we're expanding to other states now. We've got one facility in Tennessee and now we'll have one in California."

"I was just about to ask if that's what this trip is about."

"Yeah, I'm going to oversee the building site. By the time we head back to Colorado it should be well underway."

"How many of these places do you have in Colorado? What are they like?"

I smiled, warmth spreading through me at her genuine interest. I could tell she really wanted to know about it, versus just being polite. "We have three in Colorado. One in Denver, one in Colorado Springs, and one near Estes Park.

"Each building is a little different, depending on what the needs of the community are. We survey the area, talk to children and families at the schools nearby, research which children are in foster care to see what they're missing in their lives. We work pretty closely with a few social workers and other programs to run everything smoothly."

"That's amazing. Now that I think about it, I believe I remember hearing about a fundraiser around six months back your company put on. What was that for?"

"That was for raising money for specific families that had fallen on hard times, like a single parent losing a job, and we donated the money to them. The nominations came from their own communities, neighbors, or teachers that had noticed something wrong."

"What happens when the money runs out though?" The worry on her face gripped my heart. Lucy and I had talked about that very thing when we started the business, because we both firmly believed that providing a temporary fix didn't solve the overall problem.

"We find ways to help them beyond the money as well. Sticking with the parent losing their job example, we help them with a resume, find them interview clothes, set them up with employment agencies, anything we can do that they're willing to accept from us."

"That's… that's amazing, Aidan." Her eyes began to water and she sniffled quietly, holding them at bay.

"Why are you crying?"

"Honestly, I don't know. I'm not usually much of a crier. I guess it's just really touching what your company does for people. You make a direct difference in peoples' lives that need it, instead of trying to solve a major issue that can't be fixed by doing just one thing."

"That was my point of view exactly. That's why I started the company, because I wanted to be the person I needed when I was a kid." I watched her process that last statement, knowing it would raise a few questions when she figured it out.

"Wait, YOU started the company? As in, you own Rikers Foundation?!"

I nodded, letting out a small smile at her loud whisper. She looked so damn cute with her eyes widened in shock, and her full lips shaped into a little 'O'. I also loved the way her cheeks darkened with a tiny bit of embarrassment. It made me think of other ways I could make her cheeks flush.

She smacked me lightly on the arm before I could follow that train of thought. "I can't believe you let me go on thinking you were just some random employee!"

"I liked the big reveal better. You look adorable when you're just a bit flustered." I held back a laugh at the glare she gave me.

"You're a jerk." She paused. "What did you mean about being someone you needed?"

I shifted uncomfortably. I didn't like talking about my childhood very much, and I didn't feel as if this were the right time or place to divulge the not so pretty details. "Suffice it to say that I experienced quite a few foster homes before two of the best people in the world adopted me. Their last name was Rikers, so I like to think I have this company to keep their legacy going."

I could see a thousand questions waiting to burst out of her mouth, but the one she let loose wasn't the one I expected. "How old were you when you were adopted?"

"I was nine."

She nodded. "Can I just ask one more question?"

"Sure, but then your question quota is filled for the next twenty-four hours," I teased lightly.

She smiled softly. "If they adopted you at nine, why don't you have the same last name as them?"

She didn't miss much. "Long story short, McRae is my birth name. They said I should keep it." I didn't want to get into the whole messy story of my mystery biological parents, so I decided to change the topic a bit before she asked a follow up question.

Unfortunately, I couldn't think of anything to change it to. I was completely distracted by the fact that she was biting her lip, thinking hard about what I'd said. She opened her mouth to ask another question, and I did the first thing I could think of.

I leaned in closer and covered her open mouth with mine. We both jumped slightly at the spark that generated from our lips touching. I pulled away, suddenly worried that I'd just fucked everything up by thinking with the brain that wasn't in my head.

In the next second, I didn't worry about anything else. Callie grabbed my shirt and pulled me back down to her mouth. I went willingly, my body going into overdrive as I finally got to really taste the lips I'd been thinking about non-stop since the hospital. I let my tongue run across the seam on her lips and she opened wider, more than willing to let me in. She let out a soft moan as our tongues touched, and everything exploded within me at the sound. Her hands gripped my shoulders, keeping me right where she wanted me. I had no arguments about that.

I kissed her furiously, my hands going around her waist as much as possible in our two separate seats. I once again felt the urge that I'd had while sitting on her bed in her room to pull her across my lap. I knew I couldn't do that here, with other people around, and so I settled for next best. I grabbed the end of one of her long braids and pulled her head back. She started to protest my mouth leaving hers- at least until my lips reached her neck. I kissed and nibbled my way down her throat and she whimpered with every touch. I moved my head back up to meet her eyes and whispered.

"Keep quiet, or I'll have to stop." She nodded as much as she could with my hand still pulling her braid back.

I shifted so that I could grab both of her braids in my left hand. The move made it so that my right hand was free to go to her knee and slowly slide along the outside of her thigh. I gave her time to protest, but all she did was pant quietly in my ear.

She shifted in her seat as my hand reached her hip and then slowly moved its way down to her inner thigh. She seemed to hold her breath as my hand rose higher and higher.

Everything inside me burned to touch her. Her legs parted slightly, giving me just enough space to slip my hand up to cup her pussy. I paused right before contact, and Callie lifted her hips in protest.

"Ask nicely and I'll give you what you want," I said low enough for only her to hear. I nipped her neck and waited. She clenched her jaw and pulled her head up to look at me even though it tightened my hold on her braids since I hadn't moved with her.

Her eyes were a swirl of purples, the shades too mixed to pick just one. I hadn't seen this yet, and it mesmerized me. "I don't beg anyone. For anything," she protested softly. Even though I could feel the heat of her pussy radiating against my hand, she was stubborn as ever. I really, really liked that. I loved that she had a mind of her own, but it also brought out the caveman in me that needed to prove to her I was in control right now.

"You'll be begging me to touch you soon enough." I pulled my hand away. I let go of her braids but kept my hand at the back of her head while I shot forward to kiss her one more time. She bit my lip a little harder than necessary, but returned the kiss full-force. The shot of pain made heat flow through me, almost making me go back on my words, but I tamped down my desire. I wanted to play the long game, not get instant gratification. I had to repeat that a couple times in my head to convince myself, but it worked eventually.

As I sat back in my seat I checked out Callie. Despite her frustration, she had a smile on her face. I did a double-take at the look. She turned to meet my eyes and I discovered yet a new eye color- smoky purple, almost like lilac. That, along with the wicked smile on her face, told me I was in trouble.

"Maybe you'll be the one begging to touch me, Aidan. I might have amnesia but I haven't forgotten everything." She leaned towards me, and I fought the urge to lean back, swallowing hard. As she leaned forward, her V-neck shirt gaped open and I could see plenty of cleavage and more than a hint of lace from her bra. I swallowed hard, staring at the purple so dark it was almost black. "You threw down a challenge, and you're in for it now."

I looked back up into her eyes, reluctantly leaving her breasts behind. I now knew what that lilac eye color meant-seduction. I was going to have to watch myself for the next two weeks if I didn't want her to get the upper hand. She turned away, I bet to plot her line of attack. I stared down at my phone without seeing anything, and it took me several minutes to realize that the buzzing in my body was anticipation. I grinned to myself, ready for this battle. One that I'm sure would leave both of us as winners. *Bring it on, baby.*

CHAPTER FOURTEEN
CALLIE

The rest of the plane ride, all I could think about was what Aidan had done to me. I was still surprised by how quickly everything had happened. One minute we were talking, the next I was whimpering like a fool, begging with my body for Aidan to get me off. I told Aidan I didn't beg, and hopefully he didn't know how close I'd been to that very thing. Thank god I was stubborn as hell, or his hand would be down my panties by now. I frowned to myself when disappointment shot through me at the thought. Surely I didn't want Aidan fingering me on an airplane? My libido laughed at me and I told it to shut up.

Aidan had seemed taken aback when I said that I could be the one making him beg; probably not expecting me to go on the offensive. He had no idea that I was virtually clueless on how to go about that. I could talk big but I wasn't 100% sure I could follow that up. I wouldn't let him see that though; I was determined to have him on his knees before me. *In more than one way*, I thought to myself with glee.

When the plane landed and we got up to gather our stuff, I waited in my seat for Aidan to hand me my backpack. I needed the light jacket I'd shoved in at the last second. I could still feel how wet my panties were from earlier, and since I was only wearing leggings, I knew that it would be impossible to miss while walking around. I quickly stood and tied the jacket around my waist when I got it, glaring as Aidan smirked at me. I figured he'd deduced the reason for it, and I decided to pay him back for my situation. I glanced around to make sure no one was looking, and quickly ran my right hand along the wet spot in my crotch.

His eyes widened at that, and then his mouth dropped open when I lifted that hand to my mouth and flicked my tongue against my fingers, eyes hooded. I watched as his cock instantly went hard in his pants and his blue eyes darkened like they had before. I grinned, standing up and slinging my backpack over my shoulder.

"I'm ready to go if you are," I told him saucily, acting like I hadn't done anything.

He snapped his mouth shut. And then opened it again to growl, "Damn right I'm fucking ready to go."

He grabbed my hand and whipped around, dragging me out of our row and past the flight attendants as they thanked us for flying with them. I looked back over my shoulder and waved, yelling back thanks as well. One lady just winked and grinned at me, turning back to the rest of the passengers.

My legs weren't quite as long as Aidan's, and I was close to running in order to make sure I didn't fall over while he was dragging me along at his pace.

"Hell, Aidan can you give me a breather?" I whined as we passed person after person. They all gave us odd looks, but Aidan ignored them and me, and I just shrugged at the strangers as I tried to keep up. Aidan took a sharp turn into a hallway of some sort, then pushed me into a deep alcove. Before I could wonder what the purpose of this area even was, Aidan had my backpack slipped off my shoulders. He turned me to face him and grabbed my hips, lifting me up and pulling me against him hard. He pressed me tightly against the wall. I was instantly revved up all over again. I tightened my legs around his hips trying to pull him in as close as possible. I could feel his hardness pulsing between my legs, his jeans and my leggings and panties the only things separating us. Aidan grabbed my right hand and lifted it to his nose, eyes closing as he deeply inhaled. His tongue snaked out and licked my fingers once, groaning.

"I can just barely taste you. And you smell like... I don't even know but I fucking love it."

"Oh my god," I whispered, his words turning me on just as much as his actions. My panties were officially drenched. I flexed my hips, wanting to know what it felt like to have him between my legs. He groaned and thrust against me as well, wrapping his arms around my back and grabbing the ends of my braided pigtails. The sharp sensation against my skull made me moan and rub harder. Aidan slammed his hips against mine and put just enough pressure on my clit to launch me well on my way to an orgasm.

I moaned louder, and Aidan brought his lips down on mine to cover the sound and our tongues warred for control. I was hanging onto Aidan's shoulders but quickly shoved my hands into his hair and gripped it tightly. He let out a harsh noise and moved one of his hands to my breast. He squeezed, harder than I expected and I let out a cry of surprised pleasure into his mouth. I was close to the brink, ready to come and not caring about where we were. I'd forgotten about anything else around me as I strained to reach that peak.

Then he stopped. His hips pressed me against the wall tightly enough to stop me from moving at all. He let go of my hair and my breast, slowly and steadily drawing back to let my legs back down on the ground. I was in a haze, unbelieving. I had been so close, and he'd backed away completely. As it sunk in, embarrassment swept through my body.

"Aidan? Is something the matter?"

"Is something the matter?" He laughed harshly and ran a hand through his hair. "We're in the middle of the airport and you almost had me fucking you against the wall, not caring if anyone saw. Why'd you have to push me like that?"

I froze, and anger started to replace the embarrassment. Oh *hell* no, he did not just say that.

"Oh, so it's *my* fault you can't control yourself?"

He sighed, looking away from me. "Callie-"

"No." I cut him off and stepped closer to him, poking him in the chest as I continued. "You're a big boy Aidan, and you don't get to blame your lack of control on me. Yeah, maybe I took it too far, but I'd think you were man enough to take responsibility for your own actions instead of blaming me for them. So until you get your head out of your ass, you can fuck off."

I couldn't look at him as I wrapped the jacket back around my waist, unsure when it'd fallen off. I was pissed as hell and didn't care what excuses Aidan was going to come up with to explain himself. I stomped my way past people over to baggage claim, tapping my foot with steam coming out of my ears while I waited for my bag to come around.

I had the urge to check if Aidan had followed me but I thought to myself *Screw it, he can take care of himself.* My thoughts wandered back to the feeling of him between my thighs. Then I mentally slapped myself, pulling out a piece of gum from a side pocket on my backpack. *Don't fucking go there, Calliope.*

I saw my suitcase coming my way on the conveyer belt and I walked forward to get it. Before I could grab the side handle, an arm shot out of nowhere and grabbed it first.

"Hey, what are you doing?!" I demanded as I turned to see who was stealing my bag. I realized it was Aidan, who was scowling down at me. I was relieved for a second that it wasn't a stranger but then my anger ratcheted right back up and extinguished the relief. "What is your problem?" I hissed while reaching to take my suitcase back.

He jerked it away from me and started to turn back to the belt. He yanked his suitcase off the belt and started walking away.

"Hey asshole!" I half yelled it, catching the attention of a few others. It was fairly late at the airport and I was glad there weren't a ton of people around to witness this.

"Can you just shut up for a minute Callie?" He said it without even turning to look at me.

"What did you just say to me?" I picked up my speed so I could run in front of him and block him. I stood, feet apart and hands on my hips. He tried to go around but he couldn't maneuver that well with two suitcases and his carry-on, as well as some kind of tube that I hadn't noticed he'd picked up. Honestly, he looked ridiculous.

"What did you say to me?" I repeated.

He hesitated. "I asked you to be quiet."

"No, you told me to shut up. I don't care how long we've been dating, I won't put up with this shit." I reached out quickly, grabbing my suitcase away from him before he realized what I was doing. "I can roll my own suitcase. I don't need your help, and I don't want it. I just want to go to bed."

He nodded stiffly. He started walking toward a guy in a suit holding a sign saying *McRae*. He greeted the man who introduced himself as our driver. He insisted on loading our luggage into the trunk, and I asked to keep my backpack with me. He nodded politely and held open my door for me to get in to the back of a black Mercedes Benz. It was a very nice car, and I reluctantly admired the clean interior. I sat as close to the window as possible and ignored Aidan now sitting on the other side as much as I could.

I pulled my cell phone out and turned it on. I'd been too distracted to do it earlier and gave it a few seconds to receive any texts or anything I'd missed while flying. My eyebrows raised as my phone buzzed multiple times, signaling three missed calls and eleven texts. The missed calls were all from Ellinor. She hadn't left a voicemail so I went to check my texts. It said I had one from Char, five from Ellinor, and one from both my parents and three brothers, Galen, Delphineas, and Xander each. I sighed, beginning to read them and ignoring Aidan when he turned to look at me.

Char: *Fly safe princess! I'm doing an interview with that girl we talked about, she seemed really excited when I called to set it up. Give Aidan a kiss from me! ;)*

Mom: *Your father and I love you. Be safe.*

Dad: *Your mother beat me to the text. Love you anyway*

Xander: *New boyfriend huh*

Galen: *Wtf sis*

Delphineas: *Who is Aidan*

Ellinor: *HEY JERK you never called me before you left!*

I hope you fly safe

He's really hot

But you should've told me about him

P.S. Might've accidentally told G D & X about Aidan... sry

I rolled my eyes at Char's text, smiled at my mom and dad's, sweated a little at my brothers', and scoffed at Ellinor's.

No kidding, she'd told my brothers. Thankfully they hadn't tried to call, or I would've had a million more missed calls. Even though I was the oldest, my brothers were as protective and hard-headed as any older brother could be, if not more. I knew I'd have to reply to them sooner or later, but I didn't feel like it right now. I groaned quietly, also knowing that if I didn't respond I'd never ever hear the end of it. I sent a group message to all of them for now, just saying *Landed safe. Talk later. XO*

I shut my phone off again just in case they ignored my 'talk later' part. Which I was sure they all would. I smiled despite still being pissed, thankful for the support I had in my life.

Support Aidan didn't have as a child, my mind decided to butt in. *True, but he's got his business partner,* I argued back with myself. *And his parents that adopted him. He's fine, he doesn't need me.* The nagging feeling in my heart wouldn't go away, but I refused to give into it yet. I wanted to be angry for just a little longer.

I glanced over at Aidan out of the corner of my eye and noticed he was looking over at me. I turned away purposefully, hoping the car ride wouldn't be much longer.

CHAPTER FIFTEEN
AIDAN

Okay, yes, I felt like an asshole. I wanted to apologize to Callie, but both her stubbornness and mine were keeping me from saying the words. I kept looking over at her, thinking I could feel her staring at me. I saw her cut a glance at me out of the corner of her eye, but then she turned her whole body towards the window, effectively shutting me out.

She popped her gum a few times, and the smell of mint drifted over to me. I'd noticed the habit of hers when I'd gotten to her house. I don't think she realized she did it, but I thought it was kind of cute. Usually I hated that sound, but apparently I was willing to let a lot of things Callie did blow over.

Like her tendency to give me a hard-on at the most inconvenient times. I scowled again, squeezing my phone in my grip tight enough to hear a cracking sound go through the car. I looked down indifferently, noticing that my case now had webs of fractures across the back. Cheap plastic. I felt Callie's eyes on me and looked over. She was looking at the case too, her mouth hanging open slightly in shock. Her eyes met mine briefly, and she narrowed her eyes at me and turned back to the window.

Great. Now I felt like an even bigger asshole. She probably thought I'd cracked my phone because I was mad at her, when in reality it was because I frustrated that I was having such a hard time controlling myself around her. I could hardly believe that we'd gone from making out and grinding in the airport like teenagers in high school to this.

The worst part was that I knew it was entirely my fault. I shouldn't have let her teasing get to me so quickly or easily. When she'd rubbed her hand on herself and then fucking licked her fingers I'd nearly jumped her right there, in front of all the passengers and pilots and anyone else willing to stay and watch. I'd needed her taste and scent more than I needed to breathe, and I'd just taken it too far. When I realized I was about to fuck her against a wall in an airport I'd frozen. I'd pulled away. And then I'd fucked up even more by basically blaming it on her in my frustration.

Then, before I could apologize for everything, she'd run off. I'd panicked, not wanting to lose sight of her but she was damn quick. The longer it took me to find her, the more annoyed I became. I could understand her anger with me, but disappearing was childish. I only managed to meet back up with her at luggage claim. I was right behind her when she moved forward to grab her bag.

I was still hard as hell despite feeling like an asshole and was trying to do anything to take my mind off the hallway. Why did everything she do from sleeping to yelling at me turn me on? I ignored her as much as possible, but her voice only made me want to grab her and finish what we'd started and she wouldn't stop talking.

The desperation and anger finally led to me telling her to shut up. I'd known it was a bad idea when her voice went from pissed to near-violent. But it was the hurt in her voice that finally cooled me down. I figured the best thing to do at that point was not say anything else, and she apparently agreed.

And now here we were. She was pissed at me, I was pissed at me, and I'd be surprised if Callie didn't want to chop my balls off tonight while I was sleeping.

We finally arrived at the hotel, one I'd had Lucy book ahead of time because I knew it would be late by the time we got to California and we still had a long drive ahead of us in the morning. I tipped our driver and checked the time that a rental car would be sent from the company for us in the morning.

I didn't bother with Callie's bags, not wanting to piss her off any more tonight. I did hold the door to the lobby open for her and she'd muttered a belligerent thank you as she passed. I checked in while Callie looked around and she followed me to the room. We opened the door, and the first thing I noticed was the giant king-sized bed. I usually got one, since I liked to spread out when I slept, and Lucy probably hadn't thought to change it to doubles. *Or maybe she didn't think it was necessary since you didn't mention it to her and you're supposed to be dating this girl anyway.*

Callie looked at the bed, frozen, and then looked back at me. She seemed exhausted more than anything at this point, but she didn't say anything to me as she toed her shoes off. She turned away, reaching under her shirt to unclasp her bra. My mouth dried a bit and I couldn't make myself look away as she managed to take it off all while keeping her shirt on. She flung it across the room and then turned towards the bed. I was torn between following the arc of the bra as it sailed or staring at Callie to determine if her shirt was see-through at all.

It wasn't. But it was thin enough to notice her hard nipples poking through. She dared me with her eyes to say anything, and I made the wise decision to stay silent and look away

92

from her tits. She burrowed under the covers on one side, closing her eyes.

I looked around. *And your days of sleeping on the couch begin tonight, buddy.* I took my shoes off as well, setting them neatly by Callie's. I pulled some gym shorts out of my bag and went into the bathroom to change. I took my shirt off, slipped into the shorts, and made my way back out to the couch. I grabbed a pillow and stuffed it under my head as I laid back, feet and ankles extending several inches out past the arm. I struggled to get comfortable and in the midst of an adjustment I thought I heard a giggle.

I looked over to find Callie staring at me from the bed, only visible from her eyes up. Even though I couldn't see her mouth I knew she was smiling. She was probably glad I was going to sleep like shit and wake up with a sore neck. I glared at her and settled on my back, facing the ceiling with my eyes closed. I heard shifting from the bed but refused to look. I heard a couple steps come towards me and stop. I knew she was standing by me more from her warm, peachy scent than anything else. I kept my eyes closed and heard her sigh. Something, a finger probably, poked me in the chest hard. I frowned but kept my eyes shut.

"Would you look at me already?" Callie sounded amused, and a little frustrated. I sighed over-dramatically and opened one eye. I could see her trying not to laugh.

"Yes, Calliope?" My voice was over-polite and she stuck her tongue out at me.

"You can sleep in the bed. You don't have to punish yourself."

"Why, you want to do it yourself?"

"Yes. Now shut up and come to bed."

She turned and burrowed back under the covers quickly. I thought it over for about two seconds, but decided being near her would be a more pleasant torture than sleeping on this couch.

I plopped down on the bed on top of the covers. I'm not sure if that was more for her protection or my own. We lay in silence for a while and I'd just begun to drift off when I heard her quiet voice.

"I'm still mad at you."

"I know."

"Okay." A pause. "Good."

More silence. "Callie?"

"What, Aidan?"

"I'm really sorry."

She didn't respond for so long that I thought she'd fallen asleep. "I know."

I grinned into the dark. "Okay, good."

I woke up slowly, surrounded by warmth and the scent of peaches. My mouth watered and I cracked my eyes open to find the source of the smell. The first thing I noticed was the unfamiliar room. The second thing I noticed, directly after the first, was the body tangled up in mine.

I looked down and slowly realized my predicament. Sometime while sleeping, Callie had kicked the covers off and ended up halfway across my chest, our legs twined together. I had an arm wrapped around her back, clutching her to me. Her thigh was resting directly on my inevitable morning wood, and my sharp intake of breath made her slide to the side a bit, her thigh rubbing my dick roughly since she was dead weight at the moment. I stifled a groan and squeezed my eyes shut. I prayed for strength, and for her to stay asleep for a few more minutes while I tried to untangle us.

She turned out to be a heavy sleeper, which I was immensely grateful for at that moment. There would have been no way to get my arm out from under her body and everything else without waking her up if she wasn't.

I decided to shower and grabbed what I needed out of my suitcase before heading into the bathroom. I checked Callie before I shut the door and saw she was still sleeping. Her hair was fanned out around her since she'd taken her braids out at some point. Her dark chocolate waves were spread out along the pillow, tempting me to go back and twist it in my hands. Instead I backed into the bathroom and stripped, turning on the shower to as hot as I could stand.

My hard-on hadn't dissipated at all since waking, and I wasn't in the mood for a cold shower so I knew there was only one way to fix it. My hand drifted down and grasped my rock hard cock as I replayed everything from yesterday. I couldn't stop Callie from invading my mind. From her fascination with my job, to her sounds on the airplane, the smell of her on her hand, and the way she'd responded to me in the airport. I stroked myself faster and faster, slapping my other hand against the shower wall when my legs started to tremble.

Then my mind recalled that time in her room, reciting her favorite poem. I could hear her voice in my head as I replayed the words, and just as I recalled the way she looked at me when she'd finished, I finished too. My legs shook as I came, breathing hard. I was pretty sure I'd moaned her name as I came and hoped she was still sleeping.

I hurriedly finished showering and turned the shower off. I used one of the towels to dry off, and got dressed. I opened the door to the bathroom with an armful of my stuff. I noticed

Callie was awake and out of bed, and looked like she was getting her stuff together for a shower. I suddenly remembered I'd just masturbated to the thought of her and I turned away from her so she wouldn't see the rising color on my cheeks.

"Oh uh hey Callie, the bathroom is open if you nee-"

"Okay thanks," she interrupted a little too quickly. Suspicious, I turned around and ended up bumping into her on her way into the bathroom. She gasped softly as she dropped her things, and we both bent down to pick them up. She wasn't looking at me, but I could see her flushed cheeks. We both reached for her shampoo bottle, and she jerked her hand away from under mine. I didn't get a chance to ask her what was wrong before she snatched the bottle from me and shut herself in the bathroom.

I stood back up, confused. I went to run my hand through my hair out of frustration and caught a whiff of something familiar. I brought my hand to my nose and took a whiff. Suddenly I remembered why I knew this sent. I'd smelled it on Callie's hand at the airport.

Realization hit me like a wave. I knew she'd heard me in the shower, and now I knew that she'd touched herself right along with me. That was why she'd refused to look at me. She was embarrassed at the possibility of being caught! I laughed darkly in triumph at the revelation. She could run, and she could hide, but she wouldn't get very far.

I gathered all my stuff and put it back into my suitcase after calling for some room service. I was hungry, and not just for Callie. I was sure she was starving too since the only thing we'd eaten last night was what they gave us on the plane. I noticed she'd cleaned up all her stuff already, probably while I was dressing in the bathroom.

She turned the shower off just as the room service arrived, and I started to set stuff out on the table buffet-style. I'd gotten two of everything from their breakfast menu. Croissants, fruit, yogurt, a veggie omelet, muffins, and an array of butter and other spreads littered the table. I heard a hair dryer turn on, and I figured she'd be a while. I decided to eat while she finished up and then head downstairs to be sure our rental car had arrived.

I mentally ran through today's schedule while eating; drive the two hours to the set of apartments I owned, drop off our stuff, meet the building company onsite to go over the plans, make sure there were no last surprises, and then the rest of the day was free.

Callie came out of the bathroom just as I set my dirty dishes aside. I looked over and my heart clenched. I'd seen her in a variety of looks- beat up in the hospital, fresh faced for the flight, and just waking up. This time, she had her hair blown out straight except for the ends that curled just barely, with the right amount of makeup to just enhance what she already had. Thick, jet black lashes framed her eyes and her lips had a sheer gloss on them that begged me to take a taste. I cleared my throat after realizing that I'd been staring at her face for a solid minute.

"There's some food here for you if you're hungry. I'm going to go check with the front desk about the rental car."

"Okay, thank you. The food smells amazing."

"Good. I've already eaten so help yourself."

She nodded and headed over to drop off her clothes and other bathroom things into her suitcase. I watched her move, the sway of her hips graceful and enticing. Her dark blue skinny jeans flattered her body perfectly, and her light gray shirt was some kind of flowy material that hung perfectly from her breasts. I mentally slapped myself and left the room. Shutting the door behind me, I headed to the elevator all the while cursing Aphrodite for blackmailing me into this and changing everything in my life. I didn't care if she could hear; if she smote me then at least I wouldn't have to deal with all of this anymore.

CHAPTER SIXTEEN
APHRODITE

I snickered, watching Aidan stomp to a set of metal doors and listening to his inventive curses about me. Typically I would punish someone for saying the things he did, but I was in a good mood today. He was making progress whether he knew it or not. A few other gods and goddesses had a bet going on about how long it would take Callie to confess her love. I listened to them bickering behind me, placing their bets before the polls closed.

As the goddess of love and beauty, I knew that it wasn't an easy task to make someone fall in love with you in just two weeks. It seemed a little unfair, but the brand I'd inscribed onto Callie's sternum only lasted three weeks. I pushed Aidan for two, and that left the last week as a security measure. If he hasn't succeeded by the end of two weeks, then I'll tell him I'm generous enough to give him one more week, but that's his last chance. I smiled at my intelligence and planning.

"Mother."

I turned away from the vision cloud of Aidan and Callie to face my son, Eros. He had his daughter Hedone with him, and I smiled and opened my arms for her. She came and gave me a hug, squeezing me three times like she did was she was a child. It'd taken me some time to get used to her because of the history between her parents, my son and his wife Psyche, but she was such a bright happy child it was impossible to hate her.

"You realize this can't end well," Eros said quietly after Hedone went to talk to another younger immortal.

I sighed. "They're humans. Their feelings are easily manipulated. I'm not afraid of the outcome."

"You should be, you know what will happen if you don't succeed."

I shot him a glare. "Of course I know. I wouldn't have branded the girl if I wasn't sure I would succeed."

He studied me. "As long as you're sure."

Scoffing, I replied. "I am sure. Now be a dear and tell the others the polls are officially closed."

I could tell he wanted to say something else. After some hesitation, he did as I asked. I watched him walk away and talk to Hermes about closing the betting. I turned back to the vision cloud, watching as Aidan loaded their things into the car and drove away from the hotel. I had no doubt that all would go according to plan; after all, there was a reason Aidan had been there when Callie had her "accident". I was not the kind of goddess to leave these things to chance.

CHAPTER SEVENTEEN
CALLIE

As Aidan pulled away from the hotel, our luggage stored in the back, I forced myself not to wring my hands nervously or throw the door open to let the breakfast I'd eaten come right back up.

When Aidan came back up to the hotel to see if I was ready to head out, I could tell he'd been surprised to find the rest of the food gone. I was just putting on my shoes when he opened the door, and he'd glanced down at the table to see all the empty dishes neatly stacked on the table for someone to pick up.

He'd raised an eyebrow, his surprise evident, and then looked back at me.

I shrugged, not self-conscious about eating everything. "I was hungry," I said nonchalantly.

"I see," he replied but said nothing else. We headed down to the lobby in silence, and Aidan told me to go ahead and get comfortable while he loaded our things. I sat quietly in the front seat, contemplating my confused emotions. I was still mad at Aidan for yesterday, but less so now that I'd had sleep, food, and an orgasm.

I blushed, thinking about that last item. I'd woken up in bed with nothing but Aidan's scent all over me. I'd been horrified to think that I'd clung to him in the night, something that I had a tendency to do. I got cold and if someone shared a bed with me I would inevitably seek their warmth at some point.

I'd thought that him sleeping on the covers would've been enough to discourage that, but I wasn't sure the idea worked.

I had been panicking so much I didn't notice the shower running until I heard a soft groan through the wall separating me from the bathroom. I paused, heart thudding suddenly. I listened to see if I would hear anything else. Not more than a few seconds later, I heard another quiet noise. Images flashed into my mind of Aidan stroking himself in the shower.

No way, I'd thought to myself. But then I heard a loud smacking sound just above my head. My nipples stood to attention and arousal flooded my panties as I heard a louder moan vibrate through the wall. I slipped my left hand into my panties and started to rub my clit. Three circles in and all the desire from yesterday came back instantly. I heard a gasp from the bathroom, and I rubbed quicker, harder. My back arched as I felt tingles start from my toes to my hairline. When I heard Aidan say my name I let out my own sound and hit my climax. Stars burst behind my closed eyes as I throbbed with pleasure.

I lay there breathing a little harder as I came down and the shower turned off moments later. When I realized it might not take Aidan long to get dressed I jumped out of the bed, rushing around to pick up my loose items and grab what I needed to shower. When Aidan came out of the bathroom I was sure he'd figured everything out but he never said anything, then or later. Maybe I was safe.

My mind came back to the present when Aidan got into the car, shutting his door. We hadn't said much to each other since last night, and everything that we had said was all formal, polite. I felt weird, and maybe like I should say something to let him know I was over the whole thing. Then in the next second, annoyance flared and convinced me that he should be the one to bring it up, since it was *mostly* his fault. I agonized internally, switching back and forth from one point of view to another.

"Callie!" I jumped, turning to Aidan. "Are you just going to ignore me the whole two weeks?"

I flushed. "No, I'm sorry. I was lost in thought and didn't hear you."

"I said your name like three times. I was sure you decided to pretend you were on a solo vacation."

"No, not at all."

He was quiet. "What were you thinking about?"

"Oh. Uh..." I paused, realizing I had to make a decision right now about whether to bitch at him for yesterday or tell him I was letting it go. I opened my mouth but he responded faster than me.

"I'll tell you what I've been thinking about."

"Um, okay?"

"I was thinking about how beautiful you look. And that I like how soft your hair is. I was also thinking about how damn sexy you are and how much of a jackass I was to you yesterday and how little you deserved it."

He looked at me, a self-depreciating smile on his face. I was a little amazed at his honesty, but I really liked it. Which meant I had to be honest too.

"Yeah, you were kind of a jackass." I giggled and then sighed. "But you weren't wrong. I was acting like a four-year old throwing a tantrum and I feel bad for taking out my frustrations with all of this on you. You've been really understanding and helpful, and even if you were a jerk, I can forgive you if you can do the same for me."

"Of course. It was mainly my fault, so there's nothing to forgive you for really." He reached his right hand out for me to shake. "Truce? We good?"

I laughed, grabbing his hand with my left, not to shake but to hold it. I liked that feeling. "Yeah, we're good Aidan."

For the rest of the drive we compared music tastes, teasing each other about bad or surprising choices. I discovered that he was a fan of country music, which threw me off because I had him pegged as a classic-rock type. He'd hooked his iPod up to the car and played a few of his favorites and laughed when I sang along in an overdone southern accent.

I enjoyed all kinds of music, but favored rap and hip hop. He hadn't believed me until I'd pulled out my own iPod to prove it. I let him pick a song, and he kept looking away from the road to make sure I wasn't reading the lyrics while rapping along with Eminem.

The two hour drive passed quicker than I'd expected, and soon we were pulling into an apartment complex. I glanced at the welcome sign for Oceanside Apartments, very confused.

"What are we doing here?" I looked at him questioningly. He parked the car before answering.

"This is where we're staying. I own... an apartment here since I visit a lot."

"How do you *own* an *apartment*?"

"You pay for it."

I snorted. *Obviously.* He didn't give me any more information before getting out of the car and heading over to my side to open my door. His non-answer left me wondering... I'd never heard of owning an apartment before. As far as I knew, you could only rent an apartment. Unless, of course, you owned the whole complex. That realization struck, but I didn't confront him about it. If he wanted to pretend like he owned one apartment rather than the lot of them, I'd let it go.

We got out and I followed him from the car into the building, then over to an elevator. He scanned a card and the elevator started moving up. We rode it up to the top silently but without any awkwardness.

It was only four floors, but I'm sure people living higher than the first floor were grateful to have the elevator when moving in or out. Living on the third floor of an apartment complex myself, I would know. Then again, this elevator alone was nicer than my apartment. I lived in a good place, but that was in Colorado and this was California. Everything here was bigger, shinier, and more expensive.

The elevator opened and I let out a gasp. It opened directly to an apartment, like the penthouses in movies. I walked in, barely remembering to drag my suitcase with me. It was decorated simply, but it was still a homey feeling. I stopped in the middle of what had to be the living room. There were a couple couches centered around a fireplace with a good-sized TV banked into the wall above it. Along one wall was a huge window that overlooked a secluded beach leading to the ocean.

I turned to my right and saw a hallway that had three doors. I glanced back to my left and saw an identical hallway as well as a kitchen. And I'm not talking about a mini fridge and a sink, I mean it was a full kitchen with a side-by-side fridge and freezer combo and an oven with a microwave above the stove.

I turned to face Aidan, mouth hanging open with awe. He was grinning, watching me take it all in.

"Do you like it?"

"Uh, are you kidding me? How could you stand to be in my apartment knowing that you had something like this?"

He cracked up and set his stuff down. He walked over to me and motioned to my suitcase, asking if it was alright that he took it. I nodded.

"Your apartment is fine," he said teasingly. "Follow me, I'll show you where you room is."

"Yeah my apartment is fine compared to yours in the same way that a bullet to the heart is fine." I heard him laugh as he walked away and I took another look around before following.

He'd headed to the left, past the kitchen. He pointed to the doors and explained what they were as we passed.

"This is just a storage closet, feel free to use it if you need room. This door is to the bathroom; it's mostly for guests since you'll have a different bathroom attached to your room. Speaking of which..." He trailed off, opening the last door in the hall to a bedroom that looked almost as big as my whole apartment. Okay, that's exaggerating, but it was massive. A king-sized bed sat near a window, and there was a dresser, a nightstand, and an electronics center all in the same dark Cherrywood color with a simple design. The color theme of the room was all earthy, warm tones and I found I really liked it.

Aidan watched as I walked around admiring everything. I pointed to a closed door. "Bathroom?"

He smiled crookedly. "Open and see."

I opened it and turned on the light switch. I let out a small moan. It wasn't the bathroom; it was a walk-in closet made of wet dreams. I wanted to be buried in this closet when I died. "Aidan, all you had to do was tell me this existed and I'd be fine if you brought me here to murder me. Seriously, I'll

106

dream about this closet when I go back home." He chuckled and pulled me out of the closet. I didn't exactly go willingly so Aidan had to pull me harder on his second try. I ended up falling into his body, colliding sideways into his muscled chest.

My hand flew out to balance myself and it landed on a wall of hard muscles. My body warmed, admiring how built he was. Every ridge and dip tempted me to run my hand all along his torso, but I held myself back. I still didn't step away for several long seconds, and I only did so because Aidan cleared his throat.

"The bathroom is over here," he said. He pushed me in front of him to another door just to the right. He reached past me, pressing his chest against my back and distracting me again, and opened the door for me.

"Why is there so much *room*?!" I turned incredulously to Aidan after staring into the spacious bathroom. He was grinning, pleased with my reactions.

"Apparently whoever owns the buildings knew that someone would like a lot of space so they built the top floor to accommodate that. I figured why not, I'll take it."

"Yeah no shit. I can't imagine what your place in Colorado looks like if this is what your 'vacation home' is like. No wonder we always spent our time at your place!"

He chuckled. "I'll leave you to unpack, and feel free to look around. I have to leave in an hour to meet the construction company at the site to go over last-minute details before they start tomorrow. You're welcome to come with if you'd like, or stay here."

"I'll think about it and let you know before you have to go."

"That's fine. Let me know if you need anything."

I reached over and hugged him. I meant it to be a quick hug, but I really liked the way it felt to press my body against his as I wrapped my arms around his waist. He didn't even hesitate to pull me in tighter, his arms going around my shoulders.

I had my cheek pressed against his chest and I breathed in his scent deeply. I pulled away just enough to look up into his face. He was smiling at me, and the look in his eyes said he was content. I felt peaceful, and I was glad that I'd made the choice to come with him.

I stepped away and jokingly motioned for him to go. "Okay, shoo now or I'll never get my stuff unpacked."

"Yes, your highness," he mocked and walked away after a lingering look at me. I shivered, goosebumps appearing on my arms at that look. I watched him walk through to the other side of the apartment to the door that paralleled mine. Before he could turn around and see me staring, I shut my door.

It only took me half an hour to unpack everything and that was only because I lingered in the closet. I hadn't brought a whole lot since I figured I could either wash what I had or buy some new stuff. What's the point of going on vacation if you can't bring back some souvenirs anyway?

I decided to try out the bed so I fell back onto it, spreading my body out. It was comfortable and soft but not quite as cozy as mine. *Oh well,* I thought, *I suppose this place can't be completely perfect.*

While I lay on the bed I contemplated whether I should go with Aidan to the site or not. I didn't want to be in the way, but I was interested in not only seeing Aidan at work, but in how the process was done. I thought what Aidan was doing for these communities was incredible. Unlike a lot of government programs, he was able to help people in need without having to go through as much red tape. It was probably discouraging work sometimes; I'd seen how tough some people had it when I volunteered in high school at a women's shelter.

I got up from the bed and went into the bathroom to look myself over in the mirror. I didn't look too bad. My style was usually a combination of girly- which was apparent in my feminine top- mixed with a little punk, hence the skinny jeans and Cons. I shrugged at myself in the mirror, thinking that it would be fine to go with Aidan in this. I left my room and ventured down the hallway, going to the kitchen for a glass of water.

I found Aidan already in the kitchen, chugging a bottle of water. I watched him, his throat moving with each swallow. My mouth was suddenly even drier than before. He hadn't seemed to notice me, so I just watched as he lowered the bottle and breathed in deeply. He licked some water off his lip that escaped the bottle at the last second and my whole body clenched at that quick swipe of his tongue.

"Got any more of that for me?" He jumped slightly at the sound of my voice and twisted to face me.

My desire must have been obvious in my face, because as our eyes met I saw his pupils dilate. I licked my lips and his eyes followed the movement. I watched as he swallowed again, this time with a different kind of thirst. His answer made me think that we must've been thinking along the same lines.

"Are you thirsty, Callie?" His voice was low and rough, hitting all the right spots in my body.

"Practically dehydrated," I breathed out.

He wordlessly reached across the counter that separated us by only a foot and handed me his half-empty bottle to finish off. My hand landed on his as I accepted it, but he didn't actually let go of the bottle.

"Let me," he said.

I raised my eyebrow in question, but let my hand drift back down to my side. Just to provoke him, I licked around the rim of the bottle and watched as his eyes darkened. I heard the bottle crunch as his hand tightened reflexively. I would've laughed if the air surrounding us wasn't so thick.

He tilted the bottle and I leaned my head back a bit so the water wouldn't spill down my chin immediately. He slowly lifted the bottle, and the water trickled into my mouth. I swallowed a bit at a time, watching him watch me. His other hand reached over and rubbed down the middle of my throat. It's a good thing the water wasn't coming very fast or I would've choked in surprise at his touch.

He pulled the bottle away from my mouth and I let my head fall back down. His other hand was still on my neck, his thumb resting against the base and his other fingers spread to the side. My breathing quickened when he used his thumb to put pressure on my throat while rubbing up and down, up and down. I'd never realized that would be something I enjoyed, but I couldn't ignore the flutter in my belly and the tightening of my nipples. A low groan came from Aidan's throat at my obvious response, and then he pulled away.

"Have you decided about coming with me?" He placed the nearly empty bottle on the countertop and I immediately reached for it. I swallowed the rest in two gulps, ignoring the fact that he was still watching me like he was going to pull me across the counter and devour me.

"Will I be in the way?"

"No, you should be fine. If you just follow behind a bit you shouldn't be too distracting." I heard the wry tone in his voice as he turned to throw away the empty bottle I handed him.

"Well then yes, I would like to come." His eyes smoldered darkly and I belatedly realized the suggestiveness of my words.

"It would be my pleasure," he returned immediately. I flushed hotly at the double meaning but decided to ignore that too in favor of something safer.

"Do I look okay? I mean, is it alright if I wear this?"

"You look perfect. Don't worry about changing. I'll just grab the keys and we can head out."

I nodded, watching as he turned away and walked into his room stiffly. *I bet his walk's not the only stiff thing*, I thought to myself, letting a small giggle escape now that the tension had dissipated.

Then I sighed. I stayed quiet, thinking, as Aidan walked back toward me with keys in hand and I followed him out to the car. Every time things got intense between us, Aidan would back away. I wasn't sure if it was intentional or if it just hadn't been the right time. But I did know one thing: this was going to be the longest two weeks of my life if I didn't figure out a way to get Aidan to stop retreating at the last second.

CHAPTER EIGHTEEN
AIDAN

"Okay Mike, I'd like the entrance to face east, that way when people go outside for activities or events, they can see the ocean. I want it to feel like a breath of fresh air."

The project manager I'd hired nodded along with my words. I was particularly satisfied with this construction company; Mike was excited to be a part of this project, and while talking I'd realized that he not only understood the plans, but he could picture it in his mind and understood the importance of the building.

Mike had brought along his foreman and a couple of other guys who were going to be onsite during construction. When I'd noticed this, I'd almost asked Callie to stay in the car. I didn't know these guys, and I didn't trust them around her. I was beginning to feel possessive, and I was struggling between hating it and embracing it.

In the end, I knew that if I'd asked Callie to stay in the car it would've only made her want to go more- plus piss her off. I had asked her to stay close to me however, and amazingly she'd agreed without any questions or arguments.

I'd introduced myself to the guys, and then Callie. They'd all tipped their hats at her and introduced themselves as well. They hid their surprise at my bringing my girlfriend to the site well, and they stayed respectful to Callie and me. I was immediately impressed with that, and stopped worrying about whether it'd been a bad idea to bring Callie with.

We'd gone into the trailer the construction company already had onsite and I'd laid out the plans for the guys. We'd sent them mock-ups previously so they were familiar with the general idea. I went over the changes, answered some questions, and then we'd gone out to the land itself.

I'd been so deep into the conversation with the four guys in the trailer that I'd almost forgotten Callie was there. She hadn't interrupted, just quietly observed. I'd motioned for the four guys to leave the trailer ahead of me, and gave into the urge to kiss Callie quickly. She seemed caught off guard, and I hadn't lingered long enough to let her kiss me back.

"What was that for?" She'd smiled lightly as she asked, fingers going up to touch her lips unconsciously.

I grinned back. "No specific reason. I just wanted to." I'd grabbed her hand and led her outside to walk the property. I didn't let go of her hand the whole time and she seemed content to quietly take everything in. Every now and then, when the construction guys would discuss a specific detail between themselves, she'd stand on her tiptoes to quietly ask me a question about what I envisioned, or clarify some term or idea she didn't quite understand.

After making a round over the land, I shook hands with the guys and made sure they had my contact information in case they had any other questions or issues. I told them I'd be stopping by occasionally to check out the progress and they said they looked forward to it. Callie moved forward, hand outstretched to shake their hands as well.

"Thanks for letting me trail along guys," she said sweetly. That was the first time they'd really heard her say anything other than hello, and I could tell that I wasn't the only one easily mesmerized by her voice. The four of them were tripping over themselves to assure her it was their delight and not a problem at all. I watched Callie to make sure she wasn't feeling uncomfortable but she just smiled serenely back at them and waved as I wrapped an arm around her waist to lead her away. I liked these guys so far, and I didn't want to hate them just for realizing what an amazing, beautiful person Callie was so I took her away from them before that hint of jealousy started to overwhelm me.

I calmed down as soon as Callie wrapped her other arm around my back and stuck her hand in my back pocket. I jumped slightly when that hand squeezed my butt. Her little giggle warmed me and I mock scowled at her which only made her laugh more.

"That hand is going to get you into trouble if you're not careful," I growled teasingly.

We reached the car and before I could open her door for her, she leaned back against it and looked up at me.

"What if I don't want to be careful?"

I was hard as steel in an instant at her words and the heat in her eyes. I stepped closer, crowding her into the door, my hands coming up to rest on the top of the car above her head. She only tilted her head back farther, staring at me with those purple eyes. Her hands came up from her sides to slip her fingers into the belt loops on my jeans. She pulled me even closer, our hips meeting and pressing together. Her eyelids lowered in satisfaction at the full contact and even more of my blood rushed south.

She made this humming sound in the back of her throat when she felt my cock pulse against her through our jeans, and when she shifted her body to get some friction my control snapped. My hands shot into her hair, cupping her head to hold her still while my mouth crashed into hers.

Even with the ringing in my ears from the sensations rushing through me at the feel of our lips and tongues finally touching again, I heard and felt her moan reverberate through me. I bit her lip softly and she gasped into my mouth. I bit her lip again, harder.

"Aidan," she moaned softly. I loved hearing my name in that honeyed voice, and I resolved to hear it again if it was the last thing I did. I wanted to hear her say it, needy and breathless. I wanted to hear her groan it, the pitch and volume of her voice rising every time my name dropped out of her mouth. I wanted to hear her scream my name when I was deep inside her, making her come so hard she forgot everything *but* my name.

The thoughts swirled through my mind and one of my hands was making its way down her back to her ass when I registered the sounds of wolf whistles and hollering from behind me. Callie must have heard it at the same time because she pulled away from me. I caught a glimpse of reddened cheeks before she buried her face against my chest, curling her whole body into mine.

I wrapped my arms around her and looked behind me to see the guys waving at me and grinning. I was in a better mood than I would have imagined with our heated make-out session being interrupted so I just shook my head at them lightly. I realized I was grateful they'd stopped it; if- no, *when*- I got Callie naked it wasn't going to be with an audience.

"Should we head out then?" Callie's words reached my ears even though her face was still buried in my shirt. I felt the heat from her breath move across my skin and I hissed at the unexpected sensation. I couldn't see it, but I could feel Callie smile. I said nothing, but managed to help her into the car without the guys catching another look at her.

115

When I turned to get into the car from my side, I saw the guys still standing there grinning, although now silently. I couldn't help it. I grinned back over the top of the car. I'd decided it was time to stop running from this attraction to Callie. She had no idea what she'd started with her challenge, but I could promise that she would like the end result. She would like it very, very much.

CHAPTER NINETEEN
CALLIE

I watched as Aidan paused outside his door to the car. It was only for a moment or two, but it gave me the chance to take some deep breaths and tell my body to calm the hell down. While kissing Aidan, I'd felt a change come over him. He hadn't been the one to pull away first this time, content to kiss me until I passed out from the heat of it. I'd been on the verge of undoing the button and zipper on his jeans to get my hands on him when I'd noticed the racket coming from the construction guys behind us.

I'd forgotten they were still onsite. Embarrassment filled me for a moment, but after breathing in Aidan's scent while snuggled into his chest, I was ready to pick up where we left off, audience be damned. Which made me blush even more, hence the hiding into Aidan's shirt.

I glanced at Aidan as he slid into his seat. The grin he gave me caused both dimples to come out, and it only served to turn me on more. I quickly buckled my seatbelt to stop myself from leaping across the car into his lap. Which I happened to glance at, not able to help it. He still had a massive bulge, the interruption doing nothing to cool him down. At least I wasn't alone in that aspect.

We drove away from the site, the air in the car super-charged with sexual tension. The radio was off, and we didn't say anything to each other. The longer we drove in silence, the more time I had to imagine where everything could've gone just now if we'd been alone. I imagined his hand had made it to my ass, squeezing it hard enough to make me cry out. He probably would've let me undo his pants, slip my hand inside, and caress his length while he groaned and tried to move his hips closer. He would've moved his mouth from mine to nibble along my neck and-

"*Callie.*" The rough voice startled me from my daydreams and my eyes flew up from his crotch, where I'd apparently been staring, to his face. We were at a stoplight so he could easily make eye contact. His eyes burned, more intense than anything I'd seen so far. I gulped and shifted in my seat, hoping I wasn't going to leave a wet spot on the leather.

"Yeah?" I barely recognized my voice, but the rasp in mine matched his.

"I need you to stop staring at my dick like you want to swallow it whole. I'm already harder than fucking concrete, and imagining your mouth around me isn't helping at all. Plus, you keep shifting in your seat and making these whimpering noises that are driving me insane. All I can think of is pulling over and giving you what we both want."

I started panting hard, clenching my thighs together to ease the ache in my pussy. I tried to respond, to say I was sorry, but I couldn't make myself say the words. I wasn't sorry at all. I was hornier than I'd ever been in my life, and I was about to reach across for the steering wheel to do just what he'd said- pull over and finish this.

All the heat, all the longing from our previous encounters never went away. They only simmered below the surface, just to come back and intensify every experience after it that didn't end in a climax. Which, so far, was all of them. I was at the point that I believed if he swiped a finger over my clit even once I was going to combust.

I watched as his knuckles gripped the steering wheel tighter, his breathing sharp and fast.

"Aidan, I... I need something, anything." I spread my legs and I saw him watch me out of the corner of his eye. He bit his lip and stepped on the gas to move the car faster.

"Okay baby," his deep voice rang out loudly in the quiet of the car. "Spread your legs. More."

I did as he asked. He reached a hand over and put it on the thigh closest to him. He watched the road intensely while I watched his hand. It slid up my leg, the heat palpable through my jeans. His hand reached my mound and he cupped it, pressing in.

I arched my back, a needy sound escaping my mouth. I reached one hand down to cover his, making him press harder. The damn jeans were in the way of where I needed his hand to be and I let out a frustrated sound.

"God, baby, I can feel how hot you are through your jeans. Your panties are soaking wet, aren't they? I could slide my big cock right into your tight pussy with no problem and you'd let me because you want it fast and hard."

"Yes, Aidan, oh god yes." His words were dirty and I loved it. It brought me so close to the brink that I knew with another few seconds of this I'd go off like a rocket. My hand that wasn't covering his and encouraging every press into me had reached up to cover a breast. I squeezed myself, moaning with abandon now. I wanted to reach over and feel Aidan too, but he stopped me with a look.

"Don't you dare move those hands. I like them where they are just fine. Squeeze harder baby, it's fucking hot."

A small, quick orgasm razed through me, and I cried out. I heard Aidan mutter something but I couldn't understand it. He pulled his hand away suddenly and I wanted to protest.

The mini orgasm had only made my need for him that much stronger, and I felt like a wild animal.

I leaned over and reached for him again, intent on getting his dick into my hands and mouth, but he stopped me with a hand gripping my wrist hard. The heat in his eyes seared me when he glanced at me.

"Five minutes, just give me five fucking minutes to get you upstairs and then I'm going to taste that pretty little pussy of yours." He jerked his chin for me to look out the window. We were pulling into the apartments, turning sharper than was probably safe. We jerked to a stop in his parking space, and he didn't even need to let me out because I had unbuckled my seat belt and opened the door before the key was out of the ignition. He grabbed a hand and pulled me to the door. I wasn't behind him for long, moving so quickly to the elevator that I ended up basically dragging him.

As soon as Aidan scanned his card for the fourth floor he grabbed me, lifting me up so I could wrap my legs around him tightly. He didn't even bother to press me against a wall, just started shifting my center on his hardness using his hands on my ass to guide my movements. I looped my arms around his neck to hang on tightly, my head falling back and groaning loudly. I was trying to concentrate on everything at once but I couldn't. My focus jumped from the feeling of him in between my legs, to his hands squeezing my butt cheeks with every grind into him, to his mouth biting and sucking on my neck.

The elevator dinged, signaling that we'd reached his floor. I tried to unwrap my legs so I could walk, but he just gripped me tighter and stalked out. He stopped in his front room, suddenly hesitating. Fear spiked through me at being left high and dry (although maybe not so dry in my case) again.

"The couch," I whispered raggedly. I didn't know why I was whispering. Maybe I didn't want to ruin the moment. He hesitated another second, but then walked to the couch. I breathed a quiet sigh of relief and none too soon he'd sat down with me still straddling him. My knees rested on either side of his hips on the cushions and I used that leverage to move back and forth on him.

His hands roamed restlessly up and down my back, from my shoulders to my upper thighs. I could tell he was on the edge and trying to get himself under control, and I moved my hands down his chest and tugged at the bottom of his shirt.

"Off," I said. He leaned forward so he could reach behind him and pull his shirt off over his head. I loved it when guys did that in general; there was something so masculine about the way their bodies moved when pulling their shirts off from behind that made me salivate. He flung his shirt across the room and then reached for mine, easily pulling off my flowy shirt to reveal the secret I'd been hiding underneath. He sank back into the couch, running a hand through his hair and staring at the white lace bra that cradled my breasts.

The white might sound boring, but this particular bra was a demi-cup, pure white lace coming above the silky cup to hide the tips of my areola that peeked out from above. If I took a deep breath, my nipples were highly likely to pop out of the cup and play peek-a-boo with the lace above it.

So, feeling adventurous, I tried it out.

My chest expanded as I breathed in and exactly what I thought might happen did- and then some. Aidan's reaction to my little trick was to clamp his hands on my upper arms, forcing my shoulders back. That pushed my chest out towards him which only made his next move easier. He pulled me closer to him and immediately sucked a nipple into his mouth, lace and all.

My eyes rolled back in my head and I grinded harder onto his lap. I'd never experienced this before, the feeling of a hot, wet mouth manipulating the lace around my nipple to heighten the sensation.

"Fuck Aidan," I gasped out as he bit down lightly on my nipple. I could feel my pussy clench in reaction, crying for something to ease my need. He switched to my other breast, repeating what he did to the first. He was focusing so much on my breasts that he moved his hands from my arms to my back, trying to get me even closer. And, I soon realized, to unhook my bra. Next thing I knew, my bra was flying across the room to join his shirt and he'd let go of my nipple to shove his face in between my breasts.

"I fucking love your tits Callie. I could write an odyssey about them and still not be able to capture how goddamn perfect they are."

He palmed them both and squeezed lightly at first, then harder. I could only pant as I watched his big hands manipulate them to his pleasure- and mine. I was hoping that my boobs were distracting him enough that when I slipped my hands down to the button on his jeans, he wouldn't stop me this time.

He was so fascinated by my tits that he didn't notice my shaking hands trying to free his dick from his jeans until I'd wrapped my hand around it and stroked it. He'd made it easy access for me since he'd gone commando, something I hadn't expected but was very happy about. His hands reflexively gripped my breasts harder at my unexpected touch on him, and his hips thrust forward.

"Don't stop," he started to say, gasping through the words.

"Nothing is going to stop me right now Aidan." I stared into his eyes as I pumped him slowly, relishing his inability to stop his hips from following my hand. "I like the way you feel in my hand, hard and hot and pulsing." I knew my voice was making him harder, along with my words and hand. His hands grabbed onto my thighs, clenching hard as he fought the need to come.

"Your voice, Callie, how can it be so sexy? God, I feel like every time you speak it wraps another thread around me, forcing me under some kind of spell." His head fell back onto the couch, eyes shut tight.

My nipples were so hard it was close to painful. I truly felt like my namesake from Greek mythology, Aidan's personal muse that I could bewitch with my voice alone. I laughed quietly in triumph, making Aidan jerk in my hands.

His eyes were still closed when I slid back on his thighs and bent in half to lick the juice spilling from his tip.

"Ah!" His yell was one of surprise and pleasure and his hands found their way into my hair to pull my head up so he could look at my face. "You're such a dirty girl, baby. Are you going to put my cock in that filthy mouth of yours?"

"Maybe. If you ask nicely," I winked saucily at him even as his hands tightened in my hair, making my scalp tingle. I hadn't realized I liked things a little rough because so far my bedroom life hadn't been super exciting. But I was starting to think I would like anything Aidan and I did together. I was suspecting I would not even like it, but end up craving it.

"Wrap those lips around my cock, Callie. Show me how bad a good girl like you can be."

I groaned at his words, not able to tease him anymore even though he didn't technically ask me. I climbed off his lap and onto the couch next to him, leaning over and sliding his member into my mouth until he touched the back of my throat. I hesitated; I'd never gone this far before and I didn't want to put Aidan off by doing this half-assed. He reached down and stroked the front of my throat. I moaned at his touch, knowing he was encouraging me to take him deeper.

I dipped my head lower and felt him pass the spot that usually made me gag; I didn't know if it was the intensity of my desire or his hand stroking my throat but soon my nose was against his stomach, having taken all of him in. I breathed slowly through my nose and then swallowed. My throat tightened around his cock and he let out a long moan, one that didn't stop as I bobbed up and down on him. I moved a hand to cup his balls and I felt them draw up as I softly rolled them in my palm.

I choked a little when I felt a hand slip into the back of my jeans. It just caught me off guard because I'd been so focused on Aidan in my mouth. His hand caressed my bare cheek; I was wearing a matching white lace thong so most of my skin was bare to the touch. I moaned around him again when he hooked his fingers in the back of the thong and pulled it up. It rubbed deliciously on my pussy and I squirmed to get the pressure to the right spot.

"Up now Callie," Aidan said through the fog of passion clouding my thoughts. He had to pull on my hair to lift me off sucking his dick. He popped out of my mouth and we both groaned.

"Why'd you stop me? I wanted to taste you," I whined.

"You have no idea how much I want that too baby, but I need to see your pussy. Now strip."

I jolted up and got my jeans off in about half a second. He studied my body from my toes to my hair, now that I was only in my soaking wet thong. And because it was white lace, it was practically see-through at this point. It would've been obscene in any other setting, but here now with Aidan it only made me wetter.

"I hope those panties aren't important to you," Aidan commented as he fingered the lace on my hips.

"Why- oh!" I gasped as he literally ripped the panties off me. "Those were expensive!"

"Those," he said nonchalantly, "were in my way. I'll buy you new ones. And then some more after I rip those off you too."

"I can buy my own panties, thank you very much." My stubborn side was coming out despite being more turned on than I'd ever been. I watched as Aidan stood and pushed his jeans off the rest of the way. I stared, my mouth watering at the expanse of rippling muscles before me. I was a little intimidated, seeing as how he was completely ripped and I was all soft curves. But then I let it go because Aidan seemed to really like it- *a lot*.

He stalked towards me and I playfully backed up. He made a feral noise and electricity went through my body. He darted forward faster than I thought he could and I yelped in surprise. I hadn't even made it past the couch which turned out to be a good thing because he tackled me onto it. I laughed, surprised at the bit of levity in this fierce atmosphere surrounding us. He smiled in response to my laughter, but it was predatory.

He pushed my legs apart and looked down. I knew I was dripping by this time, not caring if I ruined the couch with my arousal. I felt sexy, desired, needed. I felt powerful, even though he was in control. I tilted my hips toward him, taunting him. His hands came up my sides, grasping my hips and pulling me to the edge of the couch. I was now directly in front of his face, and my breathing picked up. I tensed as he leaned forward. I thought he'd dive right into attack my clit, but he surprised me by turning his head to my thigh and licking my birthmark. I let out an incoherent noise. This was exactly what I'd been wanting for years.

"You like that, dirty girl?" His words floated up to me from his position on the floor below.

"Yes," I sighed. "Please, do it again." He did. "Again!"

He chuckled and then softly bit the mark, holding his teeth there as I threaded my hands into his hair.

"Harder," I whispered so quietly I wasn't sure if he'd heard. But his shoulders tensed and he clamped down a little harder. "Ah!"

"I have to taste you now, I can't wait anymore. You smell so fucking good and I need your taste on my tongue."

"God, yes!" I basically screamed it. I screamed again as his mouth began to devour me. I couldn't believe how amazing it felt. He pulled my legs over his shoulders and grabbed my ass to lift my hips higher. I dug my heels into his back as his tongue roved up and down my slit, slipping inside my hole and thrusting in and out. He moved back up to my clit and flicked his tongue against it.

"Oh, I'm s-so close," I moaned out and grinded my hips into his face. He wrapped his lips around my clit and started to suck hard just as he slipped two fingers inside me. I exploded at that very second, yelling my release to the ceiling. He kept sucking and thrust an additional finger in, heightening my orgasm. I shook and shook as I came hard. I finally pushed him away when it became too intense.

He came up on his knees, towering above me. He leaned in and kissed me and I could taste my essence on him. He pulled away to look at me, a satisfied smirk on his face. As for me, I was far from satisfied. I should've been, but the orgasm only made my need rise higher. I rotated my hips against his and he groaned when his cock rubbed against my wet folds.

"Shit, I need to get a condom."

"I'm on birth control, and I'm clean. I'm good if you are." The words were out before I could even think about them. Surprise filled me, realizing that I really did trust Aidan.

He grit his teeth and stared down at me. "I'm clean. But-"

"Aidan, if you don't get inside me now, and I mean right the fuck now, I won't stop teasing and torturing you until you do."

His eyes fired and he made a rough noise as he looped my legs around his arms, holding me tight as he drove his cock completely into me in one go. I whimpered, the feeling of him inside me stretching me almost to my max. He paused, breathing hard, and then slowly slid out of me until just his tip was inside, then just as slowly pushed back into me.

"Aidan, just fuck me please!" He tensed, but kept going at an agonizing pace. I decided to use my new favorite weapon on him- my voice. "You feel so good inside me babe. I need you deeper. Ah, god, I need you pounding into me hard, fast, I need you to take what is yours, Aidan. Please please please-"

Aidan finally snapped and leaned forward, pushing my legs into my chest as his hands slipped underneath my back to grip my shoulders from below. He held me in that position, making it impossible to do anything but take it as he did what I'd begged him to do. His hips moved at a frenzied pace and the sound of our skin slapping only served to drive me higher.

"You're so tight baby, you're making it hard to hold on. Are you close? I want you to come with me. Tell me what you need." He was struggling to get the words out, but it was no different for me. I was clutching onto him while he drove into me at a manic pace.

I couldn't get any words out. I wanted to say something, anything, but the beginning of the best orgasm of my life was starting to spread out through my body. I scraped my nails across Aidan's back and that must've been signal enough that I was about to explode.

He moved quickly, taking his hands from my shoulders to toss my legs around his waist as he leaned forward and bit down hard on the space between my shoulder and neck. I screamed his name out as I came hard, squeezing the life out of his cock inside me.

He plunged once more inside me, deeper than any thrust before as his warmth flooded me in spurts. He muffled his yell into my neck, vibrating the skin and making me come harder around him in reaction. He slowly released me from his bite and licked that spot once as we both came down, gasping into each other's ears.

After several minutes, I squirmed under him and felt him slip out of me. He pushed himself up on shaky arms and grinned down at me. I couldn't help but smile back widely. He helped me up from the couch and pulled me into his arms. I was surprised, but it made my heart flutter. I was about to say something when my stomach grumbled loudly, beating me to it. My cheeks flushed with embarrassment as I looked up at Aidan.

"So, I might be hungry," I commented. That made Aidan crack up and he pulled me in for another tight embrace.

"I never would have guessed," he teased and then pulled back. I stuck my tongue out at him and his eyes smoldered in reaction. "Don't tempt me Callie, it won't take me long to be ready for you again."

I noticed him beginning to stiffen against my hip and my eyes widened. *Already?* He seemed amused by my shock, but I let it go. He dropped that line of conversation when my stomach growled again.

"How about we get you cleaned up and fed, and then we'll go for round two."

"Yes to the shower and food, maybe to round two." I pulled away and started backing up towards my room, but when I said maybe about the second part Aidan started towards me. He stopped when I held up a hand to him. "Uh-uh buster, we are going to shower- and separately. Then you're taking me out to dinner."

"You drive a hard bargain." He looked me over and I saw his dick stiffen even more. I wasn't doing anything to hide my naked body from him, and I bent a knee tilting a hip down, making my breasts bounce with the movement and biting my lip. I knew I was being mean, but it felt *good*. "If you don't get into your room and lock your door right now Calliope, I'm going to forget about the shower and dinner and skip straight to dessert."

My nipples puckered and a small growl came out of Aidan's mouth. He took another step towards me, and I turned and ran, giggling the whole time. I slammed my door shut, locking it like he'd told me to. I leaned back against the door and held my breath. A minute later I heard his door slam shut too and the air I'd been holding burst out of my chest.

I wandered into the bathroom and started to warm up the water for a quick shower, still tingling from what we'd done on the couch. I'd been so turned on all day, watching Aidan take charge with the construction guys, seeing how passionate he was about this project of his. By the time he'd had me caged in by the car I'd been soaking wet for him. I'd never come across a man like him, and by the pounding and warmth in my chest I knew I was beginning to like this mysterious boyfriend of mine way too much.

CHAPTER TWENTY
AIDAN

I should've felt guilty. I should've felt terrible for basically tricking Callie into this trip, this relationship, this whole situation. But I was so sated at the moment that I couldn't dredge up the feeling. A hum of pleasure was still running through me, and even though everything I'd done with and to Callie on that couch was satisfying, I was already hard again and wanting more.

And being inside her bare… I should've felt bad about that too. I should've had more control over myself, but that fucking voice of Callie's had caught me. A twinge of remorse filled me, thinking that I should've gone for a condom anyway. But I trusted her, and she seemed to trust me.

I groaned as my hand brushed my cock while soaping up in the shower. I imagined Callie just a few feet away, running her own soapy hands along her chest, down her stomach, maybe giving in to the lingering desire and slipping her hand between her legs… I realized I was stroking myself to the images playing through my mind. I hesitated, then decided to go ahead and finish because if I didn't I wouldn't be able to make it through dinner without clearing the table to fuck her on it.

After grunting through another release while replaying everything from earlier in my head, I rinsed off and stepped out of the steamy bathroom. I went back to the front room in my towel to find my cell phone which was still in the pocket of my jeans. I gathered both Callie and my clothes from around the room, chuckling at how spread out everything was.

I walked over to Callie's door and knocked.

"Yeah?" I heard her call out.

"I've got your clothes. Do you want me to leave them here for you?"

I jumped a little as the door suddenly opened, finding Callie wrapped in a towel that (unfortunately) covered her a lot more than mine did. We looked over each other hungrily until she cleared her throat. I jerked back to reality, thrusting the bundle of clothes towards her.

"Here you go. Can you be ready for dinner in an hour and a half?"

She managed to grab her clothes without dropping anything while still staring at my chest. I had several tattoos, and this was probably the first time she'd really gotten a chance to look at them since all the other times it'd been dark or we were... occupied. I smirked, patiently waiting for her answer while her gaze drank me in. I started to tent my towel, and her cheeks reddened when she noticed.

"H-how long did you say? I missed it," she stuttered nervously when she moved her gaze up to my face.

"Hour and a half. That okay?"

She nodded once and then backed up, shutting her door. I winked at her right before the door shut and I heard a happy sigh from inside her room before I walked away.

I whistled a tune as I walked back down the hall to get ready and make a reservation for dinner. The guilt for the ruse would probably come later, but I wasn't feeling it right now and I planned to enjoy that for as long as I could.

I was wandering around the kitchen, waiting for Callie to finish getting ready when there was a knock on the door. I smiled, knowing exactly who it was as I walked over to answer it. I opened the door to find my aunt, Bethany, standing at the door, hands on her slim hips as she glared at me.

"Hi Aunt Beth," I said as I moved so she could come in. If I hadn't moved she would've plowed me over anyway. She was thin and only stood at 5'2" but she'd perfected getting what she wanted no matter who she faced. I'd fallen victim to her elbowing technique more than a few times and I was always sore for days afterwards.

"Don't 'Hi Aunt Beth' me young man! I can't believe you didn't come see me as soon as you landed here, and I know you've had the time!" She was still glaring at me, but there was a twinkle of humor in her eyes that reassured me.

I pulled her in for a hug and after only a second of pretend resistance she hugged me back. I didn't let go as I replied to her.

"C'mon Beth, I just landed last night and I was at the site all morning. You really would've wanted me to come wake you up at one in the morning just to say hi?"

She pulled back, eyes narrowed at me. "Hmph. I suppose not." She took a good look at me as she stepped back. "You look nice. Where are you off to now? I presume you aren't dressed up to come see me."

I chuckled at her pert tone. "You never know, maybe I am."

She folder her arms and raised an eyebrow at me, not believing my flattery.

"Alright, I'm going out for dinner."

"With who?" Her face lit up in excitement; we kept in touch and she'd always asked about potential girlfriends but I'd never had anyone to tell her about.

"Actually, she's-" I started but stopped when Callie's voice came down from the hall.

"Hey Aidan, I can't seem to find my purse, do you know…" She trailed off as she came past the wall and saw Beth and me standing in the front room. Her eyes went wide in surprise at finding someone besides the two of us in the apartment. "Oh, I'm sorry, I didn't mean to interrupt." Her face flushed slightly.

I leisurely looked her over, watching her flush a bit more with my perusal. She'd put on a cream colored, skin tight dress that would've looked innocent on anyone else but looked positively sinful wrapped around her curves. Her neckline didn't show more than an inch of cleavage and the skirt stopped at just above her knees, teasing at what might be underneath.

The straps of the dress sat just below her shoulders, showcasing her bare neck and delicate collarbones. The color of the dress complimented her darker skin tone and smoky eyes, and her wavy hair was piled up high on her head with some wisps framing her face. Her black wedge heels accented the black band of lace that wrapped around the waist of her dress.

Beth cleared her throat next to me, and I realized I'd forgotten all about her. I coughed once to cover my awkwardness, hoping she hadn't noticed the reaction likely visible in my slacks.

"Callie, this is my aunt, Beth. She runs the apartment complex and stopped by to say hello. Beth, this is Calliope. My girlfriend."

Beth immediately made her way over to Callie and pulled her into a tight hug. I grinned at the bewilderment on Callie's face at being greeted so warmly. Thankfully, Beth didn't hang on for too long so it wasn't completely uncomfortable.

"It's lovely to meet you Calliope. May I say, you have the most stunning eyes I've ever seen. They are incredibly unique."

"Thank you ma'am." Callie was grinning now. "And please, call me Callie. Only my parents call me my full name."

"In that case, feel free to call me Beth or Aunt Beth. That ma'am stuff makes me feel ancient." They laughed together and warmth spread out through my body watching them chat. Beth was the only family I had left, and she wasn't even technically related to me. I was glad they got along, although as they started to whisper to each other and sneak glances at me I started to fear I would come to regret them getting along so well.

"Okay ladies, stop conspiring against me and get a move on. Aunt Beth, we'll come to visit later this week if you'd like. Callie and I have a reservation to get to that I'd rather not be late for."

"Of course I'd love for you two to visit. I'd like to get to know Callie a bit more. You already know my schedule, nothing's changed since you flew here last." She turned back to Callie and they hugged again, this time with Callie participating eagerly.

Beth came over to me and gave me a hug as well, then made her way out the door, waving and grinning. She threw a wink at Callie as she left, and that made me nervous.

"She's sweet," Callie said when I turned to face her. I walked towards her without saying anything and gathered her in my arms. My mouth landed on hers, telling her how much I liked her outfit choice without words. She sighed into my mouth and kissed me back. I pulled back before getting carried away, touching my forehead to hers as we tried to catch our breath from the kiss.

"She is until you piss her off." Callie's body vibrated with laughter, only making me harder. I groaned at myself and let Callie go. "Are you ready?"

"Yeah, I just can't find my purse anywhere. I think my phone is in it, do you mind calling me?"

"Sure." I pulled out my phone and dialed her number, waiting to hear the ring. Nothing. She walked towards her room, listening as well. She came back out empty handed.

"Well, I didn't hear anything in my room. Maybe I forgot it in your car."

"Ah, yeah, that's a very good possibility. We were a bit… preoccupied earlier."

We grinned at each other and then burst out laughing.

"Alright princess, where are you taking me to dinner?" Callie teased me with the nickname she gave me in the hospital and I started to usher her out the door.

"That's for me to know and you to find out," I replied as the elevator doors opened.

"Very well," she sighed dramatically. "Distract me from the mystery then. Tell me about Aunt Beth."

I held her hand as we descended and I started the story.

"She's not technically my aunt, actually. She was a very good friend of my parents while I was growing up, so I've just always called her Aunt. When my parents died, she and her husband helped me organize the funeral. They were always there for me when I needed a parent's advice. Then after her husband died two years ago I helped her get situated here."

"Why California and not Colorado?" We'd made it to the car and I helped her in, waiting until I'd gotten into my seat and started the car before I answered.

"The four of them- my parents, Beth, and her husband, Gerald- had actually grown up here in California. They'd lost touch with each other over the years of their marriages, but then ended up moving to Colorado within a block of each other. It took them two years to realize it, but when they did they became inseparable. After Gerald's passing Beth wanted to come back home to bury him. She decided to stay to be closer to him, plus the fact that Colorado is too dry and cold for her now. She doesn't like to admit it, but I know it's part of the reason."

"Well I like her. She seems to be in good spirits and full of life."

"She's always been like that. I was afraid that when Gerald died she'd lose a little of that vigor but she stayed strong."

"Living for both of them, perhaps."

I glanced over at her, amazed at her insight. "Actually, that's exactly what she told me."

"No way!"

"Yeah," I laughed, "She was like 'Gerry would be ashamed if I withered away just because he died, so I've just got to live for both of us'."

"That's amazing," she commented quietly. She didn't follow it up with anything and seemed to be lost in thought so I let the silence continue.

She reached over and placed her hand on top of mine resting on the gear shift. I glanced over and saw unshed tears sparkling in her eyes.

"You okay?" I was suddenly worried, thinking something was wrong.

"I'm perfectly fine. I'm just really glad that you guys have each other. Thank you for taking me on this trip with you."

I smiled, heart thumping at her words. I turned my hand over to intertwine our fingers and squeezed her hand softly. "Thank you for coming with me."

We let the radio fill in the background for the last few minutes of the drive. I kissed the back of her hand before slipping my hand out of hers for the last turn of our drive. We pulled up to a restaurant that looked like a large cabin, on the top of a hill facing the ocean.

A valet came to my door and I handed him a tip and the keys. I smiled at his enthusiasm and made my way to Callie's side. I waved away the second valet that moved forward to help her out- I didn't want any other man touching what was mine. They could look all they want, but touching her was my privilege alone.

CHAPTER TWENTY-ONE
CALLIE

I could feel Aidan's eyes on my face as I took everything in. He placed my hand in the crook of his elbow and escorted me in, nodding politely at the men opening the doors for us. The hostess at the stand met us with a polite smile and greeted Aidan by name.

"Welcome back Mr. McRae! We have your table ready for you; out on the deck as usual?"

"Of course, Anna. Thank you."

We followed the woman through the restaurant, and I tried to ignore the people staring as we passed. I noticed women were raking their eyes over Aidan and it made me clench his arm a little tighter. I didn't like them staring at him like they wanted to eat him, and I didn't like that I felt so possessive. Aidan pulled his arm out of my grip and in the next second he wrapped that arm around my waist and pulled me in closer to him.

His hand tightened on my side and I looked up at his face when I heard a small growl come from him. I was looked up to see an annoyed frown on his face as he glared at someone. I followed his gaze and saw a man quickly turn away, face flushed red.

"Aidan? Do you know him?"

"No," he said in a clipped tone.

"What's wrong then?"

There was a heavy pause before he answered, like he was thinking about what to say. "He was staring at you like you were on the menu. I didn't like it."

Heat rose to my cheeks, and it surprised me how pleased his words made me. He looked down at me and his eyes darkened at the small smile on my face.

"Don't test me right now Callie." He murmured the words lowly so only I could hear. "I'm on the verge of throwing you onto the nearest table and making you come in front of everyone here just to prove that you're mine. Don't look so pleased to be getting attention from another guy, because I'm the only one that's going to be fucking you."

A wave of rebellion went through me, and I pushed his arm away from me. His words turned me on and pissed me off at the same time. He acted like I was trying to make him jealous, when he was garnering all kinds of stares from every woman we passed.

A confused look passed through his eyes when I stepped away from him and walked ahead without saying anything. I could feel his eyes burning into my back, and shivered despite my anger when I practically felt his eyes move to my ass. My body took over, making my hips sway enticingly to tempt him. I heard another growl come from him and my panties were immediately soaked.

I felt him close the distance between us and grab my hand- but we'd arrived at our table out on the patio so Aidan held back his words as she set our menus down on the table and smiled at us, politely ignoring the tension vibrating in the air. Aidan stiffly pulled out my chair for me and I sat, watching him move to his own chair. He paused only for a second before dragging his chair closer to mine so that we were both facing out towards the ocean.

Any other time I would be able to appreciate the view, but every part of me was focused on the man next to me, taking up my space and air. The heat between us scorched my body and I did everything I could not to look at him to let him see how aroused I was.

"Callie," he started in a gruff tone. The arrival of the waiter coming to take our drink order cut him off, and I saw his fist clench in aggravation. I ordered a water and Aidan ordered the same, plus a brand of wine I didn't recognize. The waiter took the hint in Aidan's short tone to leave promptly, and then we were alone, secluded in the corner of the patio outside.

"Callie," he started again, "why are you upset?"

The want in my body was pushed back when my anger arrived to the surface again. I turned to meet his gaze. "You acted like I was trying to get attention from other guys. I wasn't smiling because I succeeded in making you jealous, you idiot." I stopped, not wanting to admit why I *had* been smiling. Unfortunately, Aidan did.

"Then tell me Callie, why did you seem so satisfied to see me like that?" He just stared at me, waiting patiently for my answer. I squirmed, not wanting to say anything. I wouldn't be able to lie to him, but I didn't want him to know the truth either. I saw the patience wearing out in his eyes, and I only squirmed more at the heat as he glanced down at my mouth. I licked my lips in reaction to his stare, not able to stop myself. "Goddammit Callie."

He grabbed my chin and held me in place as he ravaged my mouth. I moaned and opened for him, allowing his tongue to slip inside and stroke mine. He pulled away as quickly as he'd attacked and I took deep gulps of breath.

"Why, Callie. Tell me, right now." His voice was demanding and pleading at the same time. I looked back up at him, studying his face. He jaw was tense with frustration and a muscle pulsed when he clenched it tighter. He was trying to control his emotions, but when I looked in his eyes I saw a hint of vulnerability- and that made the words spill out of my mouth.

"I liked that you seem to feel as possessive of me as I feel of you." My face scrunched up in annoyance. "Those women were ogling you like you were a chocolate lava cake, just waiting for the chance to dig their claws into you."

His lips twitched with a grin as the tension in his body dissipated. "I didn't even notice the women."

Happiness swelled in my heart at the words. "And I didn't notice the men. Until you started growling at them, at least." We both burst into laughter as we relaxed. My anger melted away and I realized he hadn't been trying to insult me, but then the underlying pleasure at his nearness started to fill the space where the anger had been now that there was no buffer for it.

A slow burn filled me that not even the arrival of the waiter with our drinks could tamp down. I stared at the ocean and took huge gulps of water to try and cool down, and it barely took off the edge.

"Tell me about your business, what do you do?" Aidan said thoughtfully out of nowhere.

I glanced over to him. "You don't know already?"

"I do, but you don't remember our relationship, so it's like we have to start over. You listened to me about mine, and it's only fair that you get to re-tell me about yours."

That was... surprisingly sweet. "Well, as you know, Char and I run a dating-slash-matchmaking site." I studied him as

142

he reached for his water and I continued. "The idea started as a joke, but the more we talked about it the more we decided we could actually help people. And so we started Eros."

He'd been listening with interest, but at my last words his eyes widened and he started to choke on the drink of water he'd taken.

"Oh my god, are you okay?" I leaned forward to help him in some way, but he waved me off as he gulped in air, coughing to clear his airways. I stayed close to him just in case, but sat back when his eyes finally stopped watering. "Did something I say surprise you?"

"Just that your business started as a joke. You seem to be pretty successful, since you're able to book speed dating events in popular venues."

My eyes widened. "Have you been to one of those?"

His face twisted with an emotion I couldn't identify but disappeared before he answered. "Yes. I was technically tricked into it, but I suppose I can't be upset about it… since that's how we met."

My eyes widened even more and my jaw dropped. "I can't believe I don't remember that!" He grumbled something but I couldn't understand him. "Tell me the story!"

The waiter came back then to see if we were ready to order. I flushed, realizing I hadn't even looked at the menu yet.

"Are you okay if I order for both of us Callie? Can you trust me?"

I saw a flash of guilt go across his face again at his own words, which confused me. However, I nodded gratefully and handed my menu to the waiter.

"We'd like to do the four-course meal please," Aidan told him. "We'll start with the mixed greens salad, followed by the abalone dole. The beef tenderloin and short ribs for the main, and the Valrhona chocolate ganache to finish. Thanks," he said as he handed his menu to the waiter who nodded with a smile and headed off.

I had always believed that you could tell a lot about a person with how they treated someone who worked what most considered shitty jobs. That included wait staff, retail or fast food employees, and cleaners. I was glad to see that Aidan didn't seem to have any superiority complex since he was polite to the waiter.

"You're not getting out of telling me this story Aidan," I teased.

He smiled over at me and began. "Lucy tricked me. She said that she'd signed up for a charity event but couldn't make it last minute and begged me to go for her. I gave in, and showed up to a speed-dating event in formal wear."

I covered my mouth with my hand quickly to hide the laughter bubbling inside me. Our events were nice, but not *that* nice. If he showed up in a tuxedo the women would have tried to eat him alive. A laugh escaped my throat as I lowered my hand and I coughed to cover it up. Aidan narrowed his eyes at me but continued.

"Anyway, I had just been about to escape when I saw you rushing around. I assumed you weren't part of the event as much as in charge of it by the way you were barking orders into your headset."

I gasped, playing at being offended- even though he was on the mark about me at events. I was the driving force behind the scenes and Char was the face. He enjoyed being in front of people and I most definitely did not. "I do not *bark*," I sniffed.

"Whatever you say sweetheart," he retorted and grinned. "Anyway, I couldn't take my eyes off you. I decided to stay for a bit, see if I could talk to you. Ask you out."

He paused as our first course came. It was a gorgeous salad, but I barely tasted it as he picked up the story between bites.

"I avoided talking to as many women as I could," he shrugged modestly, "but what can I say? I'm a catch." He grinned at me and winked.

I rolled my eyes. "Next part of the story please."

He chuckled. "I stayed for the whole event. Every time I caught a glimpse of you, you disappeared before I got the chance to talk to you. I knew you were busy, but it was frustrating nonetheless. I had to dodge a lot of women, and a lot of glares from the other men."

"Why did you stay if it was so terrible for you?" It didn't offend me; not everyone had the temperament for that kind of thing. It's why I believed my company was special: we did a variety of events for the different kinds of people we catered to.

He made direct eye contact with me, and my heart skipped a beat at his next words. "I knew what I wanted, and I wasn't going to leave without getting it."

The food dropped off the fork that was halfway to my suddenly dry mouth so I lowered the fork back to my plate and took another drink. This time I went for the wine.

"I stayed after everyone had left. Everyone but you. You were heading out to your car when I approached you. You told me it was surprising to see someone was still there. I nodded to you, and then said, 'I didn't get to talk to the person I wanted to tonight, and was wondering if you could help me out with that'. You looked delighted to help, by the way.

"You asked what she looked like, and I said, "She's got the most incredibly vibrant, purple eyes I've ever seen and I'm getting lost in them". We both knew it was a cheesy line and you scoffed at me, but I could tell you liked it. You had the same look on your face then as you do now, cheeks blushing and hands trembling."

I looked down at my hands to find them clutching the napkin on my lap, indeed trembling. I relaxed my hands, forcing them to stop.

"Then what?" My voice was breathier than I expected it to be.

"Then I gave you my phone number and told you to call me the following day. I said "I want you to use this, but I'm not pressuring you. However, I'll come to every single one of your events until your number pops up on my screen to tell me you'll go out with me' and then walked away."

"I didn't call you the next day." If I knew myself at all, I would've been indignant at that point rather than intrigued. I probably even threw his number away at some point that night.

"Of course you didn't. I hoped you wouldn't. I wanted to come after you, I wanted to tease you and drive you as crazy as you make me. Honestly I would've been disappointed if you'd given in so easily. Watching you run things at the event had given me the idea that you don't submit to anyone easily, and I wanted that fire from you.

"I managed to figure out that your next event was only a week away and I showed up. When you noticed me you stopped, probably startled that I had followed through on my promise. After a few seconds, you got back to your job and studiously ignored me the rest of the time. Until near the end of the event, at least. I pulled you to a more secluded spot, cornering you. I asked why you never called and you tilted your chin up at me so stubbornly that I got half-hard right then. 'I don't date assholes' you said and tried to escape. I would've let you go if I had thought you weren't interested, but when I caged you in with my arms I saw your pupils dilate and your nipples get hard under your shirt."

I felt my body respond in the exact same way now, imagining how terrifying and exciting that moment was. Aidan noticed my nipples through my dress and grinned, making them even harder. A noise escaped my mouth at the look in his eyes and the memory of what it felt like to have his mouth on my breasts.

"Yes, Callie, you made that noise too. It was then I knew I had you so I took a bit of a risk and leaned in for a kiss, almost but not quite touching your lips. You stiffened for a second against me, but then wrapped your arms around my shoulders and closed the distance. You devoured me like you'd been lost in the desert, starving and thirsty for years."

The second course arrived at that point and we pulled away from each other. I hadn't noticed we'd leaned into each other closer and closer during the story. I waited as they cleared our plates and laid down new ones, thankful for the slight reprieve to be able to breathe again.

We ate for a few moments and I could tell Aidan was waiting for me to tell him to continue. I took a few minutes to enjoy the food before getting back to where Aidan had left off.

"Alright, so after that, what'd I do?"

"You froze. Pushed me away and slapped my face."

I laughed loudly and was relieved to see Aidan grinning at my reaction. "That definitely sounds like me."

"Yeah, and I kind of expected it to be honest. You were so mad when all I did was smile at you and ask when I could take you to dinner. You stuttered for a second, at a loss for words, but then you surprised me, and I think yourself, by saying 'I'll call you and let you know'. I told you 'You better because I'll come back for you if you don't' and let you stomp off."

"How long did I wait to call you?" I grinned at him. I would bet anything he'd say four or five days.

"Four days," he admitted. "And when you did, you told me the time and place to meet you, and that this was my only chance so if I had any other plans that they were now cancelled."

Our main course arrived, and my mouth watered at the scent of the food. "The rest of the story is going to have to wait Aidan, this food smells divine and I want to really enjoy it." He chuckled softly but didn't argue. We ate in comfortable silence, and I groaned a little at each bite I took. This food was seriously amazing, and I almost couldn't wait to try the dessert. I glanced over at Aidan while taking one of my last bites and almost inhaled a piece of short rib at the desire burning in his eyes.

"Aidan?" My questioning voice was shaky at the sudden heat rushing through my body.

"Are you trying to kill me Calliope?" His voice was low and as dark as his eyes, the pupils blown to swallow the decadent blue.

"What do you mean," I whispered.

"You keep moaning and sighing with every fucking bite and licking your fork, making me hard as a rock over here. All I can think of is you down on your knees swallowing my cock and making those noises around me."

I got slightly lightheaded at the images his words invoked, and one of my hands flew down to steady myself in my chair. Our chairs didn't have arms so my hand landed on his thigh and I squeezed hard before realizing the error of my move. His hand shot out to grab mine and he inched my hand toward the unmistakable bulge in his pants. I glanced around, wide-eyed, and tried to pull my hand away.

"Focus on me Callie," he growled. "No one can see us. The waiter won't be back for a while and I need to feel you touch me. Please, Callie," he finished. With our eyes locked together, I relaxed the tension in my body and I leaned in closer to make what I was about to do look less suspicious in case someone from the dining room happened to glance our way. His breaths came out harshly as my hand brushed over his length. Then a groan sounded out when I squeezed him through his slacks.

"Now you can finish the story Aidan," I breathed out, my words whispered into his ear and made him shudder. "You talk, and I'll touch."

"God Callie… where did I leave off?"

"The date." I rubbed my hand up and down, taking my time to feel just how hard he was. His cock fascinated me, and my mouth watered at the feel of him in my hand. Aidan gulped a few times before he managed to pick up the story.

"Right. We went to Elitches."

My hand paused mid-stroke. "I made you take me to Elitches?" I covered my mouth with my hands as I giggled. I absolutely loved roller coasters, and making him take me there was only a surprise because I hadn't been there in years.

Aidan grabbed my hand and placed it back where it had been before laughing. "Yes Callie, you made me ride roller coasters with you, and I have to say it was the best date I've ever been on." He paused, leaning his head back and closing his eyes on a groan as I slowly undid the button of his pants. He breathed harshly as I slowly slid the zipper down.

"What was your favorite part?" I asked softly, sliding my hand into his pants. I shouldn't have been surprised to find no barrier between his hard cock and my hand. He'd gone commando, just like earlier. I breathed sharply as I wrapped my fingers around his hardness. I waited to move until he started talking again, his voice raspy and stilting.

"My favorite part? It's tied. I've always loved Shipwreck Falls. But the Ferris Wheel was especially interesting."

"The Ferris Wheel? I hate that one. There's no way I went on that ride with you." I stroked him just a bit faster, using the drops of pre-come from his tip to smooth the glided of my fingers. I smiled to myself as I saw his knuckles turn white around the silverware in his hands. I wanted to make him come before he finished the story, and it looked like I was well on my way to doing that as I felt his hips flex forward into my hand slightly.

"You did. I convinced you to go on with me." He looked over at me, eyed burning hotly. "Your hand feels fucking amazing Callie. I'm going to come in about three strokes if you don't stop."

"I wasn't planning to stop, Aidan baby." I bit my lip and looked down at my hand gripping him, wanting to see him climax into my hand. I felt his body tense and my eyes widened as he swelled even bigger the half second before Aidan threw a napkin over his lap and he grunted, shooting into the napkin and my hand, spurting over and over until his muscles relaxed.

We were quiet for a minute, and Aidan used the napkin to clean us both off. He pulled my hand up and met my gaze again as he kissed the back of my hand softly, thanking me silently. I blushed and smiled, then teased him as I brought my hand to my mouth and sucked my fingers, trying to get a taste of him. He groaned again at the sight.

"Do you want to know how I convinced to you to onto the Ferris Wheel with me?" I hadn't expected him to jump right back into the story, and I stumbled over my answer as the waiter popped back up at our table. I blushed furiously and mumbled a thank you as he took our plates and laid down our dessert for us. I wasn't able to meet his eyes, sure he'd see what I'd just done to Aidan under the table written all over my face. To Aidan's credit, he acted normally and thanked the waiter as well, his body completely relaxed. I snorted softly to myself, thinking about just how relaxed he was after coming all over my hand.

Aidan took both spoons before I could grab one, scooping up a bite of the dessert to feed to me. Usually, I wouldn't like it but the look in his eyes stopped my refusal. I closed my mouth around the spoon, closing my eyes at the decadent chocolate on my tongue. He growled softly in response to my low moan of pleasure.

My eyes slowly opened to focus on him, and that's when he repeated his question.

"Would you like to know how I convinced you?" I nodded, opening my mouth for the second bite he was offering. "First, I asked you to go on with me. Then you told me you hated it and refused. But then," he said, feeding me a third bite, "I told you I'd make you come so hard that you wouldn't remember you were on the Ferris Wheel, much less why you were so afraid."

His voice was low and forceful, and the words he said shot straight to my clit. I could feel it throbbing, and I shifted my thighs together to try and relieve some pressure. He glanced down and back up quickly, smirking at me.

"Don't you want to know what happened next Callie?" I nodded, opening my mouth for another bite. "We got onto the

Ferris Wheel. You started shaking when we got about halfway up while loading other people on. You had a death grip on the side wall, eyes squeezed shut. Every time we moved and the cage swung, you'd tense up your whole body and shake harder. I started to get up to hold you and you shouted for me to stop, that we had to keep the weight even on both sides. I argued that since I weighed more than you, I had to get some weight in the middle to keep it balanced."

He offered me another bite, but I shook my head. I was full, but more than that I wanted to focus on the story. He took the bite he'd offered me and his eyes widened. "Damn, that is really good. No wonder you were moaning like I had my tongue on your pussy."

I leaned closer. "I don't think your tongue has ever made me moan quite like that."

"Damn baby, you really know how to bring a man to his knees."

I smirked. "Get back to the Ferris Wheel already."

He shook his head at me and took the last bite of the dessert. I waited patiently while he swallowed and sat back in his chair. He grabbed my hand and held it as he continued rubbing his thumb across my knuckles.

"You were complaining about weight distribution, so I pointed out that I definitely weigh more than you and it would be better if I sat closer to the middle than on the opposite side. You thought about it for a minute, and then nodded quickly. You were so cute, sitting there with your eyes scrunched shut. I felt a little bad for making you get on, but then I remembered I'd promised to get you off. So, scooting towards the middle, I concentrated on doing just that. I sat right in the middle of the car and told you to let go of the cage and trust me. It took you some time but you slowly let go. I

152

told you to keep your eyes closed. Then I placed your feet in my lap and started to massage legs. When you began to relax, I moved my hands up higher. I spread your legs, moving higher and higher up your thighs, until you were tense for a completely different reason than fear. And when I slid my fingers inside your loose shorts, then your lacy panties and then your wet, hot, *deliciously* tight center you forgot where we were."

I grabbed my water, hand shaking from need. I wanted to have his fingers inside me right now. I probably would already if this dress wasn't so damn tight. The more turned on I got throughout the night the tighter this dress felt. I wanted it off, and Aidan on me. I took a long drink of water in hopes of quenching my thirst although I knew it was fruitless because lack of water wasn't why my mouth was so dry. Our waiter brought our check over and Aidan handed him a few bills, telling him to keep the change. The waiter thanked us before leaving us to gather our things. I hurriedly grabbed my purse and stood, pulling Aidan up with me. He chuckled at my effort to maneuver him.

"Where's the fire, baby?" There was humor in his voice but I was to the point where I wasn't finding this funny- at all. I turned around quickly, startling him and making our bodies collide. He almost knocked me over but wrapped his arms around my waist. The full-body contact only served to fuel the flames leaping inside me. I grabbed his jacket lapel and pulled him down so that I could whisper in his ear.

"You want to know where the fire is Aidan? It's in my pussy and coursing through my veins. I need to feel you in me, whether it's your fingers, your tongue, or your cock. So are you going to take me home and fuck me, or are we going to stand here all night?"

CHAPTER TWENTY-TWO
AIDAN

I grabbed Callie and turned her around, pushing her out through the restaurant in front of me. I needed her body to block mine since my hard-on was sure to scandalize at least a few people. I didn't even see anyone else in the restaurant, too focused on the feel of Callie's ass brushing against the front of my slacks. My hands tightened on her shoulders, and she got the message. She sped up a little and I was impressed at her ability to move quickly in those sinful heels of hers.

I reached over her and opened the door to the outside, handing my check ticket to the valet. He nodded, hurrying off to retrieve the car. I waited until he disappeared in the dark of night before saying anything. I kept Callie in front of me as we waited, and I wrapped my arms around her just under her breasts, leaning forward to talk quietly and quickly in her ear.

"I haven't quite finished the story yet; would you like to hear the ending?" She nodded. Of course, I was making this all up on the spot but I liked the scene I was painting too much to give up now. I'd told Lucy a completely different story, and now I was just hoping like hell it never came up in conversation if they ever met. "Well, I had to take my fingers out of you because the wheel turned to the point where almost anyone could look in and tell what I was doing. You started to protest and open your eyes, but slammed them back shut when you happened to look around. I pulled you forward onto my lap, on the floor in the middle of the cart. Your eyes

154

shot open as you straddled me, and you started to shake again as you looked around. I didn't want that, so I put my hand back under you skirt and inside you. I slid right back in since you were soaking wet. Your eyes shot to mine. 'Focus on me only; on my fingers and how they feel inside you' I told you.

"You swallowed hard and nodded, keeping eye contact as I curled my fingers inside you and stroked your clit. I told you dirty, nasty things Callie, and you came at the top of the Ferris Wheel, before we'd even made it around twice. I moved up to the bench and held you as you came down. You seemed surprised when the ride ended, and I held onto you as I helped you out of the car since your legs were a little wobbly."

I felt her breasts move against my arm as she breathed heavily, her bottom squirming against my crotch. I groaned and tightened my arms around her, bending my head down to her neck so I could bite her softly. A short, high moan came from her throat, and it was then that the valet showed up with the car. I reluctantly let Callie go as I tipped the valet and took the keys back. I helped Callie into the car, shutting the door for her and making my way back around. I could feel Callie's eyes watching me as I moved to my door and climbed in.

I looked over at her as I buckled in and the lust in her eyes had my dick hardening even more in my pants. I muttered to myself about the drive back being too long, and I heard a quiet laugh from Callie. I clenched my jaw and refused to look at her- if I did we wouldn't be making it home before I was balls deep in her. I drove away from the restaurant, letting the soft music from the radio fill the silence. I clenched the steering wheel in my hands as I felt Callie's eyes burning into me, silently willing me to look over. I made it about another mile without looking at her, but I saw some movement out of the corner of my eye.

I cut my eyes to her quickly- and saw that she'd peeled down the top of the dress to expose her tits to me. She was staring at me, leaning against the door to face me, as she gently and slowly squeezed them in her hands. My mouth dropped open and I jerked my gaze back to the road so we wouldn't crash. However, I kept glancing over at every chance so I could watch her.

Her moans and sighs filled the car, each one making me harder than the last. After several minutes, one particular glance had me nearly drooling- she'd slipped down on the seat causing her skirt to ride up and I caught a glance of deep red, damp lace in between her thighs. I glanced around to make sure we were the only ones on the road and took a turn onto a deserted lane. I miraculously found a spot the car could fit into between some trees, giving us plenty of coverage. I threw the car into park and turned it off.

Instantly I had Callie in my lap and she was thrusting against me, moaning as I covered one breast with my hand and biting her nipple on the other side. I used my free hand to grab a butt cheek, guiding her harder against me. Her hands flew down to my pants, undoing them as quickly as she could. She pulled my dick out of my pants and stroked me a couple times, making me moan around her tit in my mouth, biting down a little harder than usual. A strangled cry came out of her throat and I pulsed in her hand at her reaction to my roughness.

I pulled her skirt up to her waist, moved her lace thong to the side, and grit my teeth as she guided me inside her. As soon as the tip of my cock was inside her she dropped straight down, taking all of me in one go. We both groaned and stopped moving, reveling in the feel of me deep inside her.

"Aidan, you feel so good in me, so deep and thick. I want to stay like this forever," she panted out as she started to move on me. I couldn't get any words out; watching her tits bounce lightly with her bobbing was mesmerizing, as was feeling her pussy clench around me every time she bore down on me. My windows were fogging up with our heavy breathing, and that fact only brought me more satisfaction.

I leaned the seat back a little to give us more room. I moved my hands down to her ass to help guide her up and down, and on one particularly deep thrust I drew a hand back as much as I could and spanked her. She cried out, squeezing around me tighter and I did it again, a bit harder.

"I'm coming Aidan, I'm coming!" She screamed out, telling me what I already knew and I couldn't hold on any longer and I shot deep in her, coming at the same time.

She slumped forward and rocked lightly as we pulsed in and around each other. I wrapped my arms around her back lightly, kissing the top of her head. When she finally caught her breath, Callie rested her hands on my chest, pushing back to look at me. Her cheeks were flushed, eyes sparkling and I thought I'd never seen her more beautiful. She smiled shyly at me and I grinned back at her.

"You are trouble," I told her softly as I pulled out of her and straightened her panties and dress so she looked presentable, if not thoroughly fucked.

"You started it," she retorted airily. She climbed back over to the passenger side of the car and buckled her seatbelt. I leaned over and kissed her softly.

"Yeah but we both finished." We laughed as I started the car and backed out of our little cove. As soon as we pulled back onto the road I grabbed her hand to hold it. She intertwined our fingers and warmth spread through my body at the comfort of holding her hand.

"So, what's the plan for tomorrow?"

I contemplated Callie's question. "Well, we don't have to be at the build site tomorrow, so we can explore the area a bit if you're interested."

"Yeah, that would be awesome! I'll have to check with Char to make sure I don't need to do anything for Eros, but I should be good to go."

I nodded. "By the way, how exactly did you meet Char?"

"I haven't told you this story yet?!"

Shit. I have to watch myself if I don't want to give this whole thing away. "Um, no. I only just met him and hadn't thought to ask before now."

"Hmm. Well, we met in college. We had this business class together and we ended up sitting next to each other. I could always hear him making comments under his breath about the stupidity of people in the room and he always said what I was thinking. There was one moment in class where someone said something dumber than usual, and Char's mumbled comment was so perfect that I couldn't help but laugh loudly in the middle of the teacher's response. I only laughed for a second, but everyone was staring at me.

"Char just turned to me and loudly said 'bless you' like I had only sneezed. It was all I could do to keep a straight face and say thank you back. When everyone went back to paying attention to the lecture, Char leaned back over to me and whispered 'Gotta keep it in lovely, or I can't keep divulging my inner thoughts to you'. We've been inseparable ever since."

I laughed at the story, and when she finished I brought her hand up to kiss the back of it. "That's the best. He seems like a great guy to have as a friend."

"Yeah, he's been a lifesaver. I don't have a lot of friends, but Char is more than enough."

"Quality, not quantity."

"Exactly. What about you, who's your best friend?"

"His name is Nick. I met him in middle school, but we actually didn't get along very well at first."

"What? Really?"

"Yeah, the only class we had together was gym but we're both extremely competitive so we butted heads a lot." I smiled thinking back to the trouble we'd get into. "It got so bad one time that we both ended up in detention together and by the end we left as friends."

"Of course." Callie's eyes were sparkling with laughter and I let out a chuckle.

"We still tried to beat each other all the time but it was all in good fun after that. He's like a brother to me now, but he's active in the Air Force so I don't see him as much anymore. Lucy, my business partner, is his sister actually. She's become one of my other best friends over the years."

"Oh, so that's why she got into business with you? It sounds like your guys' families were very close."

"Yeah, we were. My parents loved those two like their own kids, and Lucy and Nick needed them." My hands tightened and I accidentally squeezed Callie's hand a little too hard. I noticed her wince but she didn't pull away. I loosened my grip and Callie rested her other hand on top of mine.

"What do you mean they needed them?" Her voice was soft, and I could tell she got the feeling that theirs wasn't a pretty story.

"Nick and Lucy's parents were incredibly abusive. Although they never hit their kids, they tore them down mentally and emotionally. That was one of the reasons for Nick's competitiveness- he was trying to prove he was worth something. I also think that's one of the main reasons he joined the Air Force, besides his desire to defend his country. And Lucy…" I trailed off, shaking my head. "She has a bit of a disconnect to people emotionally. She won't date anyone seriously, and even though she gets along well with people, she doesn't let anyone get close."

"So your parents were aware of all this then?"

"They were. I told them what I saw after going over to their house unexpectedly once. It horrified me to hear the way their mom and dad talked to them, and I was so torn up for them when I got home that I broke down. It'd reminded me of some foster homes I'd been in, but I knew Nick and Lucy were stuck because that was their *parents*. My mom and dad were upset but they tried to hide it, telling me that Lucy and Nick were welcome to come over any time, and that they could stay as long as they wanted. My friends thankfully took advantage of the offer, so they were able to escape somewhere safe."

"That's so sad." I could hear the genuine hurt in her voice for my friends, and it amazed me. She continued after a pause. "I'd like to meet them someday, they're obviously very important to you."

Sudden emotions clogged my throat and I had to clear it a few times before I could answer her. "I'd like that too Callie."

We reached the apartment complex shortly after that, and I led Callie to my place. When we got in the elevator, Callie surprised me by wrapping her arms arounds my body and hugging me tightly. I hugged back, knowing that she could tell I was in a pensive mood. Her comforting embrace warmed me from the inside, and my heart beat hard in my chest.

The doors opened up into the apartment and we walked in together. She started to walk towards her bedroom but I stopped her holding onto her hand tightly so she had to turn back towards me.

"I don't really want to go to sleep yet," I said then hesitated trying to read her face. "Do you want to stay up and watch a movie with me?"

She smiled widely. "I'd like that very much. I'll go change really quick and then meet you back out here."

She started toward her room again, but I held onto her hand still. When she turned to me again I closed the distance between us, placing my hands on her face and holding her there for a deep, slow kiss. She sighed into my mouth and kissed me back. It was unhurried, and a slow burn started inside me. I knew I needed to let her go if we were actually going to watch a movie, which was something I actually really wanted to do with her. I pulled back slowly and stared at her as she breathed deeply and her eyes fluttered open to meet mine.

"Thank you, Callie," I said quietly.

Her brow furrowed with confusion. "For what?"

I brushed some hair off her face to look at her better. "Just for being you." I took a mental breath and stepped back. "Now, go change and get your perfect ass back out here. First one out gets to pick the movie."

She grinned and shot towards her room, silently challenging me. I chuckled and watched her on her way down the hall. I turned back to mine as soon as she shut her door behind her and knew she was going to lose- women have too many steps to get ready and all I had to do was take my clothes off and throw on some sweats. No shirt needed.

I took a little longer than I normally would just to give Callie a fighting chance, but still opened my door less than ten minutes later to heading out to the front room. I noticed Callie's door was still shut, and I chuckled to myself as I made my way past the wall blocking the living room from sight.

I rounded the corner and stopped suddenly, taking in the vision before me. I noticed three things right away: Callie had somehow beat me to the front room; she was bending over while wearing the tiniest pair of shorts I'd ever seen; and she'd brushed her hair out so it was flowing around her in chestnut waves that begged me to shove my hands into it to test the softness.

"What the fuck?" The words flew out of my mouth before I could stop them.

She suddenly straightened and whirled around to face me, movie in hand and triumphant grin taking over her face.

"How the hell did you beat me out here?" It shocked me that she'd somehow managed to change her clothes, take out her hair and even take off her makeup all in the time it took me to take off my pants and shirt and throw some sweats on.

"You underestimated me, that's how." She ambled towards me and I scrubbed a hand over my open mouth, taking in the expanse of skin showing in her shorts and flowing cut-off tank top. I could tell by the look in her eyes that she was enjoying this, and by her heated glances at my bare chest I knew she liked what she was seeing.

"Well that's going to be the last time I do that," I grumbled as she stopped in front of me.

"We'll see about that." She winked at me and then handed me the DVD she'd picked. I took it from her and felt relief that she'd picked something I'd seen a million times. *White Chicks* was one of my favorite movies, and I wouldn't have to concentrate on the movie itself which meant I could check out Callie as much as I wanted to.

I put the movie in and sat on the couch, patting the seat next to me for Callie. She sat down on the next seat but left some distance between us. I didn't care for that at all so I grabbed her and pulled her right into my side, putting my arm around her shoulders. She turned a little so that her back was pressed against my side. That particular angle made it so that my arm rested right across her chest, hand naturally falling on her right breast. She didn't move my hand, so I decided to leave it there since that's where I wanted it anyway.

I started the movie and smiled to myself since she couldn't see me. This was going to be an interesting movie night.

CHAPTER TWENTY-THREE
AIDAN

I woke up slowly, taking a few moments to figure out where I was. I groaned quietly when I noticed one of my arms was completely numb and I had a crick in my neck. I blinked into the darkness and realized I was still on the couch with Callie from when we put in the movie. I squinted at the clock on the wall illuminated by moonlight to figure out what time it was. Barely three in the morning.

I looked down at the source of warmth enclosed in my arms. My chair reclined all the way back with the leg rest out, and Callie had taken up the rest of the couch with her body pressed against my side. She had an arm looped around my stomach and I breathed slowly so I didn't wake her. Her scent filled my nose and I tried to tamp down the rising desire it invoked.

I knew I wasn't going back to sleep right away so I decided to enjoy the moment. It felt peaceful here, just holding Callie and lightly playing with her hair. We sat through two movies, putting in Better Off Dead after White Chicks, but we hadn't really watched much of the movies. We hadn't had sex either- we'd just ended up talking through them. I might have teased her a little bit but she'd stopped that when she'd started questioning me about my tattoos. I thought back to the conversation, a smile on my face with strands of Callie's soft hair falling through my fingers.

"Aidan, what does this tattoo mean?" She traced her fingers over the tree tattoo placed on my heart. It transitioned from fully blooming and alive to completely withered and dead going left to right.

"It's a representation for family, and how it can change sometimes."

She was quiet for a second. "And what else?"

I met her eyes, startled. Her intuitiveness caught me off guard and had me telling her the rest of it despite my original reluctance to go into detail. "I got it after Serena and Caleb passed. I wasn't in a great place, so the idea behind it at the time was that beautiful things die and you can't stop it because that's life so you deal with it." I took a breath. "But later on, I realized it also meant that just because something dies it doesn't mean it wasn't beautiful, or that it can't be beautiful again with passing time and patience."

I stared at the TV screen while talking, avoiding eye contact. I wasn't sure what I was so afraid to see in her eyes, but I knew it would break me one way or the other. Callie didn't say anything after that, just leaned up and kissed the tattoo softly, wrapping her arms around me. After a hesitation, I put my arms around her as well and held her tight to me. I was grateful that she sensed what I needed at the moment and my heart pounded while I tried to sort out what was happening there. Before I could overthink and scare myself with the depths of my feelings for Callie, she distracted me with another query.

"What about this one?" She lifted herself up and rubbed a thumb across the one by my hip. The touch lit me up but I ignored it to answer her question.

"That's a tribal-style Scottish thistle. Even though I don't know my birth family, I am proud of my heritage. The flower is a representation of Scotland and its people; beautiful, resilient, and fierce."

165

"Yes, I can see why you'd be proud of it. It's just like you."

My chest swelled with pride again at the memory of her words. She'd asked about a couple of my other tattoos, and I gladly told her about them. They were a collection of who I was, and by her asking about them it was like she was asking about me. I wanted her to know me; hopefully whenever this thing with us ended she'd remember who I was and not the asshole I felt like right now.

Every moment I spent with her only made me like her and want her more. I chalked it up to adrenaline with the situation, or even possibly some kind of "encouragement" from Aphrodite to keep me on the path. I'd never felt like this about anyone, not even Lucy. It was so hard to believe that it was all genuinely coming from myself. There had to be some outside influence for why I was reacting so strongly to Callie.

She shifted against me, mumbling something in her sleep that I couldn't quite catch. It was adorable, and I grinned at her scrunched up little face that was now tilted towards me. I leaned forward a little so I could softly kiss her forehead and I lingered for a few seconds longer than I had planned to. As I leaned back again I noticed that her face had smoothed out, and a small smile was even ghosting her lips.

"Oh Aidan," she breathed out softly. She was still asleep, and my body reacted viscerally at the thought of her dreaming about me. I liked the idea of that way too much, and I'd give my left lung to know what she was dreaming exactly. She shifted again, this time her eyes fluttering open. Her hazy eyes fixed on my face and she reached a hand up and softly patted my face.

"C'mon baby, let's get you to bed," I whispered.

She nodded softly and curled into me, wrapping her arms around my neck while I gathered her in my arms and stood. I padded to her room and set her down on her bed. She didn't let go of me and a surprisingly strong tug from her caught me off guard, making me fall into bed with her. I almost squished her in my surprise, but braced my arms on either side of her head in time, heated gaze meeting hers again.

"Please don't leave me Aidan. Stay." She rasped the words out and my semi-hardness turned into a raging hard-on in a millisecond. That heavenly voice of hers would do me in every time. I hesitated for one more second and the look in her sleepy eyes turned haunted. "I don't want to be alone anymore," she whispered.

My heart seized, and I capitulated. Bending my elbows, I leaned down and brushed my lips against hers. She tilted up to meet me, but I kept the touch fleeting. Now wasn't the time to delve deeper into her. I pulled away and her arms tightened around me, silently begging me not to leave. I smiled at her before situating us so that I was spooning her. I put one arm around her and the other beneath the pillow her head was resting on.

She snuggled closer and I bit back a groan at the feeling of her rubbing against my crotch. The wildness her action called up in me was immediately calmed when a whispered "thank you" reached my ears. I waited the short minutes until her breaths evened out before kissing the back of her head and responding before falling back asleep myself.

"You're not alone anymore Callie. Not while I have you."

CHAPTER TWENTY-FOUR
CALLIE

The heat racing through the inside of my body made me moan and arch into the source of whatever was making me feel this way. Everything was hazy, the center of my focus on reaching the peak of this pleasure. Strong hands pinned my hips down, making it so that I couldn't move an inch. Fingers dug into my flesh, inciting a high-pitched cry to tumble out of me while the muscles in my stomach tightened in anticipation.

"Shit Callie, I love the way you respond to my mouth on your soaking wet pussy." The deep growl brought me out of the foggy dreamland I'd been floating in. I realized this wasn't just a dream- it was very real. A tongue rasped across my clit and I cried out louder as I shoved my hands in the hair of the man between my legs. My gaze flew down my body and met Aidan's, his full of dark desire and promises. His mouth never left me as he moved his grip to the back of my thighs, spreading me open wider and pressing my legs into my chest.

Aidan moaned against me as I tugged on his hair a bit harder. A moment later he lifted his head and my body clenched at the sight of his mouth glistening with my juices.

"Hold your legs right where they are, baby. I'm going to need both hands for what I want to do next."

I panted, hurriedly removing my hands from his hair and put them behind my knees, spreading wider in invitation. I watched his cock jerk at the site of me displaying everything for him before he looked back down between my legs. He leaned down and I held my breath, expecting him to lick my pussy. He turned his face at the last second and stroked my birthmark with his tongue. I cursed at how good it felt and Aidan bit down on it softly in response before leaning back again. Both hands came up to spread my pussy lips apart, completely opening me to him. I moaned at the expression on his face that said he was about to devour me and I rocked my hips up to him.

"Don't move," Aidan said harshly and slapped the spot where the bottom of my ass met my thigh.

"Ah!" I cried out at the sting of the slap, and Aidan smiled wickedly when he saw my wetness start to slide down between my ass cheeks. I whimpered and couldn't stop the shifting of my body. Aidan slapped the other side harder than the first, not having to tell me that I needed to be still.

"Look at how your pussy is dripping for me baby. I can tell you like it when I spank you, you're almost gushing for me. I could drink that all up and beg you for more, but I like it where it is now."

My whole body throbbed, bringing me closer and closer to the edge. My eyes widened when I realized he could probably make me orgasm just from keeping me on the edge like this and talking dirty to me. Every filthy word that fell out of his mouth felt like it landed directly on my clit, stroking me higher.

Aidan slipped two fingers into my center without any difficulty, squeezing my ass in his other hand. I dropped my head back onto the bed and grit my teeth with the effort to hold my lower body still. I wanted nothing more than to thrust into his hand, to make him move those fingers inside me faster and harder. But something in his eyes, his voice, had me burning to do what he told me even more.

"Good girl Callie. I know you like it rough and fast, but right now I'm going to take my time. I want to savor this tight little pussy."

I clenched around him tightly at his words and he groaned, putting a third finger inside me on the next thrust. He lazily delved in and out of me for what seemed like forever. I was lost in a haze from the movement of those fingers curling inside me and didn't register another finger teasing at my ass, Aidan using my arousal as lubrication. I gasped his name in shock, my hands starting to slip from my thighs and my head rearing up from the bed to search Aidan's face.

He stilled, searching my face. "Callie? Are you okay with this?"

I bit my lip, hesitating, then slowly nodded. I didn't hate the sensations but I'd never done anything like this before. I did trust him to be careful though, so it couldn't hurt to try it out at least. He leaned down and kissed me softly. When he leaned back again, my heart thumped hard at the look on his face. If I read that expression right, we were getting right back into it.

He looked back down and moved his finger up to my folds, coating his finger in my fluids. I felt my muscles clench around his finger as he started to slip in and he paused, not looking up from what he was doing before he spoke.

"Keep those hands on your fucking legs Callie. Take a deep breath and then let it out slowly to relax." Instinctively I did what he told me to; his tone brooked no argument. The finger in my ass slid the rest of the way inside me when I let my breath out and my hands turned white where they held my legs at the new, indescribable feeling.

"What are... you doing to me Aidan?" I gasped out the words as his fingers slowly thrust in and out of me in sync.

This was a definite first for me, but it was more pleasurable than I ever thought it could be. I could barely get out the words to Aidan as I hovered on the edge of a climax.

"You're going to feel me Callie. I want you to be aware every second of the day that I was inside you, that I held you in my hands and gave you pleasure like you've never had. I want you to feel me with you, with every single moment, because I for sure can fucking feel you."

When he finished talking his mouth dove down to my clit, sucking it in and flicking his tongue rapidly on it. His fingers shoved harder inside me and I came instantly, legs and tits shaking at the force of the best orgasm I'd ever had. Seconds later I was still coming when he pulled his mouth and fingers away to plunge his dick inside me. I was back to the edge instantly and three hard thrusts later I was screaming as I came again. I felt tears slipping out of my eyes with the massive amount of pleasure ripping through me. My ankles were resting on his shoulders and his hands squeezed the life out of them as he yelled out his own climax.

The feeling of him gripping my ankles only heightened my climax, dragging it out as I pulsed around Aidan inside me. He groaned quietly with every clench, and collapsed on top of me. I smiled and rubbed my hands up and down his back slowly, making him shudder. He shifted slightly so that his weight wasn't on me, but didn't pull out of me yet. We were breathing heavily as we held on to each other and a giggle escaped me.

"Nothing about what just happened should be making you laugh," he grumbled into my ear which only made me laugh again.

I pushed my head up to look at him. "I was just thinking… that was the best wakeup call ever."

Aidan looked at me with amusement and then laughed too. "Hell yeah it was," he said and grinned. He studied my face, then brought one hand up to brush the skin near my eyes. His smile slid away and he looked concerned. "Tears? Did I hurt you?"

I shook head. "No, it was just very intense. It's never happened to me before, but believe me, these are good tears."

The hand that had been touching my face sank into my hair to hold the back of my head and I was suddenly enveloped in a deep kiss. Aidan's tongue brushed against my lips, begging for entrance. I appeased him, and our tongues battled for dominance for a time before he pulled away.

"What was that for?" I asked breathlessly.

"I was afraid I'd hurt you for a second, but then you tell me you cried because it felt so fucking good. And damn," He shook his head in wonder as he stared at me, "if that doesn't make me want to get that from you again." My pussy clenched around him still in me and his eyes widened as he felt it. He shut his eyes tightly, trying to control himself. I could already feel him growing inside me, and just to test his restraint, I tightened my inner muscles and gripped him inside of me a few more times.

He rose above me, thrusting inside me shallowly as he hardened and I sighed contentedly at the feeling. He suddenly pulled out of me and yanked me out of bed by my arms. I was taken aback and gripped his shoulders as I tried to find my balance on shaky legs. I could feel our combined liquids seeping out of me and I blushed as they trickled down my thigh.

Aidan lifted me up by my ass, leaving me to wrap my legs around him as he stalked towards my bathroom. I heard him mutter something about wetness as he stepped into the bathroom. I knew he could feel everything that had dripped out of me, and that he liked it. I put my mouth on his neck, licking and biting him there.

His hands tightened on my bottom and rubbed me along his cock trapped between our bodies. I bit down a little harder when he hit a particular spot on my clit and he set me down on the long counter so he could use his hands to grab fistfuls of my hair and drag it back as he returned the favor on my neck.

"I can't believe how hard you are Aidan." He thrust against me jerkily, an automatic response to my husky voice and words. His lips and teeth trailed down from my neck to my collarbone and then shoulder as I continued. "Your cock is like nothing I've ever felt before. I love watching your tattoos move with you when you're thrusting into me. And every time I think I've come harder than ever before, you prove me wrong and do it again."

At that, Aidan bit down hard in the spot between my shoulder and neck, sucking hard enough to leave a hickey. Most people think that they're gross but I secretly loved them. I loved seeing it and knowing that my man was so into the moment that he wanted to mark me as his. I was stubborn and independent but when it came to sex I just wanted someone to take control of me, dominate me. Own me.

Aidan pulled back and stared at the mark he'd just left, licking his lips. "I hope you're ready for round two because I need to be inside you in the next thirty seconds or I'm going to be coming all over your stomach and tits."

My nipples hardened at his words, and I could almost feel my pupils dilate at the idea of that. I never knew I wanted it, but now I wanted it bad. Aidan white-knuckled the counter top and thrust against me again.

"One day I'll do that because I can see that you want it just as bad as I do. But right now I want to fuck you from behind so I can slap your ass as I watch water run down your body."

"Oh god, yes," I breathed out as I moved to get off the counter and start the shower. I jumped in, water still cold and beckoned Aidan with my eyes. "Are you coming or what?"

His eyes sparkled as he stalked to me. "Oh I'm coming alright, but not without you coming first."

I winked as he stepped into the shower and closed the glass door behind him. "We'll see about that."

A couple hours later, I was humming to myself in the kitchen while stuffing some snacks and water into a backpack for our adventures today. We'd slept in a bit later than planned. And by sleeping in I meant we spent longer in bed and then in the shower where he made me come twice before I finished him off in my mouth, but it was worth it.

I heard Aidan come up behind me but I knew he liked my voice so I kept humming. It reminded me of how much he liked me humming in the shower earlier. He'd slowly fed me his dick, blocking my face from the spray with his body. I'd started to hum a song around him and he'd nearly shot off right there. It didn't take too long after that before I was swallowing the evidence of a blow job done right.

Coming back to the present, I felt Aidan wrap himself around me from behind, resting a hand on my throat to feel the vibrations from my hum.

"What song is that?"

"The same one from the shower." His hand tightened slightly on my neck at my response. My breath shortened and I could feel my nipples start to pucker. We both groaned at the

174

same time and Aidan pulled away from me, spinning me to face him.

"If I didn't know any better, I'd think you were trying to keep me here all day and fuck me until I died from pleasure. Or exhaustion."

"Damn, you've got me figured out. I didn't think I was that obvious." He laughed and helped me finish packing the backpack.

"Seriously though, what song is that? It sounds familiar."

"Yeah, you probably know it, but I think I'll wait to tell you. Keep the mystery alive since I'm apparently so obvious about everything else."

"Fine, keep your secret then. I'll figure it out soon enough."

I laughed awkwardly, but he didn't seem to notice. I was starting to feel like I was keeping a very big secret from him, but I didn't want to voice it yet. It wasn't possible to fall in love in less than two weeks without your memory, was it? Yeah, I'd keep that all to myself for now, thank you very much.

Chapter Twenty-Five
Aidan

"Looks like we've gotten a good head start here. I'll be back tomorrow afternoon to double check the delivery dates for the rest of the materials." I spoke to the foreman but I watched Callie. She had her hands clasped lightly behind her back while staring out at the ocean. There was a light breeze today and it blew her dark, loose hair behind her, tickling her arms. It reminded me of a similar view I'd had of her by a waterfall on one of our hikes yesterday and I almost missed the foreman's reply while replaying the memory.

"Yessir." He paused. "That's quite a view you've got there."

I turned towards him. I raised an eyebrow in warning to be careful of what he said next.

His lips twitched. "The ocean, I mean. You picked a great site." He kept a serious face but I could hear the humor in his voice.

"I'm sure that's what you meant." My eyes flickered over Callie's still form again before looking back to the foreman. "Either way, you're right." I let a small smile out and he shook his head, chuckling.

"You gonna get your girl and get outta here or what?"

I laughed, glad that we were comfortable around each other. I could tell he respected me and my relationship with Callie so I took no offense to his teasing, and I liked that he felt comfortable enough to say what he was thinking.

"Yeah yeah, we're leaving. Remember, call me if anything comes up!" He nodded at me before walking off. I made my way towards Callie and wrapped my arms around her, resting my head on top of hers. She sighed contentedly and leaned back into me. We stood there for some time peacefully. Out in the distance I saw something splash out of the water, followed quickly by another couple of splashes.

Callie gasped quietly and I loosened my hold on her so she could turn. "What's out there?"

"Most likely it's a group of sea lions. They like to come close to the shore every now and then. There's a bunch of rocks nearby that they like to sunbathe on. We can go check them out if you'd like."

Her eyes were sparkling in excitement. "Yes yes yes!!!" She was practically hopping and I grinned at her enthusiasm. I grabbed her hand and started towards the car. She kept pace with me, and I heard some of the guys on site laughing. I bet it looked like we were rushing to get out of there for some *alone time*, and I couldn't help but raise my arm and flip them off. The laughter got louder and I struggled to keep my own in when Callie glared at me.

"Don't encourage them Aidan! It looks like we're running off for an afternoon delight!"

I lost it at that. "I know," I said between laughs.

Callie glared at me still as I nearly tossed her into the car after opening her door. I winked, keeping eye contact as I made my way around the front of the car.

I could see her lips moving, grumbling to herself. I wanted to know what she was saying, whether she was cursing me out or trying to stop herself from laughing too. She fell silent as I opened my door and slid in beside her. Not even hesitating, I leaned all the way over to seal my mouth over hers. Her gasp of indignation set me on fire, and I groaned as she bit my lip hard. It hurt, but it was worth it when she softly ran her tongue over the bite to soothe the sting.

I pulled back and admired her flushed face and glowing purple eyes. We stared at each other for a second, and then Callie shook her head, looking out the window. She crossed her arms and I greedily took in the cleavage highlighted with that move.

"Boys…" she muttered under her breath when she finally noticed where I was looking. I let everything I was feeling infuse my eyes as I looked back up at her, raising my gaze slowly. I saw the pulse in her neck pounding and it was satisfying to know I wasn't the only one affected.

I licked my lips and smiled when her eyes dilated at the movement. "Aww come on babe, I can tell you like it when I get all caveman on you."

I started the car and drove off to the rocks I'd mentioned. They weren't far away at all, but I knew that I could get us there faster if we took the car since I knew of a parking spot about fifty feet away from our destination.

"Hmmph," was her only reply. My smile got bigger and I knew I'd won this round. She knew she couldn't protest that without lying her face off, but she didn't want to admit I was right either. I fucking loved it when her stubbornness came out like that. It made her give in all that much sweeter.

I parked in the designated area and met Callie just as she was getting out of the car. She shut the door and stared at my reflection in the window as I came up behind her. I turned her around and kissed her softly.

"Please don't be mad baby," I said quietly, keeping eye contact and sliding a hand around her neck. I leaned forward so our foreheads were touching and I breathed her in while waiting for her reply. I could feel it in her body as it softened against me.

She let out a deep sigh and I pulled back to look at her again. I saw her lips curve into a small smile. "I *suppose* it would've been entertaining to see how fast we got out of there. Especially with how they found us kissing the other day."

I let out a chuckle. "Exactly. I'm glad you can see the humor in the situation now."

She lifted her hands to frame my face, now full-out laughing. "I was never mad at you Aidan. You're just so easy to provoke." She laughed again, and I realized that her glaring had all been for show. She'd been teasing me the whole damn time.

A choking sound flew out of my mouth at that realization, and I couldn't help but kiss her again. I couldn't go one more second without showing her just how much I loved her playfulness. The thought flitted across my mind that I'd used the term "love" with something about Callie twice in the last ten minutes, but Callie meeting my tongue stroke for stroke, moaning in sync obliterated all other thoughts.

Eventually, we pulled back and amidst our heavy breathing I heard the calls of the sea lions- what we had come here for in the first place. My mind and body warred- one wanting to pull her into the backseat and finish what we'd started, the other wanting to see the look on Callie's face when she saw the animals. My mind won when Callie looked towards the sounds and excitement crossed her face. I grabbed Callie's hand again, taking her closer to a ledge where we could watch the sea lions playing and sleeping.

She pulled me down with her to sit on the ledge and I put an arm around her waist, watching her instead of the animals.

I did the same thing yesterday when we went exploring California. I'd seen most of the places already but I loved seeing how entranced Callie was by everything.

When we'd gotten to the waterfall yesterday, she'd stood staring out at everything silently. She'd whispered something to herself, then repeated it louder when I asked what she was saying.

"I said, 'What is this life if, full of care, we have no time to stand and stare.' It's a poem called Leisure by William Henry Davies. It always pops into my mind when I see something like this and think about how much people are missing out on when they are constantly moving."

"I see what he's saying," I replied. "What's the point of life if we don't have time to appreciate life itself?"

She beamed at me and nodded. "Exactly."

I smiled again at the memory. She'd also told me she'd never left Colorado and that it was beautiful, but California had a different kind of beauty. All day she'd constantly been amazed by every new thing and she'd spouted poetry when she couldn't form her own words. I'd recognized a lot of what she recited but it was different hearing it come from her mouth.

I'd never seen someone so completely absorbed in everything around them as Callie. I was becoming obsessed with showing her something new just so I could see her reactions. A sudden idea popped into my mind for what I could show her next, and I shot off a quick text to the foreman telling him I wouldn't be by tomorrow, but the next day instead. I had somewhere to take Callie tomorrow because I wasn't going to be able to hold in the surprise much longer than tonight.

I could hear Callie humming in the kitchen three hours later, putting together the Greek salad we were bringing over to Beth's place for dinner tonight. I smiled, listening to the song. It was the same one she'd been teasing me with the last couple days since the shower when she'd first hummed it around my cock. I still hadn't figured out which one it was; it was starting to drive me crazy because not only was I trying to recall what song it was, but every time she started humming it again I'd think of the shower and get completely distracted by the memory.

I walked out to the kitchen and she glanced and winked at me, continuing to sing softly. She knew exactly what she was doing to me. So I did the only thing I could; I tried to ignore the bait.

"I was going to see if you needed any help, but it looks like you've got everything handled." I sat on a stool at the bar, watching as Callie efficiently sliced cucumbers and dropped them into the bowl with the tri-color tomatoes, olives, diced onions, and feta cheese already done.

"Thanks for the offer, but I've done this so many times that you'd only mess up my system." She added salt, pepper, and oregano before drizzling some olive oil on top.

I watched her gently stir everything together before putting a lid on the bowl to seal everything. "You look nice, by the way." She was dressed in a light blue sundress that gathered under her breasts and flowed down to her knees. The straps crossed each other in the back, letting her tan skin peek through them. Her strappy sandals were white and had a strip of blue crystals matching the dress going around her ankles.

"Thanks." She came around the countertop to stand between my open legs. She leaned forward and kissed me softly. "You look good, too."

"This old thing? Nah," I grinned. I'd put on a fitted black dress shirt, left untucked with some dark blue jeans and black Vans. I'd rolled my sleeves up and I knew that was a good choice when I caught Callie admiring my arms.

Callie rolled her eyes at my dismissal and grabbed her purse off the counter. "Whatever Aidan, you know you look good. False modesty doesn't become you."

"I know, but I love it when your eyes roll back in your head." I let the double meaning hang in the air between us; Callie's face flushed and I knew she'd caught it.

"Can't you find some happy medium between bashful and cocky?"

"I was pretty sure you liked my cock…y-ness." I grabbed the bowl of salad and followed Callie into the elevator, leaning back against one of the walls.

"Oh my god Aidan," she said rolling her eyes and covering her smile with a hand.

I started to move in on her and she backed up until her butt hit the handle running along the walls. I still had the salad bowl in one hand, so I used the other to bring her hips tight against mine.

I leaned down and lightly bit her earlobe. A low groan floated from her. "Just Aidan is fine baby, you don't need to call me God."

A sound of disbelief escaped her throat and she pushed me away. I laughed and let her shove me back. The elevator reached the lobby and she stalked out towards the car. I ate up the sight of her walking away from me, hoping that the growing erection I had would deflate by the time we got to Beth's. Knowing my body's reactions to Callie though, it wasn't likely.

Beth lived a short drive from the apartments in a small cottage that she refused to give up. I'd told her multiple times that we could renovate a space for her at the apartments so she didn't have to leave home in order to work. She refused, saying that she liked her cozy home and didn't want to live around a bunch of other people. I always gave in because I didn't care where she lived as long as she was happy there.

It was a good thing the drive to Beth's wasn't long because Callie refused to talk to me the whole time. I could tell she wasn't angry at me because she was still humming that damn song; she was doing this to torture me. She ignored my attempts to get her to talk instead of sing and I tried to ignore her voice basically wrapping around my dick and squeezing it. When I turned onto the long driveway for Beth's place, Callie must've taken pity on me because she finally started to sing the words to the song.

"I've been so busy, but I've been thinking 'bout what I wanna do with you, now it's me and you. Oh, I've been waiting; think I wanna make a move now, baby tell me if you like it."

It was Me & U by Cassie; Lucy was obsessed with that song when it came out so that was the reason I'd recognized it. I hadn't heard that song in years though so it was no wonder I couldn't place it just by the melody. The suggestive words hit me like a train and I realized Callie hadn't started to sing the words in order to help, she'd waited until I was already keyed up and at the point where I couldn't do anything to show her exactly how much I liked it.

Something began to simmer inside me. It wasn't anger, it was… anticipation. She wanted to play games did she? She had no clue what she was getting herself into. She had me all twisted up in knots over her when I was supposed to be the one in control of this whole thing. I'd let her get under my skin but I was taking the reins back now.

I parked and told her to wait for me. She did, smiling devilishly at me because she knew what state I was in. I opened her door and she put one leg down to step out. I quickly stepped between her legs and held her waist to help her out of the car. Because of the closeness, her body slid up against mine as she straightened. I slipped a hand into her hair at the base of her head and leaned forward to make my move in our little game.

"I'm going to fuck you before we leave this house tonight Callie. I'm going to find a moment where I can drag you into the nearest bathroom or closet and I'm going to turn you around and grind my hard cock on your ass before I flip up this pretty skirt of yours. Then, I'm going to pull those pretty panties I know you're wearing to the side and shove so hard and deep inside you that you start coming as soon as I'm balls deep. And I'm going to have to put a hand over your mouth to make sure no one comes to investigate why you're screaming my name."

I pulled back so she could look at my face and know I was serious. Her pupils were blown, her breathing fast, and a quick glance down affirmed her nipples were beaded tight.

"I bet your panties are soaking wet right now. If I put my hand in them would I find your pussy dripping for me, begging for my cock?"

She panted and whispered out the words of my downfall: "What panties?"

"Fuuuuck," I groaned and closed my eyes, pressing my forehead against hers. I nearly came myself at those words. An animalistic growl flew out of my mouth. I was on the brink of getting down on my knees and putting my head up her skirt to prove that she was telling the truth when I heard Beth's voice calling out to us.

"Aidan, Callie! I'm so glad you're here! Are you coming inside or are you going to stand there all night?"

I didn't move away from Callie as I shouted back in as calm a voice as I could manage. "Yeah, be in in a minute!"

Then to Callie I said, "You're such a bad girl tonight. I'm going to have to punish you before I fuck you." She let out a strangled moan that made me hotter. I pulled away before I lost control and set her to the side. I grabbed her purse and shoved it towards her, getting the salad bowl when she took her purse.

I grabbed her hand and squeezed it in mine as we made our way inside. Thank the heavens that it was a bit of a party instead of just Beth, Callie, and I. It would give me a chance to fulfill my promises to Callie since Beth's laser focus wouldn't be on us. Excitement surged through me at the thought of what trouble we could get into at this otherwise tame get-together.

CHAPTER TWENTY-SIX
CALLIE

We walked into the party together and greeted Beth like we hadn't been about to go at it like wild animals on Aidan's rental car. I was so wet I was afraid I was going to start dripping down my legs; the no panties thing had seemed like a good idea at the time but now I was starting to regret it.

"Beth this looks lovely and the food smells amazing. Can you point me towards a restroom?" Aidan smirked at me like he knew exactly why I was going. I almost glared at him, but at the last second I bit my lip and stared at him as I continued. "I have to go take care of something really quick."

His gaze darkened and I had to tear my eyes away to meet Beth's innocently when she responded. "Of course, my dear. Actually, Aidan, could you show her to one? I want to make sure I greet my guests and you know I'm horrible at explaining directions."

"It would be my pleasure to show her the bathroom Aunt Beth," Aidan said and grinned darkly at me. My mouth went dry and I realized I'd made a tactical error. I only hoped that this bathroom wasn't in a secluded area where Aidan could sate the hunger I saw in the tension of his body.

"Oh, and the upstairs one is currently occupied I believe, so the den bathroom should do. I can take the salad for you."

Aidan's grin widened at her words as he handed the bowl over and I began to shake with nerves and excitement. "You got it Beth."

"Oh, I don't mind waiting…" I trailed off as Aidan pulled me away from Beth before I could finish my protest. He casually threw an arm around my waist but I knew it was an act. There was nothing casual about his intentions. My body flushed at my train of thoughts, and at the feeling of Aidan's fingers digging into my hip as he led me farther and farther away from the other people at the party.

He led me down some stairs and when we got to the bottom I waited for him to let me know which way the bathroom was. He surprised me by wrapping the length of my hair around his hand twice, still standing behind me. He didn't say anything, just guided me around a corner and down a short hall. I was tingling from his grip on my hair and the brush of his hardness against me as we walked.

"The one on the right." We stopped and I turned the handle to the door he indicated. He pushed me into the bathroom and locked the door behind us. "It was a lot easier to get you alone than I thought it would be."

He crowded me against the counter and pulled my head back by my hair. I let out a little noise and he thrust his hips against my backside once.

"I didn't mean for you to come with me," I said hoarsely. "I was only trying to…" I broke off with another moan when he bit my neck and then licked away the sting.

"You were trying to what? Take care of your delicious pussy juice so you didn't start dripping down your leg in front of everyone?"

I flushed at his words. He got it exactly right, and his filthy words only served to make me wetter. He rubbed against my backside again, prompting me for an answer.

"Yes," I said. "I was going to make myself come and then clean up."

He snaked an arm around my body, slipping inside the top of my dress to play with a nipple. I gasped and squeezed my eyes shut.

"Open your eyes." I kept them shut, not wanting to give in to the demand. He pinched my nipple hard and repeated the command to open my eyes. I lifted my lids to stare at him in the reflection. "You were going to touch yourself? You weren't going to wait for me?"

He pulled my hair tighter and I had to fight to keep my eyes on him. "Y-yes. I didn't want to wait." Truth be told, I wouldn't have done it. Now that I'd had his hands on me, touching myself was not nearly as satisfying as when he did it. I was just trying to break this frustrating man who was driving me insane.

I had to trust him more than anyone else right now since I still couldn't remember any details of the two of us- and maybe that was why he was pulling back. It was very possible that he was holding back because of the accident, not wanting to push me too much or fast. But I didn't want to be treated with kid gloves; I wanted all he could give me. And if I had to provoke him to get what I wanted from him, then that's what I was going to do.

Aidan had been studying my face while those thoughts ran through my mind. The hard line of his mouth softened and a devilish smile lit his face.

"No Calliope, I don't think you were. You like it too much when I do the touching. You like it when I tease you to the brink. No need to protest, I'll let you hold on to your lie for now. But I'm going to fucking prove it."

His hands moved, the one playing with my breast coming up to wrap lightly around my throat. My breathing quickened and my inner walls clenched, begging for something to hold onto. The hand in my hair slid down and around my front. He bunched up my skirt to expose my bare mound. I felt the rumble in his chest against my back at the sight and we both watched as my stomach muscles tensed in response.

"Hold your skirt up so we can watch me play with you." My shaky hands did as he asked and I leaned back into him as he spread my lips. The cold air hit my throbbing clit and I whimpered.

"Look at that baby. You're glistening, and that pretty little clit of yours is practically vibrating." He swiped his fingers over it and I thrust my hips to get a firmer touch. He swiped again and again, adding more pressure each time. I was so close to the edge already that I was almost begging. He slid his fingers down farther to dip inside me. He played there for a minute, never giving me enough to get off.

I protested when he took his hand away completely, but watched avidly as he brought his fingers up to his mouth to lick them clean. He closed his eyes when his tongue reached out and lapped at his fingertips. The noises he made drove me wild and that's when I cracked.

"Aidan, please please, I need you."

"You need what baby?"

"I need your cock, I need you to fuck me right now!"

"I know you do. But you've been so bad, and I can't let that go. So you'll have to wait for my cock."

I cried out, my eyes going wild at the thought of having to endure this party in my current state. Relief almost knocked me over when he pressed me forward, making me lean on the counter and then got to his knees behind me. I moaned loudly as he spread my cheeks and started eating my pussy like it was his favorite meal.

"Keep it quiet Callie," he commanded before diving back in and I bit my lip to quell everything that wanted to escape my mouth. He rubbed my clit and thrust his tongue inside me, and seconds later I was coming hard, grinding back onto his face with abandon. His groans vibrated into me, dragging my orgasm out and tears gathered in my eyes with the effort to not scream.

I leaned more onto the counter that I had a death grip on and Aidan continued to lick me, cleaning me enough to let us get back to the party. I jerked reflexively whenever his tongue brushed against my sensitive clit, making him chuckle with satisfaction.

I sighed contently, and watched as he stood back up and wiped his mouth. He grabbed a tissue from a box nearby and wiped the moisture from around my eyes, cleaning up my smudged makeup. I moved my hand to his crotch, intent on bringing him the same pleasure he just brought me. He let me feel the outline of his hardness for a few seconds before grabbing my wrist and pulling my hand away.

"I told you that you're going to have to wait for my cock."

My body warmed at his words, but I still tried to convince him to change his mind. I sputtered out half-formed thoughts. "But... You said...I want to..."

"I know what you want, and I want that too, believe me. But every time you look at my cock- which I know you will- you're going to want it even more. You changed my game plan by being naughty. By the time we leave here, you're going to need it so bad that you'll do anything to get it. This may be uncomfortable for me, but babe..." he smiled and shook his head, "It's going to fucking torture you."

Goddamn that man. He brushed a kiss across my lips and I followed him out of the bathroom back up to the party, reluctant but anticipating the battle of wills that was about to ensue.

I wasn't paying attention to anyone that night but Aidan, trying to give as good as I got. We volleyed back and forth, using touches, glances, brushes of our bodies to ratchet it up. I'd brush a hand across my breast, lingering just enough to tease Aidan. He'd lick his lips, letting me know he could still taste me and loved it. We only lasted an hour before Aidan told Beth I wasn't feeling well and had to take me home and get me some medicine. I blushed profusely and Beth quirked an eyebrow, commenting that I did look flushed and she would bring our bowl back to us later.

On the drive back to the apartment I unzipped Aidan's pants and started to go down on him before I felt the car swerve. He made me get off him and carefully put himself back in his pants so he could concentrate on the road. He made me sit on the other side of the car while he told me in the filthiest words everything he wanted to do to me.

We finally parked, then sprinted into our building and stood on opposite sides of the elevator. We both knew that as soon as we touched again we'd be ripping each other's clothes off, so the space was necessary. Aidan stalked out of the elevator into the apartment first and I followed him towards his room. I quietly stripped off my dress and shoes on the way, and when Aidan turned back to me I was completely naked. That was the final straw for him.

He stepped forward and grabbed me, tossing me onto his bed. His clothes were off before I could finish settling, and he was inside me before I could say his name, legs thrown over his shoulders and ass gripped in his hands, bringing me towards each of his thrusts so that he was pounding deep and hard. It didn't take either of us very long to finish loudly, and

Aidan wrapped his arms around me as we cuddled and drifted off to sleep.

CHAPTER TWENTY-SEVEN
CALLIE

I woke up in bed alone. It took me a minute to realize it, but when I stretched and only touched warm sheets I heard Aidan's shower going. My heart ached from waking up alone, but I took a little comfort that the sheets were still warm which had to mean I'd just missed him being there. I sat up and contemplated whether I should join him in the shower, or head off to my own. In the end, I decided that I needed a few moments alone to get ahold of myself.

I grabbed the clothes I'd haphazardly thrown around last night on my way back to my room. By the time I finished my long shower and wrapped myself in a towel, I still hadn't figured out what the hell I was going to do about Aidan and the feelings that were growing between us. I knew I could easily fall for him and was probably halfway there already. An unusual warmth radiated from my chest at that thought and a weird panic started to set in. I had no idea where this was all coming from and suddenly it became too much. I fell down in the middle of my room onto my hands and knees, head hanging down and breath sawing in and out of my mouth. I was trying to make myself breathe normally so I didn't pass out when I head Aidan knock on my door.

"Hey Callie, can I come in?"

I tried to respond, but the breath wouldn't come. I let out a strangled, gasping noise and Aidan must've heard because next thing I knew I felt his hands on my shoulders and saw his knees in front of my face. I heard him asking if I was okay but it sounded like it was coming from the end of a tunnel. The warmth in my chest grew stronger at his touch and although it wasn't painful, something about it made tears well in my eyes. I let out a hiccupping sob, and Aidan pulled me into his lap.

I cried into his t-shirt, gripping it with both hands and releasing everything inside. All the pressure building inside since the hospital was suddenly being released. I was so confused as to what was going on, in general and whatever was happening with Aidan and me, and it was incredibly frustrating that I couldn't remember things no matter how hard I tried. I let it all out with my tears, and Aidan held me through it, rubbing my back and talking quietly to me.

My tears dried, and Aidan stopped talking although he kept rubbing my back. The warmth from before had dissipated, and my head felt much clearer. I wiped my face on his shirt and then looked up at him. His face was worried, a crease in his brown and concern in his eyes. He brushed some hair out of my face and my lips trembled at his kindness.

"What happened?" His words were quiet and I had to look away from him.

"I d-don't know." I cleared my throat of the last of my crying. "I was just thinking about everything and I guess it overwhelmed me."

Aidan pulled me tighter in his arms and kissed the top of my head, making a small smile cross my face.

"I'm sorry. I know I pushed a lot of this on you too quickly." He started to loosen his arms to let me go but I burrowed deeper into his chest. He hesitated but then put his arms back around me.

"Don't apologize Aidan. If I thought I couldn't handle it I wouldn't have come on this trip. Plus, it can't be easy dating someone for two months and then having to start over." He shifted a little and I realized his legs were probably going numb so I began to get up off his lap.

"Where do you think you're going?" He pulled me back down this time, and I gladly went back into his embrace.

"Nowhere," I sighed happily. We sat there for a bit longer until the towel around me started to make me itch.

"Alright, I have to put some clothes on." I glanced at Aidan's shirt, wet with my tears and probably a little snot. "And you should probably change your shirt since I, uh…"

"Wiped your face all over it? Yeah, I wasn't gonna say anything." I giggled at his teasing, relieved that it wasn't super awkward after my mini breakdown.

He followed me after I got up and I moved to shut the door behind him. He turned at my doorway and looked at me. "Are you good?"

I thought for a second. "Yeah I think so. Give me like fifteen minutes and I should be good to go to the build with you, if you want me to go still."

"Of course I do. But, we're not actually going there today. I have something else to show you. So hurry that perky ass up, because the drive is a little long."

"Yeah? Where are we going?"

His eyes twinkled. "It's a surprise, love. Now get dressed or we'll never make it." He shut the door as he left, giving me the perfect opportunity to freak out unobserved.

He'd called me "love". There was no way he meant it like he loved me. No. It was just a casual endearment, right? That's it. I shook my head to get it together. I pushed the thoughts out of my head and instead tried to figure out where we were

195

going to explore today. I only knew of the typical places California was known for but I couldn't figure out which was the more likely. I still had no idea by the time I was ready and Aidan and I headed out.

We drove for about an hour and then stopped for some gas and a quick break. I watched him stretch out of the corner of my eye, his shirt riding up enough to catch a glimpse of muscled abs and the dips on his hips leading to his dick like a treasure map. I was feeling a lot lighter from my cathartic breakdown this morning, but it was starting to drive me crazy trying to figure out where we were headed.

"How close are we?" I leaned against the side of the car, eating some Bugles I'd bought inside the gas station.

"Pretty close actually, we've only got about another half hour of driving."

"Oh that's not bad. Where did you say we're going again?"

He shook his head at me and grinned, those dimples almost distracting me from my question. "I never told you. Now stop trying to get it out of me."

I glared at him but he ignored me. I ate another couple chips. "What if I guessed it? Would you tell me?"

"Maybe. Actually, probably not."

"I'm going to guess anyway."

"Geez Callie, we'll be there in thirty minutes. You can't wait?" He was laughing as he put the gas pump away and closed the tank.

"You should know by now that my curiosity and stubbornness knows no bounds!"

"True. Alright, feel free to guess, but I'm going to say no even if you get it right."

"Yesss! Okay, so are we going to the Golden Gate bridge?" We climbed into the car as he answered.

"Nope."

"Yosemite?"

"No."

For the next twenty minutes of the drive I guessed everything I could think of, including Hollywood, Disneyland, Sea World, and Universal Studios, watching his reaction to see if he would give it away intentionally. And I figured out nada. His poker face was insanely good. I had to give it to him, he could keep a surprise better than I'd expected. Either that or I hadn't been able to think of what it was. I supposed it could be anything and I wouldn't know the difference since I'd never been to California before.

I gave up guessing in order to watch everything passing outside the window. He didn't talk, just let me take it all in. Music played quietly in the background and I sang along in a mindless whisper. California was gorgeous, and where we were now reminded me of downtown Denver a bit. Just a lot more people.

Aidan made a turn and suddenly we were in a parking garage. I'd spaced out a bit so I'd missed anything hinting to where we were. Figured. We were now in a line to pay the parking fee, but I had no indication of where we were going still. That is, until we'd moved ahead a few cars and I saw a sign detailing the parking fees- with a picture of Mickey and Minnie Mouse.

"No FUCKING way!! We're going to Disneyland aren't we! You lied to me! But I don't care- FUCKING DISNEYLAND!"

Aidan was laughing, the biggest shit-eating grin on his face I'd ever seen. I was bouncing in my seat, the seatbelt basically the only thing keeping me in the car. I was going to kiss this man as soon as we parked. Since I'd never left Colorado before, I'd never been to Disneyland. I didn't care that I was twenty-nine years old, today I was fulfilling my nine-year-old self's dreams.

Aidan paid the fee and we went up a couple levels to find a spot. As soon as the ignition turned off, my seatbelt was undone and I launched across the space between us and planted a big wet one on Aidan's mouth. He reacted quickly, taking the kiss deeper for a few moments before pulling away.

"I'm glad you're so excited about this. I was worried that you wouldn't be up to it after this morning."

"Aidan, I could be dead for 190 years and still be ready to go to Disneyland."

Aidan threw his head back and laughed. "That's good to know, I'll remember that in the afterlife."

We got out of the car and I kept running ahead trying to get to the park quicker, but since I didn't know where I was going I had to wait for Aidan. I had a feeling he was teasing me by walking slow on purpose and I smacked him on the ass lightly when he stopped to tie his shoes for the third time.

"Stop stalling! Your woman needs her Disney rollercoaster fix!" He chuckled and grabbed my hand to hold it. We waited in line for the transportation to take us to the gates of the park and I closed my eyes, enjoying the light breeze and leaning against Aidan's body.

When we finally got to the ticket booth I got a "first time here" button and I wore it proudly. We spent all day at Disneyland and California Adventure. Aidan let me pick everything since he'd been there before, only giving me suggestions as to which rides he thought were the best, or which rides we could take advantage of with our fast passes. By the end of the day, my cheeks and feet were killing me from all the smiling and walking, but it was so worth it. It was one of the best days of my life, and definitely the best date I'd ever been on.

On the drive back I talked for the first twenty minutes about everything, thanking Aidan for taking me a million times, to which he would either say "anything for you, babe" or just wave it off with a smile. After getting out everything I wanted to say about the park, I fell quiet and then passed out for about forty-five minutes until a bump in the road jarred me awake.

"Have a good nap?" Aidan's teasing voice filled the car and I snored dramatically, pretending to still be asleep. I yelped when he pinched my thigh; it didn't hurt but it surprised me.

"You're such a jerk Aidan." I held back the giggle that wanted to come out at the offended look on his face.

"And you're such a pretender. Did you pretend to be asleep the whole forty-five minutes to avoid talking to me? That's probably it, you got everything you wanted out of me and now you're done trying to pretend you like me."

"Yep, you're right. I got sex, the ocean, and Disneyland out of you. Which reminds me, I booked a ticket back to Colorado for tomorrow morning, so, it's been real!"

"Okay, but I've got to be at the build site tomorrow so I can't take you to the airport. Plus, I know you'll come back when you need this dick again." He made a chopping motion towards his crotch and I had to bite my lip to avoid laughing.

"Need it?" I scoffed and gave him my best in-your-dreams look.

"Yeah baby, I know you need this. You're practically salivating for it right now, even. You can't forget how good it feels deep in your pussy, especially when I pull your hair or smack that delicious ass of yours."

I hated that he was right. We'd started this out light and playful, but suddenly it'd turned into something heated and erotic. If he pulled over right now, I'd be on him so fast he'd get whiplash. But I had a verbal battle to win so I put that desire to the side as much as I could in order to concentrate.

"Hmm. Seems like you're the one who needs my pussy." I leaned a tad closer and drew out my next words in a sultry voice. "Hot... wet... tight around you..." His knuckles tightened on the steering wheel and he cut a quick glance at me. I knew my eyelids were low like they get when I'm close to coming and his nostrils flared before looking back to the road.

"Seems we're at an impasse. Maybe we can test the theory of who needs who more when we get home," he said in a gravelly voice. I tried to sound nonchalant when I responded, but I couldn't stop the breathiness of my words.

"I look forward to it."

Hours later, we collapsed onto his bed together. We were sweaty, out of breath, and I was still vibrating from the last of five orgasms he'd just given me. FIVE. I didn't even know I was capable of that in one sitting!

We were still trying to catch our breaths when his voice rumbled across the skin on my shoulder. "I think that... we're probably even."

A short laugh escaped me, then another, and more until we were both laughing so hard we were wiping tears from our eyes. Aidan eventually pulled a blanket across us, and we passed out seconds later, exhausted and completely replete.

CHAPTER TWENTY-EIGHT
AIDAN

The next morning we were back at the build site; I was currently out with the foreman checking on everything and Callie was in the main trailer doing some work of her own. She'd brought her laptop and connected to the hotspot on her phone so she could check on some profiles Char had sent over for her. Part of me wanted to keep her with me, but the other part of me knew I needed the distance so I could focus on the build instead of her.

Also, with her inside, I didn't have to worry about the guys staring at her or flirting. Not because that bothered me, but I wanted them focusing on the job, not the woman. That's what I was telling myself anyway.

We hadn't had any setbacks yet; the foundation was complete and they were working on the skeleton of the building. It was going to be big and take a bit of time, but I could see it coming together already. I'd worked on a construction crew for a few years while going to college so I was able to jump in and assist every now and then. It was hard work and I loved it. This was all second nature to me and it helped to have something to think about other than the thoughts of Callie overrunning my mind recently.

It was five o'clock before I knew it, the alarm on my phone going off in my back pocket. I said my farewells to the workers and headed back to the trailer where Callie was. I was wiping some sweat off my face when I stepped in, startling Callie when the door banged shut.

"Sorry," I apologized sheepishly. I forgot the door was heavier than it looked; I forgot almost everything else other than the dark-haired beauty reclining in the swivel chair and reading something on her computer. She'd been chuckling when I got in and the sound filled my chest- and some other parts too.

"It's fine," she mumbled, only meeting my eyes briefly and turning back to her computer to shut it down. "I didn't realize how late it was or I would've been ready to go when you got here."

I watched her gather her stuff together and something felt off. She seemed nervous for some reason. Ignoring the foreboding in my gut, I moved to grab her computer bag for her like I had earlier today.

"No, it's okay Aidan I can carry it." She spoke hurriedly and moved around me to the door. "Do you need to do anything else before we leave?"

"No," I said hesitantly. What the fuck was going on with her? When I'd left her earlier she'd been smiling and teasing me, and now it seemed like she didn't want to get too close. "Is something wrong?"

Her cheeks flushed and she met my gaze for a moment before looking back down at her feet. Warning bells rang in my head; she was never this reserved. Ever. Even at the hospital where we technically first met.

"I'm just a little tired from staring at the computer all day." She still wasn't meeting my eyes and that one small thing made me think she was lying.

She rubbed her head with a wince and concern flooded me. "Do you have a headache? Are you feeling alright?"

She quickly shook her head. "It's fine Aidan, but I'd like to go home."

I walked her way and she went out the door before I could reach her, and she kept moving toward the car. I quickened my pace until I was walking beside her. I looked over at her but she kept staring at the ground. I shook my head, mystified. The ride back home was quiet and after I only got one or two-word answers to my questions I stopped asking. Something was obviously wrong, but she wasn't telling me what it was.

The rest of the night went the same; she was unfailingly polite, but kept a distance between us and could barely look me in the eyes. We ate dinner together, had the "tell me what you did today" conversation where she gave me no real information even though she seemed genuinely happy for my project going well. It was driving me crazy! I didn't want this nice, simpering Callie. I wanted my spitfire Callie, the one who argued and teased and tortured me.

The irony of my being annoyed that she was pulling back wasn't lost on me. I'd been hot and cold and I knew it wasn't fair of me to transfer my frustrations and confusion with this whole thing onto her. Maybe she was just trying to give me a taste of my own medicine. I could understand that even if I fucking hated it. I let her go off to bed, alone, with barely a kiss to say goodnight. I sat on the couch for a while after her bedroom door closed, trying to figure out what I'd done to make her pull so far away from me. I knew she hadn't found out the truth; she would've been yelling and cussing me out, not acting like we were acquaintances.

I laid in bed for hours, trying to sleep but too stressed about Callie to do so. My final thought before drifting off was that I was going to figure out what was wrong tomorrow. I'd get it out of her sometime between going to the build site and going to bed.

CHAPTER TWENTY-NINE
AIDAN

Two. Fucking. Days. Callie and I had been stuck in this vortex of withdrawn civility since Friday night and I was ready to tear something apart. It was Sunday now, and I was on my way to pick up Lucy from the airport. Alone. I'd wanted Callie to come with to meet Lucy right away but she'd asked for some time to do work so she wouldn't have to worry about it the rest of the day.

I'd barely resisted pointing out that she'd been doing plenty of work the last couple days, and that she hadn't bothered with it at all when we first got here and started ripping each other's clothes off. I didn't want to push her any farther away though so I let it go. But I didn't have to like it.

I was in a terrible mood, and I didn't envy Lucy having to deal with my shit right now. I was mixed parts relieved for her to be here and terrified. I knew she was almost as stubborn as Callie, and when she noticed I was in a pissy mood she wasn't going to stop bugging me about why. I'd have to find a way to tell her why without telling her everything. She'd never believe that I was in this mess because of a bunch of mythological circumstances.

I snorted to myself, imaging the disbelief in her face if I told her the real story when I saw her waiting with a small suitcase, typing away on her phone. I pulled up in front of her and she looked up, smiling at me. She put her case in the back and then climbed in, giving me a quick hug.

I smiled despite being irritated as hell. She launched into questions about the project as I maneuvered us out of the airport lot and I happily answered them. I was hoping that we'd be able to talk about that the whole drive.

No such luck.

After a measly twenty minutes of work-related questions, she caught me off guard by suddenly switching topics.

"How're you and Callie?" I stiffened and didn't answer right away, and Lucy caught that. She sighed. "What'd you do?"

My jaw dropped and I looked over at her. "What makes you think it's my fault?!"

"Isn't it always the guy's fault?"

"What? How is that even-"

"Damn Aidan, calm your tits. I was teasing you." She looked at me, slightly bewildered at my overreaction. "But seriously, I can tell you're distracted and Callie's not with you so tell me what's going on."

I took a moment to gather my thoughts. I groaned and rubbed my jaw with a hand for long seconds. I decided to give her the bare minimum, and hopefully she wouldn't ask too many questions I couldn't answer right now. "I don't fucking know Lucy. We were all fine and dandy until Friday. I was out on the site and Callie wanted to do some work so she stayed in the main trailer. When I came back at our agreed time, she'd pulled away completely. She's extremely nice to me- too nice- but that's it. We've barely kissed the last two days when before that we couldn't keep our hands off each other."

"So, obviously, something happened while she was in the trailer. Unless she was being weird that morning too?"

"No! That's the thing that's driving me crazy! Everything was normal until I stepped into the trailer. And no matter how many times I ask her if everything is okay, or what's wrong, she gives me some flimsy excuse and I have to let it fly because I'm afraid she'll retreat even more."

Lucy stayed quiet. I knew she was going over all the information she had and processing it so I gave her some time. I drummed my fingers on the steering wheel, trying to be patient but needing some answers.

"Well, I don't know Callie so I can't tell you exactly why she'd do that. I'm sure she'll tell you what's wrong when she's ready. I'd suggest being patient, but persistent. Maybe if you make her snap by continuing to ask her about it then you'll get it out of her although that's not a tactic I'd suggest. I can tell you love her though."

I'd been nodding my head along with her words but choked at that last part. I denied that possibility vehemently and Lucy just looked at me with a smirk on her face.

"How could you not see it Aidan? You may look tough but you're a big softie. And the way you talk about Callie, it's plain as day to me that you're in love with her. Why else would you be ripping your hair out because of this?"

"I can't have fallen in love with her, it's only been…" I cut myself off, almost giving away the ruse. I was supposed to have been dating her already for two months before the accident, not just have met her barely over a week ago.

"You don't get to decide when the right time to fall in love is Aidan. Your heart does." She fell silent and I saw her bobbing her leg quickly, something she did when she wanted to say something but didn't know how to say it.

"Alright, I know you have something to say. Just spit it out."

She half-smiled at my wry tone. "Well... your denial about loving Callie... It doesn't have to do with me, does it?"

She was looking out the window as she spoke, so she didn't see the color leave my face.

"Uh, what do you mean?"

She glanced at me briefly. "God I hate this, it's why I've been avoiding this conversation for a while. Alright Aidan. I don't want to ruin anything between us, so I hope we get over the awkwardness of this conversation quickly. I love having you as a friend too much, and as a business partner."

"You're killing me Lucy. Stop prefacing this, and just tell me so we can move on." My hands were sweating, my heart was beating hard, and I was afraid I already knew what she was about to say.

"Fine, fine. I know that you've had a crush on me for a long time. I let it go since you never tried to do anything about it until recently, and you've been so subtle about it I was hoping that I was imagining it, or that I could act like I didn't notice."

I was speechless. I swallowed hard a few times before the words just flew out of my mouth. "It's not just a crush, Lucy. I love you." The words were a tortured whisper. Something in my chest twisted as Callie's laughing face swarmed my mind, and I thought that maybe for the first time, I was wrong about my feelings and my head hadn't caught up with my heart.

Lucy let out a short laugh. "You don't love me Aidan. Well, maybe you do, but you're not *in* love with me. You've never been this tortured over my rejection of you, and you're the kind of person that usually fights for what they want. You never fought for me. I'm sure that if Callie hadn't shown up, you and I would still be avoiding this topic."

I opened my mouth to argue, but shut it again when I really thought about what she was saying. She was right.

Goddammit, she was fucking RIGHT. The revelation blew me away. I'd fallen quick and hard for Callie like I'd never seen Lucy as anything more than a sister. All the torture that I'd put myself through because I thought I was in love with Lucy and betraying her in some way had been pointless. I was still conflicted because of the way Aphrodite had set me up with this lie, but I knew now that I was going to do everything I could to keep Callie when this whole thing went to shit.

Which, I knew, was something I wouldn't be able to avoid when this came to a head.

A relieved laugh flew out of my mouth. "Damn Lucy. What would I do without you?" I could feel the tension drain away from our relationship, and a barrier I hadn't even realized had grown between us fell away as we laughed at our ridiculousness.

"Honestly, you'd be a giant, lost little puppy." I chuckled at her words and we fell quiet again, but this time into a peaceful silence smattered with easy conversation.

We eventually turned into the lot of the apartment complex, and I drove over to the main building so Lucy could go in and get her key from Beth. She'd been here a few times with me and already knew Beth so I knew they'd be fine from here.

I put the car into park and let it idle so Lucy could grab her suitcase. She paused before getting out and we looked at each other.

"So we're good then?" She asked the question hesitantly.

"Yeah, we're good. Come on over to my place when you're ready and I'll introduce you to Callie. Text me when you head over."

"Sounds good." She leaned over and placed a soft kiss on my cheek. I smiled ruefully at her and watched until she made it into the main office. I drove over to my parking spot and sat there for several minutes, gathering my thoughts.

I blew out a big breath and my head fell back against my seat. I loved Callie. My heart skipped a beat or two as I mulled that over. Warmth spread out through me as I repeated it in my head. *I love her. I'm in love. With Calliope Drakos.* Disbelief and giddiness ran through me in equal measures.

How the hell am I supposed to get through this? I groaned at the thought of what Callie would do when she found out that this all started on a lie. I felt like I had good reason to go through with it, but small parts of me were starting to think that it wasn't the right decision.

Now I had two choices, and either way I was shit out of luck. One, I could tell Aphrodite that I was done and live with the fact that I would probably never find my family. Or two, I could follow through and make Callie fall in love and admit it to both of us. If I had managed to fall in this short time then I was hoping she could too. And, there was a possibility that she'd forgive me for tricking her if I got the chance to explain myself.

I made my decision. Gearing myself up to see Callie again, knowing I was in love with her while she was in the process of distancing us, I got out of the car and headed up to my apartment.

CHAPTER THIRTY
CALLIE

I checked the clock for about the thousandth time in the last twenty minutes. I knew Aidan was bound to be back any minute, and Lucy would probably be with him. She'd come in on a late flight and there was quite a bit of traveling involved, but Aidan had said they'd be back around 6 or 6:30. It was now 6:27. Half an hour ago I'd started pacing the room, ready to see Aidan again. With each minute that passed I got more nervous, and less prepared to see him.

I'd been super distant with him the last couple days, ever since I talked to Ellinor on the phone in the trailer while Aidan had been out working with the guys on the build. The call had taken me by surprise at first, but I hadn't exactly been in touch with anyone in Colorado since landing here. I answered the phone, but now I wished that I hadn't. For the millionth time over the last couple days, I replayed that conversation in my head.

"Hey Ells, what's up?"

"Well, first of all, does Aidan have some kind of magic dick that's keeping you from texting your family back?"

I burst into laughter, partly to cover up my embarrassment. Ellinor was never one to mince her words, and I treasured and hated it in equal parts. I decided not to encourage her so I ignored the question.

"And what's your second point?"

She huffed, acknowledging that she was aware I was avoiding the question. "Why didn't you tell me about him?" She tried to play it off as a casual question but I could hear the hurt in her voice and that sobered me up.

"I don't know Ells." She brought up the very thing that had been floating around in the back of my apparently addled mind. "I can't really think of a reason that I wouldn't tell you or the rest of the family about him. He's a great guy."

"He's very different from the other guys you've dated."

I snorted indelicately, relaxing back into the reclining swivel chair. "No kidding. I usually end up with the handsome, straight-laced suits."

"Yeah and Aidan looks like the devilishly sexy, tattooed bad boy personified. Complete with skater shoes."

I glared at her through the phone and the possessiveness came through when I spoke next. "You noticed, did you?"

She laughed. "Oh calm down, I can feel your evil eye from here. Even if he weren't yours, you know I prefer chocolate over vanilla."

Her words took the wind out of my sails. I did know that. "Yeah, sorry. You're right though. He can be a bit intense, but he's a sweetheart."

"I noticed both the sweetness and the intensity at the hospital. He barely ever left your side Callie. The fact that he seemed so focused on your well-being was the only reason I didn't give him the third degree about how he knew you."

"What do you mean by that?"

"C'mon Callie. I don't care how different he is from every other guy you've been with, or if you thought that your ever-supportive family would judge you for dating that wild-haired man, you would've told either me or Char about him."

Uneasiness prickled through me as she voiced the very thing I'd been avoiding. Even though I never really believed that I would find *the kind of love my parents had, it didn't mean I stopped looking and hoping for it. That romanticism despite my cynicism is one of the reasons that I went through with starting Eros. If I couldn't find that love for myself then I'd help others. Char's and my family's approval was a big thing to me- if I felt that I couldn't introduce Aidan to them, then why would I have been dating him for two months?*

A thought occurred to me and I clung to it. "Maybe I wanted everyone's approval more now than with any other guy, and I was avoiding the confrontation just in case it didn't all work out."

She thought about that for a minute. "I suppose. Something just feels weird about all this. I love you sis. I just don't want you to end up hurt."

I smiled. "I know Ellinor. I love you too. I'll be careful."

That was the end of the conversation, but the doubt started to niggle at me. The more I tried to figure it out, the more my head pounded. If only I could remember. I let out a growl of frustration when a sharp pain lanced through my head at my efforts and I decided to let it go for now. My Skype notification went off, distracting me from the pain. I had a message from Ellinor.

You never answered my first question.

And I never will. I was chuckling at her boldness when the trailer door shut loudly, startling me and I turned to face Aidan. He'd been wiping off his face with a small towel and I quickly took in his flexing muscles and thin sheen of sweat from exertion. He was slightly dirty too, and my panties flooded with arousal at the raw male in front of me. Then all of the doubts I'd recognized talking to Ellinor filled me and suddenly I wasn't sure of anything. I couldn't meet Aidan's eyes for fear that not only he would see what I was thinking, but fear of falling even deeper into this whole thing. Aidan asked me all night if I was okay, and I almost cried at how sweet he was being while I was being cold to him.

Yesterday hadn't been any better. We'd gone back to the build site and I'd pretended to work in the trailer while he was out on site. The whole time I agonized over the situation, trying to remember something, anything, that would make me feel better about the whole thing. All I had to answer for it was another killer headache and a night alone.

I could see the confusion in Aidan's eyes when he threw glances at me but I couldn't comfort him when I was such a mess myself. I was still confused, but I was determined to talk to Aidan about it this time. For once I couldn't stand sleeping alone, and my body ached to feel him hold me. I needed Aidan back right now, and I was just hoping that my reticence hadn't driven him away yet.

I heard the elevator doors open and I stopped mid-pace. I wanted to run to him, but I couldn't make myself move. I didn't want to make any weird first impressions with Lucy who I was sure was going to come in with Aidan. I knew she was important in his life and if I wanted to be a part of that too then I needed to stay calm.

"Callie? You in here?" I made myself walk slowly down the hallway towards his voice and when I rounded the corner he was standing there alone.

"I'm here... Is Lucy... Are you alone?"

"She's getting settled in her apartment and then she's going to come over. I wanted t-oof!"

As soon as I'd realized it was just the two of us at the moment, I'd hurried across the space between us and jumped into his arms. He reacted quickly, catching me and wrapping an arm around my back and another under my butt to steady me.

To my chagrin, I burst into tears. I cried around this man way too much, but I couldn't seem to stop it. He hushed me, rubbing my back and walking over to the couch to sit while he comforted me. It didn't take long; soon I was breathing through my last little hiccups and I lifted my face from his neck to look at him.

"What's wrong Callie?" His soft and bewildered words caused some fresh tears to gather in my eyes and I sniffled through them, trying to catch my breath to answer. He waited for me patiently, brushing away a few stray tears.

"The last two days have been miserable without you Aidan. You've been nothing but kind to me, even when I can feel you pull away every now and then, and you don't deserve the treatment I've been giving you. I missed you so much." I started to lean forward to bury my face into his neck, but he cupped my face in his hands, making me meet his eyes.

"Callie, you have nothing to apologize for. I know none of this shit is easy for you and..." He trailed off, running a hand through his hair. I loved it when he did that. "I'm not mad at you. Not at all. I definitely want to talk about what's been on your mind, but we can do that later tonight if that's alright. I don't any interruptions when we talk."

I nodded gratefully and leaned forward to press a small kiss to his lips. Heat rushed through me at the contact and a gasp tumbled from my lips still touching his. He felt it against his skin and groaned, opening his mouth to kiss me more deeply. I let him, wanting it just as much as he did. We hadn't done much of anything physically in forty-eight hours, and it had taken its toll on both of us. When he nipped my bottom lip my body reacted to the zing and my hips ground against the erection he was already sporting. We both moaned at the feeling and his hands clamped onto my hips.

"How much time do you think we have before Lucy comes over?" I asked breathlessly, Aidan shifting me back and forth on him.

He smothered me in another kiss, sending the tingles into a flurry of fireworks. We were rocking into each other when we heard the ding from the intercom, signaling that someone wanted to come up. We pulled away reluctantly.

"Apparently none," he said ruefully. I climbed off his lap and watched as he made his way over to the elevator, hitting a small button for the intercom.

"Who goes there?"

"Stop being an idiot Aidan, let me up," a light, amused voice called through the speakers. I giggled. I liked this woman already. Aidan grinned back at me when he heard my giggle. He pushed another button on the pad, approving the request for access to the penthouse.

I padded over to Aidan and squeezed his hand in mine as I waited to meet Lucy. I was a little nervous. What would Aidan do if she didn't like me?

"Don't worry Callie, she'll love you." I looked up at him, eyes wide and mouth slightly gaped. *Did I say that out loud?* "I can feel how tense you are babe. Relax."

Relieved that he was just reassuring me and not reading my mind, I squeezed his hand again as the doors opened and a gorgeous blonde stepped out. I'm not insecure about my curves in the least, and I believed that every body type had its own beauty, so Lucy's slim figure didn't threaten me. I could acknowledge that she was indeed a beauty though, and a small part of me wondered why her and Aidan had never gotten together.

Unless they did at some point, the voice in my head taunted.

Yeah well even if they did, they obviously didn't work out. He's mine, I growled back.

"Hello!! You must be Callie, I'm so excited to meet you!" Lucy made a beeline to me and enveloped me in a hug, surprising a laugh out of me. I really, really liked this girl. I'd be asking Aidan about their history later, but right now I wasn't too worried about it. She barely even threw Aidan a hello before hooking her arm through mine and leading me to the front room and asking me all sorts of questions, barely giving me a chance to answer.

"It's a good thing I showed up or you'd be bored to tears alone here with Aidan. I'm surprised you've made it a week with all your hair. Have you ever been to California before? Have you seen the sea lions yet? What about-"

"Jesus Lucy, let her take a breath!" Aidan's exclamation stopped Lucy just long enough for her to give him a glare. However, she did turn back to me without asking any more questions. I was sort of relieved Aidan had stopped her since I was starting to lose track of the one-sided conversation.

"It's nice to meet you too Lucy," I said with a warm smile and settling back into the couch cushions. "No, I haven't been to California before, but I love it here. It's gorgeous, and yes the sea lions were adorable. I've only lost a few hairs here with Aidan, but I can promise you it wasn't because of boredom."

I threw a sizzling look over to Aidan who seemed surprised at my innuendo. He even blushed a little, and I grinned back at Lucy who was cackling at Aidan's embarrassment.

"Oh my God, I'm going to keep you," she said when she caught her breath. My smile widened even more, and a feeling of happiness settled inside me. I didn't make friends easily but

I could practically see Lucy vaulting over the walls I typically kept up.

We decided to order some pizza since Lucy was too tired from all the travel to go out. Lucy and I did most of the talking with a few interjections from Aidan, but he seemed content to let us lead the conversation. Lucy and I actually had a lot in common, and despite Aidan's protests she filled me in on some childhood memories of theirs that had me in tears from laughing.

It was after one in the morning when she decided to head back to her apartment. She gave me a hug before she left and whispered, "He's a good guy. I'm glad he found you." Tears pricked my eyes at the heartfelt words and I softly nodded in thanks against her shoulder before she pulled back.

She then gave Aidan a hug, whispering something to him as well. I was curious about what she said, especially when he rolled his eyes and smiled sheepishly. She waved to us as the elevator doors closed and then Aidan came and wrapped me up in a huge hug. I melted into him, breathing in his scent and wishing we could put off the talk we needed to have.

CHAPTER THIRTY-ONE
CALLIE

"So," Aidan said sitting us down on the couch, "how's it going?"

I snickered despite my nervousness. "Way to make it weird."

"What? Me? Noooo," he said grinning mischievously.

"Whatever you say."

"But seriously Callie, what's been going on in that beautiful head of yours?" He pulled me closer as he asked the question and I blushed a little at the unexpected compliment.

"Well," I said then paused to gather my words. "I know I've been acting super weird since Friday. While you were working out on the build with the guys, I talked to my sister on the phone."

"Okay. Why is that a bad thing?" A frown crossed his face.

I shifted nervously. "Ellinor just mentioned that it was weird that I didn't tell her or Char or any of my family about dating you. Since I'm so close to them."

He paused. "I can see why that would be concerning. I wish you had just talked to me about it then though, I could've cleared up the reason why."

I finally looked up at him, surprise on my face. "Really?"

"Yeah babe, we talked about it after dating for a couple weeks."

"What? What'd we talk about exactly?"

"I wanted to meet your family because you talked about them all the time. You said it was too soon, and that you wanted to get to know me better before I met them. You also said that I was different than other guys you've dated and your family might be thrown off so you wanted to have some time to prepare them. I relented, because I figured that it was a good thing you wanted your family to like me."

"Oh." That's all I could come up with. It kind of made sense, and that's pretty much what Ell and I were saying anyway. *Good going Callie,* I thought to myself. *You just wasted days pouting about nothing.*

"You never did tell me exactly why I was so different than the other guys." Aidan's words interrupted my thoughts.

"What makes you think I'm going to tell you now?"

"Because you owe me for all the time I missed being inside you the last two days." His voice was deep and tantalizing.

"When you put it that way… Fine, I'll tell you." I moved so that I was straddling his lap, my hands curling into his hair as I hovered above him, leaving space between my butt and his lap. His hands landed lightly on my hips, willing to give me the upper hand for the moment.

"Tell me then Callie. What makes me so different?"

"First of all, I haven't dated very many people seriously. I can count them on one hand."

"Good news for me."

"Hush now, or you won't get the info you want." He pantomimed zipping his mouth shut before putting his hand back on my hip. "Better. Now, secondly, the guys that I usually end up dating are clean cut, suit wearing guys."

"So you're saying you've only dated boring, missionary-style-sex kind of guys?"

"I suppose you could phrase it like that." I tugged on his hair slightly and he let his head fall back, eyes darkening in desire. I slowly lowered my hips until we were flush. "I wasn't sure if my family was ready for a tattooed, long-haired man who looked like he could toss me around a room."

I rotated my hips slightly, grinding my body onto his already hard cock. His hands tightened on my hips but didn't slow me or push me to go faster.

"I think maybe it was *you* who wasn't ready for someone like me Callie. You dated those other guys because you could have control." At those words, he flipped us quickly so that I was laying length-wise on the couch, crowded in by his hard, muscular body. He pushed his hips hard into mine and I whimpered in pleasure. "But with me, I'm in charge. You have a certain degree of leeway of course, but I don't let you push me around. If you wanted a pussy, you'd be a lesbian."

I rolled my eyes, but he was right. I hated that he could see through me that well, but he had it spot on. With all my other relationships, I'd been in control of every situation, all the emotions, and I'm the one that cut them off. With Aidan, I not only had no idea what was going on, but he made me feel like I was being carried away in an ocean current- deceivingly pleasant and most certainly dangerous.

"Tell me Callie. Tell me you like it when I take control."

My body wanted me to spit the words out, but my brain said not to give in so easily. Instead of the *oh God, yes* that was fighting its way to my lips, "No," was the word that made it out of my mouth.

Aidan stilled against me and I opened my eyes to see him smiling down at me like the cat that ate the canary. I swallowed hard, not expecting that reaction to my denial.

"Oh, baby, I love it when you fight back. It'll make the sound of you begging me so much sweeter when you finally give in."

My breath quickened again, my panties getting wetter at his confident words. I scrambled for something to say but could only moan when he moved again between my thighs.

He grabbed my hands and held my wrists together above my head against the arm of the couch and leaned down to kiss me. Our tongues battled for a short few seconds and when he pulled away I whimpered. I loved the way he kissed me like he was starving for a taste. He moved his lips across my cheek and then down to my neck. I automatically tilted my head to the side to give him more access and he let out a satisfied noise.

He kissed and nibbled softly down my neck until he hit my magic spot where he bit down a little harder and sucked on my skin. I let out several high-pitched moans that rose in volume whenever he applied more pressure. I knew it was going to leave a giant hickey but I liked that he wanted to mark me.

He finally lifted his mouth from my neck, just to raggedly say into my ear, "Fucking love when you make those sounds."

He'd been softly grinding against me but he was now moving both my wrists into one of his hands and sliding the other down the lift my ass up so he could press into me harder. He started hitting my clit perfectly even through our clothes and my legs started to shake with the impending orgasm.

"You're so beautiful when you're on the edge like this Callie. I can tell you're close to coming and I've barely even touched you yet. I want you to come for me like this, come for me Callie. Now."

I couldn't stop my body from obeying. My back arched with a final thrust of Aidan against my clit, and waves of pleasure went through me. Aidan let go of my hands to gather me up in his arms. I loosely wrapped myself around him, still throbbing from the orgasm as he carried me into his room and to his bed. The look in his eyes told me that that was only the beginning. I grinned at him in anticipation as he stripped us of our clothes and made up for the last two days- and then some.

CHAPTER THIRTY-TWO
APHRODITE

I watched Aidan and Callie sleeping as the sun began to dawn on a new day for them. It was obvious that they'd had a busy night since they were both naked with the sheets tangled around them. I was glad I was only checking in now- I had no desire to watch them "do the nasty", as some of the other Olympians were calling it. That was private, and even though the irony of valuing privacy while I was inserting myself into their lives was not lost on me, I knew that watching them in that most private moment was a kind of intrusion I couldn't tolerate.

Things seemed to be progressing nicely, but I supposed I could give Aidan another reminder. I smirked to myself and used the enchanted pen and paper I'd gotten from Hephaestus to send off an email to Aidan like I had the week before. This pen and paper really were amazing. As long as I wrote the name of the person I wanted the message to go to, the form of the message, and signed a heart as my signature at the end of the message, it somehow got where I wanted it to go.

"Aidan, glad to see you two getting along so well," I wrote. *"Don't forget about the time limit! You have until next week to make her say those magic three words. Trust me when I say you do not want to fail."* I signed the letter appropriately, and the words began to vanish. Just as the little heart disappeared, I saw Aidan's cell phone light up on the stand next to his head.

It must have made a noise as well because seconds later his eyes squinted open as he reached for his phone.

I watched him open the email with a raised brow, and a purely masculine frown lined his face as he read the short message. He closed his phone and set it back on the side table before spearing his hand into his hair. His lips were moving, muttering some kind of obscenity, I was sure. I mentally commanded the vision cloud to produce sound. I snickered as Aidan's words filled my room.

"...I mean, who does she think she is? Stupid vows and shit."

Callie began to shift next to him and his eyes widened in sudden panic. Part of me wondered if she'd heard his words too, and my heart thundered in my chest for a few beats before a small snore filtered out of her mouth. Aidan calmed, smiled softly, and wrapped his arms around her. He pressed a long kiss against her hair, shutting his eyes in what seemed like pain.

"Callie," he whispered so quietly even I almost didn't hear him, "I love you. I hope you forgive me when this is all over."

My heart suddenly ached, and my throat started feeling tight. What can I say, I'm a sucker for love. I could only hope that Callie would fall just as easily as he had- for all our sakes.

CHAPTER THIRTY-THREE
CALLIE

"Tell 'em boy bye! Boy bye! Middle fingers up; I ain't thinking 'bout you!" Lucy and I grinned each other and belted out Beyoncé as I drove us around, trying to find the restaurant she'd found on Google for brunch. That morning Lucy had declared it a "girl's day" and we'd just dropped Aidan off at the worksite. He'd looked a little afraid at the thought of Lucy and me spending the day together. The two of us girls just smirked at each other before assuring him nothing bad was going to happen. He'd grumbled but said that it wasn't like he could stop us.

When Lucy had announced that we were going to hang out today, I'd been a little nervous but her warmth and openness squashed the nerves in no time. I couldn't remember ever getting along with someone right away like this- with the exception of Char. The fact that she loved Beyoncé just as much as I did didn't hurt.

We ended up getting a little lost because we weren't paying attention to the roads but we managed to get inside, seated, and drinking mimosas before too long. She asked me lots of questions about my life and I reciprocated, loving getting to know her. I could see why Aidan liked to have her around.

"Have you been to one of the mimosa bars in downtown Denver?"

I perked up at her question. "I have! I've been once with my sister and mom, and it was awesome!"

"Really? I've never been, but I always wanted to try it out."

"The one I went to was called Zengo. It's like thirty-five dollars because the mimosas are bottomless, and there's also food available."

"That's not a bad price at all!"

"Right! We should go sometime, if you want to." I hesitated at the end of my sentence, unsure if that would interest her.

She grinned brightly at me and jumped a little in her seat. "I would *love* that!"

Our food arrived and we ate for a bit in silence. It didn't feel awkward at all, and I was glad that neither of us felt like we had to constantly fill the space with words.

"So, what do you think of Aidan?" Lucy asked casually after a minute or two.

I could feel my face flushing and I shoved another bite of biscuit and gravy to stall answering. She laughed softly but patiently waited for my answer. I swallowed hard and washed the food down with a big gulp of my mimosa.

"I really like him. A lot. More than I thought I would, actually." I paused. "I wish I could remember the months before this though. I hate not knowing any of that and basically having to start over while Aidan's had all that time. I feel like he's got more invested into this relationship than I do right now."

"I can see that. It would be unsettling to feel like someone has known you for months, intimately, without you having the same opportunity."

"Exactly! I'm not the kind of person that trusts easily so taking this trip after knowing Aidan for less than forty-eight hours is terrifying. I don't regret it though. It's been amazing."

She considered me for a few moments before speaking. "I can only imagine how rough this has to be for you. I don't think I could do what you did. You've got some of the biggest balls I've ever seen," she paused to grin suggestively at me, "and I've seen my fair share."

We cracked up and I warmed at her compliment. When we calmed down she continued. "But seriously, I just want you to know that I've known Aidan almost my whole life. He's one of the most giving, kind, and committed people I know. I would trust him with my life, and I hope that eventually you can trust him with your heart. He deserves someone great like you."

My chest throbbed at her words, for both her approval of Aidan and me together and at the thought of giving my heart to Aidan. I would never admit it out loud, but I was already falling for him. The thought of loving anyone as intensely as I was starting to think I could with Aidan made me want to run all the way back to Denver. But the stubborn side of me would never give up that easily. I was in a bit of a conundrum. I took a deep breath and let it out slowly, reminding myself to take this one step at a time.

"Thank you, Lucy. I really appreciate that." I reached over and squeezed her hand to let her know I meant it. She smiled and squeezed back, and we both turned to our food again. My mind wandered to Aidan and how hard this whole thing had to be for him too. He'd been extremely understanding, but I could only imagine how frustrating it had to be to basically start over when he had three months of me that I didn't have of him.

I shook my head and decided to get my mind of the mess that was my life. "So Lucy, any man in your life?"

She smiled, but it seemed wistful almost. "No one specific. I'm a love 'em and leave 'em kind of girl. I don't see a committed relationship in the future for me."

"Oh? Any particular reason?" She didn't look at me as she started to push around the last of the food on her plate. I realized that was probably a really personal question and I started to backtrack. "It's okay if you don't want to answer that, you don't have to."

"Oh no, it's alright. I don't mind telling you. I just... my parents were not the best. They didn't physically abuse my brother and me, but they weren't very loving either. It was a cold, distant, and neglectful home. Nick and I fended for ourselves and each other a lot."

I squeezed her hand again, my heart breaking for her and her brother. "I'm so sorry your parents weren't what you deserved. You seem to have turned out pretty good despite that."

She looked at me, and the tension in her face dissipated when she realized I wasn't viewing her with pity, just empathy. I grew up in a home the exact opposite of hers and I had no idea what she was feeling but I could feel for her and Nick.

She let out a short reluctant, sardonic laugh. "Yeah I did okay. Nick turned out better than I did, probably because he always had Aidan. I did too, but it was different since I was the kid sister. I didn't want to intrude on their little boy's club, so I ended up by myself a lot, even when we'd go over to Aidan's- which we did a lot." Her eyes focused on me now instead of the past. "His parents would have loved you, by the way."

My throat tightened suddenly at those words, but I ignored it when she continued like she hadn't just said something extremely meaningful. "I know whatever issues I have stem from my parents' neglect, but knowing that doesn't stop me from avoiding the heartache of not being enough for someone.

So I date, but I rarely commit." She shrugged like it was no big deal.

"I can understand that. I hope I'm not overstepping my boundaries, but I hope you find someone that makes you want to commit. I used to think that kind of thing wasn't in the cards for me either, and then I woke up in a hospital with no memory of dating the most gorgeous man I've ever seen and agreeing to go with him to California for two weeks. Which is not like me at all. Maybe one day you'll knock yourself out on a parking meter and wake up dating a beautiful stranger too."

We both started to giggle- I wasn't sure if it was from making a new friend or the mimosas we'd had but I was feeling pretty damn good right now.

We paid our bills and decided to walk around for a while before trying to drive again, just to be safe. Neither of us knew the area well and we didn't want to get any more lost than we would if we were completely sober. Lucy linked her arm through mine as we hit the sidewalk. We'd ended up in a good area for strolling; there were tons of shops and other restaurants so we kept ourselves busy shopping and looking around. We found a pet store and squealed at the adorable puppies and kittens playing in their front window. We even went inside and got to play with some of the animals.

We were heading back to the car when Lucy noticed an adult shop and shouted, "We *have* to go in there!"

From the outside of the building you could tell that it was a classier shop than most stores like this were, so I agreed and we headed inside, stifling our giggles. An employee immediately greeted us and asked if we were in need of any help.

We thanked him, saying we were just looking but that if we needed anything we'd let him know. He grinned at us and nodded, whistling as he turned back to a project he was working on. Lucy and I explored everything from their everyday wear to the most ridiculously huge dildo we'd ever seen.

We stood staring at it, jaws dropped as we both imagined trying to get that inside us. Impossible. There was no way in hell that thing would fit anywhere.

"That's not a dildo, that's a fucking weapon," Lucy whispered dramatically. We both burst into laughter as we walked hurriedly away. We ended back at the area with corsets and thigh high stockings, taking our time to explore. I looked at them all, but there was one in particular that I kept glancing over to.

It was like none I'd ever seen before. It only had one shoulder strap, and the white material was pleated up to the top where a simple gold and purple accent was fastened. Gold and purple also peeked out from the insides of the pleats, with a purple cloth material that had gold threads shimmering through it the edges of the corset decorating it. The back fastened with white ribbon, and about three inches of a white gauzy material floated softly from the bottom of the corset.

I felt like it was made for me. It had a Grecian, toga style feel to it, and the purple on the corset matched my eyes perfectly. I checked the tag for the seventh time, and groaned to myself for the seventh time. It cost more than I would normally pay for lingerie, but I knew that it would be worth it. I'd feel like a goddess wearing it, and I could imagine that Aidan's reaction would be priceless.

Deep in thought about whether or not to buy it, I hadn't noticed Lucy and the employee that had originally greeted us come to stand by me until Lucy spoke, making me jump a little.

"You should just buy it."

I turned to the two of them when the man spoke in agreement. I looked at his nametag so I would know who I was talking to: Daniel.

"You really think so?" I shuffled my feet, still coming to terms with spending that much money on some underwear, no matter how obviously beautiful it was.

"I really do. The purple matches your eyes," Lucy replied, saying exactly what I was thinking.

"It's almost like it was made for you," Daniel agreed. "And you look Greek so the style would only enhance everything you've got going for you."

"I am Greek actually." I got this *ping-ping* feeling when I really looked at him, which I usually only got when my "couple radar", as Char called it, went off. I studied Daniel a little more, forgetting that they were waiting for me to decide about the corset. Daniel started to blush a bit, and I realized I was staring too quietly for too long and it was beginning to make him uncomfortable.

"Sorry Daniel, I was just thinking... are you gay?"

Lucy's jaw dropped and he let out an awkward laugh. "Umm, yes?"

I smiled big at him. "Is that a question or an answer?"

My smile must have eased him because he seemed to relax. "It's an answer. Definitely gay."

"Cool. Sorry to just come out and ask like that, no pun intended," I added when he snorted at "come out". Lucy was shaking her head at my forwardness but I could see the smile twitching on her lips.

"No biggie. I didn't expect it, but I'm not offended easily."

"That's good to hear. Are you single?"

He didn't seem fazed by my question this time, and he even folded his arms across his chest and raised an eyebrow at me. "Why do you ask?"

"I have this thing my best friend calls 'couple radar' and it started to go off when I looked at you. It hasn't failed me yet, and I run a successful matchmaking company. Since you're gay I know that it's not because of my friend Lucy here. But I think I know someone you'd get along with, and I was going to see if I could give him your number."

Both his eyebrows raised higher and higher on his forehead with every word as I met his gaze steadily. People sometimes made fun of my ability to spot people who would be good together and I used to be called Cupid in high school. It was one of the reasons I named my company Eros when Char and I decided to follow through on the idea.

"You might be crazy, but shit, why not." I took out my phone to save his number and snapped a selfie with him so I could show Char later. I showed Daniel a picture of Char as well, and Daniels' eyes widened as a smile split across his face. I could tell that Daniel was definitely interested in my proper, bow-tie-wearing bff.

A shot of glee ran through my veins at the thought of matching someone up, just like it always did. The high bled through to my decision making, and I plucked the corset of the display, telling Daniel to ring me up.

"They have some matching panties and a garter belt, you want those too?" Daniel grinned back at me.

"Hell yeah! I might as well go all in at this point!" I picked up some sheer gold thigh highs as well. I started to warm up on the insides, imagining what Aidan would do when he saw me in the outfit.

Lucy and I chatted with Daniel while he rang up our purchases, and I was loving his personality. Every moment I was more and more glad that I'd asked for his info for Char. Too bad they lived so far away, or I'd just call up Char right now. Which reminded me that I hadn't thought to tell Daniel I wasn't from here.

"Oh uh, Daniel?" I said the words with a bit of hesitation as I took my bag from him.

"Yeah, sugar?"

"Um. I forgot to mention, I don't actually live in California. I'm from Colorado, so that's where Char is going to be."

"Oh, that's okay." He leaned forward, and Lucy and I did the same even though there was no one else around to hear. "I'm a trust-fund baby. I've got plenty of resources to travel with if needed." He winked at us and straightened.

The weight in my chest lifted, and I chuckled. I sure could pick 'em. Char was gonna love this guy. We waved as we left and made a beeline for the car. We only had an hour before Aidan had to be picked up from the site, and Lucy and Daniel and I had decided together that I should be waiting for him at home in the new outfit. I rushed back to the apartment, and Lucy helped me lace up the back of the corset before she left, giving me a huge hug and telling me I looked hot.

She left, and I went to the bathroom to spruce up my hair and makeup while I waited. I paced in my room for Aidan to get back, nerves and excitement sweeping through me. The plan was for Lucy to tell him I was at home because I wasn't feeling well, so I was fairly sure that he'd come looking for me to check on me as soon as he stepped in the apartment. I was going to wait in my room, leaning up against one of the bed posts for him to devour me as soon as he caught site of me.

Suddenly, I heard the elevator ding signaling that he was here. I tried to get rid of the silly grin on my face as I slipped my heels on and posed but I couldn't stop it. I was too freaking excited.

"Baby? Callie? Are you alright?" His voice sounded a little panicked and I felt a bit bad for misleading him.

"In my room," I called out hoarsely. I didn't need to fake the voice- my body was already on fire for him, imagining his reaction.

I heard him hurrying down the hall. "Lucy said you weren't feeling well, so I..."

He trailed off as he stepped through my doorway and his eyes dilated so fast that my core clenched at the sight. My eyes roamed down his body, taking in the bulge that was already prominent.

He ran a shaky hand through his hair as he stared. I let the silence linger as I pushed off the post and walked slowly towards him in my favorite, purple spiked heels. *Thank heavens I packed these*, I thought to myself as I sashayed my way to Aidan.

CHAPTER THIRTY-FOUR
AIDAN

This woman was trying to kill me. I watched as Callie made her way towards me, slowly enough that I could take in every movement from the jiggling of her breasts in the breathtaking corset she wore to the flexing of her leg muscles encased by shimmery thigh highs and stiletto heels. The second I saw her all my worry immediately turned to dust with the arousal punching through me. My cock shot ramrod straight in an instant, and my mouth watered at the look in her eyes. Her hair was wavy, falling all around her like a dark cloud and all I wanted to do was shove my hands into it and ravage her body.

I watched as she slowly made her way around me, trailing a finger on my chest and back as she did so. That slight touch made me grit my teeth at the sensations. It was almost ridiculous how much my body craved even that small connection.

"What do we have here?" She mused huskily. She stood back in front of me, hands on her hips as she studied me. "I see the mortals have sent me a sacrifice finally worthy of my appetite."

Shocks of pleasure ran through me. She wanted to role play. I was more than okay with that, and I fell into my part easily.

"Yes, Goddess. But no one sent me; I volunteered."

"Volunteered? Do you not have brains in that pretty little head of yours? Do you not know what I do to the men who come across me?"

I gulped, partly for show but mostly because my mouth had gone dry at her tone. She was playing her part perfectly even though I knew, from personal experience, that being in charge wasn't her preference. I was okay with giving up the reigns every now and then, and what Callie wanted from me she got.

"I do, Goddess. I figured that all men die anyway, and I'd rather go out by your hands than any other's."

Satisfaction filled her gaze. "Very well, mortal. Do as I say, and I shall make it pleasurable at the very least."

She practically purred the words and I got harder if that were possible, nodding frantically.

"Strip. I like to know exactly what I'm working with."

"As you wish, Goddess." I did as she asked, impatiently shedding my clothes until I was standing tall in front of her, naked and hard.

"Mmm. I approve. And you may call me Calliope. I will allow that."

I dropped my head to hide the smile that crossed my face at her obvious need for me to call her by her name, even though it was the formal version. "Calliope, then."

I glanced up just in time to watch her eyes dilate when I said her name and it reconfirmed my theory that she liked hearing me say it.

"Good." She calmly stalked around me again, small noises of approval escaping her as she looked me over. She traced the tattoos on my body with her finger, and then with her tongue. It took everything in me to just stand there and let her do what she wanted when all I could think about was pushing her against the wall, pulling those panties of hers to the side and pounding her until we couldn't breathe.

By the time she stepped away from my body, both our chests were heaving from her ministrations. I was waiting for her next move when an idea took over in my mind. I knew that she liked it when I took over, but our current power play had reversed our situations. However, the idea I'd just had would ensure that she would still feel like she was in charge when it really was me.

I dropped to my knees in front of Callie, and a smile pulled at her lips. "I see that you are well versed in worship," she teased.

"I would love to show you exactly what kind of worship I had in mind, Calliope, if you'd let me."

She raised an eyebrow haughtily, but her legs trembled. She knew what I meant but was trying to play it off. "You may," she said. She turned and walked over to the wide arm chair that was in her room and gracefully reclined. She'd spread her legs just enough to give me a teasing view of her pussy, covered with itty-bitty panties that, even from here, I could tell were soaking.

She watched as I got up and walked over to her predatorily, less like a slave and more like a wild cat hunting its prey. I watched her throat move as she swallowed hard and took in my flexing muscles as I moved slowly but steadily.

When I reached her, I fell to my knees and hovered my hands over her thighs. In a low voice I asked, "Do I have permission to touch?"

"Yes," she choked out. I spread my fingers out on her inner thighs, close to her wet heat but not touching, and lifted her legs, spreading them farther until they were hooked around the arms of the chair. I gripped her thighs hard, making her moan and her eyes flutter closed. I took that moment to rip her panties right off her.

Her eyes flew open in shock and she started to complain. "Aidan! Do you know-ohhhh!"

I'd leaned down and ran my tongue quickly up her folds, then flicked it over her clit, stopping her protests as she automatically tangled her fingers in my hair to hold me where I was.

"You didn't… ask for permission…. to, oh my god… taste…" Callie's words made me grin. She was fighting hard to stay in charge, but she was beginning to slip. Wiping the smile off my face, I lifted my head and stared at her until she met my eyes.

"Calliope, my goddess, may I please put my mouth back onto your sweet, delicious pussy and lick you until your come all over my face?"

"If you don't I'll smite you before you can say 'please' again," she growled, her eyes full of fire.

I smirked at her words, not hiding it this time. In the next second, I was back in her folds, consuming her like she was my last meal. In this fantasy, I suppose she was. I kept my hands on her thighs, pushing against them to add some friction from her skin rubbing against the fabric of the chair and sending pulses from her tightening muscles straight into her pussy.

With every push, her moans got higher and louder, and it wasn't too long before she was shaking so hard I could tell she was going to fall apart gloriously. Wrapping my lips around her clit, I sucked hard and grazed her once with my teeth. That catapulted her into a climax that nearly drowned me with the amount of come that poured out from her. She was still coming when I leapt up, grabbing her and switching us so that I was sitting on the chair with her straddling my legs. I gritted my teeth as she wrapped a hand around my cock and held me as she sank down. She pulsed around me even as she slid down until our hips were flush. I wrapped an arm around her back and the other around her hips so that she couldn't move, her body completely sealed against mine.

"Lift your hips just a little baby," I growled out. She moaned softly as she did what I told her, the rest of her limp and hanging onto me. Her legs shook slightly and I tightened my arms around her a little more. "You don't have to do any work, just hold on."

She licked my shoulder in response and I pumped my hips up slightly. The little noise that Callie let out at the movement blasted through whatever restraint had been holding me back. I held onto her as I thrust up into her over and over, hard and fast. I wanted to feel her skin against mine so I quickly untied the strings holding the corset together until I was able to slip it over Callie's head. As soon as it was off I pulled her back to me, our chests rubbing together as I thrust up against her.

"Oh my god, Aidan, I'm going to come again." Callie moaned the words into my ear and I knew what would bring her to that point. I needed her to come again before I could let go and I was about to lose it. I moved my hand from around her hips and thrust even harder as I slapped her ass, increasing the hardness with each strike. When my hand landed the third time, Callie shattered around me, a short scream escaping her. Her climax brought on my own and I threw my head back and grunted. Both of us collapsed in exhaustion as the tension bled out of our muscles and I loosened my grip on Callie slightly as we came down.

"Best… sacrifice… ever…" Callie panted the words out and I laughed. She giggled along with me, and I groaned because it made her pussy tighten around my cock still inside her. I couldn't get enough of this woman. I had to tighten my lips in order to keep my feelings from spilling out. I knew she wasn't ready for the words, and I wanted to keep her for as long as I could. I stood, having to lock my knees to keep from keeling over as I trudged over to Callie's bed. We both collapsed and I drew the covers over us.

She traced circles on my chest and I was so replete that the soothing motion lulled me to sleep within minutes. The last thing I recalled was a soft kiss against my arm that Callie had rested her head on.

Lucy joined us in the apartment for breakfast the next morning since she was going with me to the worksite, just to check everything out. We were both invested into this project and wanted to make sure it went smoothly and according to plan. Callie had decided to stay in the apartment and do some work instead of going to the job site, that way she wouldn't have construction noise in the background to distract her or interrupt her phone calls. I gave her a lingering kiss before heading to the elevator and had to tear myself away from her before I fucked her right in front of Lucy.

Callie was blushing as I pulled away and I smirked at her, knowing that she was thinking the same thing. As soon as the elevator doors closed, Lucy pounced.

"So when are you going to tell her you're in love with her?"

I glared at her. "None of your business."

"I'm making it my business. As one of your best friends, I have the right to make sure you're happy. Plus I really like her, Aidan."

I tried to hold the glare but failed when the smile I was fighting made its way to my face. "Yeah. Me too." Then I let out a shaky breath. "But she's not ready yet. She still has amnesia, and I don't want to confuse her in any way."

"What do you mean confuse her? It's not like when she remembers everything she's going to forget that you love her. Plus, getting back the three months she can't remember is probably only going to make her like you more."

Dammit. She had a point- or she would, if Callie and I had actually been dating before she ended up in the hospital. I ground my teeth together in frustration, trying to think of another excuse without spilling the beans about the actual reason. I could feel Lucy watching me as we got into the car and left, and when she drew in a sharp breath I winced. She was too smart for her own good, and she'd obviously just figured something out.

"There's something else going on, isn't there?" I nodded but didn't elaborate. "I'm assuming that for some reason you can't tell me what it is or you already would have." I nodded again.

We drove in silence until I parked at the job site. Neither of us moved to get out though, and I stared straight ahead, hands in my lap. Out of the corner of my eye I watched as Lucy reached over and slid her hand into one of mine. She waited until I looked at her before speaking softly.

"Aidan, I know you. You're a great guy. You act and look like a tough guy but you're a big softy with a romantic heart. I can also tell when you're in over your head. Just promise me that in the end, this isn't going to leave you or Callie with broken hearts."

I choked on the emotions welling up inside me. All the love I felt for Callie, the fear that she'll hate me if I make her fall for me under false pretenses, the support from Lucy... It was all engulfing me in this moment and I told myself to control it. I swallowed hard before I could answer her. I couldn't lie, and my voice cracked when I finally pushed the words out.

"I don't know, Lucy. I want to promise you that but... I can't."

She studied me, her face soft with concern. She squeezed my hand and replied, "I'll be here for you if you need me, no matter what."

I nodded my thanks, and we sat there like that for a few more minutes while I wrestled to push my emotions back, telling myself I'd deal with them later. Right now the job needed me, and I cleared my throat to signal Lucy that I was ready.

She grinned at me teasingly. "Damn Aidan, I almost worried I'd have to go find you a mop for your tears for a second there. You know, since when you start crying you don't stop until you've flooded something."

I let out a reluctant laugh and I shook my head at her. "You're the stupidest friend I have, Lucy."

"Right back atcha, you big baby."

I chuckled at her teasing, glad she was able to put me into a lighter mood after all that heaviness. I was able to get plenty of work done onsite, and Lucy was impressed with everything the crew had accomplished. She flirted with some of the guys, and almost had them climbing over each other to get her whatever she needed by the time we left that afternoon. She blew the guys a kiss as we drove off, making me chuckle at her antics.

I dropped her off at her apartment, and grabbed her hand before she could hop out of the car. She turned to look at me and raised an eyebrow.

"Thanks Lucy." I thought about saying more, but I knew I didn't need to with her.

She smiled and slid the rest of the way out of the car. "Anytime. You know that. See you in the morning!"

She shut the door and I made sure she got into the building before driving away. I parked and walked slowly to my own building. Callie and I only had three days left before flying home, and we were going to take Lucy back to the airport in the morning since she had some other things to take care of back in Denver.

Which reminded me: I only had three days to get Callie to admit that she loved me. Sometimes I thought I saw it in her eyes, or heard it in her voice, but I refused to push her for it. If she didn't want to say the words, then Aphrodite was going to have to just fucking deal with it.

At that moment, I decided to treat this like a normal relationship. I'd let everything develop on its own terms, and deal with the consequences when they came. I also realized something else: I was ready to give up the possibility of finding my family, just for Callie. That thought hit me hard, but I figured that I was going to be okay either way. As long as I had Callie, I didn't think I'd need the family that gave me up anyway. I would just make my own. And hopefully, after everything panned out, I *would* still have her by my side. A growl rose up in me at the thought of her leaving- because if she did I'd do everything I could to bring her back.

CHAPTER THIRTY-FIVE
CALLIE

I was filled with mixed feelings as Aidan and I boarded the plane. Part of me was glad to be getting back home soon, but another part of me never wanted to leave California, and this state of bliss I'd been in. I knew reality was waiting for me back in Colorado and my chest seized at the thought of losing what Aidan and I had built while here.

Three days ago we'd taken Lucy back to the airport, and I'd been content to sit in the back and listen to the two of them chat. They'd talked about the project at first, going over future details like Lucy coming back out in order to make sure the interior was decorated correctly during the last week before the opening. I'd loved watching them interact, and I interjected my own thoughts when appropriate.

I walked the job site yesterday with Aidan, marveling at how much had gotten done in the last two weeks. The bones of the building were up, and everything else was in process. I could see everything taking shape, and I knew this was going to look amazing after it was completed. It was our last walk-through before the center opened in the next couple months.

Around 5 pm Aidan and I said our farewells to the crew guys, and I got so many kisses on the back of my hand I was sure I'd be blushing for weeks. Aidan kept a tight arm around me the whole time, but other than that he gave no outward signs of any jealousy. Every time Aidan placed a kiss on my knuckles, he would brush his fingertips up and down my side, letting me know that I was his, and only his. My body thrilled at the touches and it was the main reason for the flush on my cheeks when we left, heading to Beth's place for dinner.

The trip had been amazing, and I found myself smiling again when I recalled Beth's parting words. She'd given me a big hug, then handed me a slip of paper with her number on it. "Call me to chat anytime, dear. And let me know if Aidan starts acting up; I'll be in Colorado in a jiffy to beat some sense into him." I laughed at that image, but promised to call sometime soon.

"What's got you smiling over there?" I turned my head to look at Aidan, seeing an amused look on his own face.

"I was just imagining Beth beating you up. You lost spectacularly." I giggled when Aidan changed his expression into one of playful offense.

"I'd like to think I could hold my own against her... Or at least surrender gracefully." Another round of laugher escaped me and I clamped a hand over my mouth when other passengers still filing onto the plane gave me weird looks. I wasn't embarrassed, but I didn't want to annoy anyone either.

Aidan reached up and moved my hand from my face. "Don't do that, I like hearing you laugh."

I blushed and leaned over to give him a soft kiss. I wanted to linger, but there were too many people around so I sat back in my own seat before Aidan could pull me in deeper.

Unlike the flight on the way to California, this one was uneventful. I passed out shortly after take-off, exhaustion from the last two weeks and everything before it catching up to me.

I woke up right as we were landing and found that at some point Aidan had lifted the arm rests between us and moved me so that I could snuggle deep into his arms. I breathed deeply, taking in his comforting scent. I didn't move too much since he was asleep, something he'd mentioned he had a hard time doing on planes. Plus, I liked being near him when he was so relaxed. There were still times that Aidan seemed so distant, but the moments were fewer in these last few days. I hadn't been able to figure out why, but I was assuming it had to do with work stuff. I knew how stressful it was to run your own company.

Too soon, an announcement came over the speakers about landing and Aidan woke up, seemingly surprised he'd fallen asleep. He shifted and I lifted my body from the cradle of his arm, watching him stretch and yawn. I could feel everything in me, all the nerves in my stomach and the affection for him in my heart, rise at the dreamy, content look on his face as he came fully awake. I could feel my smile falter at the enormity of the feelings in me and I looked away to my carry-on back together. *Yeah right Calliope, you just don't want him to see all that written plain as day on your face when you can't even admit to yourself how you feel.* I scoffed at the voice in my head calling me out, but didn't reply to it.

"Callie?" I schooled my face to something neutral and turned to him at the sound of my name.

"Yeah?"

"Would you like to come over to my place tonight?"

Despite something in me warning me to get some distance, a grin spread across my face. "What, you don't want to get rid of me yet?"

"Not even close, baby." Aidan winked at me jokingly, but the look in his eyes told me he was serious so I agreed.

"Holy shit! This is awesome!" I was looking out into Aidan's backyard, amazed at the sight before me. The house

247

itself was simple, two stories with a basement turned into a movie and game space, and the upstairs with a master bedroom and guest bedroom along with the usual kitchen, living room, and dining area.

The backyard was obviously where Aidan had invested the most money. Built into the backyard was a huge ground-level pool, complete with its own diving board. A trampoline was nearby, and when I squinted I noticed something strung across the top of the pool.

"Is that a slackline?!" I nearly screamed the words in my excitement. I'd always wanted to slackline above a pool!

Aidan chuckled behind me. "Yeah, I figure if you fall into the pool it won't hurt as bad as falling on the ground."

I nodded eagerly, our reasoning the same. "How deep does the pool go?"

"Fourteen feet."

"Oh holy… that's incredible. I don't want to know how much that cost to put in- but it was worth the money."

He laughed, and since he'd wrapped himself around me while I was staring out his glass doors, I felt the laugh vibrate through my body. My body sank back into him as I took a moment to enjoy that feeling. I tilted my head back to look up at him and he captured my lips in a kiss like he'd been waiting for me to do just that.

"You're welcome to use it any time you want," he said when he pulled away.

"Good thing too, because I'd be here whether you liked it or not." He cracked up again and I turned in his arms so I could watch him. I loved the way he threw his head back and just let it out, not caring what anyone thought. My heart pounded in my chest when he looked back at me, both his dimples fully out with his wide grin.

"C'mon sassy pants, let's change and we'll go to dinner."

I obediently followed him to his room where we'd dropped off our stuff before touring his home. We changed quickly into some clothes we hadn't been traveling in and decided to go to Buffalo Wild Wings since it was nearby and we wanted something we could pig out on.

My fingers were covered in mild buffalo sauce and I'd just taken another bite that I was sure had covered my face in sauce too when I noticed Aidan looking at me intensely.

I chewed and swallowed, setting down the wing. I grabbed a napkin and cleaned off my face and hands. I could tell he was thinking about something serious, and I didn't want to have sauce everywhere while we talked. I leaned back in the booth and took a drink of water while I waited for him to speak. I sucked on the straw and raised an eyebrow at him, letting him know I was aware he had something he wanted to say.

A smile twitched at his mouth, and then he spoke. "Do you want to go with me to the Denver center tomorrow to get an idea of what the one in California is going to be like?"

"I would love that! I'm not doing anything until Monday anyway, so that's perfect."

A relieved look crossed his face before his smile wiped it away. "Awesome."

I was giddy for the rest of the night, right up until I passed out in Aidan's bed, wrapped tightly around him. In my heart I knew I was falling for him and at this point I was just hoping he was falling too. I was still frustrated by the fact that I still didn't remember things, but I wasn't going to let that stop me from being happy right now, in these moments, with him.

Chapter Thirty-Six

Aidan

I rubbed my hand on my pants for what seemed like the hundredth time that morning, annoyed with myself for being so nervous. I knew that there was no way Callie wasn't going to like the center I'd built in Denver, but fuck, I was a pile of nerves anyway. I loved this woman, and if she didn't like something I'd poured my heart and soul into, I was pretty sure I'd lose it. I'd been thinking about taking her with me for the last few days now, and had finally gotten around to asking her last night. Her response was so enthusiastic, I'd nearly told her I loved her right then.

She looked over the center with an awed expression. The center was always open, so there were plenty of people milling about and she was taking it all in. I spent a lot of time here, trying to get to know the people and what would help them the most, so I recognized a lot of them. There were always new faces, which gave me mixed feelings. I wished that these people weren't at the point in their lives where they needed help, but on the other hand I was glad that they'd found this place to help them out.

I talked to a few of the regulars- both volunteers and the needful alike- on our way in. I was proud to have Callie by my side when she treated everyone with care and love no matter how proper or bedraggled they were. If I didn't already know I loved her, watching her here would've proved it to me without a doubt.

Speaking of which, I'd gotten another message from Aphrodite while on the flight back home. Part of me had been afraid to open it when I saw the sender, but I'd never been a coward before and I wasn't going to start then. I was also a little surprised that she'd waited until then to contact me since the previous deadline was the day before. A wave of relief blew through me while reading the message; Aphrodite said that she'd seen the progress and was going to give me another week. She'd stressed that it was the final chance for me and I could tell that she was deadly serious.

The gravity of the tone in the email made me wonder if this whole vow thing was more important to her than she let on. I brushed the thought off, glad to have a little more time before everything fell apart.

"Aidan? Where next?" Callie's eager question brought me back to the present, and I hid my internal musings behind a giant smile.

"Inside, I'm going to give you a tour."

She clapped gleefully and I grabbed her hand and led her in. I knew this was going to be a long tour since people would want to be introduced to her, and I wasn't going to hesitate to brag about my girlfriend.

Hours later we finished the tour and I had a feeling Callie was getting slightly overwhelmed by all the people and activities happening. We were walking outside now, near the small skate park I'd built behind the center. All of this could be a lot to take in at once, but when I glanced over at her, I only saw her eyes shining with excitement and a big smile across her face.

When she turned that smile onto me, my breath caught and my heart almost burst out of my chest. This was it. I couldn't hold it back anymore; I was going to tell her I loved her. My heart raced and my voice was shaky as I started. "Callie, I-"

Suddenly the air was knocked out of me when I was tackled to the ground by several small bodies. I heard Callie giggle as I tried to suck in my breath and respond to the kids yelling over each other to get my attention.

"Aidan! You've been gone forever!"

"Ha! We finally tackled you! Got you!"

"Are you going to come skateboard with us?! Please please please!"

I laughed and pushed myself up off the grass, standing and grinning at three of my favorite kids, ones that came to this center all the time. Their single mom worked a lot of hours to take care of them, so more often than not, they ended up here. The oldest boy was Jake at thirteen, the second oldest was Tyler at twelve, and their sister, Anna, was the youngest at 10.

"You guys finally managed to catch me off guard. I'm impressed. Let me check with my girlfriend to see if it's okay with her that I skateboard." I winked at the kids and they giggled, waiting patiently for an answer.

I turned to Callie, who was still trying to stifle her laughter. "Will you be alright if I go hang out for a minute?"

"Who am I to stop you from being shown up by three kids again?" Her teasing voice had me tingling from head to toe, but I ignored the path my mind wanted to take.

"Watch it babe," I growled playfully. "Seriously though, you can do whatever you want around here. Feel free to wander, or stay here. Just let me know when you're ready to leave."

"Aidan, go play with them. And take your time, I'm perfectly happy to watch and cheer you on from here."

"Thanks." I went in for a quick kiss, but the moment our lips met I couldn't resist going in deeper. I only pulled away when I registered all the whistles and a few fake puking noises from the children around us.

I shook my head at Callie's wide grin, feeling a blush come across my face at how I'd instantly forgotten people surrounded us. I turned back to find the two boys with bored looks on their faces, and their little sister looking at Callie and me like we were a fairy tale come true.

I cleared my throat. "Are we gonna skate or what kids?" That made them start talking over each other again and they ran off to get our gear. I let them put their stuff in one of the lockers nearby with mine since they were here so often. We strapped into our helmets and knee pads together when they came back with their arms full of helmets, knee pads, and skateboards. I didn't typically skate with all this when I was out on roads, but I wanted to teach the children here that safety was important. I took off the flannel button up I'd worn to reveal the fitted tank I wore underneath. I could feel Callie's eyes eating me up and I struggled not to look over. If I did, then we'd be heading up to my office- and not for anything work related.

The four of us perched our boards on the edge of a small half-pipe and I counted to three before we all sprung into the air, the sound of the wheels grating on the concrete music to my ears. My brain instantly cleared of anything else but watching the kids and teaching them some new tricks. Jake, Tyler, and Anna had all taken to the skateboards like fish to water so I'd spent a lot of time with them on it. I glanced over to Callie only a few times, when I couldn't help myself. She was watching intently, a look in her eyes I wasn't able to decipher from this distance.

After a few rounds I let the kids do some skating while I watched from the side. I looked over at Callie again, and this time I noticed that she was chatting with a small girl. My jaw dropped when I realized who she was talking to. Her name was Elise, and she wandered in every now and then. Her name was the only thing anyone knew about her though, because she never talked. I'd also noticed she had an aversion to touch so I'd spread the word for others to be careful around her. I guessed she was about eight, and skinny as a stick.

And here she was, cuddling up to Callie's side, gazing at her like was a goddess. I couldn't blame her, because I felt the same. I watched the two of them interact, amazed that Elise was not only instigating the physical touch but that she smiled softly when Callie slowly reached up and ran her fingers through her hair.

"Where did you find that woman?" I looked over to find one of the volunteer counselors, Jason, staring in wonder at the same thing I was. I looked back to Callie and saw that Elise was now in her lap, letting Callie braid her hair. I watched dumbfounded as Callie talked away, apparently okay with the fact that Elise never replied.

"That's what I ask myself all the time, man. I'm glad you see this shit too because I thought I was hallucinating for a second."

"I haven't seen Elise willingly touch anyone, ever. And now your girl has her in her lap, braiding her damn hair. I've been trying to work with her for months, or even get her to talk to a female counselor, and nada. She runs every time. And within three minutes- Callie right?" I nodded. "Callie's gotten farther than anyone else."

"I know, it's a fucking miracle." I watched as Callie tied off the braid. Jason and I sucked in a breath when Elise wrapped her tiny arms around my girlfriend's waist and gave her a hug before smiling, stroking Callie's cheek, and running off.

Callie watched until Elise was out of sight, and then turned to meet my gaze. Even from here I could tell that Callie had a thousand questions for me, so I decided to call it a day. I said goodbye to the three kids, and they gave me quick hugs before going back to the half pipe.

I shook hands with Jason who still looked slightly shocked at what he'd seen. "Aidan, don't let that one go."

I smiled ruefully. "I'm not planning on it."

I headed over to Callie, stripping off my helmet and pads along the way. I nodded towards the locker and she quietly followed, waiting while I shoved the gear inside.

She handed me my flannel back and I slipped it on, grateful for it now that the slight breeze had cooled the sweat on my skin.

"Are you ready to head out?" I stroked the same cheek Elise had, and she nodded, biting her lip. "Alright babe, let's go the back way. I can tell you've got some questions for me but I'm starving. We can order pizza or something when we get back to my place if that works." I led her back around the building to a side path that led almost directly to where I'd parked.

"Yeah, that sounds good. I can wait a bit to bombard you." I grinned at her words, bringing up her hand to kiss the fingers intertwined with mine, grateful to have this time with her. I could feel the time ticking on this relationship, and I didn't know if I'd get very many more moments like this with her.

Chapter Thirty-Seven
Callie

We were sitting on the floor leaning against the couch in Aidan's living room, halfway through eating the pizza when he pushed the box away and faced me.

"Alright, you're fidgeting so much you're beginning to make me nervous. Go ahead and start asking." His voice was full of amusement, but he also seemed a little wary.

"Well, first of all you have no right looking so hot on a skateboard while wearing a helmet and knee pads." His eyes sparkled but he held back the laughter I knew was building in him.

"I won't touch that one. Plus it wasn't a question."

"No, it wasn't but I had to point it out anyway. When'd you start skateboarding?"

"Middle school. I went to a kid's birthday party at a rec center and tried it out. I was obsessed from then on."

"You're really good, obviously." I thought back to the way he'd moved, almost like the board was an extension of him. I could tell that he didn't even have to think about how to move or how to pull off a trick. While watching him, something in my brain had gone a little fuzzy, like it was trying to pull a memory out that I didn't recall. That feeling nagged at me but no matter how hard I tried I couldn't pull the memory forward. Then, the girl had sat by me and distracted me before I got a headache

"Callie? Still with me?"

"Hmm? Oh, yes I am. You saw the girl that sat with me?"

He blew out a breath. "Yeah, I definitely did."

"She said her name was Elise."

"She… she told you her name?" Aidan's eyes were wide, shock evident.

"Um, yeah. I asked her how old she was and she said she was eight, but she didn't really say anything else. She only looked at me when I asked her other questions."

Aidan was still staring at me in shock, but I had no idea why. "She told you how old she was?"

"Yes…" I was confused. "What am I missing here?"

A sound of disbelief blew out his mouth. "Callie, her name is the only thing she's ever told anyone. And I was the only one she told. She hasn't spoken a word to me or anyone else since, and she doesn't ever let anyone touch her either. Ever."

My heart pounded hard, and now I was the one surprised. I set down the piece of pizza I'd been eating, then wiped my fingers with a napkin before replying. "W-what?" I'd planned on saying something more articulate than that, but that's all that ended up coming out.

"Yeah, exactly. You can imagine my shock when I looked over and saw her happily sitting in your lap and letting you braid her hair. How did you do that?"

"I have no idea. When she first came up to me I reached out to shake her hand and she flinched really hard. I could tell that she was jumpy so I backed off. I tried to ask her questions and when she barely responded, I started to tell her things, making it easy for her to just listen instead of asking her a bunch of questions I figured she wouldn't answer. Next thing I know she's putting my hand on her head so I ran my fingers through her hair. She leaned into my hand like a cat so I asked if she'd like me to braid her hair. She jumped into my lap and well... you saw the end part, I think."

"I did. She hugged you, touched your face and then ran off."

"Yeah." Tears started to gather in my eyes just like they had when I'd watched her scamper off. "I wish I could've done something else for her. She was shaking in my lap and I just wanted to make everything better." My voice cracked at the end and I covered my face as the tears I'd been holding back spilled out.

My heart broke to think of everything that the poor girl must have gone through that caused her to be so closed off. I felt Aidan move closer to me and pull me into his lap, comforting me as I cried for Elise, and a little bit for Aidan because I knew that he'd had a difficult childhood and had to have experienced something like that little girl.

"Callie, love, please don't cry. You're killing me here." I sniffled through another surge of tears, looking up at Aidan's pained expression. "You did more today for her than anyone has been able to so far. You're amazing, and beautiful, and you have the biggest heart I've ever seen. I love you, Calliope."

A bolt of shock shot through me at those words. More tears fell onto my cheeks, and I desperately wanted to give him the same words but I couldn't make myself say them just yet. "You... love me?"

"Of course I do. How could I not? But Callie, I don't want you to say the words back to me until you're completely comfortable, until you're totally sure. I know you have a lot going on and I'm not trying to pressure you into anything. I just needed you to know that I've fallen in love with you."

I bit my lip as I stared at him. He didn't seem stressed or worried, and I could hear the honesty in his voice. I smiled shakily and nodded, letting him know I understood. He leaned down to kiss me softly, and I could feel the love between us even if I couldn't say the words yet.

Chapter Thirty-Eight
Callie

It was Monday and I was back in the office, physically at least. Mentally, I was still going over everything that had happened yesterday. What with meeting Elise and seeing how much Aidan really did for people who were struggling, to him telling me he loved me... I fell harder for him every second and I chastised myself for not telling Aidan how much I loved him.

There. I admitted it to myself at least- I was head over heels, crazy in love with this guy that I had only really known for a couple of weeks. I scoffed out loud to myself in my office, mumbling about how ridiculous it was to fall in love so quickly and yet here I was, daydreaming about waking up in his arms every day and getting married and-

"Okay, quit it with the weird mumbling, it's beginning to freak us out."

I jerked my head up to see Char and the new employee he'd hired while I was gone, a sweet girl named Allison. I'd met her only this morning, but I was glad to see that our instincts were spot on when we'd talked about interviewing her. She was able to keep up with the two of us sass-wise, and she enjoyed the work.

"Sorry guys, I know I haven't been a big help today."

"I'd find it hard to come back to work after vacationing in California for two weeks too," Allison said reassuringly.

I laughed a bit awkwardly, using the excuse she'd provided for me and looked away from them. "Exactly. Gotta get my mind back on the job."

Char snorted. "Yeah right bitch, don't try to pretend like I can't see right through that flimsy excuse. You're a terrible liar."

I flipped him off and I heard Allison chuckle at us. I gave them both a glare before turning back to my blank computer screen.

A dramatic sigh followed after several moments of silence and I stared so hard at my computer screen, I thought I'd go cross-eyed. I could see out of the corner of my eye that not only hadn't the two of them left, but they'd moved to take a seat on my couch. I watched as Allison hesitated for a second, unsure if she should be here, before Char tugged on her hand.

I blinked hard, ignoring them. This was a battle of wills I didn't want to lose. Minutes ticked by and I saw Char start to tap his foot, which meant he was about to give up. Hope blossomed inside that I wouldn't have to talk about anything right now- until the door to the office banged open. I jumped at the sound of the door slamming shut, and a shot of fear ran through me at the triumphant grin on Char's face. *What did he do??*

The question was answered as soon as I thought it. My sister's voice rang out as she came around the corner to my office and I could feel the blood drain from my face. He'd called in reinforcements.

"Calliope! You're lucky I love you because as your favorite sister, I should've been the first to know that you were back. My feelings, delicate as they are, are hurt." She stepped into my doorway at that last word, her face twisted in pain like I'd shoved a stake in her heart. Despite being frustrated as hell that I was going to have to talk about this right now, because the three of them together would never let me leave without doing so, Ellinor's dramatics made me laugh.

"You're my only sister, so that argument is invalid."

Her face cleared and she grinned back at me. "Fine- I'm your favorite sibling. Whatever. The point is, time to spill details about this little trip of yours." She plopped onto the couch next to Allison and faced her. "Hi, by the way. I'm Ellinor."

"Allison," our new hire replied with a grin. She looked at us. "I love my job."

Laughter filled the air, and some of the tension left the room. I took a deep breath and let it out slowly.

"Alright, you guys win. Aidan and I stayed at this apartment complex where he has the whole top floor of one of the buildings as his like, penthouse or something. I'm pretty sure he owns the complex, but he never admitted to it. A sweet, little old lady who was a friend of his parents basically runs it for him. We went to the site where he's building a center, like the two he has here in Colorado, quite a bit. It was actually a lot of fun to see the process. We went to the beach, saw some sea lions, went to Disneyland, and I hung out one day with one of his best friends and business partner who flew out to check on the project. Her name is Lucy and I like her a lot."

"You forgot to mention the beautiful and sweet man you found for me." Char grinned wickedly and I smiled back.

"You're still stalking to Daniel then?"

"Hell yeah. Are you kidding? Your radar is never off sweetheart." He pulled out his phone to show Allison and Ellinor a picture and they both hummed in delight.

"Good thing he's gay or I'd have to steal him away," Ellinor joked. I knew she'd like him; he was just her type, minus the whole gay part.

"Yeah right, like you'd stand a chance. Now don't think I've forgotten we were talking about you Callie, I just wanted to show off a bit." Char stuffed his phone back in his pocket, laser eye focused on me again.

"There's not much else to tell..." I petered off, feeling the blush steal across my face as I avoided eye contact with them.

"Well that could mean two things." My eyes shot to Ellinor, who was smiling happily at me. "Either the sex was incredible, or you're in love."

My lack of response drew a gasp from the three of them, but Allison surprised me by speaking out first.

"You guys, it's totally both. Look at her face!"

"I mean, it's hard not to fall in love with an incredible man," I muttered not-so-quietly. "Especially when the sex is better than... honestly it's better than anything I can even think of."

My audience whooped in congratulations, and I couldn't help but grin.

Ellinor's next question changed the mood a little bit. "Really though Callie, I'm happy for you. Despite all the weirdness of your amnesia and the secrecy behind you two dating, you deserve to love and *be* loved. He did say he loved you when you told him, right?"

I shifted in my seat. "Um, well..."

"Do I need to go kick his ass?" Ellinor grated the words out and love for my sister filled me at her willingness to fight for me.

"Calm down tiger. I was just going to say that it's actually the other way around." Silence filled the room at my words.

Char opened his mouth, then closed it. Opened it again. "So... you're saying that he told you he loves you but you didn't say it back? When you obviously love him too?"

"Yeaaahhhh." I knew it sounded dumb, like I was trying to stop myself from being happy. "I don't know why I couldn't say it back. There was something inside me that stopped the words. It's not that I don't love him, it's just... something is telling me not to say it yet."

"That's probably the part of you that's afraid it won't work out, like your other relationships," Ellinor stated. "I know that's hard to get over, but if you love him you just need to tell him. There's nothing stopping you but yourself."

I nodded, hearing what she was saying. "Thank you guys, I needed that." I didn't want to go home and be alone to think about all this, but I also knew I couldn't go spend the night with Aidan if I wanted to work through it all.

"I have an idea," Char murmured thoughtfully. "You know that event we have tomorrow night? I think you should take Aidan."

I'd totally forgotten about our "Fall for Fall" event we had tomorrow night. That was completely unlike me, since I was usually OCD about the events.

"But, how can I do my job and keep Aidan with me the whole time? You know, there's no way I'm letting some other woman even get close to him without me around. Not because I don't trust him, but because I want those hoes to know that he's taken and to find their own."

That response garnered a few laughs, but Char had apparently already solved the problem in his own mind. "That's easy; we switch spots. I think it's about time you show your face in front of the crowds anyway. Then I can run behind the scenes with Allison so she gets the hang of it and you can walk around with Aidan."

Okay, I had to give it to him. That was actually a pretty great plan. Even though I got super nervous in front of people, I'd have Aidan with me the whole time- whether he liked it or not.

"You know I hate to admit it, but that's a good idea." Char patted himself on the back at my words and I rolled my eyes.

"And that would be a perfect time to tell him you love him, too." Ellinor's words made me sweat at the thought but she wasn't wrong. The atmosphere of the event would definitely allow for it, and even though my brain pounded and my chest ached at the thought of telling him, I knew it'd be an opportunity wasted if I didn't. I looked at the three people on my couch and took in their encouraging faces.

"You're right. I'm going to invite Aidan to the event and spill the love beans." I paused. "Okay that end part sounded weird but you get the idea." Ellinor was rubbing her forehead in exasperation but I could see her smile, and Char and Allison laughed. I walked over and gave them all hugs, even Allison. She was stuck with us all now anyway.

"No matter what happens, we love you Callie," Ellinor said softly as she looked up at me in our embrace.

I choked up a little. "I love you guys too."

CHAPTER THIRTY-NINE
AIDAN

I tugged at the collar of my shirt, loosening my tie a little in the process. It was a little warm in the room where Callie was holding one of her Eros events, as a nod to the upcoming season. Last night when I called her to talk before bed, she'd invited me to go with her today, and I'd readily agreed. She'd sounded relieved and anxious when I said I'd go. I figured that she was stressed to be the face of this event for the first time, instead of working behind the scenes.

I thought it was adorable that she got nervous in front of crowds, and I knew having me there would comfort her. Besides that, I wanted to be where she was no matter where we were or what we were doing.

I loosened my tie one more time, hoping to get back the breath I'd lost when I picked up Callie from her apartment. She'd stepped out in a form fitting, jet black dress that had a shimmery quality to it, making it nearly impossible for me to look anywhere else. It was simple, but devastating to my control. Especially since I knew that she wasn't wearing any panties underneath- she'd flippantly informed me of that fact right before we'd walked into the venue.

My jaw had dropped, dick going diamond hard in an instant as I'd watched her strut away from me in a tall pair of black heels that had strings wrapping up her calves. Thankfully, the only other people there were the caterers since we were early and I didn't care if they saw my body's reaction to her statement. I was able to calm down eventually, but it was a fucking testament of strength not to show exactly how much I wanted to take Callie into the nearest empty room and check her lack of panties personally.

"Can we just go check with Char and Allison that everything is going okay back there?" Callie's nerves were getting the better of her now that we'd had a few moments to take a breather.

"Babe, take a look around. Does anyone look unhappy or uncomfortable? Do you see any sign that things aren't going well?"

In a pouty voice she responded, "No, I guess not."

I chuckled. "Then take a second to just enjoy this. You know that Char is looking out for the new girl, and that he's got everything covered."

I leaned down and gave her a light kiss on her head, feeling her take a deep breath in and out to relax. I couldn't see her face seeing as she was facing away from me, but I could feel the tension bleed out of her. Since she was standing slightly in front of me with my arm around her shoulder, that deep breath made her body expand deeper into me. Her ass pressed and rubbed against me, and my hand hovering above her chest brushed against the exposed skin. Her breath out was slow and torturous, making all the blood in my body flow below my waistline.

I also realized, too late, that she was doing it on purpose. A deep growl vibrated in my throat when I figured that out and I watched as goosebumps rose on her arms at the sound. She took another deep breath in, and that time I "casually" moved directly behind her, making it possible for me to slip both my arms over her chest. She reached up and held on to my hands, leaning back into me. If anyone looked at us, it would seem like we were posing for a romantic picture.

We both knew better. I let my fingertips graze her already hard nipples lightly and pressed my hips harder into her ass. I could feel her heart beating hard and I whispered into her ear to up the ante a little more.

"You're so fucking naughty Callie. I bet you've been soaking wet since you decided to skip the panties. If you didn't have to stay out here and mingle I'd already have you in a closet or bathroom stall, balls deep in your tight little pussy until you were screaming my name."

A small moan escaped her and I placed an open-mouthed kiss on her neck before stepping away, my hands a deliberate caress as they left her. She threw a dark, erotic look over her shoulder at me before straightening her body and heading to the microphone that was on a raised platform.

She cleared her throat as she leaned towards the mic. I'd followed her but stood off to the side to watch her. I was still hard from our little interaction so I tried to angle myself so that no one noticed. I saw her smirk at me, glancing at my crotch once to let me know she could see what effect our interaction had on me.

"Good evening everyone! I wanted to thank you all for coming tonight and showing your interest and support. It's nearing the end of the night, so I just wanted to say a few words before letting you do your thing. Eros is the brainchild of myself, my best friend Charles, and a little too many tequila shots." She paused here to let everyone laugh at her little joke and I grinned in encouragement when she glanced at me.

"I know our services are a little different than other dating avenues out there, and your willingness to try it out only proves how many people are serious about finding that certain someone to spend their time with, to go on adventures with, to love."

She glanced down at me when she said the last part and my breath caught at the meaning behind those words. She held my gaze for a few seconds and then looked back out at the crowd before continuing.

"I hope that you are all able to find that person, with or without this company helping you out. If you're here, then you're taking the search just as seriously as anyone should and I will do what I can to help you find your person.

"In closing, I'd like to remind you not to forget your personalized gift bags; inside you will find a few surprises that I hope you take advantage of soon," she said with a dramatic wink, making several whispers of excitement rise up from the crowd. "Have a lovely evening, and good luck to you all!"

Applause rang out through the crowd as I helped Callie step off the stage. I pressed a kiss against her lips and let it linger without going deeper.

"You were fantastic up there. Short, sweet, and to the point."

"You really think so? God, I just get so nervous. If I didn't have your dirty words going through my mind to distract me from everyone staring I probably would've passed out."

I leaned closer so that only she would hear me. "In that case, just let me know anytime you need a distraction; I'm more than happy to help out."

"I just bet you are," Callie teased as she pressed her hips into mine, feeling how hard I was still. "I think we could leave the rest of this to Char and the cleanup crew, yeah?"

Her breathy words had me dragging her towards the doors. She laughed behind me, calling out a hasty farewell to Char as we passed him. He grinned and gave us a thumbs up, making some of the people who witnessed our leaving laugh at my obvious eagerness to leave.

Her place was closer, so we drove there, the sexual tension in the air nearly making me pull over and take care of the first round on the side of the road. A small giggle escaped Callie but I kept my gaze on the road. I heard another giggle, and then she burst into a fit of them. I looked over, and she was curled in on herself, shaking with laughter.

Despite the desire coursing through me still, I couldn't help but chuckle with her. She lifted her head and wiped away a few tears.

"I can't believe I just let you drag me out of that event like a caveman. In front of my clients! And your face is so serious, I just can't... I couldn't stop myself!" She burst into more laughter and I realized how ridiculous we'd probably looked and was soon laughing right with her. By the time I parked at her place, we were both trying to catch our breath between laughs.

I turned my car off and we looked at each other, shaking our heads at ourselves. Slowly, the air thickened again and heated looks replaced the smiles. Callie unbuckled her seatbelt and leaned across the distance separating us. We kissed slowly, but no less intensely. She pulled away and looked me deep in my eyes. I brushed my hand against her thigh and her eyes fluttered shut before snapping back open.

"Aidan," she started and then stopped, biting her lip.

I didn't say anything, willing her with everything in me to say the words I could see forming on her lips. I wasn't thinking of Aphrodite, or the vow that got us here, only of my need to hear those words from her. I help my breath as she started again.

"Aidan, I... need you. Please take me upstairs and fuck me like you promised earlier."

Disappointment ran through me, but I didn't let it show. When she was ready she'd tell me what we both already knew.

"No, Callie. I won't fuck you." Shock blazed across her face and she started to back away, embarrassed. I tightened my hand on her thigh, pulling her back to me for another kiss. When she was nearly melting into my arms, I pulled away. "I won't fuck you because, tonight, I'm going to take you upstairs and make love to you." I was going to prove with my body that I loved her, and since she wouldn't say the words I was going to let her just show me.

Her eyes misted, but she nodded. I got out of the car and opened her door for her when I got around to her side. I held my hand out to help her up, and I brought her close into my side as we made our way to her place. I could see hear hands shaking slightly as she unlocked her door and we made our way inside.

She led me to her room and we slowly stripped together, watching with desire licking at our heels. I picked her up when we were both bare, setting her in the middle of her bed and moving until I straddled her. I kissed her all over her body, worshipping her with my lips until she was wordlessly begging me to be inside her. I slowly pushed inside her, inch by thick inch. Sweat covered us as we moved together in tandem, the only sounds were quiet moans and sighs, never breaking eye contact even as we hit the peak of pleasure together. We kissed as we came down, lazy and content.

I turned onto my back, pulling her with me so that I stayed inside her even as I softened, not wanting to break contact at all. She curled into me and hummed with content. I could feel her heart beating strongly against my chest and knew she felt mine doing the same under her hand. Moments passed in quiet content and I kissed the top of her head, murmuring a barely coherent "I love you" into her hair once more before drifting off to sleep.

CHAPTER FORTY
CALLIE

"I'm sorry I had to leave before you woke up, but I've got a morning meeting at the center I can't miss. I'd love to see you later if you've got time. Text me. I love you, Aidan. P.S. here's a key to my place. I meant to give it to you last night but something distracted me ;)"

I read the note Aidan had left on my kitchen counter again, smiling happily at it. Not that I needed any more distractions at work, but this one was definitely my favorite at the moment. I'd thought about leaving it at home, but I hadn't been able to in the end. I'd taped it to the base of my computer in plain sight. I couldn't stop the smile crossing my face every time I read it.

Guilt seeped through me at not having told Aidan I loved him last night. Whatever had stopped me from saying the words before had hit me again right as I went to tell him, and I found myself saying something else. Aidan had tried to hide his reaction, but I could see in his eyes that he'd wanted me to say those three words, so simple and yet so difficult for me.

But after the way we made love last night, I was determined to tell him tonight, when I saw him. I'd texted him after reading the note, letting him know I was free and I'd love to see him. We had plans set to meet at his house around six, and he told me to go on in to his place if I got there first.

I was planning to surprise him with dinner, so I was leaving work early in order to go home and make it, get ready, and get everything set up before he got there. I yawned, glancing at the clock. Staying up late worrying about all of this, not to mention all the sex, had wiped me out. I'd stayed awake for several hours last night after Aidan had fallen asleep, berating myself for not being able to tell him.

Only two more hours, I told myself repeatedly. *Get some shit done and then you're free to go.* I cracked my neck and put all thoughts of Aidan out of my head until that hand on the clock hit 3 P.M.

I proudly looked at my dinner display on Aidan's dining room table. I checked my phone, seeing that it was already ten minutes past seven. He'd texted me around the same time I got home saying he needed to change the time to seven instead of six. I'd agreed readily, since I'd spent more time at the store than I'd planned on.

I was glad he wasn't here yet since I still had to change out of my dirty clothes, but I was also a little worried since I hadn't heard from him. I was running a last layer of mascara on when my phone started to ring. I hurried to answer it, seeing Aidan's name lit up on the display.

"Hey!" I chirped the word, leaning towards the mirror to continue my makeup with one hand. "You almost here?"

"Not quite. I'm so sorry Callie, but we had a small issue here at the center and I have to stay and clear some things before I can head home. I'm hoping it won't take too long, but it could be a couple hours."

I looked at myself in the mirror, a frown apparent on my face. "Are you alright? What happened?"

"I'll tell you about it when I come home, but I'm okay. Don't worry about me, I'll be there as fast as I can."

"Okay, I understand. Do what you have to."

"Thanks baby. Love you."

He hung up and I sighed into the empty room. *Guess I better go put the food in the oven to keep it warm,* I thought to myself. I was disappointed, sure, but I knew that whatever was keeping him from leaving had to be important. I carefully placed everything either in the fridge or oven and decided to take another look around while I waited.

I poured myself a drink and padded around his house, admiring how clean and neat everything was. I ended up in the basement, half-heartedly playing the pinball machine that I found. I eventually moved to the couch, flipping through channels. I landed on a re-run of *Bones* so I watched it, checking my phone periodically to see if I had somehow missed any updates from Aidan.

Two hours passed, and I found myself dozing off to the sound of a paper towel commercial, my lack of sleep catching up to me suddenly.

I woke up when I felt myself being lifted in the air by a warm, muscled body. I started to protest before Aidan hushed me with a soft kiss. I was still drowsy, so I drifted off slightly until Aidan placed me in his bed. I tried to sit up and talk, but Aidan's words stopped me.

"Shh, baby. I'm sorry it took me so long. The food smelled and looked incredible, and I'm sorry we didn't get to it tonight. I put it all away for us to eat tomorrow. Go back to sleep, we can talk later."

I think I nodded, but I was already falling back asleep so I couldn't be sure. I felt Aidan climb into bed behind me, feeling his bare chest against my back as he spooned me.

He must've helped me out of my clothes, I thought dreamily before passing out completely.

CHAPTER FORTY-ONE
CALLIE

I woke up suddenly, jerking into a sitting position, making the blankets fly off. I looked around and realized I was in Aidan's bed still, and the foggy memory of him coming home after I fell asleep returned. I felt the empty space next to me, noticing it was still warm so I figured Aidan hadn't been gone long.

I looked at the alarm clock nearby, noticing it was about four in the morning. I debated about whether I should go back to sleep, wait for Aidan to come back, or just go find him. I wasn't really tired anymore, and I was too fidgety to just wait.

Decision made, I hopped out of the bed and went over to the bag I'd packed after work. I pulled out a tank top and pair of shorts, along with some fuzzy socks so my feet would warm up. I stood in the hallway, listening for Aidan but didn't hear anything to indicate where he was.

I moved down towards the living room and peered through the darkness to see if he was on the couch. Nothing. I moved over to the big glass doors and opened them to peek outside, and nothing. As I moved back inside and locked the door shut, I heard a voice. It sounded like Aidan was in the basement, which would made sense if he was trying not to wake me up. I walked over to the door and opened it, hearing Aidan's voice clearly now. He paused for a moment then replied so I guessed he was on the phone.

I couldn't hear what he was saying, but I could tell he was upset about something. Maybe about whatever had happened at the center? I started to move down the stairs, thankful that the socks helped muffle my steps since I didn't want to disturb him. I paused in the middle of the stairs when I could make out the words he was saying- and when I did, I almost wished I had just gone back to sleep instead of going to find him.

"I don't want to do this anymore. It's not fair to Callie, and it's not fair to me.... I won't. I'm going to tell Callie the truth."

My mouth was wide open, legs clutched to my chest after I sat in the stairwell and listened as he paused for a second, then continued.

"Yes. I'm going to tell Callie that this whole thing was a lie, that the first time we met was that day she woke up in the hospital, and that I've only been doing this because of some stupid vow she made and then YOU thought I'd be the perfect tool to break that vow."

What. The. Fuck. I stood up slowly, not wanting to hear anything else. My head pounded in confusion, and I moved silently up the stairs, shaking as I shut the door. It clicked louder than I'd anticipated, and I cringed, waiting for Aidan to come through any second now. I only heard his muffled voice come through the door, so I hurried through the living room to get back to the bedroom, trying to make sense of what I'd heard.

My foot caught the edge of a table I hadn't seen through the tears gathering in my eyes, and I let out a quiet sound of alarm as I fell. My knees and hands hit the carpet at the same time, and the shock that went through my body must have jogged something loose in my brain because suddenly images flooded my senses.

"God Callie, are you even listening to me?" Ellinor protested loudly into my ear, jerking me back to our phone call. The walk

277

signal came on, and I started to cross the street. Thankfully it was almost dark, so there weren't many people to maneuver around.

"Yeah, sorry sis. I was... Nevermind. What were you saying?"

"I was saying that you probably don't even need to worry about it. It's probably just a fluke or something."

"I don't think so. It felt too real to be rand-" My last word ended on a yelp as I stepped onto the opposite curb weirdly, twisting my ankle and completely losing my balance. Suddenly everything went into slow-motion as I fell. My smoothie arced in the air and I watched it come back down, right into the face of an oncoming skateboarder, all while I fell straight into a parking meter. I watched, horrified, as the skateboarder swerved and lost his balance when the shock of the ice-cold drink hit him and then my forehead smashed into the meter.

"Fuck!"

"Shit!" We exclaimed profanities at the same time on impact, and I lost sight of him as my vision went black for a few moments. I came back to consciousness for a second, only to find him lightly shaking my arm to get my attention. As I made eye contact with him, the hot pain from the other day spread in my chest again. Oh hell no, I thought to myself right before I completely passed out at the combination of the head impact and the pain in my chest.

I gasped, realizing one of my memories had come back. I must've gone to the hospital right after that, where I woke up with a concussion. *Was it a concussion though?* That kernel of doubt had me focusing again on the influx of memory. The talk with my parents flashed through my mind, the foolish vow I'd made making the same heat pulse in my chest again.

I was still on my hands and knees on the floor, and I tried to stand up to get to the bedroom as more awareness flashed through me. I definitely hadn't been dating Aidan at all, much less for months, and what he'd said on the phone was true-the first time we'd met was in the hospital when I woke up if we didn't count the part where my smoothie ended up all over him. I realized that he was the skateboarder that had been involved in my little accident, and I assumed that's how he'd ended up with me at the hospital in the first place.

Aidan's words, *"this whole thing is a lie"*, repeated itself through my mind and I didn't realize I was sobbing against a wall until a hand settled on my shoulder. I knew it was Aidan, and my heart's broken pieces throbbed while I tried to calm down.

"Callie, what's the matter? What happened?"

Tears streamed down my face as I lifted my head to face him. It took all of my strength not to break down again at the worry on his face. It wasn't real. *This whole thing is a lie. This whole thing is a lie.*

"Talk to me Callie, for the love of all that is holy, tell me what's wrong!"

"You," I brokenly whispered.

Confusion flooded his face. "What do you mean?"

"I know, Aidan." My voice got stronger as the tears started to dry and anger replaced them. "I fucking heard you on the phone, saying everything between us isn't real. When I fell trying to get away, I got my memory back. I remember every-fucking-thing Aidan."

I watched as his face slowly morphed from confusion to awareness- and then went stark white as all the blood drained from his face. He reached for me and I slapped his hands away.

"Don't touch me! You lied to me, you tricked me. You tricked my family!" I got even angrier when I felt tears start to well again. "You made me like your friends, made me believe that you loved me. And then you did the one thing I thought I could never do before ripping my heart out!" My voice went hoarse and broken with my final declaration as sadness overwhelmed me again. "You made me love you, Aidan."

A second after the words spilled from me, we both cried out loudly. The exact same pain from when I made the vow that started all this, burned through my chest as I collapsed onto the carpet again. I breathed through it and looked to Aidan to see him clutching his bare chest.

"What the hell was that?" He was panting as the fire ebbed and he stood on shaky legs, moving to me to help me up. When I flinched away from him, he slowly dropped his hand and pain filled his eyes. I looked away, using the wall to get back up and locked my knees, leaning back and breathing slowly to clear my mind.

"When I made the vow... That same thing happened. Which I guess means that now the vow has broken." My voice was dead. I pushed off the wall and met Aidan's eyes. They were pleading, in pain. My heart reached out to comfort him but I beat it back. I hardened my gaze and stood straight, willing my voice to stay strong.

"Callie, I..." He trailed off when I shook my head sharply.

"Don't, Aidan. I'm leaving. Don't call me, don't come to my place to find me. Stay away from my family. I don't want to hear your excuses right now. I don't know if or when I'll be ready to see you again so just... please, stay away."

His body stiffened until he was as still as granite as he took my words in. His cheeks flushed, and I watched as shutters came over his eyes. "Fine," he barked out. "Just go then Calliope, leave. If you don't want to listen to what I have to say, then I guess that's it." He turned sharply and grabbed his wallet and keys from a dish by the entry way, slamming the door shut behind him.

I heard his car start and his tires squealed as he tore out of the driveway. I stood there numbly for several minutes before I went and gathered all my stuff. I took the dishes with all the food I'd made with me, so that neither of us would have to worry about getting them returned.

I locked up Aidan's house, leaving the key in the mailbox for him. I drove away, not realizing where I was going until I was already parked in front of my sister's apartment. I contemplated turning around and going home, but I couldn't make myself turn the car back on to leave. I don't know how long I sat there, but I felt so dead inside that I didn't even jump when a sharp knock sounded on my window. I turned and saw Ellinor in her running gear, taking headphones out of her ears.

"Callie? Is everything okay?"

A burst of humorless laughter left me as I opened my door and stepped out. "You ever heard of Matt Baker? He writes these short poems... Anyway, he's got one that perfectly describes me right now. 'I have a very intelligent mind but a goddamn stupid heart'."

Worry overcame her, and that was the needle on my emotional haystack. Tears filled my eyes again as I lowered my head and she hurried to me. She pulled me into her arms and I collapsed into her, sobbing on her shoulder while she rubbed my back, trying to comfort me in a broken voice of her own.

CHAPTER FORTY-TWO
AIDAN

I ignored the pounding on my locked office door, cringing when Lucy's voice blasted through. I'd been avoiding her all day, not wanting to talk to anyone while I was in this mood.

"I swear if you don't let me in here right this second I'm going to kick the damn thing down!"

It was solid oak, so I doubted she'd be able to get through but I wouldn't put it past her to try. I groaned, rubbing my temples as she kept knocking and knocking.

"God! Fine! Give me a damn second!" I yelled the words and walked over to the door, yanking it open to glare at Lucy.

Her narrowed eyes widened as she took me in. I knew I looked like a mess; my hair had knots galore and my scruff was longer than normal, only wearing sweatpants and a ratty t-shirt I'd found in my car. I hadn't found any shoes in my car so I was barefoot at the moment, only adding to the whole "homeless" look.

"Shit."

I laughed humorlessly. "What, you don't like the new look? I thought it might fit in with some of the people down at the center, make them warm up a little faster. No? Don't think so?"

"Cut it out Aidan. I know you only turn into a dick when you're hurting. And I'm assuming it has to do with Callie."

Instead of answering I headed back to my desk and sat in the chair. Lucy didn't bother to shut the door behind her since it was now late at night and we were the only ones here. She stood in front of my desk, arms folded across her chest as she waited. I scrubbed a hand over my face and through my hair, grunting when my fingers got caught in the tangles and I had to push through them.

"Alright, I'm sorry. I wasn't trying to be an asshole."

"Yeah I know. So what's going on? It might help to have a female's point of view to talk through it."

"I'm not sure you'll believe me even if I told you. This is more… complicated than most relationship issues."

She raised an eyebrow and sat down in the nearest chair. "Try me."

"You asked for it." I relayed the whole story, starting from the smoothie hitting me in the face all the way to when I stormed out of my own house, leaving Callie on her own.

Silence filled the office as Lucy took it all in. She hadn't interrupted at all, but I watched the disbelief on her face turn into curiosity, and a hundred of other emotions over the course of my story. I waited with bated breath to hear what she had to say.

"Well, you weren't wrong."

"What's that?"

"This is definitely more complicated than normal relationships."

"Fuckin' tell me about it."

I leaned back in my chair to stare at the ceiling, twisting the chair from side to side while I waited for her input.

"So, an actual, real-life goddess?" I tilted my head back down to look at her, my first real smile in hours pulling at my lips at the incredulous look on her face.

"As hard to believe as it is, yeah. If I wasn't obsessed with Greek mythology and had all of that shit put into my brain about Callie and her family, I wouldn't have believed it myself."

"No kidding. I mean, it's hard to believe but I guess crazier things have happened." She tapped her fingers on her chin, thinking everything through. "First of all, this sucks ass for both of you. The only real winner here is Aphrodite."

Anger bubbled inside me all over again at those words. I had been thinking the same thing. I wasn't mad at Callie for leaving, or for wanting me to leave her alone. I mean, I was definitely frustrated that she hadn't given me a chance to talk to her about it but I did understand. I'm sure whatever she heard of my conversation with Aphrodite didn't make me look good at all. Besides, how would Callie know I was on the phone with the Greek goddess of love herself?

"Aidan, do you not understand the result of this if Callie doesn't say she loves you by midnight tomorrow?"

"Yeah I get it, but Callie is more important to me than the family that left me behind. I'd rather live my life with Callie and not know them, than to lose her and find them."

"You have no idea." She shook her head and mumbled something I couldn't understand.

"I don't want to do this anymore. It's not fair to Callie, and it's not fair to me."

"Fair? When has life ever been fair? You need to finish this."

"I won't. I'm going to tell Callie the truth."

"Oh you are?"

"Yes. I'm going to tell Callie that this whole thing was a lie, that the first time we met was that day she woke up in the hospital, and that I've only been doing this because of some stupid vow she made and YOU thought I'd be the perfect tool to break that vow."

"If you tell her, I can guarantee that she is going to feel betrayed, and she'll leave you anyway. You've gone too far to back out now.

284

I've been watching, and I know that she feels it. She's almost told you three times already! Just get her to confess, and the bond will break and you'll both be free to work everything out."

"I'm not stupid! As soon as she tells me I bet the bond will break and she's going to remember everything anyway. And that only leaves me with her knowing everything before I can tell her. Which makes me look worse! I think there's something you're not telling me. Because I've studied mythology, and I know that everything comes at a price. What happens when this expires? What happens to YOU if she fails to tell me she loves me by the deadline?"

An image of Aphrodite ripped through my mind. Fury ripped across her face, turning her beauty into something terrible before she realized her temper was getting the better of her. Ice shards formed in her eyes, almost cutting me physically as I felt the hardness of her next words   "That, dear human, is none of your concern. If you do not succeed, then I will make sure everything you have worked for falls apart. I do not care to be made a fool of. Get her to say she loves you, or else."

The vision of her faded and my basement came back into view. In fury I punched the wall, leaving a huge hole that reflected the one in my heart. I walked back upstairs, and that's when I heard Callie crying, only to leave my house minutes later with nothing left of my heart.

"Lucy, I don't know what to do." My voice gave away what a mess my emotions were.

"I can't tell you what to do. I think that it'd be good to give Callie a little time like she asked for, that way she can sort through everything and get her head on straight."

I nodded miserably. Every fiber of my being screamed at me to go after her, make her listen, make her believe that I didn't mean to hurt her. But I knew that if I went now I would only make things worse. I got up from my chair and headed towards the window, staring out at the lights of Denver and picturing Callie's face before I left. Lucy came and stood next to me, touching my shoulder softly to get my attention.

"I know that you love her. I could see it before you did, and I still see it. I know that Aphrodite has nothing to do with how you and Callie feel about each other. She wasn't the reason you fell in love, she only put you two together. Give Callie a little time, and then go get her back."

Her words lifted a burden from me, I *had* been wondering if all these feelings were a product of the vow instead of being something legitimate. I was sure Callie was wondering the same thing and the next time I saw her I was going to prove that I loved her because of her, and not some shitty trick of the gods.

I could feel the determination to fix things welling inside me, beginning to displace all the misery. A plan formed in my mind, and I hurried back to my desk to start writing things down so I wouldn't forget. It wasn't until Lucy chuckled that I remembered she was still there.

"I see you're getting back to the Aidan I know." She came over and I stood to give her a hug, squeezing a little too hard. "Ow! Geez, don't break a rib!"

"Sorry," I said and let her go with a crooked smile.

"No worries. I hope you work things out with Callie, I really like her and I don't want it to be awkward when we hang out."

"Well if you'd leave I could get started on that," I intoned as I sat back down, grabbing my pen and scribbling some more.

"Whatever. Good luck!" I waved her off without looking up and grinned at the paper as I planned.

CHAPTER FORTY-THREE
CALLIE

"What the hell do you mean *you knew!*" I was standing in my parent's living room after leaving Ellinor's place, fists clenched at my sides and betrayal sweeping through me.

"What, you think we're just going to trust some guy that says you've been dating for three months who we've never heard about? We know you better than that." My mom rolled her eyes.

"Okay but that doesn't explain why you would let him trick me into thinking that we were together, that we were in love! You knew he was lying and you went along with it anyway! How could you choose some random guy over your own daughter?"

"Calliope, *sit down*. I will not let you talk to your mother like that, and you will listen to us!"

The tone in my father's voice brooked no argument, and the little girl in me that hated to be reprimanded took over. I sat on the couch without saying anything else.

My mom spoke first. "I know you're hurting sweetheart. And I'm so sorry. If we could do anything to take that away from you, we would. When we first arrived at the hospital, we talked to one of the paramedics that rode with you in the ambulance. He said that you were in an induced coma to watch for swelling, but that your boyfriend had ridden over with you and was currently in the waiting room.

"I admit it was surprising to hear at first, and Ellinor said that he must be talking about the guy that she'd talked to on the phone and called the ambulance for you. So we went down to the waiting room since we couldn't do anything for you at the moment. We saw him sleeping and muttering to himself. We only understood one word- 'Aphrodite' and we knew instantly what was happening."

"Wait, how did you know what was going on?" I asked curiously, my anger forgotten temporarily.

My parents looked at each other and then back at me, smiles with secrets behind them on their faces. "You already know we're both from a line of oracles," my dad said, "so how do you think we ended up together? Foolish promises from both of us, and gods with a sense of humor."

"What? But you guys always said that you met on a boating excursion in Greece."

"We did, but it's not technically the beginning of our story," my mom said shrugging. "Someday we'll tell all you kids about it, but not until the time is right."

I was confused, but I had bigger concerns at the moment.

"Do you want to hear the rest of the story or not?" My dad asked, distracting me from trying to figure anything out, and I nodded.

"Only a few moments went by after we heard the goddess's name, and he woke up in a sweat, groaning as new information filtered in. What I mean," my dad clarified before I could ask, "is that Aphrodite provided him with enough knowledge about you and your relationships so that he could pull off the ruse he'd been forced into."

"Yeah, it's really uncomfortable," my mom added and my dad nodded along.

I wanted to ask what they meant about Aidan being forced into the situation, but my mom continued before I could.

"We needed to talk to Aidan, but we couldn't let Ellinor know what was happening so we sent her up to your room and had a chat with Aidan. We told him we knew, and he promised to do the best he could. He seemed so miserable, but trustworthy, so we told him we'd go along with whatever he said."

Anger rose again at the thought that they'd willingly played along with the whole thing. Then something they said clicked. "What do you mean he seemed miserable?"

"Well first of all, he was undoubtedly overwhelmed with everything, but besides that, he didn't seem to want to do it. Calliope," my dad said gently. "Sometimes we aren't given a choice. And when gods and goddesses get involved, it is highly likely that they are holding something against the people involved. In this case, I think that Aphrodite gave Aidan an ultimatum, something that made him agree to the charade."

My mom jumped back in. "Think about it Callie. Is there anything about Aidan that would make you think that he tricked you for the fun of it? Because even with the small amount of time we've spent with him, he didn't seem like the kind of person to want to hurt you."

I sat back into the couch, thinking about everything they'd told me. Logically, I knew that they were right. It made sense, and I agreed that Aidan seemed like a genuine guy who wouldn't do that unless someone coerced him. But my heart seized at the thought of seeing him again.

Although I knew that he said he loved me, and that I thought I loved him, now I couldn't be sure. What if Aphrodite had done something to make us think that, instead of trusting us to actually fall in love in three weeks? It seemed impossible. I couldn't let Aidan back in until I'd figured out if my love for him was real or not.

I sighed, standing back up. My parents followed, concern and love shining in their eyes. I gave them each a hug, trying not to tear up again. I was so sick of crying.

"Thank you for telling me. I have a lot to think about, and although I'm still hurt, I love you guys. I know it's not your fault, and that I'm the one that got everybody into this mess."

"Take whatever time you need, Calliope. We love you too," my dad said.

"Also," my mom chimed in before I opened the door, "we think you guys could be good together. Either way we just want you to be happy."

"Thank you," I whispered before stepping out and heading to my car. I drove home with the radio off for once, wanting to think about things before making a decision. It'd been a long, exhausting day and I'd been up since my fight with Aidan that morning. My head was muddled with too many tears. As soon as I collapsed into bed, I was out and sleeping dreamlessly.

"Holy. Shit." Char was looking at me with wonder, and it made a small giggle escape. I'd just told him everything that happened, and he'd been entranced with the story. He'd always been pretty accepting of things that seemed out of the ordinary, and I didn't think I could keep the truth from him anyway so I decided to tell him.

We were currently eating some takeout at the office, just the two of us. Since it was Friday, we'd told her to take the day off since there wasn't much going on that the two of us couldn't handle.

"Yeah, holy shit is about right," I replied and took a bite of an eggroll.

A sly grin crossed Char's face and I hesitated to ask what he was thinking. "Okay, what is it?"

"Well, it's probably not the best timing for the joke…"

"Oh God. Okay, just give it to me." I braced myself, not having a clue what was about to come out of Char's mouth.

"You asked for it. I was just going to say… It seems like you and Aidan… were a match made in heaven."

I choked on the bite of eggroll I was swallowing. It was a terrible joke, but I couldn't deny that it was funny. I laughed for real, glad that I had a best friend that was able to bring me out of my heartbreak funk even for a little.

"You're right, your timing is terrible. But I'll forgive you for it."

Char grinned sheepishly. "I couldn't help myself. I'm just glad it made you laugh instead of cry."

I sobered a bit. "Yeah, me too." We ate in silence until we pushed the cartons away and sank into the couch. Char took my hand in his like he tended to do when we relaxed next to each other. It was comforting and soothed the jumbled mess inside me.

"So… where does all that leave you and Aidan?"

I shrugged, watching as Char traced my knuckles with his other hand. "I honestly have no idea. Part of me understands that it wasn't his fault. But the part of me that keeps repeating the words he said can't let it go. I don't want to think that he lied about loving me…"

"But it's hard not to. I get it. And you haven't heard anything from him?"

"No, but I told him to leave me alone. I don't know if I'm relieved or disappointed that he listened to me."

Our office door opening interrupted the conversation, and Char went to see who it was. I checked my phone, seeing that it was only a few minutes before we were supposed to close so I hoped that whoever it was wouldn't be here long. I listened and heard Char talking to someone but I couldn't tell what about.

"Thanks, have a great day!" I heard Char speak, and then the door opened and closed. I sat up, wondering who it was.

"Good news and bad news," he said as he came back in the room, a small box in his hand. "Which do you want first?"

"Uh, bad news?"

"It seems as though Aidan didn't listen to you *completely*," he handed the box to me while telling me.

I read the tag attached to the ribbon tying the box shut, and my heart sped at the words. *Read it. -A*

"And what's the good news?" My voice was shaky, and I was mostly stalling opening the gift.

"That he didn't listen to you completely," he smirked.

"You're the worst sometimes."

"I know." We grinned at each other, and then Char looked down to the box. "You gonna open it or what? I'm dying here."

"Should I?" My hands shook as I caressed the silky ribbon. The box was thin and about the size of a business envelope.

"Hell yeah you should! If not for you, then for me."

I stared at the box for some time, debating with myself. *What would it hurt to open it?* I pinched the ends of the bow and pulled, untying the ribbon. I slipped it off, and then took a deep breath before lifting the lid. Inside, I saw a sheet of paper. I picked it up, unfolding it to read.

"I was breathless when you turned around
You left your mark on a fool like me
When I was hit I fell without a sound
I never saw what was coming you see.
It was love that had me and held so fast
I was trapped like a moth to the flame
Wise men have said true love never lasts
When in love you'll burn again and again.
I've often been told when falling in love
You should watch every step that you take
It's more like being dropped from above
With a heart left behind about to break.
Never make promises your heart cannot keep
And never give everything away unaware
Love can rob you of your sanity and sleep
And keep you spinning around in mid-air.
So I'm a fool in love with nowhere to go
Who gives his heart without a second glance
Will you return it to me all broken up so?
Or will you treat it gently like a second chance.
Ah! a fool and his love is always so parted
As wise men who know no better always say
It's inevitable and the fate of the broken hearted
But a fool deep in love knows no other way."

"Damnit, what does it say?" I looked up to Char through blurry eyes, and handed the poem over. I recognized it as the poem "I'm a Fool in Love" by D. Edward Barnett I'd found online once. I had it printed out in a notebook at home.

I watched Char as he read through it, his eyes misting as well. "This man loves you Callie. It's not an illusion; no man would lay his heart open like this for just anyone."

I hiccupped, trying to smother the sobbing that was trying to burst out of me. "What do I do Char? I'm so lost, and I love him so much, but I need more time. How do I keep him if I can't talk to him?"

"You take the time you need. Get away if you have to. I doubt that Aidan is going to give up on you, and things like this letter are not going to make it easier to clear your head."

Suddenly, I had an idea. "Are you sure you'll be okay if I leave? I mean, I just got back and I don't want to leave you and Allison hanging."

"Honestly love, you'll probably be useless here if all you can do is mope about. So yeah, get away from here for a few days. Turn your phone off if you have to. But keep in touch with me through email that way I know you're safe and can tell your family you are okay."

"Of course. So here's the idea I just had. Let me know what you think."

Chapter Forty-Four

Aidan

I'd been relatively calm up until now, parked in front of Callie's parent's house. I called them yesterday, wanting to clear the air as well as check up on Callie without bothering her. I know she'd said to stay away from her family, but I at least owed her parents an explanation. When I called them, they were more than willing to talk which was very relieving. It was good to know not everyone hated me.

I steeled myself and got out of the car, taking my time getting up to the front door. I only had to wait a few seconds after knocking for the door to open, and suddenly I Althea enveloped me in a hug. Stunned, I wasn't able to react until she pulled away.

"Please, come on in Aidan." I followed her into the front room where Hektor was coming towards me.

"Have a seat," he said after shaking my hand.

"Thank you for agreeing to hear me out," I said after settling into the nearest chair. "I'm assuming Callie's been here by now, and I wouldn't blame you for hating me right along with her."

"Oh honey," Alethea said sympathetically, "we don't hate you. Neither does Callie. She's just hurting."

I nodded once, my throat going tight. "I know. And I wanted to say I'm sorry for not being able to stop that from happening."

"You weren't given many options." Hektor grumbled the words, and I couldn't tell if the tone of voice was directed towards me or not.

"Can I ask you something?" My gaze moved back to Alethea's at her question.

"Feel free to ask me whatever you want."

"What was it that made you agree to go along with this?" Her question wasn't accusing in any way, only curious. I knew they deserved to hear the truth.

"A few years ago my adoptive parents passed away; Serena and Caleb Rikers were a blessing and I'll always be grateful for their guidance. I went through some pretty bad homes before they found me, and I was very lucky that I was able to find a good home. When they passed, they left me a letter encouraging me to find my biological parents, in order to find closure or something like that.

"Since then, I've been trying to find my parents but have had no luck. I'm not sure why, but they are proving very difficult to track. I want to find them, partly for myself, but also in respect of Serena and Caleb's wishes. So when Aphrodite came to me, she said that if I didn't agree to help, or if I didn't succeed in breaking Callie's vow within the given time frame, she would make sure I *never* found them."

Alethea and Hektor had slightly shell-shocked looks on their faces, and if I were in any other situation it would've been humorous.

"Did you tell Callie this?" Alethea's voice sounded choked, and I shook my head.

"She was very upset, which I don't blame her for at all. She wouldn't let me explain anything and I was so angry at how everything came out that I left instead of insisting that she listen to me."

"Oh Aidan, I'm so sorry." My throat constricted at the compassion in Alethea's voice, so I tipped my head towards her to acknowledge her sympathy.

"Well," Hektor started in a gruff voice, "I can't imagine that Callie would be so upset if she knew what you were up against. I think you should find her and make her listen. It worked for me." He smirked down at his wife, and she shot him a look full of love and amusement. I became very interested in hearing their story, but it wasn't the right time.

"That's what I was planning on. She told me to leave her alone, but I've been sending her small things to remind her of us. I haven't gotten a response yet, but hopefully it's softening her at least."

The two of them looked at each other, and then slowly back at me.

"What is it?" The expression on their faces made me think I was missing something very important. Hektor confirmed it with his next words.

"She's not in Colorado anymore. We don't know where she went, and Char is the only one that she's in contact with. We know she's safe, but that's it."

I sat frozen on the couch, taking in this new information. That meant she wasn't getting the little gifts that I'd had delivered to her office. So much for my fucking plan. I was so in my head that I didn't realize something new was happening until Hektor and Alethea stood up.

"Uh-oh," Alethea said nervously. I heard a car door slam and looked up at Callie's parents.

"What's going on?" I stood up and faced the door when I heard several voices outside.

"Brace yourself," Hektor replied, his voice slightly amused.

Before I could ask what that meant, three tall, built men burst in through the front door. They were all about my height, and each one had striking eyes that were hard to look away from. One had nearly silver eyes, and the other two, who were obviously twins, had one blue and green eye each. It didn't take me long to figure out that these were Callie's brothers and that they were pissed. At me.

Without a word, they started towards me and I straightened my spine, not giving an inch as they prowled my way. I knew they had a reason to be upset, but I wasn't going to lay down and take any shit without a fight.

"Boys," Hektor said warningly. The three men paused, glaring at me.

The tallest with the silver eyes spoke first. "Tell me why we shouldn't beat the shit out of him."

His voice was calm, but I heard the threads of anger in it, making me stiffen even further.

"Maybe because it's none of your business," I intoned in a bored voice. I wasn't going to look weak in front of them, but I had to get them engaged in order to avoid going straight into a brawl. I knew my words would piss them off, but I was hoping it would get them to talk to me.

One of the twins started towards me again, but the other held him back.

"It is our fucking business if you hurt our sister and made her leave the state because of a broken heart!" Silver-eyes' words sliced through my heart, and I made solid eye contact with all three before speaking again.

"I understand why you want to kick my ass. Trust me, if I had a sister, I'd feel the same way. I know you don't know me, but trust me when I say that I never wanted to hurt her. I made a mistake, but I'm going to fix it. I don't care how far she goes, or how much distance she tries to put between us, I'm going to find her and prove that I love her. I refuse to give up on her; on us."

They stared at me, silent and faces hard. We stood there for a few minutes, sizing each other up before Alethea broke it up.

"For the love of- stop it right now boys!" The four of us turned to her. "You three need to put your Neanderthal instincts away. There is more going on than you know about, so back off."

Her sons all looked surprised, then contrite as they nodded in agreement, relaxing enough to where I could breathe without thinking they were going to throw a punch.

"And you," she turned to me, "you go talk to Char and find my daughter. Bring her back, and bring her back happy."

"Yes ma'am," I said and grinned. "I'll stop by her office and talk to him tomorrow, since it's pretty late right now. But I promise to bring her back to you whether I'm by her side or not."

She came over and hugged me. "Ignore my boys, they're just a little over-protective," she whispered and I chuckled.

"I could take them," I whispered back and she chuckled.

I shook hands with Hektor, and then faced Callie's brothers. They were blocking my way out, and I raised an eyebrow at them, waiting for them to move.

Silver-eyes came towards me and lifted his hand. I tensed, ready for a hit, but he merely held out his hand. "Galen," he said.

I shook his hand, only wincing slightly at the tight grip. I decided not to mention that I already knew what their names were, thanks to all the information Aphrodite had given me at the beginning of this whole debacle. The other two came forward as well.

"Delphineas. I'm the better half," the brother with one right green eye and one left blue joked.

"Older does not mean better, twin. Xander," the other said. His eye colors were switched from his twin's, the right blue and left green.

"Aidan, as I'm sure you know. I wish our first meeting were under better circumstances," I shrugged, "but I've never really had good luck. Thanks for not killing me though."

The three of them reluctantly chuckled. "As long as Callie comes back happy, then all is forgiven." Delphineas and Galen nodded, agreeing with Xander's words.

"I'll do everything I can," I promised.

CHAPTER FORTY-FIVE
CALLIE

I padded into the kitchen, not bothering to smother my yawn since no one was around. I opened the fridge and stared at the contents until another yawn made my eyes water. I wasn't sleeping very well and I looked like it.

Four days ago I'd gotten on a flight to California. Specifically, back to Aidan's apartment out here. Only a week or two had passed since we left, so I could still smell him everywhere, which had made me cry randomly on my first day back. Thankfully, I'd been able to control it after a long conversation with Char and dinner with Beth.

I smiled at the thought of the sweet lady. After coming up with the idea of flying out, I'd given her a call and asked for her help. I didn't want Aidan to know where I was yet, but I needed somewhere to go. She hadn't hesitated, offering me either the apartment Lucy tended to stay in, the apartment I was currently in, and even a spare room at her place. After some deliberation, I decided that I wanted something familiar so she had an extra key for the penthouse made for me.

Dinner with her had been surprisingly relaxing. She hadn't asked many questions, waiting until I was comfortable to bring it up myself, which I did when she brought out giant bowls of mint cookies and cream ice cream. I didn't get into all the details, but she understood the gist of the problem. She'd promised not to tell Aidan I was here, but only as long as I gave him a chance to explain himself whenever he found me.

I pulled a yogurt out of the fridge and sat on the couch facing the big window savoring each bite. I'd immersed myself in as much work as possible but Char had sent me an email last night to give it a break and get outside. He knew I was avoiding thinking about everything that had made me leave Colorado, and I knew he was right that I needed to get out.

I groaned to myself, getting off the couch reluctantly and heading to the shower to make myself presentable to the public. An hour later I squinted into the sun, wishing I'd remembered to pack sunglasses. I kept my head down to avoid being blinded by the sunlight and headed out of the complex. I turned right and headed straight, having no idea where I was really going and hoping I wouldn't get lost since I hadn't brought my phone either.

I wonder how Aidan is doing. The thought was not a new one; I knew he'd been really upset when I last saw him, and then he'd sent me that poem. Char told me some other things had shown up for me at the office from Aidan. I'd told him to open them just to make sure it wasn't anything perishable, then leave them in my office for me. I could check them out when I got home.

My heart felt hollow. I wanted nothing more than to have Aidan here with me, but I was still so hurt from his betrayal. *You didn't even let him explain,* part of me cried out.

Yeah, because what kind of explanation would make me feel better about this? What could have possibly motivated him to go through with it? It just doesn't seem like the Aidan I got to know and fell in love with. So which Aidan is real?

I growled in frustration, accidentally scaring the person walking past me on the street. They jumped a little, and that made me finally become aware of my surroundings. I was near a little farmer's market, and I could smell kettle corn. I decided to investigate the source, and maybe take some time to look around while I was at it.

I was munching on some kettle corn and absent-mindedly checking out a stall of fruit when I accidentally bumped into something tall and solid. Jerking my head around, I realized it wasn't some*thing*, but some*one*. I looked all the way up a broad chest to one of the prettiest faces I've ever seen on a man. I swallowed hard, then began choking on a kernel of popcorn.

The man gave me a hard pat on my back, thankfully dislodging the obstruction to my airway and offering me an unopened bottle of water. I nodded gratefully, still wheezing as I sipped the water. He waited patiently until I was able to speak, a small smile on his face.

"Thank you, I think I almost just died." I tried to play off my embarrassment with a joke, and I was relieved when he chuckled.

"Don't thank me too much, if I hadn't surprised you then you wouldn't have choked in the first place."

"Hmm. You're right. In that case, watch where you're going buster! You don't want to be responsible for a woman's death-by-kettle-corn, do you?" My tone was mockingly upset, but I couldn't keep the smile off my face.

His lips spread slowly into a large grin, and a single dimple popped out in his right cheek. My humor faltered, that small reminder of Aidan bringing an unwelcome heaviness to the air between us.

"Hey, are you okay?" His face shifted quickly from amused to concerned, able to pick up on my change of mood.

"Yeah, I'm fine."

"Which means you're actually doing pretty terrible."

A shocked laugh escaped me, and my eyes widened at his forwardness. "I, uh…"

"It's alright, I've just been surrounded my whole life by women so I know the lingo." He paused, a contemplative look on his face. "What's his name?"

I flushed again, but for some reason found myself answering the question. "Aidan."

"Ah-ha, I was right about there being boy problems."

"What, have you caused a few of those in your life?"

His eyes sparkled with mischief, and a little something otherworldly that I must have imagined since his eyes went back to normal in the next second. "You could say that."

"Boys," I said and shook my head reprovingly, shoving some more popcorn in my mouth.

He chuckled again and shrugged. "We can't help ourselves. But sometimes we're worth it. If this is the first time that whatever he's done has hurt you, I'd say give him another chance. You seem like an intelligent woman, Callie. Don't let your heart stay broken if he has the means to fix it. 'My love, you have too many smiles left in you to be so sad'."

He quoted a line that I'd read many times before that Atticus, a philosopher, had said. Before I could respond, he stole a handful of popcorn and walked away with a small wave. It took me a few seconds to process not only how perfect his advice was for my situation, but the fact that he'd said my name. I knew for a fact that I'd never told him. I started after him, hurrying to catch up and demand to know how he knew my name, but as I rounded the same corner he'd turned down, I gaped at the deserted, dead ended alleyway.

What the… Where'd he go? I stood there for several minutes, absentmindedly eating the popcorn until I hit the bottom of the bag. I turned back around and headed towards the farmer's market and noticed that most of the booths were packing up. Still completely mystified as to what just happened, I threw my empty bag away and headed back to the apartment. Ignoring the fact that some random dude knew my name and then vanished into thin air, his advice was something to think about.

Don't let your heart stay broken if he has the means to fix it.

Maybe I should just let Aidan try. No more thinking and worrying about it. Just dive into the situation, even if it's unpleasant. I mean, it's not like I could be any more heartbroken than I was right now. I mulled that thought over the rest of the way back to the apartment. Walking into the empty space, I almost caved then and there to head back home and talk to Aidan. Or even pick up the phone and call him.

I stood by the closed elevator doors, trying to make up my mind. In the end, I figured I'd sleep on it and decide in the morning. Resolved and comfortable with my decision for the moment, I grabbed a bottle of water from the fridge and sat at my laptop resting on the kitchen bar. I swiveled the stool top as I waited for my computer to log in and checked my email.

I noticed a new one from Char, and the title made my heart skip a beat. GUESS WHO STOPPED BY TODAY. I quickly clicked on it and ate up the words.

"That's right, your sad-but-still-delicious hunk came by the office. He said he talked to your parents yesterday and they told him I was the only one in contact with you. I said I had no idea where you were, but he told me 'That's not why I'm here' so then I was like 'Well I'm taken, sorry'. Poor thing barely cracked a smile, and everyone knows my jokes are hilarious. 'Can you just pass on a message to her for me' he said so I told him sure. He wanted to let you know to stay put wherever you are, because he's going to find you and spank you until you decide to listen to what he has to say.

I'd let him spank me anyway tbh, but I digress. Anyway, just lettin'
you know your man is crushed but he's still full of fire for you-and
he's coming for you. Love ya."

Char's side comments made me laugh, but I could feel the
passion behind Aidan's message for me even from miles away
and that made my heart beat furiously. And yes, I was just
going to ignore how wet I'd gotten at the promise of a
spanking. I scolded my body, telling it to calm down. Yet, I
couldn't deny the happiness that filled me now. Change of
plans- I was definitely staying here, and I would wait for
Aidan to find me. I grinned suddenly, ready for whatever was
coming.

CHAPTER FORTY-SIX

APHRODITE

"You did what?!" I wasn't sure if I should be laughing or yelling at my son.

"I said, I stopped by Earth to chat with Callie. She seems like a very nice girl," Eros calmly replied and brushed off his tunic.

"I'm sure she is. But why does that matter? The vow is broken, and I'm free to go on about my life like nothing had ever threatened it."

"Yes, but it was a seriously close call, Mother." Suddenly his face and body went still and cold, like a statue.

"Oh, shove off. The outcome didn't worry me." I ignored the fact that the words were a bit of a lie when my name buzzed in my ears suddenly, and I shook my head to clear it. Odd.

"Sure you weren't. But there's more to the outcome of all this than where you end up. You do realize that both Aidan and Callie are hurting, broken just as much as that vow?"

A small pang of guilt hit me directly in the chest but I ignored it, as well as the call of my name again. "They're in love, they can't avoid each other forever. They'll end up finding a way."

"Not at this rate. That's why I went to see Callie. I wanted to make sure she was on the mend, but I could tell she's still running away from Aidan. I gave her some advice but I don't know if she'll listen to it before it's too late to mend the relationship."

"I've been watching them for weeks, I think I would know if their relationship could be saved or not. Plus, I know that- OH FOR ZUES' SAKE, WHO IS CALLING ME?"

Eros' face looked confused, but then his gaze traveled over my shoulder to where my vision cloud. I turned, expecting to see nothing. Shock ran through me when I noticed it was dark and stormy. I turned fully towards it and swiped my hand to clear it and accept the message that had been trying to come through.

I jumped slightly when Aidan's voice blasted through the room.

"Aphrodite! I know you hear me! If you don't get your ass down here I'm going to find a way to get to Olympus and-"

I sighed, tuning him out and faced Eros who was grinning from ear to ear. I noticed his one dimple that was identical to mine standing out and I sighed again, giving in to what I already knew he wanted me to do.

"Come with me then, son?"

CHAPTER FORTY-SEVEN
AIDAN

I was shouting Aphrodite's name, trying to get her attention and hoping that whatever had connected us while trying to break Callie's vow held enough to get her attention one last time. I was at the end of my rope and in the middle of an epic rant when my living room was suddenly occupied by two more people.

"What do you want?" Aphrodite's face was neutral, not giving anything away as to her thoughts on my demand to see her. Aphrodite and the man materializing in front of me so quickly had startled me, despite her presence being exactly what I'd wanted.

"Now, now, Mother. No need to be rude." The unknown male spoke, placing his hand on Aphrodite's back. He was wearing a wide grin, and I was so amazed to see that my shouting had worked that it took my brain a few seconds to register what he'd said.

"Mother? She's your mom? That would mean you're Cupid. Uh, I mean Eros."

"Eros is the technical term, and I prefer that over Cupid. Mostly because I'm not some air-headed cherub shooting people randomly with arrows." His dry humor caught me off guard, but I chuckled anyway. I was sure I should've been surprised, but at this point I didn't think anything could shock me.

"Yes, okay, enough with the pleasantries. I asked you what you wanted Aidan, so either tell me now or we can leave."

"NO! Please, just… I need your help. I can't find Callie, and I need to make her listen to me."

"How do you not know where she is by now? It's not like it's hard to figure out, just-"

"Mother." Eros stopped Aphrodite's words, and I nearly shouted at the interruption. He turned back to me. "Tell me Aidan, if given the choice, would you go back and refuse to comply with my mother's demands, knowing the current outcome?"

I paused to think about it, but only for a moment. "No," I said shaking my head, "I wouldn't. I love Callie and even though I wish I could've prepared her better for the truth of our relationship, I wouldn't change it. I need her by my side, but more than that, right now I just need her to be happy."

Aphrodite and Eros looked at each other, communicating silently. They nodded at the same time, and Aphrodite blew me a kiss before disappearing.

Panic gripped me. "Wait, isn't she going to help me?"

"No. But I am."

I nearly collapsed in relief, but I locked my knees to keep me upright. "How do I find her?"

"Honestly, when you figure it out you're going to kick yourself for not realizing sooner. If she's not in Colorado, how many more places does she have to go?"

"I don't know. I know she's always wanted to travel so she could be anywhere. But it's not like she'd ever left Colorado before I took her to California, so-"

I cut myself off abruptly, staring at Eros' satisfied expression. "You figure it out yet?"

"Fuck, you're right. I do want to kick myself." Relief rushed through me and came out on a choked sound. I knew exactly where she was.

Eros laughed and came over to clap me on the back. "Go get her back, Aidan. I've been watching over her, and she needs you just as much as you need her. Don't let her go."

"Thank you. I don't plan on it."

He disappeared at my reassurance, and I ran over to my laptop to book the next flight out to California.

"I'm coming for you, baby. Just hold on a few more hours," I whispered out loud as I clicked the confirmation for a flight leaving tomorrow, early Friday morning. I'd be in the same room as Callie in less than a day; and when I had her back, she was never going to want to leave.

CHAPTER FORTY-EIGHT
CALLIE

I juggled the bags of lingerie and groceries I'd picked up today as I tried to swipe the card for the penthouse. I swore softly when I almost lost a few apples, but managed to keep them in the bag while getting the elevator to start its ascent.

I was willing to wait for Aidan, somehow trusting that he would find me. However, I was getting antsy. I tried to stay out of the apartment as much as I could, and today I'd gone back to the shopping area that Lucy and I had been to while she was here. I'd gone into the lingerie store where Daniel worked, and was glad to see that he was there. We went to lunch together and got to know each other a little better. He asked a lot of questions about Char that I was more than happy to answer. When we'd gotten back to the store, I decided that I deserved some pretty panties to make me feel better.

I left the store a couple hundred bucks poorer, but a lot lighter in my heart. I'd stopped at the store for some more food and before I knew it, the sun was setting. I was trying to stuff the elevator card back in my wallet when the elevator doors opened. I knew the layout of this apartment by heart now, so I didn't bother to look up to see where I was going. Muttering about needing an extra hand, I stepped out of the elevator and turned towards the kitchen to drop off the bags of food.

"Need some help there?"

The deep voice scared the shit out of me, and I let out a scream as I whirled around to face the intruder. I stopped short when I met Aidan's gaze. He'd moved a chair to directly in view of the elevator, and I would've seen him sitting there as soon as the doors opened if I hadn't been so focused on the struggle with the card and wallet.

I lost the feeling in my hands from the shock of seeing him in front of me, eyes caressing my body from my toes to my hair, then delving into my own purple gaze. Every inch of my skin lit up at his perusal at the same time I lost hold of all my bags. Fruit and frozen meals spilled everywhere, but neither of us paid any attention to it.

"Aidan? Are you… I'm not dreaming, am I?" My voice was breathy, my body was shaking, and my panties were dripping. I knew what that look in his eyes usually meant, and I had no intention of denying I wanted it too.

"That depends." He stood up and took a step towards me. "Do your dreams usually consist of me taking an early morning flight to California on barely any sleep, hoping to see you as soon as those elevator doors opened only to find an empty apartment? Do you usually dream that I'm sitting in this chair, waiting for who knows how long to see you come home?"

"N-no." He took another couple steps towards me, and my feet automatically mirrored his steps.

"Then no, this is no dream. And it's not going to feel like a dream when I've got you bent over this couch behind me and I'm fucking you and spanking that perky ass of yours until you scream my name."

My belly clenched at his words and I didn't hesitate to wrap myself around his body as he reached me and picked me up, shoving me against the wall. His mouth descended on mine and we fought with our tongues, teeth, and lips. The kiss washed away any leftover anger I'd had inside me, instantly melting my heart. I knew we needed to have a talk, but I needed this right now just as much as he did.

I pulled his shirt up as we bit at each other's lips so I could rake my nails down his back. He let out a sexy grunt and thrust against me, pinning me harder against the wall. He moved one hand from my butt to grip the ends of my hair and pull my head back so he could bite my neck.

I let out a loud cry as he nibbled on a particularly sensitive spot, clutching his shoulders and grinding against the hardness pulsing between my thighs. He pulled back and I whimpered at the loss. He let my hair go and I tilted my head forward to meet his eyes.

"We need to talk," he said between fast breaths. "But first I really am going to fuck you on that couch. You deserve that spanking I promised days ago, don't you Callie?"

I nodded my head, wanting it just as much as he did. I needed something physical to take away the pain in my heart, and if it took his palm leaving prints on my ass, I would happily endure it.

He walked us over and I let my legs slide down his body when we stood by the arm of the couch. We quickly took our clothes off and looked each other over.

"You're so goddamn beautiful." He trailed a finger softly between my breasts and my nipples tightened more than before. He let out a soft groan at the site and I felt satisfaction surge through me. I turned around and climbed onto the couch so that I was kneeling on a seat cushion, chest resting against the back and ass pushed high into the air.

"Jesus," Aidan muttered behind me as I wiggled slightly, enticing him to get in me. "If you want me to stop, tell me right now." I kept silent and waited. I heard the sound of the first smack before I felt it, and my breath caught when the sting registered on my ass. Aidan's hand smoothed over the area for a second before lifting his hand and smacking the other cheek. As the pain transferred into warmth directly to my pussy, I moaned.

"That's it baby, I know you like the way my hand lands on that ass. I love to watch you turn pink, getting so wet that you're nearly dripping before I shove my cock all the way into you on the first thrust."

I moaned, feeling myself getting wetter with his words, and each spank he delivered buzzed all the way to my clit. Soon I was crying out with every slap, thinking that I could come just from this.

"I want you to tell me again Callie. Tell me."

My brain tried to understand what he was saying, but before I could his hand landed on me again, sharper than before. This time though, both hands gripped my hips and I could feel him rubbing his hard length against my pussy. His tip hit my clit on every slow glide and I panted wildly, my body tensing in preparation for the orgasm I could feel building.

"Don't come yet." I wailed at the command, but obeyed as he slowed his movements even more. "I want to hear you say the words baby. If you tell me, then I'll let you come."

Tears gathered in my eyes. I knew what he wanted to hear. Could I say them, not knowing where we'd end up after this? Another slow glide, and then the tip of his dick was pressed at my entrance. I tried to push back, but Aidan's hands tightened on my hips, holding me still.

"Fucking say it Callie!" Suddenly he lifted a hand and brought it back down quickly, smacking my sensitive ass harder than before and thrusting inside me at the same time. A loud, long scream erupted from my throat at finally feeling him inside me, in my pussy and in my heart. He held still, waiting for my confession and I caved. The tears fell as I yelled the words he wanted to hear.

"I love you! Gods help me, I love you so much, Aidan!"

"I love you too, baby."

He began to thrust, dragging his cock in and out of me so fast and hard and deep that as soon as his fingers touched my clit and his words registered in my ears I came, clenching so tightly around him that he yelled out, his own orgasm taking him by surprise.

He collapsed around me, hands hitting the back of the couch outside mine, still thrusting lightly to drag out the pleasure. We shuddered in each other's arms for several minutes before either of us moved. He pulled out and I groaned softly. He turned me in his arms and carried me towards the room I'd stayed in last time.

"Um, I've actually been staying in your room." I whispered the words, hiding my face in his neck to cover my embarrassment. A grunt of approval was his only response, but he held me tighter as he turned and headed the other way.

He started a bath, testing the water and adding what smelled like eucalyptus oil before settling me inside and climbing in behind me. We caressed each other lightly, not speaking. I, for one, wanted to enjoy these few moments before facing the possibility of this being our last time together.

CHAPTER FORTY-NINE
AIDAN

I turned off the water when it got near the top of Callie's shoulders. I leaned back in the tub and Callie followed, weightless in my arms. Thoughts whirled in my head, hoping that I hadn't fucked everything up by screwing her brains out and demanding that she say she loved me.

When I got to the apartment I'd been disappointed that she wasn't here, but was content to wait for her. As each hour passed, need and frustration built in me to the point that the moment I heard the elevator ding in warning I was ready to pounce on her the second I saw her.

I was throbbing in anticipation, and when I saw the desire swirling in her violet eyes I lost control of everything else but the need to be inside her. I got one moment of sanity before taking it all the way, but when I offered her the out she hadn't taken it. Hopefully that meant she was okay with all of it.

I trailed my fingers across her arms, and she trailed hers against my thighs. Neither of us wanted to be the first to break the silence, so we both took the moment to relax in the warm water.

When the water began to cool and my fingers were well past pruned, I carefully pulled Callie up out of the water with me. I stepped out of the tub and grabbed the robe hanging on the door for her, letting her use my hand for stability and then wrapped her in the robe.

"Get ready for bed, and then we'll talk." She nodded at my words, and I watched her for a minute before the cool air made me shiver. I padded to the closet in the hall and grabbed one of the extra robes kept in there. I was planning on sleeping naked like I usually did so I reclined against the pillows on the bed as Callie finished braiding her hair.

She was wearing a thin, loose tank top and her lace panties flashed me every time she lifted her arms. When she turned and headed to the bed, I did my best not to react to the shadow of her hard nipples in her shirt, holding the blanket up for her to climb under. She rested her head on a pillow facing me and I pulled the covers over us, mimicking her position. I pulled her into my arms but left enough space so that eye contact wasn't uncomfortable. She wrapped her arms low around my waist and nibbled on her lip as she searched my face.

I decided to start it off. "I know how difficult it is for you to open up to people, and how much you struggled with your feelings for me because I felt the exact same." She opened her mouth to reply, but I placed a finger on her lips to hush her. "Give me a minute to explain, and then you can talk. Please, Callie."

I waited until I had her consent to continue. I gave her a light kiss on her lips in thanks. She smiled softly and waited.

"You know I was nine when Serena and Caleb adopted me. My biological parents gave me up for adoption, so I always knew they were out there somewhere and I figured they just didn't want or need me. I never thought much about them, because if they couldn't love me enough to keep me, then I wouldn't give them the time of day it took to worry about them.

"When Serena and Caleb passed, they left me a letter urging me to let go of the hurt my birth parents had left in me, and to find them. I stalled on that request for a while. Eventually my curiosity and desire to do right by the loving people who took me in when I was an ornery kid overcame the anger and I started the search. Since I began the search, I haven't been able to get much farther than the hospital I was born in. I've been stuck, and the investigators I hired are saying they either died unidentified, or something they're doing is making them untraceable.

"I still wasn't going to give up. I believed that something would happen that would lead me to them and no matter the outcome, at least I would *know*. Then, one day I was skateboarding down a sidewalk and a beautiful woman's smoothie ended up on my face. I watched as she face-planted into a parking meter, and ended up riding along with the stranger to the hospital."

I paused, finally looking away from Callie. "In the hospital, amidst the weirdest dream of my life, I was approached by a goddess telling me that I needed to make the gorgeous, concussed stranger fall in love with me. I refused. And then she told me I had to do it or I would never find my family."

I heard Callie gasp quietly but I forged ahead. "I didn't know this girl, but I didn't want to lose the possibility of finding my biological parents. It wasn't until that moment that I realized I actually did want to find them; I wanted that closure in my life. Something inside me was drawing me toward the search and I couldn't give it up. So I agreed to make the girl fall in love with me. What I didn't know at the time," I met Callie's gaze again, "was that I was going to fall in love way before she did. And that as each day passed and we got closer to the deadline I had to get her to confess her love, the more I wanted to tell her the truth."

My throat constricted and I had to swallow before I continued. I beat back the moisture in my eyes and took a deep breath, trying to ignore the silent tears tracking Callie's cheeks.

"The morning that we fought... It was less than forty-eight hours before the day that Aphrodite had given me to break your vow. She'd originally given me two weeks, but extended it one more week when she saw I was close. I'd been in love with you since before Lucy visited us in California, although the day I picked her up was the first time I realized it. Then, watching you with Elise that day at the center, I knew that I needed you in my life more than I wanted closure with my family.

"So when Aphrodite pulled me out of sleep two days before the time limit, I told her that I was going to tell you the truth. That I was going to confess everything, and that I didn't care what the consequences were and just hope that you loved me enough to forgive me when I explained everything to you. I'd also begun to suspect that there was some ultimatum that she was dealing with too, because when I brought it up she got pissed and threatened everything I have- which included the entirety of the Rikers Foundation. I came back upstairs, heartbroken and unsure where to go from there when I saw you crying in the front room."

A sob broke out from Callie and I stopped talking as she bawled into my robe. "Shh, baby. I'm almost done." She nodded against me and her sobs quieted but I suspected the tears were still falling so I hurried with the last part.

"You tore my heart out of my chest that morning, and I was so angry at myself for letting it get to that point and so frustrated that you refused to listen to me, that I left. I've regretted that every day since. I should've stayed, made you listen, and we could've worked things out. I know that it wouldn't have been perfect right away, but we could already be past this."

I pulled once on Callie's hair to make her look at me. She obeyed, and only when my eyes held hers did I finish. "Even if you don't believe me, or can't find it in you to forgive me, just know that I will always, always love you. I don't blame you for any of this, and I never will. We both got caught in something bigger than us, and I won't let you believe I blame you for any of it."

She moved her hands up to frame my face and I let her guide my mouth down to hers, letting her take the lead in a kiss so sweet, so open that the parts of my heart began to mend back together. She pulled back and looked me deep in my eyes, her love shining so brightly that I began to choke up.

"Aidan McRae, I love you with every part of my stubborn, hard-headed, muddled being. I could never have imagined feeling this kind of love in my lifetime, but I know it will last. When I eavesdropped on your conversation, I definitely did not hear all of it. I only heard your part, and I must've only caught some of the middle. I heard you say that none of it was fair to us, that you were going to tell me the truth, and that the whole thing had been a lie and you were only doing it because of my vow.

"At that point, I was confused and I rushed upstairs. Everything was dark and I tripped and that triggered some of my memory to come back. I remembered being on the phone with Ellinor and then tripping before blacking out to your face. Then I remembered making the vow, and the fact that we definitely hadn't been dating. I'm so sorry I didn't let you explain everything, but I felt like my heart burned to ashes when I admitted I'd fallen in love with you and the vow was finally broken."

I shuddered as tears began to fall from my eyes. She brushed them away with her fingers as they fell and continued. "Thank you for telling me everything, and I'm sorry it took me so long to be ready to hear it. If you'll have me, I'd be happy to love you for as long as you want me to, as long as you promise to love me too."

"You couldn't leave at this point even if you wanted to. I owe you too much for everything you've given me."

A serene smile lit her face. "As a Persian poet named Hāfiz once said, 'Even after all this time the sun never says to the earth, "You owe me." Look what happens with a love like that. It lights the whole sky.' You don't owe me anything, Aidan. That's what love is."

A strangled laugh escaped me as I captured her lips with mine once more. Our tears and laughter mingled together, making the kiss sloppy and indelicate. Neither of us cared; I'd gotten my girl back, and she was here to stay.

"So," Callie said after our eyes dried and we were only smiling at each other, relieved to have everything out in the open, "how about we make up some more of that lost time?"

I grinned at her, rolling over so that I had her caged in my arms. I used my knees to separate hers as she untied my robe and pushed it off my shoulders.

"What my naughty girl wants, she gets," I huskily said and cherished the giggle that escaped, changing it into a sigh as my lips began the trail from her neck down to the top of her tank top that I slowly moved out of the way as I moved lower and lower and lower...

CHAPTER FIFTY
AIDAN

Callie and I stayed another day or two in California, just to catch up and get back into our own groove. When we got off the plane from the flight back to Colorado and I turned my phone back on to check for any messages, I noticed I had a text from Lucy.

Aidan, call me when you get off the plane.

I frowned, getting a sudden bad feeling. I dialed her number and turned to Callie to explain. "Hey babe, I got a weird text from Luce, so I'm just calling her real qui- Oh, hey Lucy, what's going on? Is everything alright?"

A pause on her end made me wonder just how bad her news was. She cleared her throat. "Um... I need to you to come to the office. Like, as soon as you can. There's something here you need to see."

"What? What are you talking about?"

"Seriously Aidan, just get your ass here pronto."

She hung up on me, and I pulled the phone away, staring at it.

"Aidan? What's happening?" I looked over at Callie's worried face.

"I have no fucking clue, but apparently we have to stop by my office. Is that okay with you?"

"Of course, you know I don't mind coming with."

"Damn right, because I'm taking you with me anyway." I laughed with Callie, but worry hung over us as we drove as fast as possible to my work.

I parked and we hurriedly got out of the car, making our way inside to the darkened building. I saw some lights on up on the top level, so we made our way up. I checked in my office first but didn't see Lucy so Callie followed me as I walked down the hallway to Lucy's office. I called out to her as I got closer, seeing a shadow move in the light coming from her open door.

"Lucy, what is going on? What could possibly so important that- what the hell?!" I'd stepped inside her office to find Lucy backed up against the side of a filing cabinet, caged in by some guy I couldn't see clearly but didn't immediately recognize. He straightened suddenly at my words and I noticed that we were about the same height and build. I'd kick his ass if I had to, but it would be a pretty even fight, I guessed. Still, no one fucking cornered my best friend in her office.

"What the fuck is your problem man? And who the fuck are you?" I demanded loudly and watched as Lucy peeked around his shoulder, giving me a weird look I couldn't decipher. The man slowly turned around and as he faced me, my jaw dropped at the same time Callie gasped loudly, dropping her purse. I stared at the man, taking in his face. A face I saw every day because it was my own. He smiled, hard but amused, and two dimples just like mine popped out before he spoke.

"Hey, brother."

CHAPTER FIFTY-ONE
AIDAN

I felt the blood drain from my face as my brain tried to figure out what the hell was going on. Callie's hand tightened in mine and we both stood frozen, looking at, well, me. What the guy had said when he turned around finally registered.

Brother?!

"I'll get the scotch." Lucy's dry voice rang through the silent room and she walked towards the sideboard in the office, pouring three fingers of scotch into each one and handing them out. I studied the stranger and narrowed my eyes when I realized he was carefully watching every move Lucy made. The look in his eyes was the same one I knew I got when I looked at Callie. A part of me wanted to confront him about it, but that was a problem for another day.

Right now, I had to deal with the fact that I apparently had not only a brother, but an identical twin.

"How... Fuck, I don't even know what question to start with." I drained my scotch in two gulps and dropped into a chair. Callie came and stood next to me, her hand resting reassuringly on my shoulder. I needed more than that right now though, so I pulled her into my lap. The movement startled her, but she didn't protest. I buried my face in her hair and squeezed her tight, her presence helping to calm my thoughts.

"My name is Calder. Obviously, we're twins." He paused and grinned when Lucy, Callie and I gave him looks saying that yeah, we figured that part out already. "I'm older by the way. I know that you've been looking for our parents, and I'm assuming you had no idea I even existed. Not a surprise, since when our parents gave us up at three weeks old we were unfortunately separated pretty quickly. The system tries to keep siblings together, but it doesn't always work out like that."

I grimaced and nodded, knowing exactly what he meant. I'd seen families split up before and it had always made me sad.

"I know you went through a few bad homes before getting adopted," Calder continued. "Same for me, minus the whole adoption part. I ran away from a particularly disgusting home at 14, so I ended up on the streets trying to defend myself. I was homeless, but I was happier. Freer. Lighter. I didn't have to answer to anyone, and I cherished it. I was clever and wily, not to mention I always looked older than I was so I was able to get away with a lot. By the time I was twenty, I was well versed in grifting."

"Grifting?" Callie asked the question I'd been thinking, and Calder's gaze turned to her.

"What was that, sweets?"

At his words a growl escaped me before I could stop it. Callie knew I was reacting to the nickname and she placed a hand on my chest to calm me down. I consciously relaxed the muscles in my body that had gone tense, knowing she could take care of herself.

"First of all, call me sweets again and I'll beat your ass. Secondly, what is grifting?" I grinned at her fierceness and saw a smile twitch at Calder's lips. The weirdness of staring at my face on someone else hit me again as he responded.

"Noted. Grifting is another term for swindling."

"You're a con artist," Lucy said in a flat voice. Calder turned towards her and I watched them stare at each other, something in the air changing when their eyes met. Callie turned and gave me a look and I knew she was wondering what was going on between them too.

"I *was* a con artist. But I gave that up."

"Why? You didn't like tricking innocent people into giving you money anymore?" Even I flinched at Lucy's tone. I'd never heard her talk like that to someone and I wasn't sure if that was because she was disgusted by him, or if it was because she was trying to build distance between them. From the scene that Callie and I walked into when we got here, I was guessing it was the latter.

"Not quite," Calder said and then turned back to Callie and me. "I refuse to be like our parents."

Be like our parents? It took a second for me to get it. "You mean to tell me our parents are con artists?"

"Yeah. You know how you've been looking for them for years and have found nothing? It's because they change their identities constantly. By the time anyone would start to figure things out they'd changed everything: their appearances, their information, their cars. I'm talking full reidentification. They're fucking good man, I'll give them that."

"How did you find them?"

"Pure accident. I was on a job and something about the situation was weird so I dug deeper and realized that someone in the same circle as the people I was working were also being conned. So I confronted the other grifters, telling them to stop fucking up my job. They laughed. The man had looked at me appraisingly. 'Maybe it's time you joined your parents', he said. I told him I didn't have any. The woman chuckled, and said the words that changed everything. 'We must be pretty good at this if you can't even recognize your own mother and father, Calder'."

Calder paused to finish off his drink and set it on Lucy's desk before continuing. Callie had started to run her fingers through my hair where her hand rested and I appreciated the tiny bit of distraction while I absorbed the story.

"I was skeptical, but they managed to prove that I was actually their son. That, and it was hard to deny the resemblance. I asked them about their con, and the more they told me the more disgusted I was with them. They were focused on a very rich, old lady, pretending to be a set of family lawyers that worked with the legal representation she'd been using, but that had retired. They were going to swindle her out of everything, and I had to listen to the two people who created me tell me their plans without giving away how fucking pissed I was.

"That job was challenging. I had to figure out how to con two con artists that had years more experience; thankfully the fact that their son turned out to be a grifter as well blinded them, and they couldn't see how much I hated them. They couldn't see that I'd always picked my jobs differently." He turned to look at me, and his icy blue eyes drilled into my brown ones. "I don't ever target anyone that doesn't deserve it. I mostly go after rich assholes."

Callie was the one to break the silence. "What did you do?"

"I gave evidence of their fraud to the right people, and my parents had to pack all their shit and leave quickly before they were found out. I went to confront them, and if they weren't on a time limit to get away I'm fairly sure my father would have tried to kill me. He started towards me, yelling things like 'You're no son of mine, you don't betray family'. I told him you don't abandon them either, and he punched me

328

before going back to packing. My mother looked at me with disgust, which didn't phase me at that point since I felt the same. I held no love for the people in front of me, and I wanted nothing to do with their idea of family.

"I watched our father walk out the door, and before our mother followed him out, she turned to me and spat out one last thing: 'If this proved anything, giving you boys up was the best decision your father and I ever made.' I froze at her words when I realized that she had said 'you boys', as in plural. I charged after them and caught her arm before she got into their car. 'I have a brother?' I'd asked. She must have read the dead seriousness in my tone, because she shrunk back as far as I would let her. 'Yes, you have a twin. His name is Aidan.' The shock blitzed through me and she was able to rip her arm from my grasp. She got into the car and the two of them drove off to who knows where."

Calder paused and raked a hand through his hair, a habit we apparently shared. "After that, I spent weeks looking for you. I was relieved to find that you'd kept our last name as well. It made everything easier, although not simple. When I finally found you, I wasn't sure if you'd want to see me. I didn't know if you knew about our parents and me, but watching you I saw that you were happy."

I frowned at his words. "How long have you been watching me, exactly?"

"A few months," he mumbled.

I raised an eyebrow. "What'd you do with your time while I was in California? I'm assuming you knew where I was since you seem to have been able to figure out a lot of things about my life."

Calder smiled sheepishly, but there was no guilt on his face. "I kept busy." He shot a glance over at Lucy, whose face morphed into a scowl.

"Well it would've been nice if he'd fucking shown up weeks ago. Would've saved me a lot of trouble," I muttered to myself. Callie caught the words and laughed, turning around to kiss me.

"What's so funny?" Calder asked in a confused tone and Callie pulled away to answer.

"Oh, Aidan was just saying that we could've skipped a few steps in our relationship if you had come forward earlier."

Calder was puzzled. "What does your relationship have to do with me?"

The rest of us smiled at each other, and Lucy let out a small giggle before looking at Callie. "C'mon Callie, we should let the boys have some time together, get a chance to catch up."

Callie nodded and turned back to me, silently making sure I was alright. I merely smiled at her and pulled her down to me, our mouths meeting in a simple kiss.

Well, it started off simple at least. Callie opened her mouth and let her tongue run against the seam of my lips, and everything else in the room disappeared. I reached my hands up to cup her cheeks and returned the invitation with a deep kiss. Our tongues tangled for several enjoyable seconds before Callie hurriedly pulled away and jumped off my lap and grabbed Lucy's hand.

"We'll be back in a couple hours boys!" Callie called as Lucy grabbed her purse by the door at the last second. For a moment Lucy turned back and met Calder's gaze, then turned when Callie tugged on her hand to get her moving.

With the girls out of sight, I turned to look at Calder. There was nothing else to do now but try and figure out what the hell I was going to do with a surprise twin brother.

CHAPTER FIFTY-TWO
AIDAN

I looked at my long-lost twin and felt that something I'd been looking for. My life felt complete. Right then, I knew that I didn't need to meet our parents, his word being enough for me. Part of me was pissed at them for denying me my brother, but my life would probably look very different if they hadn't made the choices they did and I wouldn't give up my current life, or Callie, for anything.

"I suppose that it's good we didn't grow up with our parents then," I finally said.

"I guess it depends on your point of view. Do you think growing up in and out of foster homes is better than having your parents around?"

"Right now? Yeah, I do believe that. Sounds like our parents were real pieces of work, so I can't imagine being happy with them either. And who's to say we wouldn't have ended up just like them?"

"You forget brother, one of us did." Self-disgust covered his face. I knew he hated the fact that he'd ended up being like our parents, but he was so wrong about that.

"No, *brother*, you didn't. Our parents chose helpless people to victimize. You did what you had to do to survive, and no one can fault you for that. Plus, you chose completely different targets. You were more like Robin Hood, not the Sheriff of Nottingham."

A reluctant smile crossed his face. "Funny, some people in my circle called me that too."

"Steal from the rich, give to the poor, eh?" I said and grinned at him

"Yeah, something like that."

"See then, you're nothing like our parents. Just because we're a bunch of persuasive bastards doesn't mean that we have to be bad."

He visibly relaxed at my sure words. "Sorry I didn't come forward sooner. You looked a bit busy anyway."

"You have no fuckin' clue brother." I sighed and shook my head lightly.

"Tell me."

"Alright, but we're going to need another drink." Calder got up to re-fill our glasses and I began to tell him mine and Callie's story from the moment the smoothie hit my face to when we walked in the room. He looked incredulous, which I couldn't blame him for. I sounded fucking crazy, talking about goddesses and visions and shit. If I hadn't experienced it for myself there's no way I would've believed it.

I finished the story and the room fell quiet. Calder and I lifted our hands to run them through our hair at the same time, prompting rueful chuckles from us both before he finally spoke.

"Shit man, that's the craziest story I've ever heard."

I laughed and nodded. "I know. And every word is true. I'm just lucky to have gotten Callie back." I tipped the rest of his drink back, deciding to tell him what I'd been thinking about recently. "I think I'm going to propose soon."

He stood up immediately and pulled me in for a quick hug. "That's awesome man! I'm invited to the wedding right?"

"As long as you don't go pick-pocketing everyone," I joked.

"Damn, never mind then." We laughed, but I was sincere about him coming to the wedding and wanted to make sure he knew that.

"In all seriousness Calder, I would be honored for you to be at my wedding. Whenever that happens. I wouldn't want to do it without you."

He cleared his throat and I pretended not to notice his eyes getting wet. "Nothing could keep me away."

I nodded, the feelings in my chest about to burst. "Ahem! Well, now that that's settled… Tell me what the hell was going on between you and Lucy when I got here."

He immediately flushed and looked away for a moment. There was a small smile on his face, but he looked slightly confused as he answered.

"That's a good question. There's something about her that pulls me in. When I first got here and found you, you two walked out of the building together. It was amazing to see you of course, but she was like a beacon. You guys hugged and I was filled with an urge to pull her away from you, claim her as mine. I had my hand on the door to get out when she pulled away, got in her car and never looked back at you.

"Watching you two interact until you met Callie, I could tell that you were interested but that she didn't feel the same. I was torn between absolute satisfaction that she wasn't into you and worry for your unrequited love to bite you in the ass."

"I did like Lucy, and I do love her. But I've never felt about her the way I feel about Callie. Lucy deserves to have someone love her wildly, and I never could have given that to her. She just realized it before I did." I shrugged matter-of-factly.

"That's good, because I would've had to steal her away from you, brother or not. I watched out for her while you were gone, had to scare off a couple of guys she went on dates with. They weren't bad guys, but I couldn't handle seeing another man touch her. Poor thing probably thinks something's wrong with her, since her dates have been getting cut short."

We grinned at each other. "Let's keep that to ourselves probably," I said.

"No shit. She'd probably cut my balls off and hang them like mistletoe in her front room if she found out." We both shuddered at the thought. "Anyway, when I got here tonight I knew that if I approached her she'd get you to come here as soon as you could. And when I knew she was alone, I came in. I knew I was attracted to her, but being close enough to smell her, hear her voice, touch her... I lost it. I barely told her my name before I kissed her like I was starving."

I had previously noticed that one side of his face was slightly pinker than the other, and I was betting Lucy had slapped Calder for that little stunt of his. "I assume that's where the glow on your cheeks came from?"

"Bingo. Little firecracker slapped me twice. Not saying I didn't deserve it, but she's stronger than she looks."

"She's taken some self-defense classes and does kick-boxing once a week, so yeah I'd watch yourself there."

"Impressive," he said. I let him mull that over before I asked him what had been on my mind, a small idea forming in my mind.

"So what are you going to do now? Stick around here, or keep up in your current line of work?"

He shook my head. "No, like I mentioned earlier I don't want to work cons anymore. I want to distance myself from our parents as much as possible. I'm not totally sure where I go from here though, since I didn't exactly go to college, although I got my GED a while back. I don't have any real job experience, so I'll probably end up at some fast food place for a bit. I've got money saved up, but if I keep renting where I'm at now then I'll run out of that money eventually."

I kept my smile hidden for the moment; he'd given me the opening I was looking for. "You know, you could come work for me if you wanted."

"You'd hire someone you just met?"

"I'd be hiring my brother. If it makes you feel better though, you can call this the weirdest job interview of your life."

"No kidding. I don't want to take advantage of you or anything, but that would be a huge help. Can I come back tomorrow to figure out if there's something I can actually do for you?"

I respected that he wanted to make sure he'd actually be doing something useful before agreeing, although I already had a few ideas of what he could do. "Of course. And if for some reason you feel uncomfortable working for your new-found little brother, let me know and I can find something else for you. I have connections everywhere and you wouldn't have to explain your lack of job experience to them."

He leaned forward to shake my hand. "Thank you, Aidan. I appreciate that."

"It's not a problem," I replied. "I don't want you to leave now that you're here, so a job is the least I can do. I finally feel, I don't know, complete I guess. I would've been happy to just have Callie, but having a brother." I shook my head in amazement. "That's more than I could have ever hoped for."

We sat in silence for a few minutes, just letting the information overload of the last couple hours settle in our brains. The sound of Callie and Lucy's giggles echoing up to us from the lobby pulled me from my thoughts.

Calder and I grinned at each other as we both stood and headed out of the office and down the hall, stopping at the top of the stairs. We watched the two of them slowly making their way up the steps, and I waited until they were about halfway up when I final spoke.

"Ladies, how much have you two had to drink?" They jumped at my loud voice, and tried to make their faces serious before replying. They didn't succeed, and their efforts and resulting giggles made Calder cover his mouth to hide the smile.

"Only a couple? Drinks, I mean." Callie looked at me, her purple eyes wide to try and make herself look innocent. Her answer didn't even make complete sense, and it was getting harder for me to act like I wasn't enjoying this. Lucy snorted and Callie elbowed her.

"Yeah, only like one or two or maybe three, but definitely not four." Lucy rambled, totally giving the real answer away.

I looked over at my brother. "What do you think Calder? They telling the truth?"

He wiped the grin off his face and stepped forward, studying the girls like he was thinking about it. "No, I don't think they are."

Thinking of all the ways I could have fun with a drunk Callie, I stepped up next to Calder and crooked a finger at the two giggling women. "Come here, Callie. Lucy, you too."

They made it up to the top of the stairs and Callie immediately came over to me and wrapped her arms around my neck. I bent down slightly when she tugged me down so she could say something.

"I'm very wet right now Aidan, and I'm thinking I want you to take me in your office and fuck me on your desk." A sharp bite on my ear followed her whispered words and my body immediately responded. I stood up straight and lifted Callie into my arms to hide my erection, turning to face Calder.

"I've got something to take care of. Can you make sure Lucy gets home? We'll lock up behind us." Calder barely hesitated, taking Lucy's hand and helping her down the stairs. I left them to it, gripping Callie tighter as I stalked towards my office to give my girl exactly what she wanted.

CHAPTER FIFTY-THREE
CALLIE

I was definitely tipsy, but that had nothing to do with how bad I wanted Aidan right now. I'd grilled Lucy at the restaurant we went to about what was going on with her and Calder, and the alcohol had loosened her up enough to tell me about him kissing her like a madman and all of the tension that had built between them from that moment until Aidan and I walked in while he'd had her pinned against her cabinet and saying dirty things to her. I totally understood where she was coming from because the object of her obsession was the twin brother to mine.

Lucy telling me about Calder only served to remind me of Aidan and everything we'd done, and by the time we'd made it back to their office I was more than ready for another round with Aidan. And judging by his reaction to my proposition, he had absolutely nothing against that. I busied myself with kissing and biting Aidan's neck while he took us to his office, making him quicken his steps and growl lightly underneath his breath. He strode through his doorway and shoved things on his desk to the side so he could place me on it. I giggled at his haste, but my laughter stopped when I met his eyes.

His blue eyes were dark and focused on me with a look so hot I thought my panties were going to spontaneously combust. I leaned back on my hands, thrusting my chest out towards him in offering. He groaned lowly, eyes raking down my body in appreciation. It didn't matter that I was still in my clothes from the flight here. I knew Aidan wanted me no matter what I was wearing.

Or not wearing, I thought to myself when Aidan reached for the hem of my t-shirt and pulled it over my head. He threw my shirt behind him and goosebumps popped up on my skin from the combination of cool air and sexual tension in the room.

"Stand up and take those pants off for me, baby." Aidan's raspy voice broke the silence in the room and I slid off the desk to do what he told me to. The tone in his voice nearly had me panting in anticipation for what was going to come next.

I slid down the zipper slowly, heart beating hard in my chest as I slipped my thumbs inside the band and pulled them down so he could catch a glimpse of mint green panties. I paused to turn around so that he could watch me bend over while I pushed them down my legs. The sound he made at the sight made my belly clench and I felt him come up close behind me.

"How drunk are you Callie?" His voice was surprisingly soft, and I realized he was checking in to make sure that I was okay with what was about to go down.

"Only slightly tipsy. Most of the alcohol has worn off. Don't worry about me Aidan, I want this."

"I just don't want to hurt you."

I straightened up and turned to face him. I stood on my tiptoes and he bent down to let me place a soft kiss on his lips.

"I trust you." Those words seemed to be what he needed at that moment. A hungry smile lit his face and he stepped back into the dominant Aidan I loved.

"In that case," he murmured and flicked the clasp on the front of my bra open, my tits spilling out into his waiting hands, "I'm going to need you to turn back around so I can take another look at that perfect ass of yours."

He dropped his hands and I let out a sound of protest. He raised an eyebrow at me and twirled his finger, demanding I do what he wanted. I huffed out a breath but listened to him.

"Mmm, that's perfect baby." He took another step closer, placing his hands on my hips and pulling me back into him. I could feel how hard he was and a small moan escaped my lips when he thrust his hips forward into my ass. I couldn't stop my feet from moving farther apart, enticing him to explore my body. He moved his hands over my stomach and up to my chest, making me gasp when he captured my nipples between his fingers and squeezed.

Before I could really get into that part, his hands changed direction again. One moved back down my stomach and right into my panties to find and rub my clit while the other came up to grasp my neck lightly, his forearm resting between my tits.

"Oh God," I moaned loudly, my hands scrambling to find something to hold onto as his fingers began to rub my clit faster.

"That's right Callie, you're mine. These tits, that ass, this soaking wet pussy I can't wait to get inside, they're mine." His grasp on my throat tightened slightly and my pulse jumped in response. "Your amazing mind, your humor, your smile, your heart. I own them Callie. Don't I?"

His fingers slid down farther and my hips bucked forward the moment he slid two fingers into me. He ground his heel against my clit and I whimpered at the explosion of pleasure.

"Don't I Callie?" Aidan demanded an answer from me and I gave him the answer he was looking for.

"Yes!" It was true. He owned me, body and mind. I'd gladly given it all to him without reservation when he'd found me in California, and he knew it. I was okay with that though, because I knew I owned him too.

"That's right baby. I own all of you." His hand on my throat moved to grip my chin and turned my head to face him. I met his eyes and saw the love shining in them. "And you've got me too. There's nothing about me that isn't yours."

I gulped and nodded, and then his mouth covered mine in a kiss that sealed his words. He took his hand out of my panties as he pulled away from my mouth and licked my arousal off his fingers as I watched, making me even wetter than before.

"Now Callie," he said when he finished, "I want you to lay across my desk on your stomach and grab the other edge."

He lightly pushed me forward and guided me down the way he wanted. I'd been standing behind his desk next to the chair, and he pushed that away to make more room. I heard the rustle of clothes and wanted to turn so I could see him undress, but something unspoken between us right now prevented me from doing it.

He placed his hand on my shoulders and moved them down my arms to make them stretch across to the other side. My fingers curled around the edge and I stilled, waiting. Aidan grasped my right leg and bent it up so that it was resting on the desk as well, my left foot the only thing touching the floor.

"Fuck, that's a pretty sight. I can see how wet you are. You're already making a mess on my desk, and we've just barely gotten started."

I dropped my forehead onto the desk, groaning at his dirty talk.

"Don't move those hands, Callie."

I clutched the desk harder just as he drove his hard cock into my pussy in one smooth glide. I threw my head back, the only real movement I could make while I was stretched and spread the way I was. I cried out loudly as he sank into me, barely giving me a moment to adjust to his size.

"Aidan, that feels so damn good!" He pulled out almost all the way and then pushed back into me, groaning when I tightened around him.

"Shit, you feel better every time. I can't believe how fucking wet you are. I bet you love that you can't move." A hand twisted into my hair and pulled my head back, taking away the last bit of movement I had.

"Oh fuck, oh fuck," I chanted as the sting brought me that much closer to orgasm. I could feel it building in my pussy and tingling through my body.

"Yes, let me hear how much you love this. I want to hear you scream my name when you come around my cock buried deep inside you."

He punctuated the words with a hard slap to my ass and faster thrusts. My legs started shaking and my fingers turned white with the effort to hold on as my climax began to ripple through me.

"Aidan! I'm coming!"

Aidan shouted out and I could feel him coming in me at the same time. He kept thrusting in order to drag out the pleasure, and leaned forward to curl his body over mine. He entwined his fingers with mine on the edge of the desk, kissing the top of my head lightly as the orgasms started to wear off.

We were both still breathing hard when he straightened and pulled out of me. I groaned quietly as he moved, my body already a little sore from my position. He carefully helped me put my leg back down on the floor, rubbing it to bring the feeling back without it going completely numb. While he did that I peeled my fingers from his desk and stretched them out to get life back into them.

Aidan suddenly picked me up off the desk completely and I squealed in surprise.

"Sorry," he chuckled.

He put me down next to his couch and then leaned over the back of it to grab something. I admired the way his muscles played across his back, smiling contentedly. The smile turned into a look of confusion when I realized Aidan had pulled out a blanket.

"What the... Why is that here?"

Aidan flushed, avoiding my gaze and explained, "Well, when you left I didn't really spend a lot of time at home. Lucy brought me a blanket so that when I crashed here overnight I wouldn't be too uncomfortable."

My heart ached at his words, and I moved into his chest and wrapped my arms around him. "I'm s-"

"No Callie, don't apologize." He made me look at him and his gaze searched my face. "I don't want you to feel bad for any of this. We did what we did, and here we are. We're in a better place than before, no lies or secrecy, and I wouldn't change anything that happened for the world. I love you Callie, for all of the good and any of the bad."

My eyes watered at his declaration, my heart about to burst from the amount of love I shared for him. "I love you too Aidan, so damn much. Thank you for not giving up on me."

He wrapped the blanket around us and settled on the couch with me in his lap, kissing me slowly in response. I pulled away some time later and sighed happily, resting my head on his chest.

We lay in comfortable silence for a while and I relaxed into Aidan's body as he played with my hair. I was just starting to drift off to sleep when something popped into my mind.

"Hey Aidan? Did you notice something weird with Lucy and Calder?"

I felt more than heard his laugh rumble through his chest.

"Oh yeah." His hand twirling my hair stopped. "Why, do you think something's going on with them?"

"Definitely. Lucy was telling me at the restaurant about how attracted she was to him, but that she wasn't made for relationships, blah blah blah. I told her she needed to go for it."

"Is that you as a friend talking, or your Cupid sixth sense?"

I laughed. "A little of both, I suppose. Man, it's a good thing I found you or else you and Calder would be fighting over her."

We both chuckled at that, but then Aidan shifted so he was looking at my face.

"I think a part of me always knew she wasn't for me. She's a really good friend and all, but I've never felt the way about her that I do about you. And from what I can tell, Calder is that guy for her. I'm sure he'll convince her that he's worth it, if we're anything alike."

I grinned at him. "Lucy's in trouble, isn't she?"

"Most definitely," he replied grinning right back. "Oh, by the way, I asked Calder if he'd like to work for me since he's not sure what he's going to do now. Now, with this thing with Lucy…"

"Are you thinking about putting them together?" The excitement in my voice was unmistakable. I could feel in my bones that the two of them were right for each other, if they just gave each other a chance.

"You don't think it's a bad idea?"

"Not at all. I don't want them missing out on what we have!"

"True. It is pretty great, isn't it?"

I gave him a light kiss. "It really is."

Later that night, as Aidan spooned me in his bed and I drifted off to sleep, I sent up a silent prayer. *Thanks for being the meddling goddess that you are, Aphrodite. Thank you for bringing me Aidan.* Aidan unconsciously pulled me in tighter to his body like he knew what I was thinking, and I smiled, knowing without a doubt that my vow was the best mistake I had ever made.

www.ingramcontent.com/pod-product-compliance
Lightning Source LLC
Chambersburg PA
CBHW021530250626
47154CB00006BA/2045